THE HOLLOW VOW

Dr. John Pierre Craig

Contents

Dedication

First and foremost, I want to thank the Most High for allowing me this opportunity to do what I enjoy so much: create stories. Writing Jevonte's story and bringing his world to life has been a dream come true. I owe the Most High everything.

I want to thank my wife, Jaazer. I could not have done this without your support. You allowed me the space to see this journey through to completion, and for that, I am grateful.

I also want to thank my children, Amaris, John Jr., Evonna, Bethany, and April. You guys mean the world to me. Thank you, Amee, for still calling me Daddy because it always transforms my heart. Thank you, John Jr., for inspiring me to work on the craft of writing with your brilliance. Thank you, Evonna, for listening to me and giving me space to share my stories (The Hobo Bear is loading). Thank you, Bethany, for reminding me where our strength comes from. Thank you, April, for looking after your dad and making sure he always has something good to eat when he's hungry!

Prologue

The music was loud. The lights and strobes were brilliantly illuminating the glee and excitement evident across the gymnasium floor. The local DJ, Mr. Magic Spinner—the kids called him Mr. Waste-hole—kept a rolling playlist of Billboard's top 100 pop hits. When the group known as Next had their hit song "Too Close" blare from the floor speakers, the kids rushed the floor, dancing off-beat, herky-jerky, spinning, sliding, bouncing, and spastically moving in every direction. But they were having fun. The principal of the school was determined to make Trinity Ridge Senior High School more diverse. The DJ promised he would play a little something for everyone to enjoy and dance to. Observing the chaos on the dance floor, Mr. Templeton mentally committed to pressing the DJ for a partial refund once the dance concluded.

In the days leading up to the senior dance, Noelle had to be taken to the hospital emergency room. Mysteriously, she had accidentally ingested some toxin that caused her to sweat excessively, and her sense of taste all but disappeared. Her vision was blurred, and her mouth was foaming. The attending physician ordered a blood panel, and it was determined that Noelle had been exposed to muscarine, a deadly poison associated with the mushroom Clitocybe. Her foster parents were mystified. Their garden, the couple insisted, was free of mushrooms of any kind. Noelle was fortunate, the doctor explained. She had only ingested a small amount and was treated with IV fluids and a dose of atropine to mitigate the muscarine that was in her system. Relieved, the foster parents brought Noelle and Talaitha home after a few hours in the ER.

The following day, the foster parents meticulously searched the garden, searching for any trace of the deadly mushrooms that had sent Noelle to the hospital. Talaitha observed from the kitchen window, grinning at the ease with which she could manipulate them. They found nothing amiss in the garden. They don't even know what they are looking for, she thought. The foster parents made their way back to the house, passing by the shaded side of the home, where the nearby wooded area had begun creeping across the property line. The decay of fallen leaves and scattered woodchips created inviting breeding grounds for Clitocybe dealbata during the fall season. Talaitha made sure they were fed well.

Noelle recovered in time to go to the dance. She and Talaitha almost came to blows in the car ride to the school, though. There was no logic to it, no reason for it; Talaitha just wanted to wind Noelle up and watch her spin out. Noelle's tolerance was nonexistent, but she was still too weakened from her poisoning to deal with her sister the way she wanted to. The foster parents threatened that if they didn't stop, they would turn around and no one would be allowed to attend the dance. Talaitha ceased harassing Noelle. She was not going to miss the dance because of Noelle.

Noelle found a spot against the gymnasium wall and began observing. Look at them, she thought to herself, fawning all over her like that. Noelle's thoughts began to race. "Why can't they see her for what she is?" Noelle muttered. They flock to her like moths to a flame. They won't see the truth until it's too late, when their bodies lie charred at her feet. "I feel sick," Noelle whispered to herself. She felt like she needed to do something, maybe warn them. I should spill her dark secrets to the world, but who am I? I don't matter, she thought. For more than a few heartbeats, Noelle watched her sister. Her thoughts repeatedly revolved around her sister's fate. She was dreaming of the day she would outshine Talaitha or rejoicing as she was lowered into the ground.

Noelle felt as if her sister had used her up to this night as a punching bag and a target for her evil rages. She even had a conversation with her guidance counselor about Talaitha and how she had been tormenting her. She shared how Talaitha had put lye in her bedsheets, set booby traps for her, and even had some boys try to attack her while they were at the bus stop. Noelle could never trust any food item coming from Talaitha, and even though she would tell her foster parents what Talaitha was doing, they never believed her. They would tell her that she was imagining things, that twins don't fight each other like this. Her counselor was not much different. The facade Talaitha presented fooled them all.

Noelle headed towards the gymnasium's exit doors. She glided along the gymnasium's wall, skirting the lights and gaggle of teen girls huddled in random cliques. As she watched her sister traipse among the crowd's admirers, she grew ever more despondent. Talaitha didn't notice her. Not like it mattered. For one, Talaitha never notices her sister unless she intends to inflict some torment. Noelle thought to herself, I'm going to show her. One day, when my feet are cooling in the dirt of her grave, I will be the one spinning around and laughing.

The intensity of the image in Noelle's mind, of Talaitha's grave, of her feet planted in the soil covering her body, sent shivers up her back and crept up her neck. One day, Noelle thought, all of this is going to change, and she's going to wish she had been kind to me.

Trinity Hope Senior High School in Sable Ridge, Maryland, was not known for its ethnic diversity. Much of Western Maryland isn't. The interstate that bisects the county is dotted with truck stops and bars. The town of Sable Ridge is not known for much beyond residents' passion for cornhole and pickleball tournaments. Tonight was different. The Barney Truck Stop was receiving an unusual inflow of traffic. Big rigs from the eastern corridor were lining up to fill up with diesel and some dinner at Momma Bell's Diner. Ms. Annebell Coughton ran the diner, but the town called her Momma Bell. Ms. Annebell cooked the best smothered pork chops in town. Truckers made a point of stopping in whenever they pulled into Barney's for fuel. The high school's lights could be seen from Barney's, and its energy seemed to flow through the truck stop. More than a few old-timers took notice. A few even hoped to see some young people amble over to Momma Bell's for a bit of entertainment.

On this Friday night, teens swayed and lip-synced in comedic interpretations of Brandy and Monica's "The Boy Is Mine." The boys were mesmerized by Talaitha. She held them in thrall and toyed with them collectively, instinctively drawing them into her gaze, then blowing them off like discarded toilet paper. She loved it. The boys couldn't help it, and the girls hated her for it. Talaitha didn't care. This game was child's play for her. These boys were too naive and innocent to comprehend what she was doing to them. She grew bored and began to stalk a few of the chaperones, who were completely unaware of the trap she was setting for them. Talaitha chuckled silently to herself. "Let the games begin," she whispered and headed to the chaperone's table.

Jack Frie intercepted Talaitha. Jack was one of the stars on the football team. He was tall, muscular, and walked with absolute confidence. "Where are you going, Tee?" Jack asked. By all accounts, the girls at the school were deeply attracted to Jack. He was on almost everyone's wish list, well, except for Talaitha's. She looked into Jack's eyes, deeply, longingly, pausing long enough to make sure there were plenty of eyes on the two of them. Then she pursed her lips and slowly moved toward him, delicately balancing on her tiptoes. Jack smiled and closed his eyes, waiting for the touch he knew he deserved.

Silence. After what felt like a full minute, Jack opened his eyes to see the whole gymnasium watching him stand alone, arms outstretched, face draped in anticipation, with nothing between his arms. The gym erupted in raucous laughter, with some even falling to the floor in a fit of laughter. Jack's teammates rushed him, slamming him on the back. Jack's face turned beet red. He felt humiliated, small, and ashamed. Several feet away, he could hear the laughter of a few girls as Talaitha made her way to the refreshments, her posse trailing her in envious delight.

Jack was furious. He rushed in Talaitha's direction, intent on slamming her through the gym floor. Like the quarterbacks he routinely wrecked on the field, Jack put a bullseye on Talaitha's back and charged. Having been anticipating Jack's reaction from the time she set him up with the fake kiss, Talaitha quickly sidestepped him. She stuck a foot out in front of him and screamed, "Leave me alone. I said no!" Jack fell flat on his face. Talaitha started adjusting her top, moving her bra strap back underneath her blouse. A crowd gathered around, and some teachers who were present also joined them. Jack's coach, Mr. Simons, also rushed over. Jack lay on the floor, and when he rolled over and sat up, Coach Simons was standing over him with a look of incredulity and disappointment draining from his face.

"Get up, Jack," Coach Simon said. "Let's go, and I don't even want to hear any excuses. I can't believe this. What has gotten into you, young man?"

Jack was frozen in place; he could not understand what had happened, but he eventually rose and followed his coach. Before he left the floor, he looked back at the crowd and caught Talaitha laughing among her girls. Meeting his eyes, she blew him a kiss and turned towards some of the parental chaperones mingling near the DJ's stand. Mr. Rustin looked intriguing, so she marked him.

As Talaitha made her way to Mr. Rustin, she caught a glimpse of Noelle standing at the exit door in the gym. Odd, she thought. No one was posted at that door because it was locked for tonight's dance. Fire code violations really didn't matter in Sable Ridge. Usually, by the time the fire department arrived, the structure would be ash. They were just too far away, and the local fire brigade was a mighty force of three men and a blind dog! So, to keep people from sneaking friends into the dance, the school staff would lock at least one door and post someone at the other exits.

Noelle stood at the door, taking a moment to gaze back at all the young people who were dancing and enjoying themselves. She scanned the dance floor one last time, hoping to find Talaitha. Was she really hoping, though? No, she thought. She saw what had transpired between Talaitha and Jack. It was classic Talaitha. Sometimes, Noelle envied her sister. She admired that much about her that she always seemed ten steps ahead of everyone else, always in control of things. In many regards, Noelle was just like her sister. They were both calculating. They were both focused. They both had near-flawless memories, but where Talaitha was spark and fiery retaliation, control and manipulation, Noelle was icy calm and quiet simmering, a coiled spring of potential fury. They were very much alike but different in how they saw themselves. Talaitha loathed Noelle for reasons she didn't understand and didn't care to. Noelle hungered for Talaitha, and this desire hurt her deeply. She didn't understand it and spent countless sleepless nights trying to understand why.

The twins locked eyes briefly. Talaitha smiled with disgust. Noelle rolled her eyes before the tears could escape. There was a universe between the two teen girls. For a brief moment, the gymnasium was cloaked in darkness, and the void that stretched between them was absolute. A moment more passed, and Talaitha resumed her stalking of Mr. Rustin. With that, Noelle walked out into the cool of the night, never to be seen again.

1

The Severing

Jevonte's vision begins to clear, but his head is aching. His thoughts are muted; a whirl of disjointed images vie for space in his mind. Pain racks through his body, causing his limbs to tremble. He is disoriented but struggles to sit up. The bed he's been chained to begins to creak in protest. He can't feel his legs. He's numb from the waist down, but his feet are feeling the effects of nerve endings as they wake up and announce their presence. Nothing seems to be working. His fingers are numb, and he struggles to get a grip on the bedsheets. He can't quite get into a good position to sit up. He strains to sit, but his body is so weak that he can't even manage a semi-crunch. The effort alone is taxing all of his strength. He feels completely helpless.

The despair is crushing. It feels like a herd of elephants is partying on his chest. His head is spinning, and he hears a tone—no, a ringing—in his ears. He must be concussed, he thinks to himself. He tries to turn over, but his ribs hurt, and his spine feels like it's laced with fire. He has to breathe in short, shallow breaths to keep his chest from moving too much. He feels warm. It must be a fever, he thinks. Dying of thirst, he tries to get a better look around his room, but his neck is sore, and he can barely turn his head.

"God, how long have I been here?" Jevonte mutters. The darkness in the room remains placid and heavy. There is no reply. She must not be listening, he thinks.

The bed is sticky and warm. It's slightly damp under his back. Did I piss myself? He wonders. Through the dim evening light coming from the bedroom window, he can see dark stains on the sheet that covers him. Is that blood? Panic starts to take hold of his spirit. The room smells damp and musty, and an acrid, metallic odor hangs in the air. The sun's waning glow casts shadows across the room's walls. Nothing is clear in his mind. The ringing in his head that stirred him to consciousness has increased in intensity. He tries to call out, but his throat is parched, the dryness torching the back of his throat like vengeful fire. He stops struggling and lies flat on the bed. His breath is now shallow, and he feels like he's about to pass out from the effort.

Jevonte lets the evening light consume him. He continues to steel himself against the darkness filling the room. As his heartbeat finally slows, his breathing becomes more controlled. His eyes adjust to the twilight surrounding him. With a renewed effort, Jevonte turns onto his stomach.

He rests for a moment before trying to push up to a kneeling position. He fails, and his face collapses into the pillow. He slowly shifts himself to the edge of the bed, moving his face to keep from suffocating. He manages to move his right leg over the edge of the mattress. Using the weight and a little momentum, he pushes with his left arm and slides ungracefully to the floor. The wounds on his abdomen and lower extremities open from his collision with the floor. His thoughts are so clouded, he barely registers the pain. Everything hurts everywhere, all at once.

Jevonte wasn't sure what his plan was when he rolled out of bed. He had no plan. He knew that he didn't want to remain in bed. He tried to concentrate and think, but he couldn't get his thoughts together. He was in too much agony. Every movement made him want to give up. At least my body seems to be coming back online. He can move his right arm fairly well, at least.

Outside of the small bay window, Jevonte can hear a car door close. He can hear voices. There is someone near the house. He opens his mouth to cry out, but nothing escapes. His brain finally starts to recognize what his body is screaming about. The fire erupting in his loins is severe, pulsating at first before exploding up through his body like an angry volcano intent on destroying the world. His whole frame is convulsing with torment as he tries with all of his might to make a sound, anything to get the attention of whoever is outside his window. The effort is too much, and Jevonte starts to pass out from the sheer torment and trauma of the moment. With his body bleeding, Jevonte surrenders to the cold embrace of the floor.

When Jevonte wakes, he's still on the floor. He's still in a great deal of pain, but the tremors and explosive echoes rippling from his midsection have calmed—somewhat. At least he can think a little more clearly. His eyes move to the left side of his room, his cell. He can barely make out the outlines of a door. It's one of those divided doors where the top can be opened while the bottom half remains closed. He wonders quietly, "When did she get that?" His eyes continue, following the door to an adjacent desk and chair. It's a small student's desk, not something you'd see an adult using. The room is dark, but he sees what appear to be carved, wooden animals scattered across the desktop. He continues his survey of the room and locates the source of the shimmering starlight pressing into the space. A single bay window frames the wall, and its light paints the foot of the bed he had been shackled to. It's all strange. Jevonte struggles to place the desk or the toys in his mind. None of it makes any sense. She never mentioned children or a desire for any.

Jevonte lies still once more. The slightest movement triggers avalanches of anguish and waves of repressive, nauseating pain in his stomach and groin. With his right hand, he reaches into his ragged pajama pants to check himself. He can't see what's happened to him because it's too dark, but he can feel it. Jevonte shudders and starts weeping slowly as his fingers trace over testicles swollen like grapefruits. He can't find his penis! He can't even feel where it is. This mess can't be right, he thinks. There is a mass where his junk should be, but what his fingers find feels more like a clump of stiffened jelly. His left ankle is immobile. He can't move it at all. He uses his right foot to feel around his ankle, where he finds a heavy chain wrapped around it. The chain rattles as he slides it away from the bed, but he doesn't get far before his groin and midsection demand an immediate halt.

Jevonte discovers cuts and bruises all over his torso, along with rippling scabs and painful lesions crisscrossing his chest. He's glad he can't see what he must look like. He reaches up to feel his face and head. There are lumps on the top of his head and spots on his face that are too painful to touch. His right eye is swollen shut. He notices something else. He can feel his chin, but it feels wrong. With his tongue, he searches his mouth and lips. His teeth are all there. He starts to rub his forehead, and that's when he notices that he's missing a finger; his pinky finger is gone!

A broken, terrified howl finally manages to escape from his throat. Jevonte starts to heave and vomit, and his injuries intensify their assault on his senses. He has never felt so much misery and so much pain, and he has never been as afraid as he is now. He doesn't know what to do. What can he do? As Jevonte lies on the floor, the starlight streaming in steady ebbs of subdued blues and white light, he tries to conjure up memories, memories that might help him understand how he got here. He has to focus on something else besides his condition.

Slowly, the beginnings of some memories tease their way back into his mind. Most of them are just jagged recollections, jumbled together, out of order, vague, and still too distant to seem real. Her face, however, is clear in his mind. Her smile was gentle and inviting. The depth of her brown skin, her green eyes, the strength in her arms, and her glow captivated and mesmerized him from the start. Her hair hid the night, and she wore it like a mantle of power and divine authority. She reminded him of an ancient African queen, commanding armies and binding her enemies in the wake of her train. Everyone bowed down before her. Everyone desired her riches, her bounty, and her mercy.

Jevonte willingly surrendered to the shackles of her passion, as it liberated him.

He swore to his family that his love for her was genuine, arguing that it was not a fleeting affair. The moment he stepped into her presence on the cruise, he fell for her. She was not like any other woman he had ever known. He told his uncle Roscoe that there was magic in her hips. She commanded both him and his heart, leaving him with no choice but to obey, which he did with wanton abandon. Of course, his family didn't understand. They constantly questioned his rashness and the speed at which he was attempting to make her a permanent part of his life.

His friends thought he was being corny when he told them that she was the song his soul was destined to sing. She was the one. There was no doubt about it. Everything with her was effortless, and this state of bliss validated him and his decision to propose to her. There was nothing they wouldn't do for one another. He'd finally found someone who understood what he wanted and what he needed and someone willing to fight for him. He had never had that. She fought for him. She was always where he needed her to be, and that comforted him beyond measure. Although they did not understand her, Jevonte did, and that was all that mattered to him—back then.

As Jevonte lay in the dark, he also remembered how passionate their lovemaking had been. She felt supernatural to him. She paced him. She was surgical in her control of his energy, holding him back until she was ready. She orchestrated their love play in ways that defied all understanding. There were nights when he actually believed that she was a goddess, someone divinely appointed for the communion of their flesh, and he always craved her until it hurt.

His thoughts shift to his family. He closes his eyes and tries to think about his mom. "What was it she tried to tell me?" he whispers to himself. In a gentle whisper, Jevonte cries, "Mom, why didn't I just listen?" I should have paid attention to you and Dad. My God, what have I done! "Uncle," Jevonte utters softly. "I need you to find me, please."

Jevonte's body starts to grow cold, lying on the damp floor. He is shivering now. He wonders how much more of this he can endure when the door shudders loudly and violently against its frame. The sudden shock of the sound jolts Jevonte into alertness. He clearly cannot move, but he does all he can to squirm closer to the bed, trying to gain some distance between him and the door. He stares intently in the door's direction, as a soft, delicate knock rattles against the top door half. The old wooden door registers three knocks, then silence. Three more knocks, then the quiet of the room fills the entire space. Jevonte's heart starts pounding. He knows that knock. In an instant, memories of her bat and the blows it delivered to his body—the garden shears—flooded his mind like an enraged, bloodthirsty mob. He is again in the thrall of her terror. He is once more lost in her hurricane of madness, just so much debris tossed to and fro and at the mercy of her unrelenting, torturous love.

Jevonte believed he had found his soulmate—until the woman he married gradually transformed his body into a prison of pain and his mind into her favorite weapon. With the knock announcing a new round of horror and dread, Jevonte's thoughts flash back to just a couple of short years ago, when everything made sense before it all fell apart.

2

Alone Among Lovers

It's early in the evening, and the summer heat has settled into a comfortable lull. A gentle breeze drifts ashore, and Canton Waterfront Park is just beginning to welcome its first few visitors. Parking is still available, much to Jevonte's relief. Typically, this time of year, the park is pretty congested. He finds a spot close to the water and parks.

At first, he's content to sit in the car and listen to some music. But the weather is nearly perfect, and the walking paths look inviting, so he bites. I can't be the only guy out here by himself, he thinks. Jevonte looks up the path. "Yep, I am. How pitiful," he mutters. "It doesn't matter. I mean, who's watching? Who even cares?" I need to get out of my head. The day is fine, and I'm right where I want to be, he thinks, stepping out of the car and onto the path.

Jevonte begins his walk, seemingly carefree, but there's a slight slouch in his back. His shoulders are heavy, burdened. His thoughts drift, and all the beauty of the bay slips past him like the breeze. He's so disconnected that he nearly walks into a couple of lovebirds holding hands along the path.

"Oh, I'm so sorry. I didn't see you," Jevonte says, embarrassed.

The man tilts his head and offers kindly, "It's okay. No harm, no foul."

"Thank you. Every time I come here, I end up lost in my thoughts. You two look lovely together. Are you a couple?"

"Married, six years last week," the woman smiles. "We come here all the time, until the bay starts smelling from all the fishing boats and whatnot."

They wave goodbye and continue down the path, hand in hand, joy in their every step. Jevonte watches them a moment longer before resuming his walk. That kind of happiness... that's what I'd love right about now. It's what I really need, he thinks solemnly.

As he rounds one of the inclines, Jevonte sees several couples sprawled across picnic blankets on the lawn. Some have baskets, charcuterie boards, and wine. Others are playing games or laughing together. One couple is nestled close, gently stroking each other while Luther Vandross croons softly from a nearby radio. He slows his stroll, barely catching Cheryl Lynn's voice:

"If this world were mine, I would make you a king with wealth untold; you would have everything if this world were mine."

Jevonte is spellbound by the harmony and intimacy of the moment. The lyrics grip him so securely he can't look away; he doesn't want to—until the man finally notices him staring. Snapping out of his trance, Jevonte waves weakly in apology and resumes walking.

How embarrassing. I must look like the biggest loser right now. I bet they're laughing at me, he thinks. He doesn't look back. He can feel their eyes mocking him and branding him a lost soul.

He takes a seat on an empty bench. Foot traffic has picked up. "More couples? Really?" Jevonte whispers under his breath, his inner torment building.

A mixed-race couple strolls by in perfect sync. He can't quite place the ethnicity of the second couple, but they begin a slow jog in the direction he is heading. Two older Black women push a baby stroller down one of the side paths, heading toward the public restrooms. Near the pier, a group of young people gather, looking across the bay and pointing out the nearby yachts anchored on the harbor side. He can hear the excitement in their voices. Jevonte thinks about the couples who are making plans, discussing dreams, and hoping for a better future. If they only knew how lucky they are, he thinks.

People are everywhere—tuned in, connected, laughing, loving. "Just look at them," Jevonte mutters. Countless voices tickle his ears—laughter, whispers, and the soft, hungry sighs of intimacy. It feels almost cruel. I need to find a new place to chill. Let me stop, he reflects. Look at them, though—carefree, unbothered. I wonder just how many of these people are really happy. Like, how much of this is just a show? Who knows, at home they might be fighting like cats and dogs. God, I hate this.

Jevonte lowers his face into his hands, his fingers pushing through the short hairs of his beard. As he rests against his knees, the pointy elbows of his arms make them ache. "This trip wasn't a good idea," he admits. I thought getting out, getting some air, and changing the scenery would help. But I feel worse than ever. Maybe what I need is to go home, pour a stiff drink, and call it a day. Staying here is only making me feel worse.

He begins his walk back to the car, retracing his steps past all the same entangled souls. No one notices him, not even the man who caught him staring earlier. As he passes the same couple, Teddy Pendergrass's "Love T.K.O." is playing on the radio. The lyrics hit like a body blow, and

Jevonte stumbles slightly. A wave of nausea rises. He hurries to the car.

Inside, he pounds the steering wheel. "I can't. I can't do this. It's too much." Looking up at the roof of his Jeep Grand Cherokee, he groans, "I'm a grown man. Why am I feeling so overwhelmed? It's just people. It's just life right now. So what if I don't have anyone? I've been doing just fine on my own. So why the hell am I feeling like this? I'm not going to be alone forever. Or, maybe I will be. Shit, this is just sad and pitiful."

He closes his eyes, holding back tears. But when he opens them, a little white girl is pointing at him, talking to her mom and dad. The father chuckles. The mother gently takes her hand, and the family walks off toward the park. Jevonte lets the tears come.

At home, Mrs. Elleanor is sweeping her stoop, humming along with Grover Washington Jr.'s "Just the Two of Us" on 107.9 FM. Jevonte notices her as he pulls into his driveway.

"Hi, Mrs. Elleanor. Good to see you out and about. How are you?" Jevonte braces himself. He winces inside, anticipating that she is going to start again. Mrs. Elleanor had taken a fall a few months ago and had nearly broken her hip. She was a fixture in the neighborhood, constantly sweeping her stoop and tidying her yard. People had noticed her absence.

"I'm good, young man. Thanks for asking," she says with a smile. "And how about you? Have you met anyone yet? Son, you've got to get out and meet people. It's not good for a man to be alone, you know what I mean?"

"Yes, ma'am. I'm working on it," Jevonte says weakly.

"Well, look, we're having a singles night at the church in a few weeks. You ought to come by and mingle. We've got some wonderful young ladies at our church. God-fearing women. I'm sure there's someone just right for you."

Jevonte breathes deeply. "Thank you, Mrs. Elleanor. I'll think about it. And thank you for thinking of me."

She resumes sweeping and humming as Jevonte enters his house, closing the door softly behind him. He grabs a beer and sits at the kitchen bar. The microwave clock is flashing.

Great, he thinks. The power must've gone out.

As he rises to reset the time, his phone rings.

"Hi, Dad."

"Hey, son. I called earlier, but the phone just kept ringing. You okay?"

"Oh yeah, I was just out for a bit."

"You need to get yourself an answering machine. You never know who might call with something important."

Jedidiah Greene was blunt with his son. Stern, but loving. Jevonte found him to be a bit pushy at times, but he was always dependable. He and Jevonte's mother, Ruby, had been married for 38 years. Through all the storms they weathered over those years, they stayed together. Jevonte envied that.

"I know, Dad. You always remind me. I will, eventually. What's going on?"

"Your mom and I were talking about a social event we saw online, and your old high school friend, Mercer, came up. Remember him? He's hosting something we saw on Facebook. It looks like many people you used to hang out with are planning to go."

"Oh yeah, I remember him. We haven't really talked since Howard. I'll have to check it out. I haven't been online in a while, my calendar's been a mess, but if I can find the time, I'll look into it. How's…"

Jedidiah cuts him off. "Son, I'm not trying to tell you what to do, but we're worried. You've been alone for so long, cooped up in the house. Are you seeing anyone?"

"Well, there it is. You said you would rather not get in my business, and here you are doing just that," Jevonte says with a smirk. "I'm fine, Dad. I don't need dating advice right now. No disrespect, but it's different these days. People don't date the same way you and Mom did back when woolly mammoths roamed the earth," he joked.

"Jevonte, we're not bloody dinosaurs," Jedidiah chuckles. "You make it sound like your mom, and I grew up in the 20s. I get it, but I'm telling you, as you get older, the doors don't open as easily. You catch my drift?"

"My goodness, Dad. If I wanted to get some, I could," Jevonte says, laughing. "That's not my problem, old man."

"I'm your father," Jedidiah says in his best Darth Vader voice. "I just don't want that thing to fall off before you give us a grandkid!"

They both burst into laughter. For a moment, Jevonte forgets the loneliness that stalks him.

"I appreciate the concern, Dad. I do. I'll check out Mercer's thing later tonight. Tell Mom I'll call her."

"Will do. And one more thing, get an answering machine!"

Jevonte hangs up. The blinking microwave reminds him there's more to reset than the time. Maybe it's time to reset everything.

He pulls out his laptop and logs into Facebook. It's been so long that he has to reset the password. Finally, he finds Mercer's event. It's a simple house party to kick off their upcoming high school reunion. Jevonte missed the last one, so the prospect piques his interest.

Most commenters are unfamiliar with him, but quite a few women are chiming in. That's encouraging. Still, he can't help but notice one name missing. Maybe she just hasn't seen it yet. Jevonte opens his Outlook calendar, creates an entry, and sets a reminder two days before the party. Then, eyeing his wardrobe in his mind, he resets it for a week. "I need to buy some clothes," Jevonte exhales in exasperation. This is why I don't like to go anywhere; I hate this.

He logs off his laptop and heads back to the kitchen, not sure that he's even hungry. The bareness of his pantry and fridge exacerbates the emptiness he's already feeling. "Dang, dude, when was the last time you bought food?" Depressed, Jevonte heads for the couch and turns on the TV. "Just another night of mind-numbing late-night talk shows," he sighs.

Nothing is on, and Jevonte quickly loses interest in channel surfing. "Maybe watching a little porn will help me sleep," Jevonte says to the glowing TV screen. The desktop whirls to life again. Clicking on the "Juggs for Thugs" link under his browser favorites transports Jevonte to one of his favorite porn sites. Three hours later, Jevonte falls out of his desk chair, and his keyboard slides out of his lap. "Dammit. I fell asleep again. Shoot," he fumes. The microwave clock is still flashing. The microwave clock's glowing red zeros contrast sharply with the darkness of his kitchen space. Jevonte rises and notes the time on his computer screen. It's 2:54 a.m.

He shuts down his desktop and shambles off to his bedroom. He has to meet with a client at 9:00 a.m. to provide an estimate for a sunroom remodeling project. Two weeks have already passed since the project began, and the client is starting to show signs of trepidation. I need this job. The funds and dividends are getting on the low side, Jevonte thinks.

Jevonte slides under his sheets and lies on his back. The quiet of his room is noticeable, but he feels calm right now. "I have to find a better way to still my thoughts. I'm going to have a phenomenal day with the client. I will book this job. I will find the perfect shirt to wear to Mercer's party—shit, Mercer's party! I can't go to that thing. I mean, I don't know anyone, and Mercer probably doesn't even remember me. I did make a promise to the old man, though. Fuck!" Jevonte says with consternation.

He closes his eyes and fights to escape his anxiety, but his thoughts about the party, the park outing, and everything except sleep continue to evade his every effort. So, he reaches into his nightstand and pulls out his liquid silk. The jar is almost empty, but the single pump of pleasure goo is enough. Five minutes later, Jevonte is expended. His mind surrenders to the night as his body relaxes under the tutelage of the dopamine coursing through his brain.

3

Blueprints and Blind Spots

Jevonte is up early despite the very late night he had. He grabs his gear, his booking notes, drafting stock, and keys. He pauses at his barren pantry and stares into the space along the shelves. "Note to self, make a stop and buy some bloody food," he says to himself.

Before he turns to head to the door, he picks up the phone to call his client, James Rueberry Carlton. James was among Jevonte's first clients when he embarked on his independent career as a contractor. He had been doing random jobs as a carpenter when James saw the work he had done for a few friends. Jevonte received a commission to refurbish dilapidated row houses. When Jevonte finished with them, they looked almost like newly constructed homes. The detail Jevonte created in the woodwork was what really captured James's attention.

"Hello, Mr. Carlton, this is Jevonte."

"Good morning, Jevonte. Haven't I told you to call me Carl? Please, no need to be so formal with me. Your work has certainly earned that privilege."

Jevonte chuckles humorously before responding, "Sir, now you know how my mom and pops raised me. They'd have my backside if I ever presumed to call you by your first name."

"Well, if you say so, that's fine. I can respect that. Now, what can I do for you? Are we still on for this morning?"

"Yes, sir, that's why I was calling. I just wanted to confirm and let you know that I was on my way."

"Excellent, I will be here waiting for you. I'm really looking forward to seeing what you want to do with the sunroom and basement area."

Jevonte pauses slightly, not sure he heard Mr. Carlton correctly. "Ah, sir, did you say basement? We discussed your sunroom, but not the basement."

"Oh, I thought I would add it to the project. We've been looking to get some work done on the basement for years. Bryan could never make up his mind about that space, and I am running out of patience," Mr. Carlton laughs. "Look, just take a look at the basement area and see what improvements you can make with it when you get here. We've budgeted for the renovation, and I'm sure we can make it worth your time."

"Yes, sir. Give me a few more minutes, say thirty? I'll need a few more items to work up an estimate and project plan for the basement. It shouldn't take me long at all."

The two men hang up, and a large but worried smile spreads across Jevonte's face. Basement! Basement now, he thinks excitedly, imagining the potential payday ahead. He might be able to invoice this job for at least $65,000, maybe more, depending on the extent of the basement upgrade. Jevonte grabs his car keys and heads out the door. The lights on his microwave blink steadily as he closes the door.

Mr. Carlton's house, which Jevonte would describe as a mansion, occupies a large three-acre lot on the outskirts of Baltimore City. The home was magnificent. Jevonte doesn't think it needs any upgrades, but Mr. Carlton has money and likes to spend it. Jevonte believes he is a bit too generous with his largesse, but it is his dough. He laughs at the thought of calling Mr. Carlton by his first name. James always ends up paying him significantly more than he is invoiced for, especially for the last few jobs he completed. Jevonte doesn't want to take advantage, even though he's more than happy to keep the overages!

The morning proceeded as planned. Jevonte provides two project plans for Mr. Carlton. Mr. Carlton writes two checks to get the project started. He even offers to pay for everything in full, but Jevonte refuses. "Half is fine and is all I need for now," he reassures Mr. Carlton.

As Jevonte is packing his equipment, Bryan arrives home. "O Lord, what has that man done now?" James asks grumpily.

Bryan and James have been sharing a life undercover for almost a decade. Friends and family know who they are to one another, but publicly, neither man disclosed very much about their personal lives. Bryan is a tenured professor at Towson University and teaches in their African American Studies Program. James is a named partner at the law offices of Dwight Strong, James Carlton, and Harry Lewis. James isn't the managing partner, but his billable hours dwarfed those of his other two partners combined. James knows he can take the named position whenever he wants because of his client lists and the vast white whales he serves, but he also knows that life is worth more. He and Bryan have built a quiet, settled life together. He doesn't need the extra demands a named partnership will require.

"Hello, Mr. Butcher," Jevonte says politely as he continues to load his gear into the back of his Jeep.

"Now, young man, please, please, call me Bryan. You are practically family, what with all the projects my dear friend has cast upon you over the years," he smiles.

"I appreciate it, but a rule is a rule, and my momma didn't raise no hellion!" Jevonte extends his hand and waves goodbye to James.

On his way home, Jevonte pulls into the Towson mall. He's riding high, feeling good about the money he's about to make, and he's famished. The food court is crowded, but he doesn't care. He orders a three-entree meal from Bourbon Wild Grill and finds a seat at a table along the periphery. It isn't the ideal spot, but he has a good view of passersby. The afternoon's entertainment is already underway. During the summer months, it's literally clothing optional at this mall. Some of the wildest outfits one can imagine make their appearances during this time of the year.

Jevonte starts digging into his noodles and beef slices when he spots someone he thinks he knows. "Mercer, is that Mercer?" he thinks out loud. Mercer is walking into the Men's Warehouse situated across from where Jevonte is seated. The man looks like Mercer, but at this distance, Jevonte isn't sure.

Jevonte rushes through the rest of his meal and guzzles his Sprite. Tossing his leftovers in the trash bin, he cuts across the food court and makes a cautious beeline for the clothing store. Inside, the man he believes is Mercer is casually perusing some of the off-the-rack suit combinations on the sales rack. He's taking his time. Jevonte makes a mental note of which items catch Mercer's eye. The man was always a snappy dresser back in the day, and Jevonte finally has the chance to watch him at work.

Jevonte is carefully shadowing Mercer. He starts walking down an aisle parallel to Mercer when he bumps into a sales clerk. The clerk drops all of the display materials she was carrying for a new frontside showcase. The materials sprawl across the aisle, attracting the attention of several patrons, including Mercer.

"Oh snap. I'm so sorry. I didn't see...," the clerk interrupts him.

"My goodness! Everything is everywhere now," the clerk snarls. "It took me all fucking morning to locate these, shit."

Jevonte is petrified. No, mortified. It feels like the whole store is looking directly at him. But in reality, it's only Mercer who is staring blankly at Jevonte, a growing, inquisitive look spreading across his face.

"Jevonte? My man, is that you?" Mercer laughs out loud as he crosses the aisle to where Jevonte and the angry clerk are standing.

"Hey Mercer, what's up?"

"You, apparently! I wasn't sure at first that it was you, but then I remembered that no one is as awkward in life or with women as good old Jevonte Greene. How are things going, my man?" Mercer asks, a sly smile still beaming across his face.

"Mercer Shephard, in the flesh! You look good for a retired pimp!" Jevonte replies as he stoops to help the clerk pick up the display materials. The clerk scowls at Jevonte before grabbing the spilled items and walking off. Jevonte and Mercer move out of the center aisle and resume their conversation.

"Retired? Man, please. Actually, I am reformed. I've dedicated my life to the straight and narrow these days. Believe it or not, I'm a one-woman man. I left that life in the rearview mirror years ago, and I don't miss it. Since walking away from that life," Mercer grabs his package, "the Bible is the only sword I sling, man. What have you been up to? Still square biz these days?" Mercer jokes.

"Merc," Jevonte shifts to the school nickname Mercer used to wear fondly around the halls of Carver

Vocational-Technical High School, "I've been working hard, man. I have my own company. Well, it's just me running it, but it's still mine, you know what I mean?"

"Sure, sure, that sounds really good, though sorrowful, man," Mercer jests. "Look, let's do some catching up really soon, ok? What does your busy company schedule look like these days? Can you pencil me in?" Mercer asks, a trace of merriment lacing his words.

"I like that. We should, but I've been swamped with jobs lately. Let's exchange..." Mercer stops him in mid-sentence.

"I tell you what, I'm having a little party thing at my place next Saturday. Why don't you swing by, and we can do a little catching up then?"

"I... I... sure," Jevonte stammers. "I can probably make that work."

"Dude, it's on a Saturday. Who works on a Saturday? C'mon, you can do this. Besides, I have some cool friends stopping by, mostly single people. You're not seeing anyone, right? It will be perfect!"

How does he know that? How's he just going to assume that I'm not seeing anyone? Jevonte thinks to himself. I really don't feel like doing this, but I did promise

Pops. "Sure, I can do that. Here, write down your address and phone number on this."

Jevonte hands Mercer part of a paper receipt he had from Bourbon Wild Grill. The two men exchange some dap, then Jevonte starts toward the store's entrance.

"My man," Mercer calls after Jevonte. "Aren't you going to buy something? What did you come in here for?"

Jevonte stares blankly before replying. "I can't make up my mind, so I'm going to look around at some other stores. See you Sat…" Mercer turns and continues to inspect the clothing racks as if he were alone in the store, ignoring Jevonte before he can finish speaking.

Jevonte spends the rest of the afternoon going from one clothing store to another. It's been so long since he went to any social event. He has no idea what to buy or what he should wear. His grown-up life has been one of hard work and sacrifice. He has work clients like Mr. Carlton and his partner, Bryan, and his mom and dad, but no hangout friends. I need some advice. This kind of life is pathetic, Jevonte thinks.

He finally settles on some jeans and an Old Navy sweatshirt. He decides he'll clean up his Tims and wear them. He usually wears them for his carpentry gigs, but they clean up nicely once he gets the wood scarring and glue off.

The following days are a blur. Jevonte has started rough sketching Mr. Carlton's job and completed some quick work on Ms. Elleanor's guest bathroom. Of course, he works on the bathroom quickly and finishes before Ms. Elleanor can return home from grocery shopping. The last thing Jevonte wants to hear is another pitch for her church's singles event, which she was trying to involve him in. He really liked the old lady, but she could be pushy, and he already got enough dating and relationship advice from his mom and dad.

On Saturday, Jevonte arrives early at the address Mercer gave him. The condo was very chic and upper-middle class; "bougie" was the word that came to Jevonte's mind. It is nice and exactly what Jevonte expected to see for Mercer. He definitely would not stay long. He would meet and greet a few people and then flee the premises!

Three hours later, Jevonte is standing alone out on the balcony. The scotch in his hand is nearly gone, and he is lost in his thoughts, watching the lights of the city below shimmer with unrealized promise.

"My dude! What in the hell are you doing out here?" Mercer asks as he walks away from the raucous noise erupting in the party room inside. Closing the door behind him, Mercer approaches Jevonte, gin and juice in hand.

"Nothing. I just needed some air. Great party, by the way," Jevonte replies somberly before turning back to the scenery below.

"Well, it can't be that great since you're out here all by yourself, and some of the finest women on this side of Baltimore Street are in there," Mercer points with gusto toward the party room.

Quiet descends on the two men and threatens to engulf them when Jevonte says, "I appreciate the invite, and yeah, you are right, there are some real fine ladies in there, but..." he pauses, his words stumbling, constraining his throat.

"But what? You looked like you were doing okay in there, from what I could see. I mean, please don't take this the wrong way, but Barbara mentioned that you appeared a bit out of place in there. Well, I was told that you looked cute, but it seemed like you were dressed for a Baby Gap convention or something. I didn't hear anything else negative, except for Thurnesia; she mentioned, or so I was told, that you smelled like her dad. Mercer stepped closer to get a whiff of Jevonte. "Man, is that Brute? Please tell me you don't have that shit on, please!"

"So. I like the way it smells."

Mercer drops his head while shaking it slowly. "My dude, my man, come on now."

Jevonte sets his drink down on the banister. "I tried to get involved in there, but it just didn't feel right to me. I was just out of my element." Jevonte's downtrodden eyes cut a sour look towards the party room. "There were some very intriguing women in there, but no one who interested me. I don't think I appealed to them. They showed no interest in me, or I didn't pick up on any interest from them. There was one lady; I think her name was D'Queshon or something like that…"

"That was Deeshawn," Mercer corrected. "We call her microwave… I'll explain why later," Mercer laughs.

"Well, she was nice, but she kept yawning when I told her about my company. I didn't sync with anyone in that crowd."

"I think you're judging the situation too harshly. Everyone is a stranger in there, right? You don't know them, and they don't know you. It takes a little time for people to warm up to each other."

"That's true, but I realized I was in the wrong place when you brought out that Urban Trivia game. I was excited to play at first, until you made everyone form teams of three.

Man, it was worse than those days in the gym when no one picked me for their team. Here I am, 36 years old, feeling as though I am back on the playground, without friends and disliked by the other kids. It just made me feel like shit, you know. Do you understand what that feels like? No, I bet you don't. You've always had your fun, had the best girls, and got to do just about whatever you felt like doing."

A brief silence separates the two men, and Mercer looks out over the city before slowly turning to Jevonte.

"Jevonte, you are right. I got what I wanted, who I wanted, and when I wanted it. Not because I was the most suave or debonair. I was, of course, but that wasn't the reason I succeeded. I won on the outside because I was winning on the inside. I figured out that at the end of the day, no one really cares who you are. I mean, yeah, your parents care. The pastor cares, and maybe some teachers care, but mostly, no one cares who you are. People are too focused on their own survival to care about others, and that's the truth. Sure, words get spoken, and people say a lot of things about caring for each other because they know they are supposed to say those things, but when the rubber meets the road, and the chips are down, you see who they really are. Are you feeling me?"

Jevonte picks up his scotch and empties the glass. The intense brown liquor burns its way down. "I hear you, but what are you really trying to say to me? I don't seem to remember seeing you down a single day when we were in school."

"Jevonte, I'll say it again, I was winning on the outside because I was winning on the inside. I felt invincible, and that gave me the confidence to transform how I saw the world around me."

"Oh, so what you're saying is that you had a positive outlook on life and…"

"No, dude, no," Mercer interrupted. "Let me ask you one simple question. Do you love yourself? Do you love who you are unconditionally?"

"What kind of question is that? Of course, I know who I am. I have been running my independent contracting company for the last five years. I stand on my own two feet, and I have managed to make my own way in this world."

"Jevonte, that is not what I asked you."

"Do I love myself? Merc, that's a silly question. Yes, of course I do. How could I not? I mean, how can anyone not love themselves, right?"

"Listen, I'm no shrink, but what I learned about people, about myself, is that when you truly love yourself, when you love that man in the mirror, inside and out, unconditionally, you will draw like energy. You will attract the love you feel inside for yourself."

"Merc, you are definitely right about one thing. You are no shrink," laughs Jevonte. "Listen, I understand what you're saying, but that stuff sounds like something straight off of an Oprah Winfrey show. No offense, but I think you've been watching too much TV."

Mercer exhales. "Ok, Mr. Happiness. Have it however you want; believe what you want, but I am telling you, you won't find love out there," and Mercer points his gin glass towards the city lights, "until you find it in here," and Mercer points at the center of his chest, drawing a circle where the heart is.

"I'm done preaching, and I need a refill. Why don't you come back inside and get one too? Perhaps I'll explain how Big Dee got her nickname, ha," Mercer chuckles as he starts towards the party room.

"I'll be in soon," Jevonte replies.

For the next ten minutes, Jevonte stands alone, reflecting on Mercer's question and their conversation. Yeah, maybe if I were still in high school, it might make sense, but I'm a grown man. I'm old enough to know who I am. If I didn't love myself, why would I work this hard to accomplish what I have accomplished?

Facing the city lights, Jevonte contemplates whether the real question isn't if he loves himself. Maybe the better question is: why hasn't he taken a vacation in the past 10 years? Mulling it over in his mind, he's worked nonstop since forming his contracting business, and perhaps that's why he's so out of sync and so out of rhythm with the women he meets. He doesn't blame them for not being interested in him. He has no life outside of his work! A light comes on in his head, and it all seems to make sense now. What he needs is a vacation!

4

Screams Beneath the Surface

Jevonte, waiting in the customs line, thinks, I'm in the line to hell, man. I didn't know the wait would be this long or slow. This deal was too good to pass up, and who knows when I'd get another chance like this? Passengers are forming in various queues on the boarding deck. Excited children are whining and playing in line. Frustrated parents are pulling, yanking, and scolding, hoping that the lines move faster so they can get their charges safely tucked away in the cabin.

Jevonte continues scanning the boarding area. It all looks like utter chaos, but the lines are moving, luggage is getting dropped and processed, and passengers are slowly making their way to their designated decks. Despite her age, the Vision of the Seas still strikes an impressive pose while docked at the harbor.

Jevonte has never taken a cruise. This was a spontaneous decision. He couldn't decide where to vacation, but when he saw the ad while surfing online, the seven-day getaway was priced right and would let him see multiple places in one trip. Also, he disliked flying and preferred not to drive his Jeep for this vacation. The Jeep would remind him too much of work, and he wanted to escape that for now.

Once inside his cabin, he stepped out onto the balcony and inhaled deeply. The salty sea air comforted him. "This," he said to himself, "is going to be a great trip. I know it."

Stepping back inside, he starts putting his things away, moving his cruise sets into the cabin's storage spaces and setting up his toiletries. The bathroom is small and seriously cramped, something he hadn't anticipated, but he manages to make the space work. "Squared away," Jevonte smiles. The moment reminds him of his Uncle Roscoe, who would always use that phrase. The thought reminds him of family. When he booked this cruise, he told no one, not even his parents or his uncle, that he was getting away for a bit. He wasn't sure why. He just didn't, but now he felt like calling someone to say goodbye and let everyone know. The thought struck him as peculiar. As he thought about it more, he reasoned that in some small way, he just wanted his family to know that he was an adult and that he could do things for himself. He smiled, thinking that he was sending his family, mainly his mom and dad, a message that if he could go on a vacation by himself, he could also find a woman without their help. He knew they meant well, but too often, they over-parented, and he was a grown-ass man now.

A series of announcements blares over the ship's intercom. Jevonte focuses on the meal and dining locations mentioned in the announcement. He worked up a big appetite getting himself together and making it to the pier on time. He locks some of his valuables in the cabin safe and heads towards the buffet area. The ship is huge in Jevonte's mind. Getting around is proving a little confusing, but after 20 minutes, Jevonte finds the buffet breakfast area. His eyes go wide with the variety of food to choose from. It's a bit overwhelming at first, but Jevonte gathers some delectable French toast and strawberries before taking a table near one of the huge deck windows. From where he is sitting, he can see the front of the ship as it begins its transit away from the port of Baltimore. Jevonte's spirits are rising as the voyage gets underway.

Later in the morning, while the ship is well underway, Jevonte ventures down to the eatery to grab some brunch. A trio of college-aged Black women moves through the buffet line, scooping up various fruits, and then heads over to the omelet station. Their laughter and joy are infectious, immediately capturing Jevonte's attention. He's staring, mesmerized by the air of freedom and happiness emanating from them. They gather their breakfast plates and take a seat adjacent to Jevonte's table. One of the young women glances briefly in Jevonte's direction, and he breaks off from his trance, embarrassed. My God, what's wrong with me? He thinks.

The women speak in hushed tones, and Jevonte detects a little laughter from the trio. He finishes his meal quickly and then departs the breakfast lounge. Damn. Jevonte thinks to himself. He assumed the women were laughing at him. "Well, I had hoped this vacation would be an improvement. I guess not," and he exits the dining area.

Before evening, Jevonte has explored the entire ship and signed up for a couple of excursions when the ship arrives at Belize in two days. The chance to see and walk through some of the ancient Maya ruins is irresistible. Jevonte had never heard of the Cahal Pech or Xunantunich ruins. Hence, the opportunity to learn about this royal acropolis-palace, home to an elite Mayan ruling family, intrigued him. His attendance at Howard was an outstanding educational experience, but none of his studies ever gave him a clue to South America's vast cultural richness.

Passengers disembark at Belize City. The tour bus is packed. The city is busy. Tourists are moving throughout the shops, grabbing up souvenirs as they go. The weather is warm but muggy. It's the rainy season, so most of the town is wet, and the streets are braced with channels of running water. However, Jevonte is well-prepared. He's a planner by nature and vocation. He carefully packed a spare set of clothes in his backpack and waterproofed everything. He made sure to keep his passport and identification papers dry inside.

Most of the disembarked passengers are traveling in pairs or groups. Jevonte is alone, but he stays relatively close to a group of women he recognizes from breakfast at the start of the cruise. Their energy remains high, and Jevonte remains unobtrusive. He doesn't want to draw too much attention to himself.

He goes unnoticed as the group boards a bus bound for the Cahal Pech ruins. The trip lasts just over two hours. The bus driver is being extra cautious navigating the winding roads leading to the ruins. The rains have made travel by vehicle arduous, and more than a few tour buses and local taxis have slid off the muddied dirt roads. Jevonte's group was in luck. Their driver was well-experienced and adept at dodging the life-threatening sinkholes forming along the mountainous portions of the trip.

The tour group finally reached the ruins and found a place to park, though it was still a decent hike to the actual site. Jevonte was one of the last of the passengers to leave the bus. He was excited, and as he took in the expansive plateau surrounding the ancient city of Cahal Pech, his breath caught at its impressive beauty. The city was obviously not what it once was, but even with a bit of imagination, one could see how amazing the place was. As with almost everything, commercialism was on full display just outside of the ruins. All kinds of souvenirs were being hawked to the tourists as they made their way to one of several paths that would wind their way through the heart of this once former royal center.

I love this place, if only they didn't have all this other stuff going on here. It just detracts from the primal beauty of this place. Mom and Dad are not going to believe this, Jevonte muses, then begins snapping pictures with his Canon Rebel T7.

He shoots all three rolls of film he brought for this excursion. Just in time, he thinks as he scans the horizon and the rapidly setting sun. The tour guide starts escorting the group back to the parked tour bus. Jevonte has lost track of the ladies he was shadowing. He was so caught up with the majestic scenery that he didn't even notice that they had disappeared.

Out of his periphery, one of the three women emerges from behind a row of huts positioned at the entrance of the tourist site. Her companions are nowhere to be seen, and she looks panicked. Jevonte halts and watches her make her way around the huts and the open areas where the souvenirs were being sold, then suddenly she stops. Her hand is on her forehead, and she looks panicked.

Jevonte cautiously approaches the woman. "Ms., um, is everything alright? I couldn't help but notice that you really look worried. Is there anything I can do to help?" Jevonte's face is kind, and while bald, Black men can sometimes appear intimidating; the gentle, soft lines of his face and his neatly trimmed beard give him a very approachable and warm presence.

The woman takes a deep breath, holds it for a few seconds, then releases it with her eyes closed. "I lost my purse somewhere out here or up in the hillside," she says, swinging her arms across the trails that lead up into the ruins. I never took it out, not even to buy any of the useless trinkets they've been selling since we got here."

"Wow, I'm sorry to hear that."

"You and me both. I can't believe it. Someone may have lifted my purse, but I didn't think there were pickpockets here. I should have known better; they are everywhere."

"My name is Jevonte; what's yours?"

"Synthia. Thank you for checking on me. I was out here with my girls, and it looks like they've abandoned me now because I don't see them anywhere out here, heifers!"

Jevonte laughs and quickly cuts himself short, not sure whether Synthia is in a laughing mood after losing all her money. She smiles at Jevonte and giggles at his gaffe.

"Is there something in particular you were hoping to buy out here? I haven't bought anything myself, but I'd be pleased to help you out if there is something really catching your eye."

"Jevonte, that is so sweet of you, but I couldn't possibly take advantage of you like this." Synthia pauses before saying, "I was on my way to that stall over there, which has a really awesome headpiece that would be perfect for my living room, when I discovered that I had lost my purse."

"Listen, I made the offer, so you are not taking advantage of me." I'd love to help you out. It's not a problem at all. It will be my good deed for the day."

"Rescuing a damsel in distress, is that it? Well, who am I to deny you the opportunity to show how chivalrous you are, but I can only accept if you allow me to pay you back with dinner when we get back on board."

"I humbly accept, Madam! Lead on, please."

The pair moves on to the stalls, stopping between them to discuss the various pieces on sale. Synthia grabs Jevonte's arms and intertwines her arm with his as they walk. The conversation is light and easy, and Jevonte is feeling the most relaxed he's been since the cruise began. Synthia's playful laughter puts Jevonte at ease. They finish in time to hear the tour bus honking loudly, warning the tour group to wrap things up and make ready for departure. Seated next to Jevonte, Synthia watches her girlfriends board the bus and take seats towards the rear. They exchange no words. Jevonte thinks that's strange, but doesn't give it much thought.

The rains have started again, and the bus takes much longer to get back to the pier. The weather is not as muggy as it was in the morning. The freshness of the night air and the cool mist of the rainfall are energizing, and Jevonte is filled with hope as the bus begins to pull into its designated area. He and Synthia have been in one another's ears the whole ride. Their bond is so real, so fulfilling to Jevonte, that he doesn't even care that he spent $500 on junk for Synthia. She is impressive, he thinks, and he is so glad that he took a chance to approach her, which isn't his norm. No, relationships have never felt this effortless. He thinks to himself, maybe this relationship will be different. Synthia is different, and with that thought, Jevonte smiles wide enough to silence the moment of self-doubt that attempts to creep into his thoughts.

The pair boards the Vision of the Seas, and together as they are, the casual onlooker might believe they were hopelessly in love. Synthia's girlfriends walk past both her and Jevonte without speaking, and Synthia remains silent as well. Jevonte asks, "Are your friends pissed at you? They just rushed by without saying a word. I hope it wasn't me."

"Don't worry about them, skank hoes. They're just mad because I found a man and they haven't," Synthia responds.

A man? Jevonte's mind freezes. Did I hear that correctly? "Aw, well, I hope they don't stay upset. I'd hate to be the reason things turned sour between you and your friends."

"Jevonte, don't worry about them. They will be fine. Let's not waste any more time on that, ok? Shall we meet on the promenade later this evening for drinks? I need to get out of these sweaty clothes and shower. You wanna help a girl out?" Synthia says devilishly.

Jevonte is lost for words. He can feel a flush coming over his face with every breath. Slow down, man, slow down. He feels paralyzed. Why can't I say anything?

He feels like a child right now, and before he collapses in on himself in complete humiliation, Synthia whispers in his ear, "Don't worry, love. I can wait. We have the rest of this trip to play!"

"Ah, yes, yep, right," Jevonte stumbles. "May I help you with your packages to your room?"

"I've got it," she says with mischievous eyes, "So save your strength for later; you're going to need it."

It's 10 pm, and the promenade is full of bodies. People are moving in rhythm to the music playing in the background. Drinks are flowing, and the stars are shining bright in the sky. Jevonte has been on the promenade deck for an hour, and Synthia has yet to make an appearance. He ambles around the deck, taking in the scene of merriment and joy spreading all around him.

"Well, this evening is a bust," Jevonte says to himself. He walks over to the bar and has one more Scotch, but after finishing that one, he finishes the evening with four empty shot glasses staring him in the face. It's late, and while patrons are still enjoying the night's vibe on the promenade deck, Jevonte staggers back to his cabin alone.

He collapses on his bed, in his clothes, and feels nothing inside. He knows that he will regret drinking so much in the morning, but he doesn't care. All he wants to do is not feel anything. He doesn't even want to dream because he's tired of being disappointed.

The morning comes and fades into the late afternoon before Jevonte stirs from his slumber. His head contains a dozen bursting bombs, all firing, exploding, and wreaking havoc with every cell in his brain. His vision is hazy. Damn, did I drink that much? What's wrong with me, shoot. I haven't been nearly this blackout drunk since Howard.

He attempts to rise, but after the cabin flips upside down and slaps him in the face, he reconsiders. He lies back down, but no sooner than his head hits his pillow, he starts heaving and rolls over to vomit all over his cabin floor. He can't even think about racing to the bathroom. His head is pounding, and his stomach feels like it's in a vise. All he can do is lie still and pray that the boat sinks. "I know, that's a bit extreme," Jevonte pleads to the heavens to end his suffering.

After a few more hours of rest and plenty of water, he finally begins to feel like a human being again. He showers and gets cleaned up, and he is grateful to the stewards who came in and cleaned his cabin while he was in a coma. They earned a generous tip for that selfless act alone.

Extremely famished, he makes it down to the dining hall to grab some dinner. None of the usual suspects is having dinner right now. He had hoped to catch Synthia during the dinner hour. Perhaps he missed them, he thinks. As he finishes his meal, he notices a placard on his table. This evening, the All-Star Club is open, and it's two-for-one drink specials until closing. Jevonte's head hurts just thinking about drinking, but maybe a certain someone will be there, and he'll have another chance to connect with her.

The club is really jumping, and it's crowded. They knew what they were doing when they advertised the two-for-one deal. Not that cruise passengers needed any excuse to drink; most were in a near-constant state of inebriation while the ship was underway.

It doesn't matter. Perhaps this trip was not the right time for us to connect, Jevonte muses. "I'll just find someone else. There are so many people here. Maybe this situation will be just like the Maya ruins, and someone will need me, and maybe they'll need more than my money," Jevonte fusses to himself. He is not too sure or confident that this night will end any better than the last.

Jevonte moves around the All-Star nightclub. With a drink in hand, he finds himself uncertain about where to begin. He approaches a few women, only to face outright rejection. He offers to buy a woman a drink at the bar, but she turns him down. She's waiting for someone and doesn't want to talk to him.

For Jevonte, the night's sequence of rejections continues to repeat itself. Every attempt he makes seems to be met with rebuff. In his mind, he is scrambling to understand this, straining to explain why he can't connect with anyone, anybody at all. He's a good-looking Black man. He has his own business. He is independent and compassionate. He treats women with respect. He loves his momma and honors her. So, what the hell is wrong with him? The question remains unanswered. A certain depression begins to seep into his spirit as he dwells on the state of his single life. In a room full of souls, he's never felt so alone.

Still sitting alone at the bar, he orders a slew of drinks for himself. By the time he's finished, the nightclub music has stopped, and the place is almost empty. Jevonte doesn't even know if he can make it back to his cabin. Where is his cabin? What deck is he on? No matter, he thinks to himself.

I'll just start walking and walking until I find someplace to lie down, and that will be my cabin for the night.

Somehow, he reaches the tail end of the ship. He doesn't know how long he's been walking, shuffling, and bouncing along the halls to get to this point. Nonetheless, he made it. The hum of the ship's engines and the cool breeze of the night seas help settle his mind into a calmer space. He sits on one of the lookout benches that line the observation area at the stern of the ship. The gentle rocking of the boat is relaxing, and Jevonte can barely keep his eyes open. As he sits alone with his thoughts, his mind replays the events of the last few months. It seems like, from the time of Mercer's party, meeting Synthia, and tonight's nightclub tragedy, there appears to be no room for love in his life, not even the fleeting, artificial kind that should have been possible on this cruise. Maybe he's asking for too much.

Jevonte grew up watching his mom and dad move in perfect harmony. They are the standard, and what they have is what he wants. However, despite his best efforts, he couldn't establish a relationship like theirs. It never worked like that. He could remember sitting with his dad and asking him how he met his mom and how they maintained their relationship. It always looked effortless between them. He even asked Mr. Carlton how he and Bryan managed to cement their love so thoroughly, especially in the climate of hate that gay couples often faced. His dad would always joke that Jevonte's mom just took pity on him and tolerated him, that he was just a blessed man and had lucked out when he found her. Mr. Carlton was equally unhelpful.

The night begins to draw near to midnight, and Jevonte has the entire stern of the ship to himself. No more couples are walking hand-in-hand. There are no more lovebirds snuggling deeply into the folds of the deck chairs. There is just silence wrapped in the steel embrace of loneliness, filling all the open spaces of the stern. Not even the ship's engines disturbs the sound of breaking seas against the hull. Then it hits Jevonte, and the answer seems as clear as the midnight sky above. He's tired of hurting. He's just so tired right now. He's tired of not being seen or felt. He's tired of not being heard. He's tired of the endless rejection. The rail is so low, so tiny. One faulty step and it would be all over. The sea beckons and promises not to reject him.

Jevonte stands, wobbly, and stumbles his way to the railing lining the stern of the ship. He peers over to see the safety net jutting out from the ship's hull. Beneath the safety netting, even in the dark of the night, he can still make out the churn of the ocean under the power of the ship's propellers. His head is swimming. One decision will be all it takes, and he will find the peace that has eluded him all his adult life. No one will see him go in, and no one will save him; in this thick darkness, they won't find him.

Jevonte steps over the railing. A substantial leap, and he's sure he can clear the safety net. As he prepares to launch himself into the deep, a firm hand grabs his arm.

"No, no, don't do that, my brother," says a commanding yet soft feminine voice. Her other strong hand reaches around Jevonte's waist, hauling him back upright as he nearly tumbles over. "King, we simply cannot allow that to happen, okay? Come, sit with me for a while. Talk to me for a while. Can you do that?"

Jevonte can't tell whether he's dreaming. His head is thick, and he is feeling ill. He's on the verge of collapsing and tries to stagger towards the bench where he was previously seated. His mystery rescuer helps him to the bench and takes a seat next to him. "Now, my beautiful Black man, tell me, why did I just have to stop you from becoming one with the ocean a moment ago?"

Jevonte sits in silence. His head is hanging low, and he's looking at his feet, not sure how to respond. "I don't know," Jevonte responds. "I just want the pain to stop."

The ebony stranger places a hand on his head and strokes his brown skin slowly. "I hear you. We all do, right?

I'm going to help you, ok? My name is Talaitha. Let's get out of here, and let me take care of you tonight. We can work on what's eating at you in the morning. Is that alright with you?"

Jevonte nods slowly, still not sure whether he's alive or just dreaming with the fishes below.

5

The Need that Unmade Him

Time slows down as they make their way to Talaitha's cabin. It's quiet in the passage leading to her space. Her cabin is in the interior. The room is dark except for a bathroom night light. Jevonte is still wobbly and has to lean on Talaitha to keep from falling. She holds him upright easily. With her arms wrapped around his waist, she turns him slowly until he's facing her. She carefully leads him back towards the bed and guides him into a seated position. One by one, she removes his shoes and socks, then unbuckles his pants. She slides them off his waist. Then she uses her left hand to pull his head into her breasts as she reaches for the back of his shirt to begin pulling it over his head. Jevonte doesn't resist or object. He's still not sure what's happening, but he feels safe.

After removing his shirt, Talaitha guides him to lie back on the bed. She closes his legs, removes his underwear, and tosses them into the corner. Pulling back one edge of the down comforter, she maneuvers Jevonte until he's lying half-in and half-out of the sheets. Jevonte closes his eyes. His head feels heavy, but he doesn't feel sick. He's just watching Talaitha move around the cabin. She's smooth, quiet, and looks like a wraith in the darkness of the room. Against the dim bathroom lighting, Talaitha's silhouette takes on a life of its own. He watches in awe as she removes her skirt and stands in the calming light. She enjoys being watched, he realizes. But he also enjoys watching. He doubts he'll remember any of this in the morning, though he doesn't care. At this late hour, Talaitha's eyes look like they are glowing like cats' eyes when caught in beams of light.

Jevonte can't tell for sure because the darkness of the cabin refuses to relinquish control to his sight, but she looks like she's looking straight through his soul. Finally, she moves, delicately removing her blouse. She tosses it alongside Jevonte's pants. The bathroom's soft glow betrays her, and Jevonte can see the roundness and fullness of her breasts as she moves toward the bed.

His heart begins to beat triple time. He is afraid that he won't be able to perform. The alcohol has ruined whatever chance he had at experiencing this goddess. In his mind, Jevonte is praying for a miracle, anything, something to awaken his body—urgently! Talaitha crawls into bed, beginning at his feet and then sliding up his body like a python scaling a tree. She pauses at each thigh, kissing them before moving up to his stomach. Along the way, she blows gently on his groin and penis. She lingers for a moment, and in that time, Jevonte is quivering with hope and anticipation. He's still limp, but miracles do happen, he thinks to himself.

Talaitha moves away from his midsection, and Jevonte doesn't know whether he should feel sadness or relief. She nestles under his arms and rests her left hand on his chest. She drapes her left thigh across his midsection, allowing the weight and warmth of her leg to press against his manhood. The pressure is welcomed and helps relieve some of the tension Jevonte is feeling. Talaitha doesn't move, lying still and allowing their breathing to synchronize as the ship begins a series of gentle rolls.

The cabin is still, and the darkness finally begins to give way to Jevonte's night vision. He feels warm and safe, not ashamed of what he did at the ship's stern. He doesn't know why, but he feels like he can trust Talaitha. There is something about her that is welcoming. She doesn't feel like a threat. It's almost like he's known her his whole life. He knows that it is insane, but he can't help feeling like they may have met in another life. He decides to throw caution to the wind. He can blame it all on the alcohol in the morning.

"Talaitha, thanks."

"King, you don't have to thank me. Wounded souls need each other."

Jevonte continues speaking, not fully catching what Talaitha said. "Until tonight, I had never considered ending my life. It just never occurred to me before, but lately, I've been feeling the hurt more than ever."

"Pain, especially when it's prolonged over an extended period, can really impact our mental health. I'm here. Talk to me." Talaitha moves her hand across Jevonte's muscular chest, briefly massaging the short curly hairs on his chest.

Jevonte, who has always had problems speaking to women about his feelings, opens up fully with Talaitha. Over the next hour, Talaitha learns about his parents, his favorite uncle, his business, and his profound loneliness. She hears how he has lived with constant rejection and his bouts of hopelessness. He shares how hurt he was when Synthia ghosted him and maybe used him. At the end, Jevonte's so tired he isn't even sure his words are making any sense. Talaitha simply kisses his neck and continues to rub his chest and stomach. The pair falls asleep, locked in each other's embrace.

It's midday when Jevonte awakens. Under his arm lies Talaitha, still snuggled tightly against him. She is still asleep, and he dares not disturb her. He looks down the side of her silky smooth body. Her skin is perfect. So brown and rich, she is a sleeping masterpiece. Her body is warm, pulsing with energy. Jevonte wonders to himself, Who is this creature?

Jevonte recounts the events of last night in his mind. It all seems pointless now. None of it matters at this moment, right here. In fact, how could I have been so stupid, Jevonte thinks. I'm lying next to a gift from God, fallen straight from heaven's throne room. We didn't even have sex," Jevonte muses.

Almost on cue, Talaitha yawns and places her hand under the covers to hold Jevonte in her hand. The heat of her touch is electrifying. Jevonte's blood is flowing again, rushing through his body. With a little more encouragement from Talaitha, Jevonte is reborn, and his confidence rises like the sun. The midday passes, and by the time the lovers have exhausted themselves upon each other, the scheduled dinner with the ship's captain is but hours away. The two cling to one another, not wanting the day to end.

"Listen, get dressed for dinner. Come back here and pick me up. You should probably bring your things here because you're not going to need your cabin anymore," Talaitha says with a sly smile. Jevonte is at a loss for words, but he nods in obeisance and rises to use the bathroom before leaving Talaitha's cabin.

I haven't hurt this good in a very long time. Did this really happen? Man, I think I'm dreaming. I have to be. Should I even leave? No, she is definitely not Synthia. At least I know where she is staying. Man, Jevonte thinks in the quiet of the bathroom. Before leaving the cabin, Jevonte embraces Talaitha as she lies in bed. She holds him tightly, reluctantly releasing him to head to his cabin.

At the captain's dinner, Jevonte and Talaitha are enjoying some steak and lobster at an open table for six. The other dinner guests have not arrived, and they have the entire space to themselves. Jevonte is talking more than he has all cruise, and Talaitha is attentive, nodding, and showing concern and understanding. The couple is oblivious to everything around them and doesn't notice the trio of women who take seats at their table. Jevonte isn't even paying attention and doesn't hear the question one of the women asks as she gathers her silverware.

"Hello. Jevonte, right?" asks Synthia politely. Jevonte and Talaitha pause, taken aback by the sudden interruption.

"Ah, yes, hello. Hi. You are?" Jevonte asks, slightly bewildered because he doesn't recognize Synthia at first.

"Synthia! We met a few days ago on the Maya ruins excursion. You were so kind to help me out that day. Don't you remember?"

Jevonte hesitates for a brief moment, and then the light comes on. "I'm so sorry. Yeah, yes, now I remember." Synthia looks different now. She's wearing a mini-skirt and a silk blouse. Her hair is freshly braided, and she's wearing some of the golden jewelry Jevonte helped her purchase on the excursion.

Talaitha interrupts, saying, "Jevonte told me all about that little deal; it's nice. It looks like you did pretty well for yourself." Talaitha's eyes grow cold as she meets Synthia's.

"Um, I was thankful Jevonte was there to help a sista out. Experiencing such a situation was truly embarrassing. You read about it and try to prepare, and they tell you what to expect, but sometimes you just don't think about it. Never again," exclaims Synthia as she spreads her dinner napkin across her lap.

"Oh, I know what you mean, and that's why I love this man so much. He's truly one of a kind." Talaitha smiles and touches Jevonte's cheek softly while looking him in the eye.

She loves me. Did she just say that? Jevonte replays the words in his mind.

"And I am the one who is truly blessed here. I've never met anyone like you, ever," Jevonte responds passionately. Once again, they immerse themselves in each other's presence, allowing time and space to envelop them completely.

"Well, you two are cute," Synthia says sarcastically before turning to her companions to discuss the next morning's arrival at homeport. Jevonte hungrily returns to his lobster, but Talaitha's eyes silently track Synthia's every movement.

The final evening of the cruise comes to a close, and Jevonte and Talaitha return to her cabin. They pack Jevonte's belongings and arrange his luggage next to Talaitha's. The cabin stewards have provided information they will need for the next morning's arrival in Baltimore harbor. The pair becomes one throughout the evening and into the early morning hours. When Jevonte wakes, Talaitha is gone. Her things are still in the room, but she is not. Jevonte's heart quickens a bit. There is no note, nothing. He rises and uses the bathroom. Her toiletries are still there. As Jevonte throws on his clothes and heads to the door to look for Talaitha, she walks into the room with two fresh coffees in hand. Jevonte breathes a sigh of relief.

"Oh, there you are. I was just about to get a search party together," Jevonte jokes lightheartedly.

"King, now why would you do that?" Talaitha laughs. "I think we're going to need a little caffeine after last night. Mr. Man, you wore your girl out!"

With a beaming smile, Jevonte responds, "Me? No, ma'am, I'm the one who can barely walk this morning!"

Debarkation runs smoothly. Jevonte and Talaitha retrieve all their luggage and find some shade while they wait for the shuttle to the parking garage. Jevonte is feeling a little downcast because he would rather not say goodbye. He doesn't want this newly formed thing, this new experience, this miracle to end at all.

"Hey, why don't we…" Before Jevonte can finish, the sound of sirens from a Baltimore Medical Center ambulance startles the pair as it enters the pier-side taxi area. EMTs rush into the receiving area and meet several of the ship's staff. Several minutes pass, and two Baltimore police SUVs arrive. The officers head toward the ship and confer with more of the ship's officers. A white sheet-covered body emerges from the ship after what seems like hours. Onlookers line the exits from the ship's deboarding area. Gasps can be heard as part of the sheet is blown off the body, and the disfigured face of a Black woman can be seen before the emergency medical personnel can reposition and cover the woman's body. Behind the EMTs, the police are speaking with two Black women, taking notes and consoling the women, who are obviously distraught and in tears.

"Oh God, that looks like the women who sat with us at dinner last night," Talaitha says, breaking the silence that had ensued between them after the ambulance arrived.

"I can't be certain. It looks like them, but that would mean that the person under the sheet is Synthia. I don't see her with them. Wow. I wonder what happened."

"That's sad. So close to home, too." Talaitha grabs Jevonte's hand and arm. "There will likely be news coverage about it tomorrow, or we may never find out what happened. Poor thing," Talaitha finishes.

Jevonte shakes his head in agreement, then the thought strikes him. "I don't know where you live. I want to see you again, Talaitha. This has been the best seven days of my life. I'm not kidding. I have to see you again, ok?"

"I feel the same way, King." Talaitha smiles at Jevonte and pulls a business card from her purse. Call my office in a few days. I'm having some issues with the home phone line, so you can reach me at the office.

"Talaitha Mercedes, Psychiatrist! Should I call you Doctor Mercedes now?" Jevonte laughs. You never mentioned that you were a doctor.

"Well, we were very busy with other things, wouldn't you say? Besides, we all have our little mysteries to maintain, right? Trust me, we will have plenty of time to get to know one another better. I, for one, am excited for this new exploration. Aren't you?" Talaitha asks with a gentle pleading in her voice.

"Absolutely! Jevonte draws Talaitha into his arms, and the two kiss deeply, then wrap each other in a hot embrace that leaves them both wanting to find privacy from prying eyes.

Talaitha's taxi arrives first. The pair embraces and kiss once more. Jevonte helps load Talaitha's luggage and watches as the taxi pulls away. Jevonte is alone with his thoughts, waiting for his taxi to arrive. He is filled with so much raw energy that he could almost run home, carrying his luggage on his back. This is the kind of thing that only happens in the movies. Jevonte pulls out the business card

Talaitha gave him and stares at the name, Talaitha Mercedes, Psych. He hit the jackpot. Wait until I tell Mom about this. She's going to be thrilled, he thinks. "She better be," he laughs to himself.

Several days pass, and despite leaving thirty messages for Talaitha, Jevonte does not receive a single call from her. He is crushed and devastated. "How could I be so stupid to believe that miracles like this happen?" he says in frustration. What an idiot I've been, acting like some stupid high school teenage boy, damn.

The emptiness of Jevonte's living room offers him little comfort. Not even the blinking microwave can distract him from the melancholy. He racks his brain trying to come up with explanations for why Talaitha isn't answering any of his calls. Maybe he just needs to go to her office. He could just show up and demand an explanation. No, he would never do something like that, he thinks. Maybe she's married, and what we experienced on the cruise was just a fling for her, a distraction of some kind, or a diversion she needed—at his expense.

Jevonte decides to concentrate on work. He has been putting off several jobs he needs to close out. With a planner in hand, he sits at his computer and begins organizing his work schedule for the next two weeks. A news flash triggers a briefing alert in his web browser. Jevonte clicks on the alert to read:

News Flash: Tragedy Strikes Aboard Cruise Ship Returning to Baltimore

Baltimore, MD – May 5th, 2018

Authorities are investigating a gruesome discovery aboard Mainstay Caribbean's Vision of the Seas cruise ship early Monday morning after the body of a woman was found brutally strangled and disfigured in her cabin just hours after the vessel returned to the Port of Baltimore.

The victim has been identified as Synthia Livingston, a 32-year-old African American woman from Middletown, Delaware. Livingston, a graduate of Morgan State University, held a degree in criminal law and psychopathy and was described by friends and former classmates as intelligent, driven, and passionate about justice.

The Vision of the Seas had just completed a seven-day voyage to the Eastern Caribbean, docking in Baltimore in the early morning hours, when the ship staff reportedly discovered Livingston unresponsive. Emergency services were called to the scene, but she was pronounced dead shortly after their arrival.

The cause of death has been confirmed as strangulation and severe trauma to the head and face, and authorities are treating the case as a homicide. Federal and maritime investigators, along with the FBI, are working closely with local law enforcement and Mainstay Caribbean to piece together the final hours of Livingston's life.

Officials have not yet identified any suspects, and no arrests have been made.

A spokesperson for Mainstay Caribbean expressed condolences to the family and pledged full cooperation with the investigation.

Anyone with information is urged to contact the FBI's Baltimore Field Office or Crime Stoppers.

This is a developing story. Updates will be provided as more information becomes available.

Jevonte sits stunned. He's thinking about his last conversation with Synthia at dinner when his phone rings.

"Hi, King. I'm sorry I haven't been able to return your calls. I was away at a few conferences, and my service did not get your messages to me. How have you been? I hope you haven't forgotten about me," Talaitha's soft, firm voice fills Jevonte with relief.

"Talaitha, is that really you?"

"Yes, man, I missed you. I'm free the rest of this week, so how about we have dinner this Friday? Let me do something nice for you."

That moment heals Jevonte's entire world. All his doubts and fears recede, and everything starts to look brand new once more. Jevonte replies with a sense of relief and happiness, "Yes, love. I'm free for you whenever you want me."

6

Under Her Command

It's 7:30 pm, and the city's streetlights have begun painting the walkways in a warm, amber glow. The evening is cool but comfortably so. Jevonte waits patiently outside the Ruxton steakhouse. It took him months to get the reservations, but based on everything he had read, it was well worth it. It had been challenging to find time to spend with Talaitha. Maybe two out of seven calls would connect him with her. It was a rare occasion when he would actually get to see her in the flesh. Sometimes a whole week would go by before she returned one of his calls. Jevonte was beginning to wonder whether she was interested in their relationship at all. Just when he was about to walk away from her, she would re-emerge and spark new life into their time together. Despite how fickle and inconsistent their time together felt to Jevonte, he could not imagine never seeing or hearing from her again. He couldn't walk away yet.

Jevonte walks into the steakhouse and is seated at his reservation table.

"Sir, what can I start you off with? We have notable house wines we could start you off with," says the waiter.

"I need a few moments. Let me peruse the wine list, and I will let you know," Jevonte answers.

"As you wish, sir. I will return in a few minutes to check on you. Are you expecting another party?"

"I am, and here she comes now."

Talaitha strolls through the restaurant doors; her toned, bare arms stretched to open the way for a couple who are leaving. She wears an elegant, shimmery emerald dress that falls just below her mid-thigh. The dress holds her fit frame perfectly. Clutch in hand, Talaitha scans the area before the maître d' greets her.

"I'm good; I see my handsome friend right over there," and Talaitha moves past the maître d' and makes a beeline for Jevonte.

Jevonte stands and reaches for her before she gets to the table. "You are a vision."

"My eyes are very pleased this evening, my king," Talaitha replies jovially. "I hope I haven't kept you waiting too long, my love."

"No, I just sat down," Jevonte lies. "I do have an appetite, though. Work was…" Talaitha cuts him short.

"Where are the menus? You haven't ordered our drinks yet?" Talaitha asks, disappointedly. Jevonte takes a moment to stare at the drink menu. His brow is fallen, and he's feeling a little uncomfortable, like someone just threw cold water in his face.

"I… I haven't ordered any yet. I was…"

"Waiter," Talaitha waves. After reviewing the wine list, Talaitha boldly says to the waiter, "Bring us a bottle of your 2005 Domaine Bonneau du Martray Corton-Charlemagne Grand Cru, please. We'll be ready to order after our first glass. Thank you." The waiter nods politely and scampers off to the restaurant's wine cellar. While Jevonte watches the waiter hurry off, he thinks to himself, That sounded like a very expensive bottle of French wine. What the hell!

"So, have you managed to get your messaging service straightened out? I can never seem to get you when I call." There is a pause before Jevonte adds, "I'm assuming you didn't get my calls and messages?"

"Lover, listen, I got the calls," Talaitha responds with no further explanation. "You said you were famished when I arrived. What do you have a taste for?"

"Ah," Jevonte responds slowly before picking up his menu. "The steak here is really…" Talaitha stops him in mid-sentence.

"Do you see this? They have swordfish on the menu. I've never tried it, but I hear it's to die for. Let's try that, ok?"

"Swordfish? Where do you see that on the menu?" Jevonte asks, grinning.

"My god, some people are just stupid," says Talaitha under her breath. "It's right there," and Talaitha points at her menu sharply. Jevonte stares intently at the menu; although he feels bruised emotionally, he conceals the growing sadness that threatens to overwhelm him.

"I just need my glasses; that's fine. I'm leaning more towards the ribeye. This place is known for its steak dinners."

The waiter arrives with the bottle of wine and two glasses. Talaitha, nodding at Jevonte, says, "We are ready to order now."

The waiter turns his attention to Talaitha. "Very well. Ladies first. What would you like?"

"We'll both have the swordfish with roasted asparagus and the Mediterranean salad. No bread. Thank you." The waiter nods in obedience and gathers the menus.

Jevonte smiles politely, says "Thank you," and takes some of his wine. There is a pointedly uncomfortable silence at the table, and Jevonte, looking into Talaitha's eyes, asks, "Talaitha, why did you do that? I didn't want the swordfish."

Talaitha drinks some of her wine and then slowly places the glass down on the table. "I just want us to stop eating red meat." It's really not healthy for you. Did you know that? I care about you, my king. I don't want you to drop dead on me, not now when things are so good in our lives."

"But I don't think consuming it in moderation is a bad thing. I mean, my dad, he…"

"People always say that, but after their heart stops and they've blown out some arteries, they wish they had heeded medical advice and the research that proves how harmful consumption of red meat can be. So no, we won't be eating red meat anymore, end of the story."

"If you say so, dear," Jevonte smiles widely, attempting to draw out Talaitha's humor. But he meets silence from Talaitha. Instead, she turns her attention to the bar, where a well-dressed man is seated. The man, clad in a suit and tie, holds a glass of scotch. Talaitha leaves the table and walks over to sit next to the gentleman, not explaining to Jevonte. The two begin having a quiet conversation.

Talaitha starts to laugh and throws her head back in merriment. The bartender brings a drink to her, and the well-dressed businessman gives him a nod in thanks. The pair continues to converse in mutual admiration.

Seated at his table, Jevonte's mind and thoughts begin to churn. What in the world is she doing now? Uh, hello, I'm right here. Did you forget we were having dinner? Jevonte thinks angrily. He watches them at the bar, as if they are the only two people in the restaurant. After twenty minutes, Jevonte searches for the waiter to get an update on the swordfish but ultimately decides instead to join Talaitha and her new friend at the bar. Just then, the waitstaff starts bringing out the dinner order to his table.

The staff begins plating the orders. Talaitha abruptly ends her conversation with the businessman and walks back over to Jevonte's table. One of the waiters pulls out a seat for her. Talaitha adjusts her dress and exclaims, "Oh my goodness, this food smells so good, doesn't it, babe?"

Jevonte is quiet. He can't find the words to say. He is humiliated, confused, and uncertain about his ability to formulate words because he fears that his voice might crack. He starts to feel a little ill. His stomach is beginning to feel queasy, but he slows his breathing and closes his eyes for a count of five. He doesn't know why or from where he learned to do this, but it has always helped him calm his anxiety. It works.

"King," Talaitha speaks soothingly. "Are you alright? Is it your weak stomach again?"

"No, it's not that. I'm fine. Who is that at the bar?"

"Who?"

"That man you were sitting next to, speaking with intimately, or so it looked from here."

"I think you should try the swordfish and stop worrying about trivial matters. We discussed this, if you recall. You always take things the wrong way. You always make assumptions that turn out to be wrong, and you end up with hurt feelings. Now do as I say and try the swordfish. It really is wonderful, my God!" Talaitha exaggerates.

After the pair finishes the meal, Talaitha abruptly stands and walks over to Jevonte's side of the table. "I have some early client appointments in the morning, so I need to leave."

"Sweetheart, I thought we could hang out at my place after dinner? Let me get the check, and we can head over…"

"Honey, I wish I could, but I have too much to prepare for, and I can't do what I need to do over at your place. I'll call you later tonight, ok? Thanks for the dinner. The swordfish was perfect!"

At home, Jevonte is lying in bed staring up at his ceiling. It's after 11:30 pm, and Talaitha hasn't called. He can't sleep. His thoughts are keeping him up. "What am I doing here? Maybe the question should be, What am I doing wrong?" Jevonte whispers to the empty room. "I'm going to have to visit her tomorrow. This, the way she is treating me, makes no sense. It's like she is a whole different person from the woman I met on the cruise."

Jevonte's last thought of the night is of Talaitha, snuggled under him, their bodies in harmony and flowing together as one. She fit. They fit together. Her passion inscribed his heart, and he knew she was the one he'd been searching for, the one gift from heaven he never thought he was good enough to receive.

The morning sun is pouring through Jevonte's bedroom window when he awakes to a call from his mom.

"Hey Mom, what's up? It's early for a call, isn't it?"

"Son, it's never too early for a mother to call her son," Ruby chuckles. It's been more than a few moons since we last saw you, and I haven't heard from you in a couple of weeks. I thought it a good idea to call and make sure my son was still in the land of the living!"

"Mom," Jevonte replies, exasperated. "I'm still here. I've just been so busy. A lot is going on. I was planning on calling you."

"When? Next Spring?…"

"I met someone, Mom," Jevonte interrupts. He really hadn't planned on telling his folks about Talaitha yet. He didn't want all the questions, especially now when things seemed uncertain between him and Talaitha.

"You met someone? Who is she? Is she anyone we might know?" asks Ruby with hope and anticipation in her voice.

"No, Mom. I met her on vacation a little while back. Her name is Talaitha, Talaitha Mercedes, and she is a psychiatrist."

"Well, now, a psychiatrist. I'm impressed, son. Is it serious? When do we get to meet her?"

The question Jevonte was dreading stared him boldly in the face. "We're taking things slow for now. We're still trying to feel things out. Don't worry; when the time is right, I will bring her around to meet everyone."

"Don't wait too long, you hear? I want to meet the woman who is monopolizing all of my son's time. Is she on

Facebook?" Ruby asks, and Jevonte can almost see her biting at the bit to start searching for her profile.

"Mom, I have to go. I have lots of work to catch up on. I love you. Tell Dad I said hello, and I promise, I will come by for a visit soon."

Ruby hangs up the phone and stares across the kitchen table at Jedidiah. "Your son has a girlfriend," she says flatly.

"A what?" Jedidiah asks, his face shocked.

"He said he met her while he was on vacation a few months ago. He says that they are still getting to know one another but that he will introduce her eventually, which means we won't meet her for another decade or so," Ruby laughs.

"What's her name? I take it she's from or lives in Baltimore?"

"Her name is Tailshehah, or something like that. I think he said her last name was the same as that luxury car you keep talking about; you know, the one you were supposed to buy me four birthdays ago!" Ruby teases.

"Beamer? Audio, no Audi, or was it Winnebago?" Jedidiah mocks.

"Stop playing, man."

"I know, I know, Mercedes?"

"Yes, Mercedes, and she's a psychiatrist."

"Oh Lord, so she's a quack that plays head games with people. Your son had better know what he's getting into with that one."

"I think his father should talk to him then and get him to come for a visit sooner rather than later. Now what do you want for breakfast?"

Dr. Talaitha Mercedes's office was located on the discreet third floor of the Baltimore building on East Lombard Street. Her office was nestled toward the far side of the building, away from most foot traffic, which was perfect. Talaitha's clients appreciated the nondescript facade and the unassuming nature of the entry space. Legal offices, IT workspaces, and management offices dominated the office, providing most of the day's hustle and bustle. In fact, the casual observer would not even know that Talaitha's office space was there unless someone were seeking her specifically. So, when Jevonte arrived at the Baltimore building, he had difficulty finding her office. There was no office number, and the building's directory did not identify her office by name; it displayed 'Therapeutic Rescission Support & Counseling Service.' Jevonte guessed that the location might be Talaitha's office, so he took the elevator to the third floor.

When the elevator doors opened, he stepped out into the hallway more confused than ever. He easily located the listed law office of Brent & Turner, the Technical Review Office, and the Intrepid Management Firm. They each had clearly marked office numbers and names, but there was no Therapeutic Rescission Support & Counseling Service.

Jevonte walked up and down the hall and even poked his head inside the law office to ask for information. No one seemed to know about the counseling service. As he turned to head back to the elevator, the door opposite the tech firm's office opened, and a disheveled, middle-aged man came shuffling through the door. Sweat trickled down his forehead, leaving his receding hair slicked and wet. Jevonte couldn't be sure, but it looked like his nose had been bleeding. The man abruptly slammed the door behind him and stormed off towards the stairwell exit. As Jevonte stood waiting, the elevator arrived, and a young man exited. The man looked to be in his twenties. He was thin and frail-looking. The back of his basketball jersey bore Larry Bird's name and number. The young man didn't look well. His skin was pale, almost jaundiced. He ambled past Jevonte and opened the same hallway door the middle-aged man had exited. He opened the door and went in with practiced ease and familiarity.

The door had no markings whatsoever. These people obviously knew where they were going, but where did that door lead to, Jevonte thought. Is that her office? He wondered. He approached the door and attempted to open it, only to find it locked. Wait, he thought. That young man just opened the door and entered the space.

This was not working and only added to the confusion in his mind. He would just go back home and try calling her again. Maybe he would tell her he tried to visit, or perhaps he wouldn't. At this point, it was becoming harder to see himself staying in the relationship. The elevator doors opened, and there was Talaitha. She stepped out into the hall, a cup of Starbucks coffee in hand.

"Jevonte! What a pleasant surprise. What are you doing here?"

"Ah, I, well, I came to see you. I wanted to surprise you. It was hard to find your office. It's not exactly marked clearly on the building directory."

"As it should not be, Jevonte. The work I do here is very sensitive, and the patients I see trust me to protect their privacy and ensure their safety. You being here has severely jeopardized that, by the way. Please tell me no one saw you here, and you didn't ask about my practice, did you?"

"Sorry, but I asked for information about Therapeutic Rescission Support & Counseling Service at the law office over there," and Jevonte points at the law firm's door. "No one seemed to know anything about the counseling service," Jevonte explained fearfully.

"Damnit, Jevonte. You don't understand. The counseling service is not a real office here; it is a front. My clients know what and where it is. The directory name is a cover that lets them seek my specialized services without stigma, which you just ruined. I have to go now. Please just leave. I'll call you later," and Talaitha walks toward the hallway door, murmuring to herself, "This is just not going to work."

The elevator door shuts, leaving Jevonte by himself in the hallway. He presses the button again. His heart is aching more than ever now. He doesn't know what to think. What did I do? What in the world did I do wrong?

Later that night, while Jevonte is preparing a frozen dinner, his phone rings, and it's Talaitha.

"Hi Jevonte. Look, I owe you an apology. I was way too harsh on you at my office. It wasn't fair to you, and I want to come over if that's ok with you."

Jevonte is stunned into silence—a very short silence. "Oh, it's ok, love. I shouldn't have just shown up like that. I'm the one who owes you an apology. I just missed you so much, and I haven't been able to reach you by phone."

"I understand. I'm on my way to your place, and when I arrive, I hope you're wearing nothing but a smile. Do you understand?"

"Loud and clear, my queen," Jevonte says and hangs up the phone.

After Talaitha arrives, the two retire to the bedroom. There is minimal conversation. Talaitha takes control and instructs Jevonte to remove his clothes and lie on the bed. Then she removes her skirt and blouse, leaving her bra and panties on. She mounts Jevonte and pins him to the mattress. Carefully, she grips his jaw in her hand and stares him in the face. "Most of my patients have attempted to harm themselves in ways you couldn't even imagine. The pain they experience is so profound that even the slightest inconsistency in treatment or the smallest disruption in their routine could likely lead to catastrophic psychological harm. Even seeing someone new in a space they had grown accustomed to as a solitary haven could be enough to make them doubt the stability of the reality I had created for them. So, my love, don't ever come to my office again unless I call for you, and then never come to the third floor of the Baltimore building," Talaitha speaks calmly but sternly.

Jevonte nods his head slowly. "I really am sorry. I just had no idea…"

"Be quiet," Talaitha commands as she begins to grind slowly against him. She maintains eye contact with him while gradually sliding her panties to one side and positioning him until he is inside her. Talaitha remains atop Jevonte until she is nearly spent. She can feel the urgency in Jevonte's hips as he rises to meet the rhythm of her hips.

Jevonte moans in ecstasy and cries, "I'm coming, shit, I'm coming…"

"Not yet. Don't you dare," Talaitha growls. "I'll tell you when to let go."

"I can't hold it, babe, I…"

Talaitha slaps Jevonte across the face. The shock of the strike brings tears to his eyes, but Talaitha continues to grind toward orgasm. In miniature thrusts against Jevonte, Talaitha's hips tremble and her back arches. She freezes briefly, her back arched, her chin lifted to the ceiling. She looks as if she's about to howl at the moon before sliding from atop Jevonte.

Jevonte lies in complete silence. His breathing has slowed dramatically. Talaitha's body is shimmering with sweat, and she sounds as if she's run a marathon. In minutes, Talaitha has dozed off, her back turned to Jevonte. Jevonte is still rigid, and as he looks down at himself, he contemplates finishing himself, but the slap has paralyzed his mind. He can't bring himself to touch his body at all. All he can do is lie still as if waiting on another command to move or to breathe.

In the morning, Jevonte wakes to an empty bed. In his kitchen, he can hear the sound of plates and utensils moving. He can smell coffee—and bacon! The aroma energizes him, and he quickly rises and dons his robe. He casually strolls out into his kitchen to see Talaitha working some eggs over on the stove. The scene is almost surreal to Jevonte. Talaitha is moving with such elegance and precision. She moves with a dancer's grace, gliding from stove to counter, shifting her body between poses with the absolute grace of a jungle cat.

"Take a seat, my king. I'm going to feed you and then get ready to meet some new clients. I made some calls this morning and confirmed two of your meetings today. Your planner is clear for the rest of the week. Let's go, let's go now, don't just stand there, love."

Jevonte is speechless, but he obeys and takes a seat at the kitchen table. Talaitha sets his breakfast in front of him and kisses him deeply on the mouth. She swiftly makes her way to the master bathroom, where the sound of a steamy shower soon fills the air. Jevonte sits staring at his plate. Everything looks perfect and delicious. He pauses for a moment and looks back toward his bedroom. Was I dreaming? Did last night actually happen? Jevonte thinks quietly. He reaches up to rub his face, which is still puffy from the slap. "Yeah, last night was real alright."

7

The Sundress and the Cage

Jevonte finds himself distracted at the brownstone renovation site. The work has helped, but that's not what's distracting him right now. Talaitha has been in and out of contact with him, and he can never really pin her down unless it's on her schedule and terms. His thoughts drift back a few weeks to the dinner date at the Ruxton. He never got a clear answer about the identity of the gentleman Talaitha sat with at the bar. She's been so secretive, never disclosing much about herself or her work. Usually, Jevonte would find this odd lack of transparency off-putting and cause for alarm, but it's different with Talaitha. Jevonte would be more critical of someone who accepts such treatment if he were an outsider, but he isn't. This is his life, and his feelings cloud and dampen the panic alarms that are going off.

Mr. Stroud, a close acquaintance of Mr. Carlton, pulled up to the work site to preview the refurbishment. Mr. Stroud was an accountant with the Danberry firm of Baltimore. He and Mr. Carlton often tapped local talent to work on revitalization projects in the city. They recommended masons, electricians, plumbers, mechanics, and general contractors to each other, as well as to members of various civic organizations that served the city as a whole. They played a crucial role in fostering economic opportunities within the Black community.

"Hey there, Jevonte, how've you been? How's the job coming along?"

"Good morning, sir. So far, everything is proceeding as planned. Before I start refinishing the lower stairs, I wanted to ask you about the waste trolley at the back of the home. Are you sure you want it pulled out completely?"

"Yes. It's an eyesore that has to go. I thought about developing it into a working laundry chute, but with the washer and dryer upstairs, I don't see the point. Is it going to be difficult to remove?"

"No, sir. It will add a bit of a delay and some extra costs, but if you're ok with that, I can get it done."

"Perfect, perfect. I've got some calls to make before heading back to my office. If you need anything else, just call me there."

Jevonte waves, and Mr. Stroud pulls off. Even with the modification to remove the waste trolley, he could complete the refurbishment ahead of schedule. Jevonte had nothing but time on his hands, so he worked until his body was exhausted. He had nothing better to do.

A car drives past the worksite and stops at the two corner homes south of Jevonte's project. A lone passenger steps out of the vehicle and starts walking towards the worksite. Jevonte is busy scribbling notes on his work schematics, so he doesn't notice the woman until she stops in front of him. Talaitha clears her throat. Jevonte looks up, surprised to see her.

"Talaitha! What? What are you doing here?" Jevonte asks, startled by her unexpected appearance.

"I came to see you, King. I was missing you and decided to cancel my appointments today so I could come and surprise you. Did I?"

"Definitely, but I'm glad you did. I have been thinking of you all week." In reality, Jevonte has Talaitha on his mind almost constantly. There hasn't been a time when he hasn't been obsessing over her. It is one of the reasons he is working nearly 12 hours a day. He doesn't want any downtime because then he'd get lost in his thoughts about her: what she was doing, what she was wearing, and who she was talking to. It was overwhelming. Hammering nails was about the only relief he could find from the constant intrusion of this woman in his every thought.

"You've been thinking about me, huh? Well, here I am, so what are you going to do about it?" Talaitha asked with purposeful mischief in her voice.

Jevonte's eyes brightened, and his spirit instantly lifted. Just seeing Talaitha in the afternoon's sun, her sundress flowing like a living thing around her, was mesmerizing, and Jevonte couldn't focus on much else. "How about I give you the VIP tour inside? I can show you what I've been working on."

"Lead the way, King. Show me how you work on things on the inside," Talaitha says with a sly smile.

Once inside the brownstone, Talaitha moves across the foyer into the living room. The owners had most of the furniture covered or moved so that Jevonte could work unencumbered. The absence of most of the furnishings gave the lone bearskin rug particular prominence in the living room. It is at its center that Talaitha pauses and turns to face Jevonte, who is walking towards the rear sitting room of the large home. Jevonte stops when he notices that Talaitha is not following. As he turns back, his jaw falls open. Talaitha was in the process of kicking off her panties and dropping her sundress to the floor. She stood there, naked. Her body is smooth and light brown—radiant. The visual sent Jevonte's thoughts all the way back to their time together in her cabin aboard the Vision of the Seas.

Talaitha stood statuesque. She wasn't moving, but Jevonte could almost feel the energy shimmering around her, or maybe it was just in his mind. He couldn't be sure. He is feeling somewhat off-balance, as though his senses have been overloaded. Experiencing so much of her all at one time made Jevonte feel like exploding! She was in control, and when she looked up to meet his gaze, his body obeyed without a word. Before he could reach her, Talaitha pointed with one finger at his belt and motioned towards the floor. Jevonte quickly removed his belt and trousers. Talaitha then pointed at his shirt and gave the silent command to discard it. He obeyed without hesitation. Jevonte stood naked before the bearskin rug and Talaitha—save for his socks.

Over the next two hours, Jevonte and Talaitha melted into each other. Jevonte was ravenous—starved. The two lovers rolled and twisted, each one searching for leverage, seeking the deepest part of one another. Jevonte was desperate to mount Talaitha, to pin her deep into the soft white fur of the carpet, but she would have none of it. She curled a leg around Jevonte's waist and rolled him to his back. She held him firm and slowly ground her way to a second orgasm. Jevonte could feel the urgency within his body to release weeks of pent-up energy and desire. He could feel his groin tighten, his back begin to stiffen, and every muscle in his body start to grow taut, coiled, and ready to blow like a geyser.

Talaitha reached down and took him firmly in her hand. "No," she whispered as she withdrew him from her body.

Time stood still for Jevonte. His eyes were wide. His body trembled as it sought permission to let go; none was given.

"Please," Jevonte groaned in a soft, quiet, whining voice.

Talaitha held him firmly and began to position herself between his legs. She kneeled and bowed down to place her head next to his rigid penis. Still holding Jevonte tightly, she looked up into his pleading face and said, "Wait."

"My love, please. It hurts; it really hurts." For the next few minutes, Talaitha said nothing. Jevonte's entire body was inflamed, and when it didn't seem like Jevonte could endure anymore, Talaitha released him and began to stroke him firmly but vigorously until all the disappointment, frustration, and heartache spilled from him in heated spurts of long-delayed passion. Talaitha crawled up Jevonte's spent body and found a long, familiar nook under his arm. In minutes, the two lovers fell asleep, nestled together in the warmth of the bearskin rug.

Jevonte awoke to find Talaitha gone. Very little remained in the space they had inhabited for the last few hours except for the fragrance of their lovemaking. Jevonte sat on the carpet, alone with thoughts of what he had just experienced with the absolute love of his life. But why did he feel hollow and sad, as if something had been stolen from him and all he could do was watch the thief run away with his prized possession? He was so glad Talaitha had come to visit him at his worksite, too. She was everything he wanted, but she was also his jailer. She would go by and feed him, let him out for some sunshine and exercise, but at the end of the day, she would march him right back into his cell and lock him in for the night.

As Jevonte dressed and gathered his tools, he contemplated a shift in plans. He needed to do something, and he needed to do it soon. Then it hit him as he secured the brownstone for the night. "I've got to lock her down once and for all," Jevonte said to himself.

Early the next day, Jevonte heads over to the Baltimore building. This time, he remains in the lobby while he attempts to call Talaitha's office. To his shock, Talaitha answers.

"Hello, this is Dr. Mercedes." Her voice is cold and clinical, and even over the phone, she sounds commanding and robotic.

"It's me, my love. Can you come down to the lobby, please? I have something for you."

"Who is this? I'm sorry. Who are you trying to reach?"

"Talaitha, it's me, Jevonte." The line grows quiet for what feels like an eternity.

"Hi, Jevonte. I was not expecting this."

"I know, and I apologize for just showing up like this. Do you have time for a quick chat? It won't take long, I promise."

Talaitha huffs quietly before relenting. "Listen, I only have thirty minutes before my next client, so this better be quick. I'll meet you in the C-wing over by the coffee shop. Be seated and order me a small chai latte with almond milk.

"Thanks, my heart. I can't…" Before he can finish speaking, a dial tone fills his ear.

Talaitha exits the elevator and descends the stairs to the lobby. She finds Jevonte seated. Her chai latte is positioned in front of the empty seat next to Jevonte, waiting. He rises as Talaitha approaches and stands behind the empty seat. Talaitha takes the seat, and Jevonte scoots her forward.

"Jevonte, I don't have a lot of time. What do you want?" she asks impatiently.

Jevonte considers his thoughts carefully before speaking. He isn't sure he's making the right decision, but he feels he must do this. "I've been giving this desire of mine a lot of thought. I love you, Talaitha. I love you more than anyone, ever. I can't even think straight when you're around me, and I can't concentrate when you're away from me. You are a problem for me, and the only way I know of solving this thing is to make sure I never have to be without you. I want to make you the happiest woman alive. I want to make you as happy and fulfilled as you have made me. I want to dedicate the rest of my life to loving you completely, fully, and for as long as we both shall live."

Jevonte stands and takes a knee before Talaitha. "My heart, will you honor me with the pleasure of becoming my wife?" He then pulls a small ring box from his shoulder bag.

The coffee shop grows deathly still as patrons stare, hopeful for Talaitha's response. Jevonte and Talaitha lock eyes, and then, without a word, Talaitha stands and walks away, headed back to the stairs in the lobby. She pauses at the elevator and looks back at Jevonte, who remains on his knee, a look of horror and trepidation shrouding his face. The elevator doors open, and before stepping inside, Talaitha mouths the word "yes" and disappears as the doors close behind her.

"Well, what did she say?" asks an elderly Black woman who witnessed the proposal.

"She said, 'Yes!'"

The days that followed were heaven for Jevonte. Although Talaitha didn't appear to embrace the proposal, Jevonte couldn't be certain that she was happy about it as he reflected on her reaction. However, this was Talaitha, and her true nature would always remain a mystery. Maybe that's why Jevonte loved her so much. He wouldn't concern himself about that now, however. He received the answer he wanted and hoped for. Now, he resolved to get a better, more meaningful ring for Talaitha to wear. He had bought the ring in haste. He just wanted to have something to show her when he proposed. He hadn't really given a lot of thought to the ring, but now he knew what he needed to do.

The brownstone project is finally complete on Friday, and Jevonte is filled with excitement. After arriving home, he walks into his kitchen to grab a cold beer. Funny, he thinks to himself, something is off in here. Jevonte looks around, and everything seems to be in order; nothing is missing. Not that he owned much kitchenware or decorative pieces for the apartment. Ruby had been hounding him forever to buy a few things to spruce up his place. He simply never had an interest in purchasing decorative items for his apartment. He liked to keep things simple, clean, and airy. Everything had its place, and there was a place for everything. Jevonte's motto was "no muss, no fuss." However, now he would have to make room for someone else. He would have a wife! The thought filled him with happiness and relief. He would no longer be alone. He would finally have someone to share his life and his dreams with.

Jevonte leaned back against the counter and faced his cabinets. He was picturing them full of dishes, glassware, coffee cups, and whatever else Talaitha wanted. Then he noticed something odd. The microwave had a set time. He had not set it. He persistently postponed it, and upon returning home from a tiring day of renovations, he was too exhausted to bother. Oh well, perhaps he forgot.

He walks to his computer, sits at the console, and checks his emails before hitting the shower. Why is the desktop fan running? Jevonte reaches down to touch the side of his desktop. It's warm, very warm. Could some background programs have been running unattended while I was at work?

He turns on the monitor and waits for the screen to come to life. He logs in to the system and, before he can launch his browser, notices that his screensaver has changed. His desktop background has also changed, but he wonders how it happened. Someone has been on his computer, but who?

Even if someone had broken into his apartment, Jevonte doubted they would be able to log into his system.

After a cursory search of his folders and files, Jevonte shuts down the system, but not before changing his login password and screensaver. He rises, worn out and more than ready for a hot shower. He walks into his bedroom and instinctively reaches for the light switch.

"Hey, King, it's about time you got home. I've been waiting for you all evening," purrs Talaitha. She pulls back the sheets to reveal her soft, warm, naked body. Jevonte is frozen in place, speechless, and painfully aware of an erection growing under his jeans.

"Babe, what? How? What are you doing here? When did you get here, and how did you get in? I was planning on giving you a key, but I…"

"I have been thinking about what you asked me. I apologize for the way I handled that situation. I have so much to tell you. I have things I need to share with you, and I wanted to spend more time with you before letting you know about my life and my baggage. Before you commit to me, you should know my past. But first, please take that much-needed shower. You stink, man," Talaitha laughed.

After Jevonte washes the stink of the day's hard work from his body, he joins Talaitha in bed, and the pair embrace.

Jevonte takes Talaitha by the hand and prepares to listen to whatever she has to say.

"We will have time to really talk, my love. Right now, I'm hungry," she says and rolls on top of him.

"Babe, wait, let's just…" Jevonte protests weakly.

Talaitha firmly covers his mouth with a hand. She goes to work, and his body, helpless underneath her grinding fury, yields and responds in earnest to its master.

8

Signed, Sealed, and Silenced

It's the July 4th weekend. To manage the surge in new projects, Jevonte has recruited several new subcontractors and extra carpenters. The business is expanding at a steady pace. And he wants to take full advantage of the revenue increase because he anticipates a large wedding ceremony and reception. While he may enjoy a frugal lifestyle, he is aware that Talaitha does not. She is quality from head to toe, and he's certain his mom and dad want to join in the celebration in a significant way. Nevertheless, Jevonte has prepared himself and his finances to cover the wedding expenses.

On his way home from inspecting Mr. Carlton's office extension, Jevonte calls his mom's house, constantly thinking about the man's ongoing expansion projects. No one answers. He was going to share the news with her and Dad, and he wasn't going to leave it as a voice message, so Jevonte tried to reach Talaitha at her office. It's late, but they can still grab some dinner at the Ekiben. Chinese food sounds very appealing to Jevonte, and he hopes Talaitha agrees.

"Hello. This is Dr. Talaitha Mercedes."

Jevonte is still shocked that he actually reached her. "Hey, love. Feel like a little Chinese for dinner tonight? I can come by and pick you up. Ekiben's should still be open if you have a taste for some Chinese food this evening."

"Chinese does sound good, and I missed lunch today. So, yeah, we can do that. I can meet you there as soon as I finish up here in the office."

"Love, I can come get you. I'm not that far away. We can go together."

"And what am I supposed to do about my car? Just do as I said, and I'll meet you at the restaurant, say, in twenty minutes?"

"Alright, that's fine," Jevonte replied, his feelings ruffled. "I need to get home and get cleaned up a bit. We just finished…"

"My God, man. You mean to tell me that you were going to pick me up from my place of work smelling like a garbage pit and then sit with me for dinner looking like some refugee hobo bear?"

"Babe, I don't smell…too bad. I was conducting inspections today, and I…"

"I don't want to hear it. Go home, shower, and use the Creed Aventus I bought you. I want you to wear that outfit I picked up for you last week."

As usual, Jevonte arrives early at Ekiben's, while Talaitha arrives very late. They sit near a window. The night is quiet. There aren't many customers or vehicles on the road. Jevonte can hear his thoughts for a change.

"Babe, you look great. How was your day?" asks Jevonte.

"Did you order some drinks yet?" responds Talaitha curtly as she begins to scan her menu.

"Yes. I have the Merlot you love and a Cognac for me."

Talaitha stares blankly at her menu and slowly shakes her head. "I'm too tired to argue. The Merlot is fine, but that's not what I wanted." She pauses, testing the air. "Well, you managed to do at least one thing right," she says, a bit exasperated.

Jevonte decides to ignore the barb. He's starting to develop a little skill at slipping her jabs. "I wanted to talk to you about the wedding. I tried to call my mom today to break the news, but she…"

"Please tell me you did not tell your parents about the wedding. Who told you that you could do that, Jevonte?" Talaitha's full attention is on Jevonte now. Her tone and body posture are erect and tense.

"Sweetheart, I just wanted to tell my mom. It's no big deal. I'm sure she would…"

Again, Talaitha cuts him off. "I'm not going to repeat this. You will not tell anybody about the wedding until I tell you to. I'm not playing with you, Jevonte." Her words are cold, sharp, and drip with authority. Jevonte grows still, not sure how to respond.

"I. I don't understand, babe. So, when are we going to tell anyone?

"Until I say so, Jevonte. I am in the middle of crucial clinical trials, trials that, if disrupted in any way, will jeopardize the health and safety of many of my patients," says Talaitha in a more relaxed, concerned tone. Having tamped down her responses, Jevonte begins to relax.

Cautiously, Jevonte asks, "So then, how or when do we say anything to our families? As for the families, I still don't know much about yours, love."

Talaitha returns her eyes to the menu, and a long silence ensues. She gestures for the waiter. "I'll have the roasted duck with chestnut stuffing. He'll have the duck, sausage, and shrimp gumbo. Thank you." Jevonte starts to protest, but decides against it.

After the pair finishes their meals, Talaitha gathers Jevonte's hands across the table. She holds his hands gently, massaging the back of his hands with her thumbs. She stops and looks him directly in the eye.

"I know it's important to you that we include your family in our wedding plans, and I want that, but my work is at a very significant point right now, and I need you to understand this. I know you may be having some doubts about us, and I promise I will share a lot more about my family soon, but I need you to be patient concerning the announcement until after we return," Talaitha says with a smile.

Jevonte is slow to respond. His brain is slowly processing what he heard. "Return? From?"

"Hawaii, King. We are going to Hawaii for our honeymoon!" Talaitha says with immense joy.

Jevonte sits stunned. "Hawaii, babe—that sounds great, but how are we going to honeymoon when we haven't wed yet?"

"I've already made arrangements with the city justice of the peace. We're scheduled to meet at the courthouse at 1:30 pm sharp."

"What?" Jevonte raises his voice in surprise. Talaitha's eyes open wide at this sudden outburst. "I apologize, but could you please let me know when you were planning to share this information with me? What if we hadn't seen each other tonight?"

"I'm telling you now. Isn't that all that matters after all? We're going to become one unit after tomorrow, and we will never have to miss one another again. What, you would rather not get married now?"

"Yes. Yes, I do. But love, I was just hoping we could include our folks and have them share in our joy. Plus, Hawaii, did you already put that together?

Talaitha withdraws her hands from the table and sits back in her seat. "I see I was wrong then, so I'll fix it. I'll call down to the courthouse and cancel it. Hawaii is not a problem. I need a vacation, so I'll just go by myself. In fact, some of my girlfriends could use a few nights away, so this will be a great opportunity for them." Talaitha motions for the waiter. "Check, please."

"Talaitha, please, no, I want to get married, I really do. Don't cancel any…"

Before Jevonte can finish pleading his case, Talaitha rises and walks out of the restaurant, leaving Jevonte to pay the waiter. After the waiter returns with his receipt, Jevonte stays at the table, wondering what just happened. He begins to experience nausea. He's feeling panicky, not sure whether he should chase after Talaitha or wait until tomorrow and try speaking with her about this whole thing. He decides to go after her.

Outside the restaurant door, Talaitha is standing at the street's corner, alone under a dimly lit street lamp. Her arms are folded across her chest, and her chin is lifted to the night sky. In the faint glow of the lamp's light, Jevonte can just make out the glistening streak of a few tears on her face. Jevonte rushes to her side.

"My love, are you okay? Please don't cry," Jevonte says soothingly.

"I don't want to lose you, King. I wanted this desperately, and now it's all gone. I really thought I had found the one man, the one man who could love me as I loved him," Talaitha says, her mouth thick with saliva, her throat tight with raw emotion.

"No way, my heart. You could never lose me, ever. I am fully yours, completely. It doesn't matter when or where we get married. I just want you. I just want you to be my wife, forever. Nothing else matters to me. No one matters to me the way you do. I'm sorry. I was just bugging out back there, but I'm feeling better now. Let's get married tomorrow at the courthouse."

"Are you sure, man? I know I can be a bit difficult to swallow sometimes, but if you're sure, I am too."

"I am—no doubt about it—none."

"Good. Tomorrow, a tux will arrive for you. It should get to your place at 8 am on the dot. I'll send a car for you and meet you at the courthouse. Are we clear?" asks Talaitha sternly.

"I will be there. Horses could not drag me away."

The couple embraces and enjoys a long, passionate kiss. They are oblivious to the passersby and gawkers. They are breathing for one another, roiling in the heat of one another's passion. The intensity of their embrace almost drives them to the ground before Jevonte breaks contact. "Let's save some of that for Hawaii, shall we?" he whispers, a giant grin spreading across his face.

Check-in was uneventful, and after getting into the room, Jevonte began to relax and feel more at ease. Much of his discomfort with how quickly Talaitha had arranged the wedding and the honeymoon had faded. The main point is that they have reached this moment; they are finally married, and he could not be happier. He hoped that as they took more and more time to get to know one another on deeper levels, he would finally get to see the soft side of Talaitha. He hoped that she would let her guard down and invite him into her secret spaces. Besides that, he would have to reconcile this whole matter with how his parents were treated. They were completely isolated and left out of the entire thing. Ruby would not forgive him anytime soon for that, and Jevonte knew this as clearly as the sun burns bright in the sky. This was going to hurt her deeply, and he also knew his dad would be very disappointed.

No matter. Jevonte would figure out how to make things work and please his family. They would have to understand; after all, this is what they always wanted for him, right? Jevonte arranged the luggage closer to the dresser and started to unpack his things when Talaitha called him to the balcony.

"King, come out here and sit with me. These views are to die for." Jevonte hurriedly closed the distance to the balcony where Talaitha sits with nothing but a sheer shawl draped across the front of her body. She's wearing shades and smiles as Jevonte takes a seat in the lounge chair beside hers.

"Oh my, this is a gorgeous view," Jevonte exhales.

"Yes, now aren't you glad we came?"

"Definitely. I've never been to Hawaii, but I've always heard it was a honeymooner's dream. I can't wait to see..."

"I have a few excursions planned for today and tomorrow. We're going to kick everything off with a couple's massage at Kapalua Bay. This should get us ready for the hike in the afternoon."

"Hike?"

"Oh yes, love. The rainforests here on Maui are extraordinary. I hired one of the best guides, so we can look forward to visiting the waterfalls and the Haleakala Crater."

"That sounds like fun, but I really wanted to..."

"Oh, and I have some time set aside for us at the Maui healing retreat. I attended an off-site professional conference there a few years ago, and I can assure you that the psychic readers and yoga instructors there are genuine. They stretched me in ways I never thought were possible. You're going to love it, trust me."

"I've never been to a reading. I have my doubts about those things. I just feel like it's all a sham," replies Jevonte.

"Do you, now? Psychics are real people, and they do have gifts. I am one. Bet you didn't know that, huh?"

"Stop," laughs Jevonte. You're a psychiatrist; surely you don't believe in that nonsense?"

Talaitha smiles, then removes the shawl covering her toned, naked brown hips and waistline. Drawing her knees up, she massages her hamstrings slowly, deliberately. "I can tell you exactly what's about to happen right now, King!"

Jevonte's eyes trace the soft curves of her thighs and the tight bunching of Talaitha's six-pack. He rises and takes his position at the foot of her lounge chair. He notices a bath towel has already been positioned underneath her hips. Talaitha closes her eyes as Jevonte obeys her silent beckoning. She palms the top of his head and leans back to rest her head against her raised hand. Twenty minutes pass with Talaitha controlling Jevonte's head like a joystick. She stops him when she gets close to finishing, then drives him into complete immersion when she's ready to climb the mountain again. Jevonte's back is aching, and his mouth and jaw grow tired, but Talaitha's control is firm, and she does not allow him to adjust his position. His back is on fire from being bent so awkwardly, and Jevonte tries to stand and break contact, but Talaitha clamps her thighs tightly around his head and wraps a leg across his back.

In a panic, Jevonte tries to cry out to warn Talaitha that he can't breathe, but he can't get any air to speak. His voice is muffled, so he grabs her knees and tries to loosen the vice grip he's in. Talaitha finally relinquishes her hold on his head as her body is overcome with waves of orgasmic release. She continues to hold his head with one hand, not wanting to disturb the rush of pleasure flooding her whole body.

"Be still, King. Don't you move," Talaitha moans. Jevonte relaxes and begins to sag. His vision is blurred, and he is just barely conscious. Talaitha shudders and releases Jevonte finally, and he collapses onto the balcony floor, breathing heavily, working to gasp as much air as possible. In a still, quiet, sultry voice, Talaitha croons, "I told you I was psychic, my love. Now, let's get ready for dinner. We have a reservation at Tony's in two hours."

After dinner, Talaitha and Jevonte walk along the beach before heading back to their bungalow. The two are in harmony, laughing and teasing one another. The moon is full and bright, and its light shimmers across the slowly breaking waves on the beach. Jevonte is feeling so content and fulfilled. Talaitha is opening up and sharing things with him for the first time. She explains some of her clinical work and practice, sharing that she's been working with several patients who society at large would probably classify as homicidal maniacs, psychopaths, and people who pose a serious threat to the community. Jevonte can see how excited she is about her work. She's excited and completely in the moment as she shares her career and how she became a mental health professional.

"I was in the system as a young teen. I don't talk very much about that period of my life. It's just too painful." Jevonte continues holding her hand. He doesn't interrupt her. "Something awful happened, and I had to be removed from my parents' home. Please don't ask, because I need more time to work on those memories," Talaitha said softly.

"I understand," replied Jevonte.

"I suffered a lot of abuse and trauma growing up. I made money for one set of foster parents, lots of it. Other men in the neighborhood used me for their pleasure. They passed me around from one customer to another. It sickens me to even think about it."

"My love, I'm so sorry this happened to you." I believe I'm starting to understand why she's the way she is now, he thinks.

"Don't feel sorry for me. I completed medical school at Johns Hopkins and established my boutique practice in Baltimore. I have found my life's calling in helping people who have had struggles similar to mine. I'm extra sensitive about it, too. Nothing can disrupt my care of the delicate minds entrusted to me."

The pair continued in quiet conversation, finally making it back to their suite. Talaitha undressed and headed to the bathroom for a shower. She paused at the bathroom door and said, "King, I am grateful you are in my life the way you are. I needed someone like you, and now that I have you, I will kill to protect what we have. Now get naked, because when I get out of the shower," she said seductively, "you better be ready, sir!"

She's insatiable, Jevonte thinks, but that's alright with me. Jevonte sat on the bed and started undressing, but he stopped. Let me make a quick call before she gets out of the shower. Jevonte grabs the room phone and asks the front desk for an outside line.

"Hi, Mom, how are you?" Jevonte begins.

"Oh my Lord, Jevonte, is that you? You sound so far away. Where are you?" asks Ruby excitedly.

"Mom, I'm in Hawaii."

"Hawaii!!! My goodness, what are you doing there? How long have you been there?"

"Mom, I don't know how to say it, so I'm just going to say it. I'm married now. We are in Hawaii for our honeymoon," replies Jevonte before holding his breath in anticipation of Ruby's reaction.

A long silence ensues before Ruby asks, "I don't even know what to say, son. Who did you marry? Was it that girl you met on the cruise a few months back? What was her name, Tabitha?"

"Yes, Mom. Her name is Talaitha. I told you and Dad about her a while ago."

"Yes, I remember, but son, did you marry her? You got married and didn't tell me? Did you tell your dad at least?" Ruby asks, pain and disappointment evident in her voice.

"Mom, I'm so sorry. I wanted to, and it all happened so fast. Actually, we couldn't say anything because it was necessary to keep quiet to protect the sensitive nature of Talaitha's work."

"I don't get it, son. That does not make sense to me, and I know your dad is really going to be disappointed about this. But you're a grown man. You do what you want, but I have to say, this does hurt. We would have liked to be there to support both of you."

"I understand, Mom. I really do. I have so much to tell you guys. When we return, let's plan a get-together, such as a cookout or another gathering. I can bring my wife to meet the family and introduce her to everyone. Once you meet her, you will love her; I just know you will," says Jevonte, his voice earnest and hopeful.

"Well, alright, we will see. When do you expect to be back from Hawaii, and where are you guys going to live now?" Before Jevonte can respond, the shower stops.

"Look, I have to go, Mom. I will let you know when we get back in town. Please tell Dad that I'm sorry I couldn't say anything or share my plans earlier. I'll talk to you soon," Jevonte whispers into the handset and then hangs up.

Talaitha sits on the bath stool. She has been out of the shower for the duration of Jevonte's call, listening, fuming, and growing darker in mood. She straightens up, applies some bath oil, and conditions her face and pores. She stands for a long minute in front of the mirror. Her rage is building, and in her mind, she watches as her fists shatter and destroy the steamed-up mirror. Finally, with several deep breaths, she relaxes and finishes her skincare regimen.

Talaitha walks out of the bathroom and immediately goes to the dresser, where she removes her nightclothes. She gets dressed without saying a word to Jevonte. She doesn't even glance at him as he sprawls naked on the bed.

"Babe, what are you doing?" Jevonte asks, surprised. Talaitha does not respond. She stands in front of the dresser, facing the mirror with her back to Jevonte. She says nothing.

After a few more moments of silence, Jevonte again asks, this time with pleading in his voice, "Love, what's wrong? Talk to me, please." Talaitha remains rigid and unresponsive and then proceeds to grab a comforter from the closet and walk out to the balcony. She lies down on the chaise and closes her eyes.

Jevonte sits up in the bed, stunned and confused by the sudden shift in Talaitha's behavior. He walks out to the balcony and sits opposite where Talaitha is lying down. "Talaitha, I don't know what's going on, but if I have said something to upset you, please tell me. Talk to me." Talaitha rolls to her side, facing away from Jevonte. She remains silent. Jevonte moves to sit on the edge of the chaise, near Talaitha's hip. He places a hand on her waist and gently attempts to roll her onto her back. Talaitha goes limp and does not resist. She lies on her back, her eyes staring blankly into space. She looks like she isn't breathing, and Jevonte starts to panic.

"Babe, babe, are you alright?" Jevonte asks while shaking her. Talaitha's body moves back and forth under Jevonte's efforts; her eyes remain blank and uncaring. She just lies there, and when Jevonte stops shaking her, she looks him in the eye and rolls back onto her side and curls up into a ball. Silence ensues for the space of a few minutes as

Jevonte remains seated next to Talaitha. Before he rises, Jevonte says, "I'll leave you alone. I'm sorry. I'll be in the bedroom if you decide you want to talk about whatever is bothering you."

Jevonte kisses Talaitha on her shoulder and returns to the bedroom, where he sits at the foot of the bed, bewildered at what is happening. Maybe in the morning, she will feel like talking to me.

Jevonte wakes early. He couldn't sleep, thinking of his new wife, who was on the balcony on their honeymoon night. He gets out of bed and walks out to the balcony, hopeful that Talaitha is feeling better and ready to talk. She's gone. She neatly folded the comforter she was using and placed it at the foot of the chaise. Talaitha's luggage is gone. She has also removed her toiletries. All of her clothes have been removed from the closet. All that remains are Jevonte's things. In a panic, Jevonte rushes to get dressed and heads to the resort lobby.

As he approached the check-in desk, he saw no one. He impatiently rings the front desk bell. A desk clerk walks out from the back office and greets Jevonte with a fake smile.

"Hello, sir. How can I help you this morning?"

"Um, I need to see whether my wife has checked out of the resort, please," Jevonte asks, worry and concern on his face.

"Just one moment, sir." The desk clerk turns to his computer screen and logs in. "What is the room number?"

"507," answers Jevonte.

"Can I see your ID, sir?"

"Sure." Jevonte reaches for his wallet and pulls out his driver's license. "Is there a problem?"

"No, no, sir. I just can't give that information out unless I verify the ID." The clerk takes Jevonte's license and says, "Sir, I don't have anyone under the name Greene registered for that room."

Jevonte, confused, stares blankly at the desk clerk. "What do you mean 'no one named Greene' is in that room? My wife and I are on our honeymoon. My wife made the reservation. We've been here now for three days!" Jevonte's voice is strained.

"What is your wife's name, sir?"

"Talaitha Mercedes," responds Jevonte.

"Ah, yes, okay, well, we do have a Mr. and Mrs. Mercedes in the room. There have been no check-outs for that room yet." The desk clerk pauses, staring intently at his computer monitor. "Sir, it does show here that there was a second reservation made early this morning for Mrs. Mercedes."

"What room?" Jevonte demands hurriedly.

"Sir, I really need to see some paperwork confirming that you are married to Mrs. Mercedes." I can't give you the room number without confirming that."

"How am I supposed to do that? I don't have the marriage license on me right now. Please call the room so that she can confirm it. The situation is very urgent," Jevonte pleads. The desk clerk nods his head and dials the room.

"Good morning, Mrs. Mercedes. This is the front desk, and a gentleman here is insisting that he is your husband. I told him we cannot divulge your room number unless we can confirm that he is indeed your husband," the clerk says politely. There is a long pause before the clerk responds. "Thank you, ma'am, and I am sorry to have disturbed you this morning. I'm sorry, sir. The lady said that her husband is deceased and that she has no idea who you are."

Jevonte is cut, hurt, and deeply confused. He stands at the counter, his hands falling slowly to his sides before turning away. I don't know what she's playing at, but this is not funny, Jevonte thinks.

Before Jevonte can walk away, the desk clerk asks, "Sir, that ID is not registered for the room you say you are staying in. Do you have a key for the room?"

Jevonte turns to face the clerk. "Yes, I do. Why?"

"Since you're not allowed in that room, please give me the key."

"Are you insane? I'm not giving you my room key. All of my things are in the room. I'm telling you that we checked in together. I didn't know that she made the reservation under her maiden name, but we are married."

"Sir, I'll have to call security unless you give me that key."

"I don't believe this. This is some bullshit. All you have to do is check the room. You will find all of my things; my luggage and toiletries are there. If it weren't my room, how did my bags get in there?"

"I am sorry, sir. Mrs. Mercedes has requested the removal and cleaning of the room. I will have resort staff bring any of your property, if there is any, down to the lobby area. You can wait in the lobby for your property, but please understand that we will need to confirm that it actually is yours. I apologize for any inconvenience."

"I don't believe this is happening," says Jevonte, and he tosses the room key across the counter before walking to the lobby waiting area.

Thirty minutes later, a bellhop approaches the front desk, and he's pushing a luggage cart with all of Jevonte's things neatly stacked on it. The desk clerk points in Jevonte's direction, and the bellhop nods and begins walking towards Jevonte.

"Hello, sir. Can I see some form of ID, please?" Jevonte remains seated, but he pulls out his driver's license and hands it to the bellhop. "Thank you, sir. I can see that your luggage tags match your ID, and I found a copy of your boarding pass on the dresser. They all confirm that the bags are your property. But, we still cannot let you back into the room without Mrs. Mercedes's permission."

Jevonte sits in silence. He is utterly confused and hurt. What should he do now, he wonders. He rises and begins to walk back to the concierge. Maybe they have another room he can reserve. Their flight back to Baltimore is tomorrow, but he will need somewhere to sleep for the night. Before he can reach the counter, the elevator in the lobby opens, and out steps Talaitha. She ignores Jevonte and motions for the bellhop to take her luggage to the shuttle. She points towards Jevonte's cart and instructs another bellhop to load it as well. She pauses briefly and then stares at Jevonte as if to say, "Let's go. What are you waiting for?" She then walks out of the lobby and boards the shuttle.

Jevonte finds himself speechless. He looks at the concierge, who quickly breaks eye contact with Jevonte. Jevonte, with sadness and hurt on his face, grabs a paper from the check-in desk and follows the bellhop, who is pushing his luggage cart towards the shuttle. He takes a seat next to Talaitha, who remains cold as ice, staring outside the shuttle window.

"Honey, why…why are we leaving now? I thought check-out wasn't until tomorrow." For a full two minutes, Talaitha says nothing as the shuttle heads toward the airport.

"I changed our departure time. "I have important business matters to address, so I need to return earlier than originally scheduled," Talaitha finally responds.

"What business? Is it your practice?

"No, King. I have to speak to my lawyer."

Jevonte grows quiet. He sinks into his seat and asks no further questions. A small tear begins to form in his right eye. He closes both eyes and starts feeling depressed. His mind and spirit are tumbling into an abyss of turmoil and despair. He knows this dread. He is very familiar with it, but he didn't think he would ever have to face it alone again, not with Talaitha in his life.

"We are closing on a house. My lawyer advised that I return early to meet an early deadline. Tomorrow, I aim to sign the closing documents to expedite our move-in. You will love this house. I'm excited about it." Talaitha exclaims, and her happiness and enthusiasm invigorate Jevonte, pulling him out of his depression.

"House? Closing? I don't understand. What house? When did you do all of this?"

"It was before we departed for Hawaii, King. I had been interested in this property for a long time, and it finally came on the market just before we left, at a price that matched what I was willing to pay. I didn't want to say anything to you in case it all fell through."

"Can we talk about last night, my love? I mean, I'm happy about the home, and I do have some questions about that too, but shouldn't we talk about what happened last night?"

"No. Maybe you can just call your mom again and talk to her about it," says Talaitha sarcastically.

"Love, I'm sorry. I understand you didn't want me to inform anyone about the wedding earlier, but by the time I called my mom, it had already happened. She's happy for us, you know. I didn't see the harm in it. In fact, they want to throw a party for us when we get back."

"You snuck behind my back and called your mom after I explicitly told you not to. You hurt me by doing that. I don't know whether I can trust you now."

"I understand, Talaitha. Please, I won't let that happen again. I promise. Your happiness brings me immense joy. I just want to make you happy. If that's okay, I'll tell my family the party's off, and we'll reschedule for later this year.

"Fine. I forgive you, but don't let that shit happen again, ever."

Jevonte nods, "I promise. You have my word. Now tell me a little about this house." How much did it cost, and where is it located?" Jevonte asks. His heart flutters, and his mind feels at ease, as if he's averted a huge catastrophe. The shuttle proceeds toward the airport as the couple draws closer in whispered conversation. Talaitha laughs, and Jevonte's eyes are filled with joy again as he listens to the happiness in Talaitha's voice.

"King, once we complete the remodeling, we can have your folks over for dinner. It will be fun and special. I want to make sure everything is in place before I meet your mom and dad. It has to be special. I want to make a big impression on the two of them."

9

Ghosts Don't Stay Dead

Supplies begin to arrive at the new home in Accident, Maryland. The shippers had difficulty locating the property and, for that matter, the town. With a population of just over 450, the town of Accident doesn't see much commercial traffic or interest. The residents of Accident are mostly quiet, unobtrusive, but friendly folk. People minded their own business and took little interest in strangers. How and why Talaitha chose this area remained a mystery to Jevonte. He and his bride were the only Black people, from what he had been able to observe, in the whole town.

Still, on this picturesque morning, none of that mattered to Jevonte. On this warm August day, he felt energized and ready to start his planned renovations. The house looked like it had been plucked from the pages of a forgotten New England folktale—timber-dark, secretive, and half-swallowed by the forest. Its wood-shingled exterior bore the stain of years and silence, whispering tales in the evening breeze. The screened-in porch, covered in ivy and shadows, looked like a watchful eye, with a faded red door only slightly ajar.

Soft light spilled from the interior windows, casting long fingers across the stone patio—an odd comfort amidst the stillness. The courtyard was meticulous, too meticulous. Brick pathways led nowhere in particular, and the wrought iron chairs surrounding the table looked like no one had dared sit in them for years, though the cushions remained untouched by dust or weather.

The house was beautiful, yes. But it was the kind of beauty that watched you; it remembered things you'd rather forget. This place wasn't a home. It was a setting. Jevonte didn't know why Talaitha had chosen it or how she'd managed to close the deal without him ever setting foot inside. But as he stood by the red umbrella and listened to the woods press in behind him, he realized something else— he hadn't chosen any of this. Jevonte hadn't chosen the sudden wedding, nor the trip, nor the house. He hadn't even chosen the person he was gradually transforming into.

Jevonte was a master craftsman, and he considered himself an artist when it came to remodeling homes. Despite the Craftsman/Cottage hybrid's age, he was confident in his ability to revitalize both its interior and exterior. All that mattered to him was creating a space that he hoped Talaitha would love.

Jevonte's plans called for a complete rebuild of the patio and replacement of the shingled roof. He wasn't worried and thought he could finish that part of the project before fall. His deeper concern was with the basement. Talaitha had expressed how important a fully finished basement was. She also let him know that the greenhouse needed to be a priority. Over the coming weeks, he faced a challenging task, but now that the supplies he had ordered had finally arrived, he was eager to begin.

Jevonte thought to himself, the greenhouse will take a lot of time and crowd out my other projects before winter. Just then, Talaitha opened the screen door and walked out to her car.

"King," Talaitha says softly. How's everything going? I saw the delivery truck. Did everything arrive as planned?"

"Yes. I'm reviewing now. I believe I can get started on the roof this afternoon. I intended to call my uncle to see if he could lend me a hand. With his help, I'll finish ahead of schedule for sure."

"Oh, no. Don't. The house isn't ready yet. I don't want anyone to see this place until we've transformed it."

"As you command, my love," responded Jevonte playfully.

"I do," laughed Talaitha.

"I've been thinking about this place and its proximity to most of my contracts in Baltimore. It's going to be a challenge to maintain the work there and get this remodel completed."

"It's not going to be a challenge, King. I informed your clients you wouldn't be available this summer or anytime soon.

"You what?" replied Jevonte incredulously. "Babe, you can't cancel my jobs like that. I have signed contracts with most of my clients—long-time, faithful clients. I can't do that to them."

"It's already done. Besides, it's not an actual cancellation but more of a delay—an extended one. You can restart those projects after you finish this job." With that, Talaitha headed for her car and started the engine. She took her time adjusting the seat and mirrors, setting the GPS coordinates for the shortest route to a new office space she was reviewing at the edge of town. She backed out of the driveway and blew Jevonte a kiss before driving down the long, isolated road to the connected Interstate.

Jevonte stood silently next to the pallets of supplies that lined the side of the cottage. "What the hell did my wife just do to me?" Jevonte mused out loud. He stepped back inside the house and grabbed a cold beer from the fridge. He sat at the bar and opened up his contacts. He would call his clients to assure them he would honor their contracts. He was not going to lose or jeopardize these client relationships, which had taken years to cultivate. There was no way he was going to throw all of that hard work in the garbage.

There was no signal. Accident was a tiny town, and apparently, there was very little infrastructure in place to support cellular equipment. Jevonte didn't recall seeing any cell phone towers along the way into the town, nor did he remember seeing any cable or power lines. Still, he had assumed that some communication infrastructure was in place. There had to be. It was 2018, for God's sake. He couldn't contact his clients, and Talaitha had not connected the home telephone service yet. Jevonte wondered how she managed to call his clients to cancel the contracts.

He was stuck.

To combat the emerging feelings of isolation and frustration, Jevonte dove into the work. There was nothing he could do about the questions hounding his mind at the moment. He had faith that these issues would resolve themselves eventually. As he began offloading the pallets of wood and shingles, he reminded himself that he was getting the woman of his dreams, who was very complicated. His heart was full, and so were the nights he shared with the most amazing lover he'd ever experienced.

The next few weeks were a blur of activity around the home. Jevonte managed to get the new roof up and dressed. He had laid the foundation for the greenhouse and began wrapping the basement to waterproof it. He was exhausted most days, but it was a satisfying feeling. He could see how happy the work made Talaitha feel, and that was his reward.

Since the home telephone landline hadn't been installed yet, Jevonte, having remembered seeing signs about the town's library, determined in his mind to find it and visit. He loved how small and quaint Accident was, but living there also made him feel like he was moving backwards in time, losing ground, and being left behind by modern civilization, not to mention the isolation. It could be crippling sometimes. Talaitha had taken an afternoon nap after the couple's mid-morning lovemaking, and so Jevonte used that time to walk to the library.

The Accident Public Library was small, just like everything in town. It only had five shelves of books and a reading room. What was most important to Jevonte was having computers and an Internet connection. It was also free.

After signing up for a library card and logging into the computer, Jevonte navigated to the Lowe's website. He needed to order additional supplies to complete the work in the basement. Jevonte loaded his cart and navigated to the online checkout.

The purchase failed.

Jevonte tried again, carefully entering his bank information.

The same results appeared on his screen. Jevonte navigated to his bank website to review his account. There was no way he was broke. His business account was flush with cash after his last project with Mr. Carlton.

The memo that greeted Jevonte after he logged into his bank's website sent chills down his spine.

This account has been locked. Please contact your business account representative for instructions. You may call during business hours at 1(800)435-8897, or email us at Tristarbanking@ibank.com

Jevonte quickly wrote down the contact number and email address. He logged out of the banking page and navigated to his email account.

His login and password failed.

He attempted to log in again, but the system rejected his credentials. Maybe I'm using the wrong password. Jevonte thought, I don't understand why this is happening, so let's try this again.

Jevonte submitted a password reset request, and the reset code was sent to embarkanew@mercedes.com for verification. Jevonte sat stunned. How was this situation even possible? The email address embarkanew@mercedes.com was not the backup email address that Jevonte used for his primary account. Was this Talaitha's account? How did she get into his account and change his preferences without his knowledge?

Jevonte's allotted time was up, and he needed to get home. He needed answers, and he was dreading having to ask them of Talaitha.

On his way home, he thought about how he would approach this situation with Talaitha. By now, he is used to her controlling nature. She can be—he searched his mind for the right word—bipolar at times. No, that's not it, Jevonte thought. Jevonte believed it was related to personality, but he lacked sufficient psychological knowledge to describe Talaitha's condition accurately. There were times in the relationship when her anger would be inappropriate and very intense. She operated like an on/off switch, instantly switching to morbid silence and isolating herself from him and everyone around her. He planned to take a peek at some of the books she held in the library-office he built for her after they moved into the new home. Until then, he would just have to brace for the storm.

The curtains Jevonte just installed in front of the house are drawn closed. As Jevonte walks through the front door, the interior is dark and very still. He pauses to listen. The partially closed-off kitchen emits the sound of cookware. Jevonte was demoing the cabinets and the wall separating the breakfast nook from the living room.

At the stove, Talaitha is stirring a pot of something good and aromatic. Oxtails are braising in a pan, and she is slowly preparing the roux, collecting around the meat. The fragrance fills Jevonte's nostrils, and his mind instantly goes back to when he was a boy watching his mom cook. He is so distracted that at first, he doesn't even notice that Talaitha is wearing nothing but an apron. Her back is facing him, and all he can see is the smoothness of her skin and the delicate but pronounced musculature of her back and shoulders. She spreads her legs slightly, the shiny darkness of her heels evoking mysteries yet to unravel.

She never turns her head, but after a few moments of rapt silence, Talaitha acknowledges Jevonte's presence. "Hey, King. Did you get what you needed at the library?"

"How'd you know I was at the library?" Jevonte asks as he strolls up beside Talaitha. "I should have left a note for you. I didn't think I was going to be gone as long as I was."

"Here, taste this," and Talaitha scoops a small ladle's worth of the brewing roux up to Jevonte's lips.

"Babe, that's fantastic," says Jevonte, licking his lips for more. "It reminds me of home and the way my mom used to cook oxtails."

Talaitha slowly lowers the ladle down into the sink and places her hands on the countertop. She lowers her head to look down at her apron. Jevonte can't be certain, but it almost sounds like a whistling sound is emanating from her midsection, or maybe it's her throat. It's a slight, quiet sound, so faint it's hard to tell where it's coming from, but Jevonte can feel the atmosphere in the kitchen has drastically changed. "Tal, are you okay?"

Talaitha does not respond. She slowly lifts the pan of oxtails from the stovetop and holds it suspended over the fire. Her eyes are blank, and the whistling noise has ceased. Jevonte holds his breath, not sure whether he needs to be ready to duck or run. Then, without saying a word, she dumps the entire pan of oxtails into the garbage. The smoldering meat sears the bottom of the garbage bin and melts some of the plastic liner.

"Hey, sweetheart, why did you do that? I was really looking forward to trying those! Babe? Talaitha, what's wrong? Did I say something to make you upset?"

Talaitha begins walking out of the kitchen. She ignores Jevonte and pauses in the hallway that joins the kitchen area and living room long enough to untie her apron. She lets the garment fall to the ground around her ankles. Jevonte walks over to where she's standing and wraps his arms around her.

"Lover, where are you going?" Jevonte whispers gently into her ear.

"This was a mistake," Talaitha replies.

"What was?"

"This. This marriage was a mistake."

Jevonte unwraps his arms and takes a step back. "Talaitha, what? Why would you say that? Why do you think our marriage is a mistake?"

"Maybe I should bring your mom out here, and she can cook you some oxtails since you love hers so damn much."

"Babe, c'mon now, I didn't mean to imply that my mom's cooking was better. I wasn't making a comparison. I..."

"Whatever you say, Jevonte. Look, I have to head down to the Baltimore office for a few hours. You can cook something for yourself."

"I don't understand Talaitha, but okay. I'm sorry. I didn't mean to upset you or offend you." Talaitha begins to turn and head towards the bedroom. "One thing, babe. Did you get into my business account and change my preferences? My account was blocked, and I couldn't order supplies for the remodel."

"Come here," Talaitha's voice trails from the end of the hallway.

Jevonte moves down the hallway and enters the bedroom. Talaitha is leaning against the back bedroom wall. Her hands are clasped behind her back, and her legs are crossed. "Remove your pants and get on the bed," Talaitha commands; her voice is strong and confident.

"Babe, you haven't answered my question. This is serious, my love..."

Talaitha moves quickly and closes the distance between her and Jevonte. She grabs his belt and unbuckles it, and pulls his trousers down until they're bunched around his ankles. She shoves him backwards, and Jevonte loses his balance, collapsing with a dead bounce onto the queen-size mattress.

With cold eyes, Talaitha straddles Jevonte and lowers her face to his. "Don't worry about your business account. We are now one unit, and I will handle the finances from here on out. I need you to trust me and know that what I am doing is for the best. If you need money, let me know, and I will give you what you need. If you need to order supplies, use the card I left for you in your desk drawer."

Soon, Jevonte's thoughts are quiet, and his real hunger emerges as Talaitha bears down on him. Her hips don't move up and down but take on a life of their own, moving in a halted, jerky rhythm and plunging strokes against his pelvis. Talaitha climaxes suddenly and thrusts Jevonte's hands away from her waist as he attempts to match her body's shuddering movements.

"Wait, babe. I'm almost there, I…"

Talaitha slaps Jevonte hard across the face.

With her other hand, she quickly grabs him around the throat and palms the back of his bald head with her free hand. Talaitha draws Jevonte's head forward to meet her own. Their foreheads touch, and she pulls her legs into a squatting position with Jevonte still inside of her. Talaitha slowly and forcefully whispers into his mouth—still open from the shock of the slap—"King. Oh, my beloved King, I didn't permit you to finish. I didn't say you could cum." She begins to slowly grind and rock back and forth against Jevonte's tensed body. "Do you understand me?" Talaitha hisses through gritted teeth.

Jevonte nods. His body is tight and ready to explode. His face tingles from the slap, but he relinquishes all control to Talaitha. He is under her power, and as he lies under her hips and thighs, he finds contentment. More important than his pleasure and needs is her happiness. In this moment, though he feels diminished and emptied, he feels satisfied because she is getting what she wants and needs. This is how they will stay connected. This is how he will remain tied to her. This is how their love will thrive and grow.

The evening air in Baltimore is remarkably calm and cool for this time of year. Dr. Mercedes has seen the majority of patients with appointments and has secured the office for the night. As she heads towards the elevator, she misses the man waiting at the far end of the hall. He remains silent and watches while intentionally staying out of sight of Talaitha's office. Anyone nearby who sees him would likely stop and notice his attire. He looked like a detective, one of those characters one reads about in a true crime novel. His trench coat collar is turned up. The brim of his hat is sloped forward and covers his eyes. His wingtip shoes are flawless and coordinate perfectly with his pinstripe trousers. There is an air of detachment around him, and someone meeting him might assume he belonged to the mafia or some kind of organized, old-world crime family.

After the elevator doors shut and Talaitha is gone, the man in the trench coat begins cautiously moving along the wall towards Talaitha's office. He pauses at the office door and listens. The hall is quiet, and the adjacent offices are now empty. The stranger adeptly removes a zippered pouch from the inside pocket of his coat and removes a few delicate tools from its interior. In less than thirty seconds, he is inside Talaitha's office. He walks over to her desk and sits down. Her computer is still warm. The intruder jiggles the mouse, and the monitor brightens, and the system desktop appears.

"What have we here? Not even a password login. Are we that sure of ourselves now?" The intruder whispers. "Let's open a few emails and do some digging, shall we?" The stranger culls several of Talaitha's file folders until he finds what he's looking for. He pulls a thumb drive from his pocket and begins transferring entire folders to it. Satisfied with what he's copied, the stranger starts rifling through

Talaitha's desk drawers and file cabinets until he comes across a folder marked "RESTRICTED_FYEO_NOELLE." Inside the folder, there is a compact disc with the same folder's file name and a date written on it. October 7, 2008. He pauses, staring at the CD case and the highlighted date. A deep breath is drawn, held, then slowly expelled through glitched teeth. He pockets the CD in his trench coat and leaves the cabinet open, its drawer fully extended. He then walks over to Talaitha's library wall and pushes on two sets of books. A soft click can be heard as he stands back from the bookshelf. A small recessed drawer emerges from under the bookshelf's second shelf. The man grabs a stack of prescription pads, then heads for the door, leaving the shelf extended. A giant grin of contentment spreads across his face as he pauses at the door. Looking back over the office space, the man utters one word—"soon."

As quietly as he entered, the stranger exits Talaitha's office. Moving with deliberate speed, he takes the stairs down to the lobby floor. A few late-departing personnel from the tenant offices give him a fleeting glance, mainly due to what he is wearing. One security guard commented to her partner, "People in Baltimore will wear anything no matter the season," and shook her head in amusement. The stranger's trench coat shrouds his small frame as he makes haste, leaving the Baltimore building.

The next day, Talaitha arrives at her office early. As soon as she opens her office door, the sight startles her. Her space, her inner sanctum, has been violated. She walks over to her desk and notices the file cabinet is open. Her desk is a mess; it's out of order, nothing is where she left it, and she begins to fume intensely. The file cabinet has been pulled almost all the way out. In a panic, she inspects the folders, moving through them in order, and stops when she notices that a special file is no longer where she placed it.

Talaitha stands in sullen silence. She takes a seat at her desk, clicks her mouse, and the monitor refreshes. Her computer desktop becomes visible, and she clicks on the icon labelled 'Sessions.' She selects yesterday's date, and video clips appear in date-and-time order. There is a 45-minute gap between the last two file date stamps. She opens the very last file, and the video launches.

She watches the stranger move through her office and rifle through her desk. She can see that he has inserted something into the USB port. She makes a mental note to scrub her folders later. The scene changes, and the violator is now perusing her file cabinet, fingering her files, and pauses at one in particular. He removes it and examines it closely. He withdraws the folder, and then Talaitha watches him as he locates the false book switch that triggers a hidden drawer on her bookshelf. How did he know about that? He cannot use my prescription pads without my pharmacy license code, which is not listed on the pad; only my business address and email are included, Talaitha thinks. Sharp, jagged strands of fear begin to lace through her mind. There is only one person in this world that would know about my obsession for hidden compartments, and she's dead, or she has been to me since she disappeared from the senior dance eighteen years ago, Talaitha recalls.

It's August 12th, and the summer heat has not yet relinquished its hold on the town of Accident. Jevonte was relieved to have the greenhouse completed for Talaitha. It was one less thing he had to worry about. Besides, the completed greenhouse would allow for a peaceful segue into an outdoor space that would go a long way towards massaging Talaitha into a more agreeable mood. The layout is exact to her specifications, and Jevonte triple-checked them all. Why does she want such a big greenhouse, Jevonte wondered to himself. This place is big enough to get lost in. The greenhouse occupied 195 square feet of the backyard space, which seems small until you consider that the backyard itself was only 726 square feet. The greenhouse wouldn't leave much space for backyard activities.

No matter. Talaitha was going to have her greenhouse, and Jevonte couldn't wait to show her the finished project. Upon observing the remaining yard space, Jevonte felt a slight unease. The basement remodel hadn't gone exactly according to plan. It was finished and sealed, but Jevonte had to leave a portion of the basement floor uncovered. Over Jevonte's objections, Talaitha insisted on leaving a section of the basement floor bare in one darkened area. She said she needed it to cultivate some of her herbs that could not tolerate direct sunlight. Jevonte thought the move was strange because the greenhouse he had poured significant labor into building could accommodate shade and protection against sunlight overexposure. He didn't argue the point. He was just happy to be finished.

He heads back inside the house to find Talaitha signing for several medium-sized boxes that UPS has just delivered.

"Hey, hon, what have you got there?" Jevonte asks as he makes his way from the kitchen.

"Nothing really. I got in touch with a satellite dish company, and they will provide Internet and phone services here. This equipment is part of the initial package."

"Babe, your knowledge always amazes me. I'm married to a tech genius!"

"I can't afford to lose contact with my patients, and the system will allow me to monitor them and hold telehealth evaluations with my patients no matter where they are." Talaitha didn't tell Jevonte about the office break-in. "I need to have the company come out to finish preparing this equipment and to hang some of the boosters that will be needed around the exterior of the house. Are you certain that the roof is complete and ready?"

"Yes, but you know, I could hang those myself. No need to have the company…"

"Don't be stupid. This is their job, and they are being paid to do it. I left some bills on the kitchen table. Please pay the technicians after they finish the install." Talaitha heads toward the master bedroom, and over her shoulder, she says, "I have a conference to attend in D.C. I have to leave for the train station early," her voice echoes down the hall.

"Conference? Babe, what about the visit to my folks? We talked about it the other night, remember?" Jevonte says. His hope is dying quickly because he already knows what's coming. "How long will you be gone?"

There is no response. After a few minutes, Jevonte heads toward the bedroom. Talaitha almost knocks him over as she's leaving the room. "Hey, King, slow down. Are you trying to take me out before I leave?" asks Talaitha jokingly. "Listen, I should be back in three days. These conferences pop up from time to time, and I have no choice but to attend if I want to stay current in my practice."

"I suppose, but when are we going to take some time to see my folks? I haven't talked to them in a while now, and this whole incommunicado thing is making things hard."

Talaitha faces Jevonte and saunters up to him until her forehead is nearly buried in his chest. Jevonte is still in his sweaty gym shorts. His musk is in her face, and Talaitha inhales his fragrance deeply. She pushes him up against the wall slowly and reaches a hand into his shorts to grip him firmly. She presses her body into his and looks up into his helpless eyes. She is savoring the moment, holding his rapt attention, listening to his breathing become erratic and shallow. With his gaze locked on her, she says, "Can your mommy do this for you?" Jevonte groans. "Or, maybe," Talaitha whispers into Jevonte's neck, "you want her to?"

"Love, I..." Jevonte responds, his firmness complete in Talaitha's hand.

Talaitha releases him and heads toward the shower. "Make sure you receive the technicians when they arrive. I want the equipment prep completed before noon tomorrow."

Jevonte slides to the floor. His gym shorts are stretched and awkwardly bunched together, his brow is sweaty, and his pulse is struggling to return to normal. He sits in the hallway; his mind is blitzed and confused. He's horny as hell, but without an invitation, he doesn't dare join Talaitha in the shower. His thoughts carry him to the work he's completed and the greenhouse he never got to show Talaitha. Maybe he was the one who needed that space. Perhaps he was the one who needed to plant something of his own.

10

The Stillness Between Knocks

Talaitha rose early in the morning. She fixed a few snacks to take with her on the train. Jevonte was still asleep, and the house was as quiet as a crypt. She liked the quiet, the stillness of the early morning, when energy was just beginning to percolate and set the rhythm of the day. She sat down at her desktop and logged into her monitoring software. The screen showed several rooms, and Talaitha rotated through each of them. She then checked the exterior of the home, all sides, and especially the rear space. There was a small blind spot there that she would have to address when she returned. She was still thinking about the stranger who visited her office several weeks ago. Her inquiries hadn't turned up anything actionable, but she was not going to let her guard down, not now. She would have time to conduct a deeper, more thorough investigation once she returned.

"Hey, honey, why are you up so early?" interrupted Jevonte as he strolled and yawned his way into the kitchen.

"I'm just verifying a few details. "I want to make sure all is in order before I leave," replied Talaitha.

"Babe, your train doesn't leave for another four hours."

"While I'm gone, be sure to keep an eye on that neighbor's dog. Somehow, he keeps getting out of the fenced area and loves to shit all over my yard."

"What dog, sweetheart? I haven't seen any strays out here. Strange, I haven't seen much wildlife at all, and that's probably the weirdest part of all, seeing as we practically live in the woods," Jevonte chuckled. "I haven't seen any deer, not even a squirrel."

"Well, just watch for that mutt. I swear, if I come back and see another pile of dog shit, I'm going to end that mongrel's life," said Talaitha, a tinge of anger coating her words.

"As you wish, my love. So, you still haven't told me where you'll be staying for this conference. What's the name of the hotel you're going to be at?"

"Once I check in, I'll send you the details." Talaitha looks at Jevonte, walks up to him in the kitchen, and wraps her arms around him while he pours his coffee. "Are you going to miss me, poor baby?" Talaitha teases.

Jevonte places the coffee carafe down on the counter and shifts around to return Talaitha's embrace. "Now you already know I will. I'm missing you right now, and you haven't even left yet. I still don't know why I couldn't come with you. It would be fun, just the two of..."

"I've already told you, and I am not going to repeat myself about how sensitive and important my work is. Besides, you still have work to do on the guest bedroom, don't you?"

Talaitha releases Jevonte and turns to leave the kitchen, but Jevonte takes her by the wrist and pulls her back into his arms. Staring down into her emerald eyes with deep longing, Jevonte says, "I just can't bear to be without you, my love. I just want to be wherever you are. I love you, Tal." Jevonte moves to find her lips with his, but Talaitha turns her head and twists out of Jevonte's grasp with apparent ease.

"I want the guest bathroom completed as well before I get back," Talaitha says, starting for the door.

"Guest bathroom? How did that get on the project list, babe?"

"I swear, sometimes you can be so dense. How can I have your mom and dad over as guests if the guest bathroom isn't ready?" Talaitha responds, then walks out the front door.

Jevonte is speechless. Did he hear her correctly? Did she just tell him that his parents were coming over? Jevonte can hardly believe he heard her say this—or that she implied his folks were coming, but he didn't care! This news changes everything, he thought to himself. Jevonte finished his coffee and went to the garage to start planning the guest bathroom. He was ecstatic with joy, so much so that he only slightly felt the ache of Talaitha's departure.

Mr. Gerald Harper Jefferson was like most of the residents of Accident. His routines were unimaginative and straightforward. He enjoyed a cup of coffee every morning. He took pleasure in gathering his morning paper. He let the dog out to do his business. He walked the block once and noted the yard violations for the next community council hearing. On this morning in August, Gerald decided to pause at 52 Riverrun Drive. The home had new tenants, and it no longer appeared to be a candidate for demolition. There was a new roof, and the porch had been completely rebuilt. The landscaping was nearly impeccable. Gerald could not believe the amount of work the new homeowners had put into the home. This home was definitely worthy of Yard of the Month in the Accident Gazette.

Jevonte walked out of the garage to find Mr. Jefferson standing in front of his house—his dog, Skulky, bent over intently, straining to make a smelly, steaming deposit. "Uh, good morning, sir. Can you not have your dog do that in our yard, please?" Jevonte asked politely.

"Oh, I'm so sorry, young man. This old man cannot be stopped when he needs to go outside. He has weak bowels due to his old age, as you can see. Say, who did all of the work on the home? Are you the owner?"

"Yes, yes, we did all of the work ourselves," Jevonte lied. My name is Jevonte. My wife, Talaitha, and I just moved in a few weeks ago."

"I know, and I apologize for not coming over sooner. Skulky and I noticed when you guys started moving in, it was kind of hard to miss. You don't often see your kind around these parts, if you catch my meaning. No offense meant by that, and I hope you don't take any."

"None taken," Jevonte replies, a hint of disdain in his voice. "We were under no illusions when we first moved in."

"Accident is not so bad. I mean, things have improved since the time I was a child growing up here, and for the better, if I say so myself."

"So, you've lived here all of your life, then? I bet you know where all of the bodies are buried, then, uh?" Jevonte laughs gently.

"I know quite a bit, actually. For instance, I knew the previous occupant of this home before you moved in.

"Really? Who lived here before us?" Jevonte asked.

"Well, we weren't best friends or anything like that, but he was alright. He was a doctor. He worked with those psycho, whacko-kind of people, I think. If my memory serves me correctly, his name was Dr. Robinson. Yes, his full name was Dr. Samuel Robinson. My mind is still a steel trap to this day," Gerald laughed.

"I'm impressed, sir," Jevonte grinned. "Do you know why he moved? Was he married? Family? Children?"

"No, he was single and very reserved. He really didn't interact much with the community. He might have been the first Black resident of Accident. I don't really know, but what I remember was how he stayed to himself, and whenever I saw him, he always seemed to be having conversations with himself or with someone the rest of us couldn't see. Catch my meaning?"

"What did he do? Maybe he had to move because of his job."

"I think he was a psychiatrist or possibly another type of mental health professional. I believe he worked at the Sable Ridge State Hospital. There were times when he looked, and I don't know for sure, but he would look troubled a lot, like he was plagued by troubles—or something."

Jevonte's mind started searching for where he had heard that name before. Sable Ridge State Hospital, if his memory was accurate, had a dark past. He remembered watching a documentary about the state's history of abusing psychiatric patients. According to the film he saw, the hospital began its life not as a place of healing, but as a mechanism of control. Established in 1873 on the grounds of the former Ridgeview Plantation, the institution was initially chartered as the Maryland House for the Feebleminded and Morally Wayward—a euphemism designed to obscure its role in continuing the forced captivity and exploitation of Black people under the veil of state authority.

According to the documentary, following the Civil War, Ridgeview's enslaved population was "transitioned" into indentured laborers using Black Codes and vagrancy laws as cover. Many were funneled directly into Sable Ridge, where they were declared mentally unfit or delinquent by local justices and committed indefinitely. Within its iron-barred wards and crumbling stone corridors, generations of Black men, women, and children vanished—lost to experiments, exhaustion, and silence.

"I do believe I saw something about that hospital on TV. Is it still operating?" Jevonte asked, looking directly at Accident's resident historical expert.

"I believe it is," answered Gerald. "I've never actually been there myself. Dr. Robinson was the only person I had ever met who was from that place. Look, I need to continue my rounds. I have a few more homes to review, and you've put me behind schedule," Gerald remarked and walked off in a huff.

Jevonte grinned and laughed to himself until he began reflecting on the rest of the documentary about Sable Ridge State Hospital. Jevonte started walking back to his garage when he recalled the words of the documentary narrator:

"In the early 20th century, Sable Ridge became a key node in Maryland's eugenics movement. Funded by state grants and private philanthropists, the hospital partnered with medical schools to perform neurological surgeries, sterilizations, and behavioral modification experiments. All without consent. The victims were overwhelmingly poor and overwhelmingly Black."

The thought sent chills up Jevonte's spine. Just as he started back to his front door, a white, paneled utility van pulled up to the front of the house. On the side of the van, a bright red-and-blue star logo read "Tech Shop Express Services" in embossed, heavy lettering. The logo also features a chubby, bearded, cartoonish figure popping through the center of the star with a toolbox in one hand and wires and cables in the other. The driver exited the van and opened the sliding side panel to reveal a mini-workbench and shelves stuffed with every imaginable bolt, nut, and crimp, and rolls and rolls of electrical tape. On the van's floor lay a row of boxes of different sizes, each labeled with Talaitha's name and address. Jevonte waited at the front door and waved at the driver. The driver nodded, grabbed two of the boxes, and started towards the house.

"Hey, can I give you a hand with any of those?" asked Jevonte.

"No, sir. I have to handle these myself. Is it all right with you if the door can remain open? It will make it easier for me to bring these inside."

"Oh, yes, of course. I'll just get out of your way. Please let me know if you need anything. I'll be in the back of the house."

The technician thanked Jevonte and then began bringing the remaining boxes inside the house. He returned to his van and climbed inside. He shut the side door and pulled out his cell phone to make a call. After a brief conversation, he confirmed that the materials had been delivered as instructed and hung up. He grabbed his toolbox and then proceeded with the installation.

The job was finished in just over two hours. Jevonte didn't go back into the house until the installation was completed. When he entered the kitchen, he noticed the technician seated at Talaitha's desktop computer. He quietly observed the man work, typing on the keyboard and moving the mouse across the screen intermittently.

"Hey, excuse me," Jevonte started, moving through the kitchen towards the technician. "What are you doing? I don't think you need to be on my wife's system, do you?"

The technician was startled and quickly clicked off the monitoring software he had been using. "Yes, sir. I have to add a patch to your wife's system to fully integrate it. Now that I've patched the system, you guys will have access to all our satellite services. I won't have the actual dish up and running until the new unit arrives, but that will be a separate install and will be easy. I have all the interface adapters in place and wired now. You guys will love this new system," the technician said as he logged out of Talaitha's desktop.

"Technology is really something else," responds Jevonte. It's not until after the technician drives off that Jevonte realizes the question of how he managed to log into Talaitha's system. I don't even know the login password, Jevonte thinks to himself. He makes a mental note to discuss this with Talaitha when she returns, which reminds him that he hasn't heard from her all day.

The evening descends, and Jevonte has wrapped up his work in both the guest bathroom and some minor patchwork in the basement. He walks out to the front porch and takes a seat in one of the oversized deck chairs. He dials Talaitha's number, but gets no answer. There is very little signal, and Jevonte's frustration grows. So he decides he's had enough of the isolation and grabs some gym clothes. There is a 24 Hour Fitness location thirty miles outside of Accident. Despite the inconvenience, he will at least have access to cell phone service in that civilized area.

After adjusting his seat's position a few times, Jevonte pushes the ignition button, but nothing happens. His Jeep Grand Cherokee is as dead as a doorknob. There are no lights or any other signs of life. "What the hell is wrong now? I just had this thing serviced last month," Jevonte says out loud. He hops out of the jeep and lifts the hood. Although Jevonte is a gifted carpenter, he is not very skilled as a mechanic; however, he hopes that the problem with the jeep is obvious and something he can easily fix. No luck. His untrained eye spots nothing amiss, so he shuts the hood and stands in front of the vehicle with his hands on his hips. After contemplating what to do for several minutes, Jevonte turns to go back inside the house, disappointed and feeling helpless.

Inside the home, Jevonte sits at Talaitha's desk and attempts to log in. He tries all the obvious passwords, then realizes that one of the most common—her birthday—is a mystery to him. He has no idea what Talaitha's birthday is. Why don't I know that? Jevonte muses to himself. "We've been dating each other for well over a year, almost, and I have no idea when my wife was born," Jevonte mutters to himself. He gives up and decides to head back to the library. He could use a walk and some fresh air. He'll send Talaitha an email while he's there. He's missing her terribly. Jevonte makes it to the Accident Public Library with 45 minutes to spare before closing time. He logs into his chatbot account and sends Talaitha a text:

> Hey, love, how are you doing? I haven't heard
> from you, but that might just be due to the poor

cell service we have here. Have you tried texting or calling me?

There is no response.

Babe, I am starting to worry about you. Please tell me that you are alright.

What hotel are you in now?

The Jeep won't start.

The technician arrived as you planned and installed everything. I wish he had installed the full system. I'm still stranded, lol.

I have to go, but when you get these texts, please let me know something. I miss you so much, and it's a ghost town here. Oh, by the way, I met Mr. Jefferson; Gerald is his first name, I believe.

Ok, well, I just want you to know that I love you, and I miss you so much. Please respond soon.

Jevonte waits a few minutes to see if Talaitha responds. She doesn't, so Jevonte starts surfing the web. He stumbled upon a story about a New York hospital nurse who faced a conviction for euthanizing patients. Before Jevonte can learn more about the story, memories of the documentary he discussed with Mr. Jefferson flash through his mind. He enters Sable Ridge State Hospital and a few other search terms. What he finds stirs his curiosity. One passage in one of the articles he was reading caught his attention:

…The hospital's Lower Wing, long since sealed, was rumored to house a subterranean chamber known to staff as "The Deep." It was there, according to decades of hushed reports, that unregistered patients—often children from state-run orphanages—were subjected to clinical procedures not found in any medical textbook. Some survivors who later emerged described rooms without windows, voices that weren't their own, and a feeling of being "unborn and remade. By the 1960s, a series of disappearances and patient deaths drew national attention. A federal investigation ensued but was swiftly closed after several records mysteriously vanished in an overnight fire. No one was charged. Sable Ridge was renamed, restructured, and presented as a modern neurobehavioral facility.

Jevonte had just enough time to print the articles so he could finish reading them at home. He didn't have enough time to look up Dr. Samuel Robinson; that would be a project for another day.

After five days, Talaitha returned home. At first, Jevonte doesn't hear her arrive; he's been working in the garage over the last couple of days, trying to work on some furniture he's planned for the back porch and greenhouse. Talaitha drops her bags in the bedroom and immediately heads to the bathroom for a shower. Jevonte stops what he's doing to listen. When he hears the water running from the bathroom window, he hurriedly rushes into the house and towards the master bedroom. There he finds Talaitha's bags, and the bathroom door is shut.

"Honey, when did you get back? I was out back and didn't hear you come in." Jevonte tries the bathroom doorknob. It's locked. Confused, Jevonte knocks on the door gently. There is no reply from within. "Babe, can you hear me? Why is the door locked?" Jevonte asks, his voice sounding shrill and desperate. His only response is the sound of water splashing in the shower stall. Jevonte stands in silence at the bathroom door, his forehead pressed against it.

Finally, the shower stops, and after several minutes, the door opens, and Talaitha emerges wrapped in a towel. She walks past Jevonte as if he is invisible, then sits at her vanity and starts drying her hair. She says nothing and doesn't even acknowledge his presence.

"Um, my love, did you get my texts?"

"Yes."

"So, why didn't you respond?"

"I was working, Jevonte. I didn't have time to pacify you," Talaitha snaps.

"I asked you to let me know where you were going to be staying, and I wanted to know that you had arrived safe and sound; that's not pacification, love."

Talaitha stops patting her hair dry and turns to face Jevonte, looking at him dead in the eye. "I thought I married a full-grown man and not a child I needed to pamper and cuddle every damn minute." She turned back to face her mirror and resumed drying her hair.

Jevonte's heart stings with the venom of Talaitha's words. Before a tear can begin to well up in his eyes, he turns and walks out of the bedroom.

Evening comes quickly, and the dinner table is quiet. Not a word is exchanged between Jevonte and Talaitha. After they both finish eating, Jevonte remains seated at the table, and Talaitha clears the dishes. He watches her as she rinses the plates and loads the dishwasher. After starting it, she walks over to her desk and fires up the system. She still hasn't said anything to Jevonte, and the silence is eerily familiar.

What is happening? Why is she not speaking to me? Jevonte asks himself. He decides to try one more time.

"Babe, I don't understand why you're ignoring me and giving me the silent treatment, but I want to know what is going on and why you're acting this way. I mean, you haven't said two words to me since you've been back. Did something happen? Did I do something wrong? What's going on?"

Talaitha straightens at her desk; her computer is loading a new program as a result of the patch the technician installed. After the program downloads and the installation is complete, she shuts the computer down, stands, slides her chair back under the desk neatly, and then briefly organizes her desktop. She turns and walks back to where Jevonte is still sitting, his eyes pleading for some answers.

"Everything is fine, King. There is nothing to talk about, and I'm exhausted. Take me to bed, please," she replies in a soft, silky voice. Talaitha heads down the hallway to the master bedroom, her silk robe falling around her feet.

The pair lie in bed, still and silent, until Talaitha reaches under the sheet to find Jevonte's penis, but Jevonte removes her hand and turns on his side to face her. "What's going on, Talaitha? Talk to me."

"I already told you, nothing is going on. I just had a long day, and the conference was intense. I just want you inside of me tonight. I don't want any more words from you. Now, move your hand," Talaitha commands, her voice now a little more impatient.

"I don't feel like having sex, Talaitha, not right now. I don't like how you're treating me; it's hurtful. I've been missing you so much these last five days, and when you come home, you don't greet me or speak to me. In fact, you head straight to the shower like you can't wait to scrub the dirt off. What kind of conference was this?" Jevonte asks, his breath short and shallow.

"Forget it. I'm too worn out anyway," Talaitha responds and then turns over, her back now facing Jevonte.

Jevonte exhales and says, "My goodness, babe, I just wanted to know how things went for you. I just wanted you to know how much I missed you. We're married now, and we should share these things, or so I thought that was what we were supposed to do." Talaitha remains silent, and soon Jevonte turns his back to her as well. The pair remains motionless for the rest of the night. Talaitha is fast asleep within the next ten minutes, but Jevonte is troubled, and his thoughts are cascading furiously over every imaginable thing that could have happened with Talaitha. For the rest of the night, Jevonte never really falls asleep.

Jevonte wakes up in the morning to discover Talaitha has already gotten out of bed. The lovely smell of bacon greets his senses, and he heads to the bathroom to pee. After washing up a bit, Jevonte walks into the kitchen and finds Talaitha has prepared breakfast.

"Good morning, King. I wish you had stayed in bed. I was bringing breakfast to you. I wanted to surprise you." Talaitha sets the plate of eggs, bacon, and wheat toast in front of Jevonte. She brings him a small bowl of fruit and pours him some coffee.

"My heart, this is too much. You really didn't have to do it, but I'm glad you did. This food smells and looks fantastic," Jevonte says with exuberance.

"I did have to do this, King. I realize that I acted badly last night. The conference work stressed me out, but I shouldn't have treated you that way. I just want to make up for that, so eat up and enjoy."

"I love you, Tal. I really do. Thank you for this." Jevonte lowers his head to say a silent prayer and blessing, and then pauses while staring down at his plate. "Babe, what are these dark specks in the eggs?"

Talaitha looks at his plate and smiles, "Those are just a few special herbs and spices I have been cultivating. They will give those eggs a real boost. Taste them and tell me what you think."

Jevonte forks a mouthful of eggs into his mouth. A huge, expressive smile breaks out across his face. "Oh my

God. Oh my God, babe. This dish is incredible. I love eggs, but I don't think I've ever tasted any as delicious as these." Jevonte resumes eating and, after a few more mouthfuls, says, "My momma didn't cook eggs this good." With that comment, Talaitha grins and lowers her head shyly.

After the meal, Talaitha logs on to her computer to check some patient files. Jevonte clears the breakfast dishes and loads the dishwasher. He sets it to run on a 4-hour delay, then heads to the garage. Before he shows Talaitha the progress he's made on the backyard space, he wants to clear some of the spare plywood and two-by-fours he left in the yard.

Mid-stride, Jevonte feels his chest burning intensely. His legs immediately lock up, and he falls to the floor clutching his chest. His breathing becomes very shallow, and he can hardly speak. His windpipe is constricting, and only wheezing sounds escape his lips. His vision is hazy, and his head begins to throb intensely. His body starts to convulse and thrash on the kitchen floor, and the sound of his head banging against the dishwasher's door startles Talaitha into action. She launches from her desk chair and rushes over to Jevonte's trembling body.

"King, King, what's wrong? What happened?" Talaitha cries out. Jevonte's eyes begin to roll up in his head.

His convulsions subside, but he starts to foam slightly at the corners of his mouth. His tongue is slack, and his body is burning up. Talaitha grabs her keys and her purse and heads out the front door. She's calm and focused. She quickly starts her car and rushes back inside to Jevonte.

Remarkably and with enormous effort, Talaitha hoists Jevonte up into a fireman's carry and carries his feverish body to the back seat of her car. He is unresponsive and unconscious. The nearest hospital is thirty minutes away—Talaitha makes the trip in twenty. Talaitha pulls into the emergency entrance of Sable Ridge State Hospital and honks her car's horn until emergency personnel rush to her car to render assistance.

Inside the emergency room entrance, Talaitha begins filling out intake forms for Jevonte. Hospital staff wheeled Jevonte's comatose body into one of the bay's examining rooms to await the attending's arrival. Talaitha sat alone, pen in hand, her thoughts frazzled and disorganized, a feeling unfamiliar to her. The situation was a new development and one she had not thought possible. She had never seen Jevonte looking so weakened and vulnerable before. He had to recover. He just has to. There is so much more we have to do, so much more that remains unfinished, thought Talaitha.

Talaitha walks up to the nursing station to give the intake staff the forms she completed and her insurance card. The driveway still needs to be done. He's got to get better soon; Talaitha's thoughts are so loud in her head that her face must have broadcast them out loud. The intake nurse looks up at her and asks, "Ma'am, did you say something?"

Talaitha replies, "No," and returns to the waiting area.

11

The Wound and the Remedy

The corridors of Sable Ridge State Hospital are filled with medical staff moving from nursing stations to patient examining rooms, doctors issuing orders, and specialists conferencing in huddled corners. Jevonte's room is the center of attention. Test results are not looking good, and his condition is not improving. The attendee is at a loss to explain why he is still in a coma. His vitals were growing weaker by the hour, and the doctor said to Talaitha that if they could not reverse Jevonte's decline, in all likelihood, he was not going to survive.

Talaitha accepts the news with little concern until one of the nurses attending to Jevonte mentions a special blood panel the doctor was getting ready to order. "This panel," explains nurse Bridgette, "will screen specifically for organic toxins."

"Toxins?" Talaitha responds.

"Yes. Your husband is not responding to our protocols for nutritional deficiencies or genetic conditions that could explain his illness. So, the doctor wants to take a closer look at organ function and test kidney, liver, thyroid, and heart function. Some toxins can cause severe impairment of vital organs. We just need to rule them out."

"Of course, that all makes sense, and I want you to do everything possible to save my husband. He's all I have in this world." Talaitha looks away, feigning despair. Looking out of the hospital room's window, Talaitha begins to think back to the last time she experienced something like this. She meant to harm Noelle back in high school. She didn't mean to cause this much damage with Jevonte. In her mind, Talaitha retraces everything over and over again. The amount of Clitocybe mushrooms she used should not have put him in a coma.

Talaitha is puzzled and in deep thought when the attendant enters the room and asks, "Mrs. Greene, does your husband suffer from allergies? Is he allergic to anything that you are aware of?"

"I'm not sure. I don't think so," replies Talaitha, but in her mind the pieces start to come together. She has never seen Jevonte eat mushrooms with any of his meals. Perhaps he is allergic to them, and that may be the cause of his reaction to the muscarine. Before the doctor could ask another question, Talaitha blurts, "Atropine! Can you administer that now? Now that I think about it, his mom mentioned something about needing to give him some after a picnic they were at a few years back. She just didn't say what his allergic reaction was to."

"Well, we don't normally do that unless we have test results that indicate a need for the atropine. I'd like to know more about what he ingested and what may be causing the decline in organ function."

"Please just give him the shot. You can run more blood tests later. Besides, the atropine won't hurt him," says Talaitha firmly.

"Mrs. Greene, we run the risk of creating adverse conditions that could further harm your husband. We don't know what his sensitivity is to atropine. We only have a partial medical history for your husband, and..."

"Either you give him the shot now, or I'm taking him out of here. I'll sign whatever waiver you need, but I want my husband to get some help. I know the history of this hospital, and I know how badly you all treated Black people in the past. I hope your recalcitrance is not indicative of a re-emerging culture of harm," Talaitha says with cold eyes.

"I am aware of this hospital's history, and I assure you, nothing of the sort is taking place in your husband's case. I just want to be careful not to harm him further, but with your consent, I will..."

"I did already. Now, please, give him the atropine."

Within the hour, Jevonte's vital signs stabilize and show improvement. The doctor orders a transfusion to counter the loss of blood components and bolster liver functioning. Talaitha remains by his side for the entire process. By the end of the day, Jevonte regains consciousness.

"Mrs. Greene, I believe your husband will be ready to go home in the morning. He's recovering nicely," remarks one of the CNAs.

"I want him released as soon as possible. I want to take him home today."

"Oh, I understand. I'm sure the doctor will sign off on his discharge really soon," the CNA responds.

"I'm only going to say this once. Bring me his discharge papers now. This is not the doctor's decision; do you understand me?" Talaitha stares daggers at the smallish CNA. "Did I just stutter? Are you stupid?"

"I, I," the little CNA begins to stutter. "Yes, ma'am. I'll be right back," and runs out of the treatment room.

"Babe, is that you? What? What's going on? Who are you fussing at?" asks Jevonte in a still weak, small, trembling voice.

"King, oh, my beloved king! Don't worry. I'm getting you out of here, and we're going home, where I can take proper care of you. The staff here should all be fired for incompetence and malpractice."

"Tal, what did the doctor say was wrong with me? Has he been by to see me?"

"King, he doesn't know. I told you, they are all incompetent. It's no wonder they could only get jobs here at this hospital. It's shameful. I will explain it all to you when we get home. I just don't want you to worry about anything for now, do you hear me? Your health is all that matters to me.

Talaitha rubs his temples and begins to stroke his chest and abdomen softly. She reaches for his hand to hold it firmly and warmly, and then looks into his eyes with joyful tears. "I'm just so grateful that you're alive and recovering. I just want to take care of you and make sure you heal. Nobody can do this for you but me. I was so scared I was going to lose you, King."

Jevonte, buoyed by what he hears, smiles broadly, and a soft tear puddles in his eyes. "I've never felt so sick. I can't believe this happened to me, as I never get sick. I can't wait to see those test results."

"Don't worry about that. What's important is that you rest and recover. I've got you, and as soon as that silly nurse thingy gets back with the discharge paperwork, we are out of here."

"As you command, my love. I'm in your hands, babe." Jevonte closes his eyes and relaxes under the weight of the hospital sheets and blanket. He's still very weak and can barely move, but he is not worried. His wife is watching over him, and he feels secure. Seeing how careful she was to get him settled in, seeing her address the hospital staff in charge of his care, and seeing how she touched him and stroked his head, it all made him feel like he was whole. Whatever illness had hit him, he felt confident that Talaitha would help him recover from it completely.

The certified nursing assistant returned with the discharge nurse. "Well, it's about fucking time," uttered Talaitha, scorn and contempt etching lines in her face.

Talaitha supervises the medical staff while they secure Jevonte in her car. She stows the bag of prescription medications Jevonte will have to take for the next couple of weeks. On the drive home, Talaitha holds Jevonte's hand and starts the CD player. The gentle melodies of Earth, Wind & Fire cascade through the car. Phillip Bailey's falsetto voice plays softly as he sings his signature hit, Reasons. Talaitha's intentional act deeply moves Jevonte. He squeezes her hand back, and their fingers interlock.

As Talaitha heads towards the interstate, she suddenly veers onto a small, seemingly deserted road. A couple of abandoned mobile homes line the single-lane road. She continues down the path, rounds a curve, and comes to an area shrouded by a few trees with low, overhanging branches. The bend in the road circles a small pond. There is a small shack and a dilapidated boat dock that's barely standing out of the water. Along the edges of the pond, a few ducks are paddling toward the deeper parts. The approaching car has disturbed their family time.

"My heart, what are we doing here?" asks Jevonte, gently roused from his nap by the car's bouncing along the country road. Talaitha says nothing. She rolls both their windows down and sits in silence for the space of a few breaths. The duck family's perturbed quacking resonates from the middle of the pond.

"King, you don't know how much you scared me. Watching you fall and seeing you convulse like that on our kitchen floor… it was more than my heart could bear. Seeing you hurt, seeing you helpless like that—it almost killed me," Talaitha said. Jevonte turns his head to look directly at

Talaitha. She was more earnest, more sincere, and warmer than he could ever remember her being since they first met.

"Babe," Jevonte says as he takes both of Talaitha's hands in his. "I don't know what happened to me, but this I do know. I will always fight to come back to you, no matter what. I will never leave you, even if death stands in my way; I know that sounds corny, but I feel very strongly about this. I love you beyond life and death. In you, I know that I have found what I have been searching for my whole life."

Talaitha holds Jevonte's gaze and then exits the car. She appears as a vision of beauty, illuminated by the setting sun, moving gracefully, and her hips ignite Jevonte's passion. As she moves around the front of the car, Dru Hill sings confidently through the car's sound system, filling the surrounding area and drowning out the discontent of the watching duck family.

"I don't know how much longer
You're going to be here,
So I say my prayers
Every night

One for my mother
One for my father

And one for the love of my life

So if you decide to leave today
Then leave tomorrow at the door
And take only
Half of yesterday
And forget all hope for the present
Cause it just went away."

Talaitha is now standing at Jevonte's open door. Somehow, he lost track of her while she was moving towards him. He was enraptured. When did she undress? Jevonte thought. Talaitha's cocoa-brown skin glistened in the setting sun's light. She was completely naked and unafraid, standing there like a demi-goddess in the open air. The slight breeze of the fast-approaching evening carried her heat and made her intent clear. Jevonte silently prayed. No help was forthcoming.

Talaitha deftly lowered the passenger seat to a fully reclined position and slid it as far back as it would go. Jevonte stared in awe, speechless, and happily powerless to object. He started to untie his shoes, but Talaitha stopped him. She removed his shoes and socks, then unbuckled Jevonte's pants and pulled them and his underwear off in one swift movement. She climbed into the passenger side of the car and knelt between Jevonte's legs. Jevonte could hardly breathe. He didn't want to. He stared down at her as she sat motionless, scanning the length of his body hungrily, eager to consume him. He started to open his mouth, to speak, to say something, but she gave him a silent command to cease, and he did. Talaitha remained as still as a statue and narrowed her eyes to focus on Jevonte's swelling appendage. No words were exchanged, but the language spoken was very poignant.

Talaitha doesn't touch Jevonte. She just hovers above him, tracing the bend of his penis with her lips, never brushing too close to his skin. Jevonte can feel her breath against him. He is soon hard as a rock, and he feels his skin tighten. His testicles are pulled tight against his body. He ached so much. He doesn't know how much more of this torment he can endure before he explodes. In his mind, he is pleading, begging Talaitha for release, but he knows better than to speak.

Talaitha runs her fingers along Jevonte's hips. Her hands begin to massage his stomach, and she kisses his pelvis, allowing his hardened, engorged member to brush against her cheek. She alternates kissing each side of his stomach, allowing the valley of her warm, full breasts to enfold his manhood lightly. She pauses above his penis and starts moaning and whispering as though she were conversing with someone apart from Jevonte. He was so lost in the moment that he almost didn't hear her say, "I promise."

The blood is pounding so loudly in his ears that he fears his head might split open. Talaitha grows silent and places one delicate kiss on the left side of Jevonte's straining penis. His organ was now visibly throbbing, and the urge to paint the roof of the car in opaque white was imminent. Sensing the moment, Talaitha closes Jevonte's legs and straddles him, pinning him firmly. She begins to slide up slowly against his body, making sure her mound of soft, carefully trimmed pubic hair grazes his midsection. Neither is breathing; both are suspended in thick anticipation. Talaitha hovers; the heat between her and Jevonte is subsumed by the pungent fragrance beckoning with ever-increasing intensity from Talaitha's descending love flower.

In an instant, Talaitha engulfs all that Jevonte is, has been, and will ever be. There is no daylight between them; no quarter given, just a desperate need to erase time. Again, she thrusts and rocks firmly against Jevonte, who is struggling to meet her in heaven. His arms are pinned along his side, and he's still too weak to lift her, so he desperately holds her buttocks in his hands. Jevonte feels faint and lightheaded, as if all the blood is now pumping beneath his waist. The car is now rocking, the suspension warning the nearby duck family that the earth is about to move.

Talaitha moves with deliberate speed and urgency, drawing Jevonte's forehead to meet hers. Her breathing is halted, her muscles all along her pelvic floor signaling the beginning of major orgasmic convulsions. Jevonte cannot hold it in any longer and opens his mouth to beg release, but Talaitha grabs both sides of his face and moans into his mouth, "Not yet." She continues to rock against him until her body explodes in waves. Jevonte begins crying her name, but Talaitha is in his mouth, sucking on his tongue, refusing to give him back the power of speech. She holds him in her mouth, probing all of his tongue with hers and moving her lips to seal his mouth. They exchange breath for a moment, and then Jevonte explodes inside Talaitha. She does not release him. She can feel him throbbing violently inside of her and presses her hips harder against him. The duck family has grown silent, and all time seems to have stopped around the little pond community.

For three minutes, the lovers remain still and connected, their bodies glistening with sweat. Talaitha slowly rises, allowing Jevonte's depleted organ to pull out from her engorged haven. They can both feel the heat escaping from Talaitha's body when Jevonte completely withdraws from her. She sits across Jevonte's knees, allowing the flow of their love to find a small puddle on the car's floor. She then turns and leans back to lie in Jevonte's arms, snuggling up under his armpit. Jevonte wraps his arms around Talaitha, and the two fall asleep under the stars and the watchful eyes of the duck family.

Jevonte rolls over in the large queen-sized bed, reaching across the sheets for Talaitha, but he finds her missing, and her spot feels cool to his touch. He starts to get out of bed, but his legs feel unsteady and wobbly. He notices a slight tremor in his hand and fingers. He lies back down and begins rubbing the sleep from his eyes. His mouth is parched, and his throat is parched. "Did someone get the license plate on that truck that just ran over my head?" Jevonte says to himself. "Tal, where are you, babe?"

Hearing no response, Jevonte struggles to get out of bed. Slowly, he plants both feet on the floor and bends slightly at the waist. He has to wait for a moment until his head stops spinning. Then it hits him; the aroma of bacon and fresh-brewed coffee wafts carefree across his senses, and he is instantly awake with hunger. With considerable effort, he stands while holding onto the footboard of the large queen bed. He manages to stand upright, if unsteadily. First, one step, then three, and Jevonte starts trudging towards the kitchen.

Talaitha is sitting at the counter, reviewing documents and organizing papers in a file folder. She barely acknowledges Jevonte as he enters the kitchen. There is a pot of warm grits on the stove, a pan of bacon strips, and a saucer full of fruit. Jevonte shuffles up beside Talaitha and bends to kiss the side of her temple, but she rises abruptly and walks over to the computer at her desk. Jevonte doesn't take offense. He knows she's not a morning person.

"How'd you sleep last night, love?" Jevonte asks, making his way over to the stove. He reaches up into the cupboard for a plate and his coffee mug, since nothing had been set out for him.

Without returning a glance, Talaitha replies, "Fine. Look, I have a lot of work to complete today. I am woefully behind with my cases because I've been here taking care of you. It looks like I'll need to go into my office in Baltimore to get most of this done, and I have to reschedule some of my patients." Talaitha grabs her briefcase and says, "Lord only knows what state some of them are in because of you."

Jevonte doesn't quite hear that last part and asks, "What was that, babe?" Talaitha ignores his question. "By the way, did the doctor call with any of the results on those tests they ran? I still feel like crap, and my legs feel uncoordinated. I feel like an old man walking around here," Jevonte chuckles.

Talaitha doesn't respond at first. She is looking at her computer screen and moving the mouse, then she answers, "Yeah, they called, and there was nothing in the blood panels they ran. They screened for Lyme disease, too, but that came back negative. They recommended that you get plenty of rest and hydrate." Talaitha rises from her computer desk and walks over to stand by the kitchen counter. "I'm going to be home late tonight. There is plenty of food, and I want you to make sure you finish with those closets. They still need to be adjusted, and the extra shelving needs to be installed."

"Whoa, babe. I don't think I could lift a hammer right now if I tried. I still feel a bit dizzy, and like I'm going to fall. I know I need to get some rest, and I…"

"My God, Jevonte. Stop being such a whiner. You've been lying around for a full day. There is nothing wrong with you. In fact, check the fridge. I made a few natural juices for you. Make sure you drink all of them today. They will help restore your body's electrolytes and give you some more energy."

"Tal, are they those nasty green drinks I see you with? I am not about to drink that stuff," replies Jevonte jokingly. "All I need is a little more of you, babe. I'll be right as rain then." Talaitha looks Jevonte in his eyes, and her face is an arctic blizzard of indifference. "Don't be a weak man, King. Just make sure to get those closets done. You want your parents to visit, don't you?" Jevonte's smile vanishes, and he tries to stand up straight, the counter next to the stove bracing him.

"Oh yeah, I almost forgot about that. You're right. I will get it done—somehow. Listen, I..." And before he can ask about the computer login, Talaitha is walking out of the front door. "Ok then, goodbye to you too."

Jevonte grabs some coffee and bacon. He retrieves one of the juices Talaitha made for him and takes a seat at the table. He finishes the bacon and coffee in short order. The juice takes a minute to get down. The taste isn't unpleasant, but it's thick and a little chalky. Nonetheless, Jevonte finishes it, and as his wife said, he can feel his energy pick up in the late morning.

Jevonte dresses and prepares to tackle some of the small projects that were delayed due to his illness. He mentally commits to calling the doctor's office as soon as he locates the number. Looking down at his legs and feet, he notices that his skin still looks discolored, and he can see some of his veins in his lower legs. They don't look normal to him. Walking to the mailbox, Jevonte sees Mr. Gerald walking past his house and waves. Mr. Gerald stops and greets Jevonte.

"Long time no see, sir. How have you been?" asks Jevonte.

"Are you ok? You look like death warmed over, son."

Jevonte grins. "Well, that's always nice to know," laughs Jevonte. "I was hit with some kind of bug. I was down hard for a few days. It was pretty awful."

Mr. Gerald takes a couple of steps back. "Sorry to hear that. Is it contagious?"

"Oh no, it's not contagious like that." I think it was something I ate or was exposed to in this old house. Some of these old homes have severe mold infestations, and you never know. I didn't find any mold in the house, but I may have missed it during the basement demolition. Right now, I just want to get my strength back and get back to work finishing these renovations."

"Well, I hope you feel better. You know, you should see that doctor I was telling you about, that Dr. Robinson guy. He could probably fill you in on the house's history better than anyone; I mean, he did live there for a while."

"That's not a bad idea, but I have no contact information on him. He may not even work around here anymore."

"Let me ask around. I think I know how to contact him. I'll get a message to him that the new occupants of his old house have some questions about the house; how's that sound?"

"Thank you, Mr. Gerald; that would be wonderful."

"Well, you get better soon. I'll let you know as soon as I get in contact with Dr. Robinson." Mr. Gerald resumes his mid-morning stroll while Jevonte gathers the piled-up mail.

Talaitha observes the interaction between the two men as she sits at her desk. She only has video from the mailbox location and notes that the system should be upgraded to include audio in more of the external spaces surrounding the home.

"Dr. Mercedes. Dr. Mercedes! Are you listening to me?" asks Wilber, his big eyeglasses magnifying his stare of concern and angst towards Talaitha.

Talaitha refocuses her attention on her patient, but in the back of her mind, she's not happy about the contact Jevonte has had with the neighbor. Something will have to be done about that, she thinks to herself.

The week finally concludes, and even though Jevonte continues to struggle with his health, he has completed the basement retro work and updated the closets per Talaitha's demands. Although his appetite has not returned to its pre-coma level, he eats the meals that Talaitha prepares for him. He has managed to cope with the chalky juices, too. They still don't taste good, but he is getting an energy boost from them, though he noticed a few traces of blood in his bowel movements. Concerned about his health, Jevonte asks Talaitha for the doctor's office contact information, but she informs him that she has already scheduled a follow-up appointment for him. She is just waiting for a return call to confirm the day and time.

The next few days are a haze for Jevonte. His energy is good, but he's feeling weak, and the veins in his legs still look weird. He has started noticing that his feet feel numb in the morning. Talaitha is going into the office in Baltimore more and more now. She had him set up an ample office space in the home so she wouldn't have to travel as much, but it seems she is traveling more than ever, and he still doesn't have log-in credentials for the home computer. His Jeep still isn't running, and he just hasn't felt like dealing with it, but Jevonte knows he will have to soon; otherwise, he'll be stuck in the house forever. In his present condition, Jevonte doubts he can walk to the library, where he can reach out to his family. His only contact at this point is Mr. Gerald, and that thought makes him even more depressed.

Weeks go by, and the routine is the same. Talaitha is less and less accessible to Jevonte. Some days it feels like he doesn't see her until she slips into bed. He feels like a stranger to her. The two exchange very few words before Talaitha heads off to her office in Baltimore. Jevonte has lost weight, and his clothes are hanging off him. While shaving his head one morning, he notices how old and ragged his face looks. Staring at him in the mirror is the visage of a man ten years older than Jevonte's actual age. Bags under his eyes greet him as he shaves. Some of the nails on his fingers are starting to look blackened and discolored. They remind him of the accidents he had with his finishing hammer while learning carpentry. Occasionally, he'd miss and hit a finger, causing bruising underneath the fingernail. "I really do look like death warmed over," Jevonte remarked to the ghostly figure in the bathroom mirror.

Then one morning, to Jevonte's delightful surprise, Talaitha decides to work from home. Although she is physically home, he feels that she is emotionally distant. She remains cold and unreadable to Jevonte, so he tries another tactic to reach her.

"Honey, I'm going to cook for you this evening, ok? I just want you to relax and let me do all of the work. How's that sound?"

"Do whatever you want. I have work to get to and don't want to be disturbed, so please don't."

"No problem, babe. I need your car, though, because I need to pick up some groceries to prepare the meal."

Talaitha does not respond; instead, she grabs her coffee and heads to her in-home office. She stops at the door and faces Jevonte. "If you can't fix dinner with what we have in the house, don't. I'll take care of it like I do everything around here." Her office door closes behind her with a finality that shames and wounds Jevonte.

I don't understand her. What have I done except break my back getting this house put together just for her? Who is this woman? Because I feel like I don't even know her anymore, he thinks.

Jevonte sinks into the sofa and stares at the ceiling. The silence in the living room is deafening. He can't even hear the signs of life just outside of the home, which is normally abuzz with birds and squirrels rampaging throughout the yard and trees. Jevonte begins thinking about his family, wishing he had a way to contact them, to hear his mom's voice. His dad's big laughter used to get on his nerves, but now, Jevonte would give anything to hear it. They have to be worried about him. Jevonte folds his hands together in his lap, and one of his fingernails falls off. Jevonte stares at his index finger in despair. The tips of his fingers are numb now.

There is a knock at the front door, and Jevonte is startled upright on the couch. Talaitha comes rushing out of her office and looks at Jevonte, who shakes his head and shrugs his shoulders weakly. Talaitha walks to the front door and opens it. An older Black man is standing at the door. He's wearing a dingy-looking tan sports coat and khaki pants. His salt-and-pepper mustache and old, tired face greet Talaitha with a look of recognition. "Hello, pardon this interruption." He pauses, not sure if he should pretend he doesn't know who Talaitha is. "My name is Dr. Robinson. Is there a Jevonte Greene here?"

Talaitha is taken aback by Dr. Robinson's piercing eyes and responds to his question with a look of surprise and then dismay. "Um, yes. Jevonte is my husband." She follows Dr. Robinson's lead. "What, may I ask, is your business with him?" She eyes Dr. Robinson, silently questioning why he is breaching her privacy like this. Jevonte has shuffled over to the front door and peers over Talaitha's shoulder.

"Are you Dr. Robinson?" asks Jevonte.

"Hi. Yes, that's me. I got a message from a former neighbor saying you had some questions about this house, and I was in the area, so I thought I'd drop by to answer them. I apologize for arriving unannounced, but I didn't have your email address or phone number to contact you beforehand." Dr. Robinson appears awkward, as though he wasn't expecting to see Talaitha at the address.

Talaitha now understands what Jevonte and Gerald must have been discussing, having observed them on her monitoring service that one morning, though her thoughts still swirl with questions. "We're fine, Dr. Robinson. My husband has fixed everything that needed repair here. Thanks for stopping by, but now is not a good time."

Jevonte squeezes past Talaitha, who had blocked the entire doorway. "Please, Dr. Robinson, come on in." Jevonte reaches for Dr. Robinson's hand, and the two men shake hands as Talaitha steps out of the way, suddenly alarmed by Jevonte's forcefulness. "Can I fix you some coffee? I have a fresh pot on now," says Jevonte.

"Yes, that would be fine. I prefer my coffee black, if that's alright with you." Talaitha closes the door and remains in the entryway. Jevonte glances back at her, a puzzled look on his face.

"Babe, is everything alright? We won't disturb you." Talaitha says nothing and stares blankly at the two men. "Here, Dr. Robinson, please take a seat here, and I'll get us set up shortly."

"Please, Mr. Greene. I don't want to put you out. I thought I could help you and your wife by sharing some history about this place and this home since I'm nearby." Talaitha starts moving again. She walks into the kitchen feeling nervous and unsure, standing close by Jevonte. This behavior is different, thinks Jevonte.

"Here, King. Let me get that. Go ahead and sit with our guest. Dr. Robinson, have you eaten anything? Can I fix you something to eat this morning?" asks Talaitha.

"Coffee is fine. I don't normally eat in the morning. I know I shouldn't skip breakfast, but I'm just not a morning person."

"I understand. I'm not much of a morning person myself," says Talaitha. "Where do you practice, if I may ask?" Talaitha starts feeling claustrophobic and uncomfortable because she already knew the answer.

"I used to run a clinic at Sable Ridge before they closed the mental health unit. I was responsible for the behavioral health wing there for almost twenty years."

"Oh, you're a psychologist, then?" interjects Jevonte.

"Psychiatrist," answers Dr. Robinson.

"Oh my, so is my wife," chimes Jevonte. "Perhaps you guys have been to the same conferences. My wife just attended…"

"Jevonte, I'm sure Dr. Robinson doesn't want to hear about that. Besides, those things can be so big; you never know who will be there, especially if they're not presenting a panel or paper," Talaitha interjects.

"Please, call me Samuel, and it's ok. I don't normally attend those. After they closed my unit, I've been on my own, publishing here and there. I am currently writing a book that explores bipolar dissociative disorders in middle-aged women of color. It's a really fascinating topic," Dr. Robinson said with excitement, his focus slowly shifting to Talaitha.

"I bet it is," replies Talaitha as she places two cups of coffee on the table.

"My wife also works with people with special mental health disorders. She's very modest about her practice, but I'm so proud of the important work she's doing," offers Jevonte.

Talaitha stoops to kiss Jevonte on his brow. "My love, please. Remember, Dr. Robinson didn't come here to hear about my practice. So, Samuel, what can you tell us about this little old house? What's your connection here?" asks Talaitha as she pulls out a chair to sit at the table.

Dr. Robinson shares the home's history with Jevonte and Talaitha. He shares how he came to buy the house and how he managed parts of his practice here during the early days of Sable Ridge State Hospital. Dr. Robinson retells how the fire of '93 almost ended his practice and practically wiped Accident off the map. He tells them that he has deep roots in the hospital. Over the next hour, Jevonte and Talaitha learn that Dr. Robinson was born in 1963 and raised in Baltimore by a single mother who once labored on the Ridgeview estate. He tells them that he grew up hearing chilling stories about the land's haunted past—tales that now echo in the hospital's crumbling corridors. He shares that he was once an idealistic mental health practitioner and that he joined Sable Ridge under the promise of reform, but soon uncovered a legacy of abuse, cover-ups, and vanishing patients. Today, he tells them, decades after coming to work at Sable Ridge, he is both caretaker and captive, burdened by secrets he can't unsee and haunted by the knowledge that something unnatural lingers in the sealed Lower Wing.

"Lower Wing?" Jevonte interrupts the silence that ensues.

"Yes, the Lower Wing was a specifically designated area of the hospital where ad hoc clinics were scheduled to deal with particularly troubled patients. The reality was that these patients weren't troubled as much as they were just Black and poor," answered Dr. Robinson. "But I digress. You wanted to know about this house, didn't you?"

"Yes, sir. My friend Gerald, our neighbor, mentioned that you would know if there are any maintenance issues or mold problems. I told him that I didn't find anything during the remodeling," said Jevonte. "I recently experienced a health emergency and wondered if something I inhaled or ingested from the house could have caused it."

"Honey, come on now, I doubt that anything in the house caused your illness. I mean, really, that sounds crazy. Pardon the unscientific use of that pejorative, Dr. Robinson," said Talaitha.

"It's ok. I hear it all of the time, as I'm sure you do. Honestly, mold and the spores it produces can be extremely problematic when inhaled. They are living organisms, as you know, and tough to kill. But I had no issues with mold of any kind while I lived here. If I were in your position, considering the foliage and wooded area near the home, I would be more concerned about the wild mushrooms that may have taken up residence nearby."

"Dr. Robinson, there's no need for concern on that front. The setback for the house is pretty clear, and we've taken steps to weed the area quite thoroughly, haven't we, love?" asks Talaitha, looking directly at Jevonte. "The hospital conducted numerous tests, and I recently received Jevonte's results."

"Babe, you did? You didn't tell me. What did they say?" asks Jevonte. "Where are they?"

"It was nothing. Somehow, you contracted a mild case of MRSA, which affected your nervous system. The condition worsened while you were at the hospital, ultimately leading to the coma. The doctors were either unable or unwilling to explain where or how you came into contact with MRSA. They likely want to avoid potential legal issues, given the widespread presence of MRSA in many hospital environments. We should probably sue them. Sorry, Dr. Robinson."

"No need to apologize. It wouldn't be the first time the hospital has had legal problems. The hospital never learns from its past mistakes, and MRSA is a serious issue that warrants careful consideration. Two years ago, while I was covering for the Chief of Mental Health at John

Hopkins, the hospital experienced three deaths due to MRSA. So, I get your concern."

Jevonte sat in silence, both stunned and relieved to have a name for what had him so sick. Still, in his mind, he couldn't help wondering about these lingering issues he was experiencing.

"My love, it's ok. Everything will be fine now. And Dr. Robinson, thank you so much for stopping by and sharing so much of the hospital's history with us. It was a real pleasure meeting you," Talaitha fakes a smile as she stands from the table.

Jevonte stands up as well and extends his hand to Dr. Robinson again. "I'm really glad you made the stop. I will be sure to tell Gerald that you came through for a visit. You should stop by his place to say hello. I bet he'd get a gas out of seeing you again."

"You know, I just may have to do that. Does he still take those walks in the morning, inspecting the neighborhood like he's the resident sheriff?"

"Of course, and he loves it," Jevonte laughs.

"Look, if you ever have any other questions or need anything from me, here is my card. Don't hesitate to reach out to me. Most days, you can reach me after 5 pm." Dr. Robinson is careful not to make direct eye contact with

Talaitha, but nods in her direction subtly letting her know that he won't breach her privacy again.

After Dr. Robinson pulls out of the driveway, Jevonte asks Talaitha, "Babe, I wish you had said something to me earlier about my test results. I've been so worried, and I'm having issues with my veins and nails. Can MRSA really do that to someone?"

"Jevonte, it's a bacterium. Who knows what effects it can have on the human body? Just keep drinking those juices I prepare for you. I'll add a few smoothies as well, in case you need some variety. I do not doubt that those side effects will clear up soon. I need to get back to my patients. Are you good here?"

"Yeah, I'm okay, but can I get the login for the computer before you go? I don't feel up to walking to the library to read my emails."

"Jevonte, I have proprietary files and information on the system. I need to make you a new login, but I don't have time now, so you'll have to wait."

Talaitha returns to her office, shuts the door, and begins searching for information on Dr. Robinson. He was either very sly or completely slow-witted because he acted like didn't remember her at all, and that by itself was practically impossible. Jevonte begins clearing the kitchen, feeling hopeless and despondent. Jevonte holds Dr. Robinson's business card, committing his phone number to memory.

12

Veins of the Damned

The mail carrier arrived early at Ruby and Jedidiah's home. Phil had managed this mail route for the last ten years, and both the Greenes and Phil knew each other by name. He only had one letter this Tuesday afternoon, addressed to Jevonte Greene. Ruby took the letter from Phil, and they chatted a bit before he made his way to the next few addresses on his route.

"Ruby, what did Phil bring us this morning?" asked Jedidiah from the study.

"It's a letter from Sable Ridge State Hospital, and it's for Jevonte."

"Well, open it and let's see what it is," barked Jedidiah.

"I don't think we should do that, man. It's for Jevonte, and it might be private."

Jedidiah walked out of the study and took the letter from Ruby. "Please, if it's from a hospital and it's about our son, it's our business too. The question is, why did they send the letter here?"

Jedidiah and Ruby examined the letter together, and it read:

SABLE RIDGE STATE HOSPITAL Department of Clinical Toxicology 1291 Briar Hollow Road Ashville, VA 23804 Phone: (804) 555-2134 | Fax: (804) 555-2135

August 17, 2019

Jevonte Greene 343 Wren's Hollow Lane Accident, MD 21520

RE: Follow-Up Required—Environmental Toxin Exposure and Inconclusive Testing Results

Dear Mr. Greene,

We are writing regarding the medical evaluations and laboratory testing conducted during your recent stay at Sable Ridge State Hospital. After a full review of your diagnostic panels, imaging, and toxicology screenings, our findings remain inconclusive at this time. While no definitive diagnosis was made, there is substantiated concern that you may have been exposed to extremely dangerous environmental toxins that could have delayed or cumulative effects on your neurological, respiratory, or cognitive functions.

Given the potential severity of such exposure, our medical team strongly urges you to return to the hospital for immediate follow-up testing and extended observation. Additional diagnostics may help us determine the nature and extent of any exposure and initiate appropriate treatment if required.

We must also inform you that, as per hospital policy and legal guidance, you were not officially discharged by a licensed medical doctor, and your departure was recorded as leaving against medical advice (AMA). As such, Sable Ridge State Hospital cannot assume liability for any complications, injuries, or medical deterioration that may have occurred after your release.

This letter is not meant to alarm you but to encourage prompt medical action. Your well-being is our top priority, and we trust that you will treat this matter with the seriousness it deserves. Please contact our admissions office at (804) 555-2134 no later than August 27, 2019, to schedule your return visit.

If you are currently experiencing unusual symptoms—including dizziness, confusion, skin lesions, memory gaps, or sensory disturbances—we urge you to proceed to the nearest emergency room immediately.

Sincerely,

Dr. Elaine R. Mendez,

MD Director of Clinical Toxicology

Sable Ridge State Hospital

"Oh my God, what has happened to our son?" Ruby pleads, worry gripping her spirit in a vise.

"Let's give this Dr. Mendez a call and find out. I haven't been able to reach Jevonte in a long time, and I'm worried now. He tends to keep to himself, but the silence is too much."

"I haven't heard from him since he and that woman bought the house. I mean, it's like he has disappeared off the face of the earth now that he's with her," Ruby says with concern in her voice. "Don't call that doctor until I try to reach him a few more times. I don't want to butt into his business unless we have to."

"We're already in his business, Ruby," says Jedidiah, holding up the letter.

"Old man, you know what I mean. Now, cool it, but don't lose the letter. What do you want for dinner tonight?"

"Do we have some of that roasted lemon chicken you did from the other night? I could do with more of that."

Ruby heads into the kitchen and begins pulling some of the leftovers out. She stands at the pantry door, worry lines forming across her face. In her bones, she can feel that something is wrong with her boy. Call it mother's intuition, a sixth sense, or the Holy Ghost, but she knows that something is not clean in the milk. She leans against one side of the pantry and begins to utter a prayer for her son.

"Father God. Precious and holy art thou in all of thy majesty and power. No one but you can redeem us. I call upon you in the name of your only begotten Son, the Lord Jesus Christ; please hear my prayers. Please entertain my pleas in this hour of need. My son needs you now. I need you to send heaven's armies to him right now, Father. Whatever state he is in, whatever danger faces him, please, oh merciful God, do not delay rescuing him; do not stretch out the time. Right now, mighty God, please do it right now!" Tears stream down Ruby's face, and she begins to sing a hymn of deliverance and praise to God, standing in her pantry.

Evening arrives, and Ruby and Jedidiah are relaxing in their living room after dinner when Ruby's phone rings.

"Well, hello, Melanie. What a pleasant surprise to hear from you! How long has it been now?"

"It's been at least a year now, ma'am," said Melanie.

"Has it been that long?"

"The time has really gone by fast," said Melanie

"It seems just like yesterday you and Jevonte were heading off to Howard for your freshman year."

"I hope this is not a bad time. I know it's late."

Ruby adjusted the phone in her hand. "No, this is as good a time as ever. You're not interrupting anything. Jedidiah and I just finished dinner, and we've been watching the news, which is so depressing sometimes."

"By chance, have you spoken to Jevonte lately?" asked Melanie.

"No, I haven't really spoken with Jevonte in a long time. In fact, we just received a letter from Sable Ridge Hospital about him. Hold on a second. In the letter, they said he may have been exposed to a deadly toxin, and they want him to come back to the hospital for more testing."

"Jesus! So, you haven't talked to him since then?"

"No, sweetheart. Neither of us has been able to reach him at all. Since he hooked up with that person, we haven't heard a thing from him."

"His new wife has been keeping him to herself, I guess," said Melanie with a bit of disappointment in her voice.

"I know, but something is off about her. I can feel it in my bones."

"Woman, stop maligning the poor woman! You don't even know her yet, sheesh," interrupted Jedidiah, ear hustling on the conversation.

"Hush, and stay out of grown folks' business. No one asked you, anyway," said Ruby with vinegar.

"Does Uncle know her?" asked Melanie.

"Honey, no, he doesn't know her either. He just wants to butt in on my conversation," replied Ruby.

"Ok, well, will you please tell him I called, and I'm trying to get in touch with him?" asked Melanie.

"Yes, sure. I will let him know as soon as I hear from him."

"Have a good night, and I'll talk to you soon."

"You too, baby, and please tell your mom I said hello. Uh-huh, good night to you too, darling."

Ruby hung up the phone. "I see you are already working your mighty works," Ruby says to herself with a smile.

"Woman, what are you over there grinning about?" asks Jedidiah.

"The Lord is working it out, old man, but you don't know anything about that!"

"Woman, please, and who are you calling old? Come on over here, and I'll show you old!" Jedidiah laughs out loud.

"Man, just watch TV. Don't make me come over there!" They both chuckle together and then resume watching the evening news.

In the cool of the den, Jevonte has found respite from his aching legs. Propped up on an ottoman, the elevation is easing his discomfort. Talaitha hasn't spoken two words to him most of the week, and she hasn't commented on his condition even though he knows he must look horrid. Mirrors don't lie, so how can she not see what he sees? For now, Jevonte immerses himself in an old favorite book he's carried with him since graduating from Howard—The Other Woman by Eric Jerome Dickey. He's always been fascinated by the way Joni navigates the complicated, emotionally charged world of relationships, infidelity, and personal growth in the book. The infidelity, the betrayal, and the final journey of self-discovery and empowerment depicted in

Joni's life constantly stir Jevonte to believe there is more in life, more that is worth pursuing for himself, despite how upside down things may appear.

He is alone on an island in this house, Jevonte thinks to himself. At least within the pages of Dickey's novel, he can find relief and escape from the disappointment and sorrow crowding out the light in his life.

Jevonte is so engrossed in his reading that he misses the doorbell. He puts his book down and prepares to push himself up out of the loveseat, but Talaitha has already reached the door. She's like a phantom, moving through the house unseen, taking care not to disturb the living.

The technician is back with the remaining components and the dish needed to complete the system install. Jevonte breathes a sigh of relief, and his heart warms with hope. Finally, he will have a means of contacting his family. They must be worried sick by now, Jevonte muses.

The installation takes less than thirty minutes to complete. Talaitha and the tech guy hover around her workstation, exchanging documents. Talaitha signs the technician's clipboard and escorts him to his van. When she comes back inside the house, Jevonte is standing weakly next to the workstation, moving the mouse and looking for a login screen. The monitor is on, but the screen is black.

Talaitha strolls by him and walks into the kitchen, oblivious to his efforts. She pulls out one of the smoothies and grabs a bottle of water, then she returns to the workstation and hands Jevonte the smoothie.

"The phones should be working now. I got a tone from them after the system was initialized, but there is no login for you yet. Here, drink some of this. You look like shit." The smoothie hangs in midair between them, Talaitha's hand outstretched towards Jevonte, and his hands suspended at his sides, limp and dangling. "Jevonte, what is the matter with you? Stop acting so helpless. It's depressing," Talaitha says with acrid disdain in her voice.

"Tal, it's not an act. I feel horrible. I can barely…"

"Please go sit down then, please. I feel sick just looking at you. I think you should go call your mommy or something," Talaitha mocks. "This is definitely not a good look, and I am not about to treat you like some overgrown man baby," Talaitha responds, then turns and heads back into her office.

Despondent, Jevonte shuffles to the living room, smoothie in hand, and sits on the couch. The landline is perched close to the armrest. He stares at it and then begins to cry quietly at first, but the tears begin to fall in a flood of emotional pain and hurt. Jevonte doesn't try to stop it. He doesn't try to hide it. He lets it all come rushing out in an avalanche of pent-up torment and sorrow. His shoulders heave up and down as his body shakes with anguish, but he can't do anything else. The void he's feeling is just too deep and too wide. He can't close it down, so he doesn't try.

From her office, Talaitha launches the internal monitors and observes Jevonte's breakdown. A smile graces her lips, and she sits back in her plush office chair and hums delicately to herself. She is at peace right now. She feels whole. Her spirit is light, and so she begins making plans to visit her Baltimore office tomorrow to test the new satellite connections from there. Before she can close the surveillance application, she observes Jevonte on the phone with someone. The tears are gone, and he's clutching the phone line as though his life depended on it.

Talaitha clicks a few buttons, and the call audio begins playing through her computer's speakers.

"Mom, they said it was MRSA. I was in a coma for a while. I'm not even sure how long I was out," says Jevonte.

"Jevonte, oh my God, son. A coma? Oh Lord, thank God you made it through that," Ruby responded. "So what else did they say? What are you supposed to do now?"

"I don't know. Talaitha is scheduling a follow-up appointment for me, but I don't think it's been confirmed yet.

All I know is that I feel so weak, and I don't think my legs are healthy. I mean, there are veins in my legs that are pushing out, and they look green. My fingernails, some of them, have fallen off too."

"Baby," Ruby stopped herself because what she wanted to say was, "What has that woman done to you?" Instead, Ruby said, "What have you been eating? Maybe you just need to change up your diet or something. I don't like this, Jevonte. I don't like this at all." Ruby's temper was rising, and she was about to lay into Jevonte's new wife when Jedidiah picked up the other line in their home.

"Son, what do you need?" Jedidiah said in a firm, clear voice. His dad, the Marine, was now on the line. Just hearing the strength and conviction in his father's voice, the confidence and authority it carried, strengthened Jevonte's resolve—and straightened his backbone.

"Dad, I'll be alright. I was feeling low, but I feel much better now, much better."

Ruby jumps in and says, "Ok, boys, enough of all that mushy stuff. Guess who we spoke to just a few days ago, son? Your old flame, Melanie. She…"

Talaitha disconnects the call, and Jevonte's line goes dead. Jevonte stares blankly at the handset. "Mom? Dad? Can you hear me?" Silence ensues. There isn't even a dial tone in the handset. Jevonte returns the handset to the cradle and sits back on the couch. There are no tears now, just a small smile that erases the decrepit seeds of doubt and fear that sought purchase inside his mind. He got a chance to hear his momma's voice, and for that, he is so thankful and relieved.

Over the coming days, Talaitha stops bringing Jevonte smoothies and her special juices. She sits in her Baltimore office, fuming, recalling how lively Jevonte sounded on the call with his parents. Her thoughts grow increasingly darker as the morning stretches into the afternoon. She has three sessions scheduled with a few complex patients, but she is considering canceling them all so she can return home to work on a new project.

Her receptionist, Isabelle, knocks at her door and then opens it. "Dr. Mercedes, your 9 o'clock is here. Are you ready for him?"

"Shit," murmurs Talaitha under her breath. "Send him in, but I think I am going to cancel the rest of today's sessions."

"Yes, ma'am." Isabelle closes the door, and Talaitha can hear her giving the client instructions before the session begins. Talaitha pulls a legal pad from her cabinet and then notices an amber light on her monitor indicating that someone is calling the house. She clicks on the surveillance program and dons her headset to listen in.

"Hey there, it's really great to hear from you. How have you been?" A melodic female voice asks.

Jevonte, with obvious enthusiasm in his voice, responds, "Melanie, it's amazing to hear your voice. I can't believe it's you! How did you get this number? Did Mom? Nope, I already know," laughs Jevonte.

"Well, Ruby is always looking out, you know. She told me that you had a real scare there. What happened?"

"MRSA, in a nutshell, is the culprit. Somehow, I became infected with MRSA, and it severely affected my health. I was in a coma for a while, and I am still not fully healthy or feeling right. Something is wrong with me, like my body is still going through some battle with something, but I have no idea what that could be. I've lost about thirty pounds now. I'm just a mess, girl."

"Jevonte, no, I just hate to hear that. What are the doctors telling you? Have you had any follow-up with them?"

"Friend, I haven't received any information, although my wife did hear from the doctor, and that's how we found out it was MRSA."

"I saw the letter from the hospital, the one they sent to your mom's house."

"What? Did they send a letter there? I wonder why they didn't send it here. Can you email it to me? I have no real contact information for the doctor or the hospital staff that assisted me."

"Of course. If I remember, the doctor's office number is in the letter too. Hey, so please tell me what you've been doing. Where are you and your bride living now? When can we see you? I have so many questions!"

"It's been crazy. I have so much... Oh, hold on, Melanie; my wife is calling on the other line. Hold on, ok?"

"No problem. I'll be here."

Jevonte clicks over to the incoming call. "Tal, hey. What's going on?" Jevonte asks, his voice low and unsure.

"Hi, King. I was calling to check on you and see how you were feeling. You were on my mind."

"I'm good. I still feel like crap, but what else is new?"

"Listen, I have some new recipes I want to try on you. I think they will really help with your legs and your skin quality. In fact, I'll bring home some of that organic coconut oil from the Hoodoo store near where I work. They have some of the best ointments, and they're all natural and organic."

"That sounds good, babe. I appreciate that, and at this point, I'm willing to try just about anything. If you haven't noticed, I look a little like one of those walking dead zombie things," Jevonte jests. "Hey, I have to run, but thanks for calling."

"Where? Why are you trying to get off the phone right now?" Talaitha reacts with anger.

"Babe, I'm not going anywhere. I need to get a shower and try to get cleaned up. I think I'll feel better if I do."

"If you say so." Talaitha hangs up abruptly, and Jevonte clicks over to Melanie's call.

"Sorry about that. That was Talaitha, and she wanted to check on me, which is very out of character for her. Lately, she's been everywhere but here with me."

"I'm sorry to hear that, Jevonte. It can't be easy for you, or her, for that matter, seeing how you guys just got married and this health scare popped up out of nowhere. Listen, I'm not due to return to the hospital in Middle River for another few days. Would you like to get together for lunch so we can catch up properly?"

"Count me in! What do you do at the hospital? I didn't know you were in the medical field."

"Well, yeah, you wouldn't know, seeing as you dumped me after graduation, Mr.!"

"Dumped you? I don't think so, ma'am. As I recall, somebody was not ready for a full-time commitment at the time," Jevonte shot back.

"Uh, sir, I do believe you need to get your facts straight, Mr. "I need to figure things out for myself," laughed Melanie.

"Ok, you got me on that one," and Jevonte joined her in the laughter. "It feels good to laugh a little; thank you, Ms. Melanie Decartes."

Talaitha had heard enough and clicked on the button to disconnect the house system. She was boiling inside, filled with a sudden, unspeakable rage. She opened up the file she had assembled on her desk. She dialed the listed number.

"I need this. I need it soon. No, I don't want to wait any longer. You have my instructions. I'll send what you asked for once we have a resolution, once I'm positive I won't have to contend with them anymore. Am I making myself clear? Good," and Talaitha ends the call.

Two weeks have passed, and Ruby, true to form, is at church. Church Emanuel is not as packed as it usually is on Bible study night. Pastor Cecil was a wonderful teacher, and most Tuesday nights, the pews are full. This evening, perhaps because of the severe weather, only the hardcore Bible thumpers were in attendance; Ruby was proud to be one of the few. She tried, as she always did, to get Jedidiah to come with her. Her husband was a so-called believer; he just wasn't a practicing one. He was probably lying on the couch watching some game on television. I bet he's knocked out cold on the couch, Ruby thought to herself.

After Bible study ends, Ruby commiserates with some of the elders and members of the usher board about next Sunday's processional. She spoke with Pastor Cecil and asked him to pray for her husband. He promised he would and told her to let Jedidiah know he was going to come by to visit. They both chuckled about that comment.

The rain had slowed quite a bit by the time Ruby pulled out of the church parking lot. There was very little traffic now, but navigating the two-lane back roads still required caution. Ruby especially hated driving in the rain. The wiper blades just never seemed to do a perfect job. How many times had she told Jedidiah to replace them? They were practically rotted off the blade shafts.

Two miles from the on-ramp to Highway 83, a set of blinding lights flashed in the rear of Ruby's Lincoln MKZ. She raised a hand to shield her eyes, but the glare was too intense. With her free hand, Ruby tried steering the Lincoln onto the side of the road to let the other vehicle behind her pass by, but she didn't see the deep water that had pooled along the edge of the road. The steering wheel jerked out of her hand when the car's right tire struck the puddled surface of the rain-drenched road. The vehicle swerved and started to fishtail along the country backroad. Ruby grabbed the wheel with both hands and attempted to regain control of the car.

A savage blow struck Ruby from behind as she began steering the Lincoln back onto the roadway. The impact drove the Lincoln off the road and into the water-filled drainage ditch, which had overflowed from the earlier torrential rains. The Lincoln lay on its passenger side. The hood and nearly the entire front windshield were submerged. Rudy struck her head against the steering wheel when the car plowed into the ditch. She was dazed and disoriented. Her lap belt did its job and kept her from flying out of the car, but now she was stuck, and the seatbelt release was jammed. Ruby looked around the car's interior; the water had filled the entire right side, and the passenger seat was covered entirely.

"Oh Lord, where is my phone? I need your help, sweet Jesus, I need your help," Ruby cried. Ruby continued to silently pray when she heard the sound of splashing and sloshing behind her. She couldn't see what it was, but she could tell it was getting closer. "Help. Is anybody there? I need some help, please. Can you hear me? I'm stuck inside, and my seatbelt is jammed," Ruby yelled.

A dark figure stood in waist-deep water to the rear of the Lincoln and said nothing as he approached Ruby's side of the car. There was little room to maneuver, as the vehicle was wedged tightly along the bank of the ditch. The stranger climbed on top of the side of the Lincoln and slid down to Ruby's door. Her window was down, and the interior was filling slowly with more water.

"Oh, thank God," said Ruby. "I'm stuck in here. Can you help me get out, please?" She pleads softly.

The stranger reached down and patted the back of Ruby's head, brushing her hair back and away from her face. The stranger looked her in the eyes and then shoved her head towards the center console, which was underwater. Ruby, initially shocked with disbelief and then terror, began to struggle against the stranger's grip, but his hold was like steel, unmoving, taut, and unrelenting. Ruby fought with all she had. Memories of Jedidiah and Jevonte flashed before her eyes as she let out the last bit of air she had in her. Her light went out with her last desperate gasp for air. Her lungs filled with the putrid roadway runoff that now filled the Lincoln. The stranger released his hold on Ruby's head and withdrew from the car.

The backcountry road remained deserted. The stranger climbed into his truck and left. A map lay on the passenger's seat, and a bright red circle illuminated the little town of Accident.

Jevonte and Talaitha rose early. Jevonte is struggling to get out of bed, but Talaitha has already set the breakfast table. She's been cleaning the basement and making preparations for a new in-home garden. She brought home several seed bags and tincture bottles. She had Jevonte build her a special workbench where she can store her clippings and seeds. Jevonte didn't understand why she needed the basement space, especially after all the work he put into building her a greenhouse in the backyard. But, like most items on his honey-do list, he carried out his wife's wishes, and that with a smile.

"Here, babe. Sit here. I brought up some very special herbs that I'm sure will fix you up in no time. These are all homegrown, none of the processed junk the supermarkets sell. No fillers, just raw organics all around. You will feel like a new man in no time," said Talaitha.

"Jevonte said weakly, "This all looks yummy, babe. Thank you."

Within minutes of finishing breakfast, Jevonte was doubled over in excruciating pain. Talaitha came rushing out of her office when she heard dishes crash to the kitchen floor. "King, what happened?"

Jevonte was foaming at the mouth and convulsing violently on the floor. His eyes began to roll up into his head as he lost consciousness. Talaitha stood fixated a few feet away from Jevonte's unmoving body. Her expression was emotionless, blank. She looked down at Jevonte. He was so still, so small. Saliva was spilling from the side of his mouth, and his chest was barely moving. Talaitha moved slowly and kneeled beside him. She placed two fingers against his neck. A pulse was there, but it was weak and fading.

She rose calmly and walked over to her desktop computer, and started checking the feed. She watched Jevonte eat the scrambled eggs, bacon, and toast she had made him, then she saw him sprinkle something over the bowl of fruit she had prepared for him. What is that? Where did he get that bottle? Talaitha mused. She glanced over at the kitchen table and saw one of her tincture bottles, and panicked. Talaitha rushed to Jevonte's side and began shaking him, patting him, and then slapping him across the face, but there was no response.

"What have you done, Jevonte? What have you done, you fool!"

At Sable Ridge, the medical staff worked desperately to stabilize Jevonte's vitals. He coded twice while they had him in the examining room.

"Mrs. Greene, your husband is in a medically induced coma. We've stabilized him for now, but his blood tests are not very good. Can you tell us what's been going on with your husband? Preliminary results of our tests show his blood has been exposed to heavy metals and some toxins we haven't been able to identify," said the attending physician.

Talaitha thought carefully for a minute and responded with confidence, "No, nothing besides the usual. We ate breakfast together. I had the same breakfast as he did. I do know that a few months back, this hospital infected him with MRSA, and he is still recovering from that debacle."

"I saw that in his chart, but it doesn't explain what we're seeing now. I'm really concerned about his heart at the moment. We will continue testing and monitoring him closely. I'll be back in a few hours to update you when the labs fully process everything."

Talaitha sat at Jevonte's bedside. The monitors were recording his heart rate, blood pressure, and his heart's rhythm. It all looked so clinical, antiseptic, and cold. Jevonte's body was cool to the touch, and his breathing was so shallow that a casual observer would have thought him deceased. The day passed with little update from the medical staff. As evening approached, Talaitha was informed that they would be keeping Jevonte for the next few days and that they could prepare a recliner bed for her so that she could remain close to him. Talaitha contemplated accepting the offer but declined. She needed to get back to the house to make sure everything was put away properly. The tincture Jevonte used contained three times the normal dosing she used in her garden for the special herbal mix she was experimenting with. She still didn't know how he got his hands on it in the first place. I've never seen him go into the basement since he completed the refurbishment down there, she thought to herself. This close call was more troubling than the last, and this time, Talaitha feared she might lose everything.

On day three, Jevonte's vitals are becoming stronger, and the medical staff is encouraged. The attending notifies Talaitha at home, and she heads over to the hospital. She hasn't been back since he was first admitted. The doctor informs Talaitha that they will try a series of infusions now that Jevonte is showing signs of recovery. They slowly bring him out of the induced coma, and he wakes to find Talaitha holding his hand and looking at him with enormous concern.

"Babe, please tell me I didn't catch MRSA again, please," Jevonte moans.

"I wouldn't be surprised, King, but no, it wasn't MRSA. Again, they don't have a clue, but they have informed me that they are going to give you some infusions to help your system purge itself of whatever is causing this," Talaitha replied. "But, before they get started, there is something I need to tell you." Talaitha paused for a few moments, then she took Jevonte's hand in both of hers. In a mechanical, clinical tone, devoid of human emotion, Talaitha said, "Ruby is dead."

Jevonte reacted slowly, not sure he had heard Talaitha correctly. His eyes began to lose focus, and he turned his head to see Talaitha better. "What? What did you just say?"

Talaitha was detached and robotic. "Your mom is dead. Ruby is dead."

"No. You have to be mistaken. I don't... I don't understand," Jevonte stuttered. "How do you know this? When did this happen?" Jevonte began to struggle to sit up in his hospital bed; his arms were trembling and weak. "Tal, what are you talking about?" Jevonte demanded, tears forming in his eyes.

"Apparently," Talaitha began, analytically retelling the details as she believed them to be, "Ruby was in some ecstatic state or experiencing a religious hallucination. She lost control of the car she was driving and crashed into a ditch full of water. She drowned."

Jevonte's mouth gaped open, and he began sobbing, then choking because he could barely swallow. His air was cut off, and he couldn't breathe. The monitors in his room started beeping, and the blaring alarms carried them out into the hospital corridor. Nurses from the nearby station rushed into the room and started working to clear Jevonte's airway. Talaitha moved to the back of the room and stared. Her face was a stone. Her eyes never registered any humanity or compassion for the suffering and pain Jevonte was enduring.

Again, Jevonte was stabilized, and his vitals began to stabilize. He lay on his back, looking up at the ceiling, tears streaming down his face. Talaitha watched as his chest and stomach rose with his anguish. The nurses did their best to calm and reassure him, but he turned his head towards Talaitha, pleading through tears for her support. He stretched out his hand to reach for her, and the nurses moved out of the way and left the room. Talaitha hesitated at first and then walked gingerly to take Jevonte's hand.

"My love, how did you hear about this? When did it happen?" Jevonte started.

"All I know," said Talaitha in hushed tones, "is that she was in an accident, and they held her funeral two days ago."

"Funeral?" Jevonte cried out, his voice strained and weak. "Already! Oh my God. Oh my God, Talaitha! I wasn't there…"

"King, you were still in a coma. There was nothing you could do, and I was not going to have them bring you out of it to receive this news. This episode was worse than the last time. There was no way. There just was no way to do this. For now, you need to rest and regain your strength. I'll take you home as soon as the doctor says I can. I'll be back," Talaitha said with finality.

"Now? Where are you going, Tal? Baby, I need you! Don't leave me," Jevonte whimpered in anguish.

"Jevonte, just stop it, please. My goodness," exclaimed Talaitha. "I'm going to pick up some clothes for you and get more information on where they have buried your mother. Is that ok with you?" Jevonte said nothing and returned his sullen gaze to the ceiling. Talaitha scoffed and left the hospital room.

Two days have passed since Jevonte found out that his mom was killed in a car accident. His appetite is nonexistent, and even if he could eat, he probably couldn't keep it down. His whole body just feels sick. Talaitha hasn't come by or called. She isn't answering the phone. As Jevonte sits up in his bed, he starts wondering how his dad is doing. Does he even know that I'm in the hospital right now? Jevonte wonders.

The doctors and nurses have been keeping him company, and the results of the battery of tests they have been running indicate that the infusions have been helping him a lot. His doctors tell him that they expect to be able to release him in one or two days. Jevonte is finally able to get out of bed and use the bathroom on his own. The veins in his legs still look weird, but they aren't bulging like before, and his fingernails look almost human.

Standing in front of the bathroom mirror, he could see a person again, someone resembling a member of the human race, and his spirit improved. He dabs a little water on his face and dries it before walking back into his hospital room. To his wonderment and joy, Melanie is standing in the

middle of the room waiting for him to come out of the
bathroom.

13

Poison Secrets, Bloody Soil

Jevonte's stay at Sable Ridge has stretched into a week, much longer than the medical staff originally planned for, but Jevonte has been buoyed by Melanie's daily visits. Melanie consistently remains attentive even after visiting hours conclude, and Jevonte's recuperation continues to progress. His mental and emotional state has benefitted from Melanie's calm reassurance. Melanie has been helping Jevonte with a little of his physical therapy, helping him navigate the various exercises the medical staff has directed. Though Jevonte is not on a full-blown rehab program, Melanie has been using her nursing experience to encourage him and prepare him for what's to come.

"You know, Melanie," Jevonte smiles, "I think I can work out my bathing situation on my own now."

"I don't know, Mr., you almost fell the other day, and I had to swoop in for the save!"

"Hey, that was not on me. The floor was wet. I have to stay on top of these nurses around here…"

"Now wait a minute, Mr. Jevonte Greene. Don't lay that on my fellow nurses. We are not the maids, sir!" Melanie replies lightheartedly but sternly.

"Haha, just kidding, just kidding. Melanie, I can't begin to tell you how much your visits have meant to me. Honestly, I don't think I could have gone through this if it were not for you; I mean that."

"Jevonte, I'm just glad I was able to get away. I need to think carefully about what I want to say next," Melanie says, pausing. "I have to be honest with you, too, Jevonte. I just felt like I needed to see you. I've always felt like there was so much unfinished business between us, stuff we never really had a chance to get closure on. It's so funny sometimes the way God works."

Jevonte sat down on the edge of his bed across from where Melanie was seated. "Definitely, but what do you mean by unfinished business?"

Melanie crossed her legs and relaxed into her seat. "I feel like we were connected in college. I honestly thought we would continue down the path we were on after graduation. I mean, I pictured a future together, and I really thought you did too, or was I just… wrong?" Melanie asks, shifting slightly in her seat.

Jevonte stares at Melanie blankly, then turns his gaze to the hospital window. The day is turning out to be a gorgeous one, and Jevonte can feel a change coming as surely as the warmth of the sun touching his legs. "Mel," and with that short name, Melanie knew Jevonte was speaking from someplace softer towards her, "You are not wrong, not at all. I know we wanted the same thing, but…"

"But what, Jevonte?"

"I was scared. I mean, I kept tripping over my own inner stuff, going back and forth, doubting myself about whether I could actually be in a real, long-term relationship. I think college was easier because I had a routine and knew what to expect. After we graduated, a plethora of new fears swept through me, overwhelming me with anxiety and doubt. I became lost, and I didn't want to bring you into my little circle of confusion. I looked at you, and I saw so much brightness, so much possibility, and I knew that I couldn't match that, not at that time anyway." Jevonte averts Melanie's eyes and stares at the hospital monitors.

A good long moment of silence fills the room, followed by a single, lone tear on Melanie's cheek. "Jevonte," Melanie stops. She stood and walked over to sit beside him. "There is nothing I wouldn't have faced with you, nothing. I wish you had trusted the love we hold. I could have carried you through that until you found your footing. I know you're a good man. You are worth the effort, and I would have gladly helped you shoulder the burdens you felt you were under."

"Mel," Jevonte says as he takes her hand in his, "I think part of me knew this, but another part wanted to get myself together enough so that I could contribute to what you were bringing to the table. I just wanted to fly with you—not drag you down."

"Jevonte, you really don't give yourself enough credit. I know you are married now… And I'm no home wrecker, but I can't let the matter go; I won't. So, let me ask you something. Where is your wife, Jevonte? You almost died. You've been in this hospital for how many days?"

"It's been over a week, I think. She has a bustling practice in Baltimore. It isn't easy to get away. She has patients undergoing some kind of acute, critical care under her guidance," Jevonte replies.

"Ok, well, has she been here once in the last five days?"

"Mel, no, she hasn't, but I didn't expect her to either."

"You didn't expect your wife to take out some time to see about you? You don't feel like you deserve that much attention from your wife, Jevonte?"

"I... I do, Mel. Well, I don't know. I don't feel as important to her as I once did, but I'm needy, and I know that much about myself."

"Jevonte, you lost your mom for goodness' sake! What's going on here?" asked Melanie, exasperated.

"None of your motherfucking business!" Talaitha interjects as she strolls into Jevonte's room.

In an instant, the room feels darker to Jevonte. The sun even seems to dim its light as Talaitha takes up a position at the foot of Jevonte's bed. Melanie, startled by Talaitha's entry, stands to face her. Jevonte's jaw grows slack, but he musters the courage to respond to Talaitha's rudeness.

"Talaitha," he barks. "What's the matter with you?"

"What's the matter with me? Who is this bitch, Jevonte?" Talaitha says, staring directly at Melanie.

Melanie doesn't say a word, but she returns Talaitha's ice-cold stare and then turns to look at Jevonte directly. "Listen, I'm going to head out. Don't worry, though; I will be back. We have a lot to discuss," Melanie smiles and then walks past Talaitha as though she were invisible.

Talaitha's hands are clenched into balls of maddened fury. She is standing in the center of Jevonte's room, her feet spread shoulder-width apart and her knees slightly bent. She is tense, and her body is coiled and ready to explode at the slightest provocation. It's only when the door closes behind Melanie that her posture changes. She walks over to Jevonte's bed, his eyes fixed on the door. Looking at Talaitha, Jevonte imagines that if she were a cat, her tail would be a blur of whipping fury.

"Who was that fat hoe, Jevonte?"

"Talaitha, please. She is not a hoe. Her name is Melanie, and she is a very good friend with whom I went to college. She heard about my situation and what happened to my mom, so she came to visit with me so I wouldn't be so alone," says Jevonte, his voice appreciative.

"Well, it didn't look or sound like she was a friend," replies Talaitha.

"How long were you listening? If you had heard the whole conversation…"

"I heard enough, and I don't like her."

"You don't even know her, Talaitha."

"I don't need to. I know her type, and she's trash." Talaitha wants to test Jevonte's reaction. "She's fat and slobbery. She looks desperate, and I bet that's why she was here. She heard about you and wanted to make a move on you, take advantage of your weak ass," Talaitha snorts.

Jevonte doesn't respond, but then he says, "She was here at least."

Talaitha walks over to the hospital room's window and places both palms on the sill. Looking out over the parking lot, she spots Melanie, a handful of papers in hand, walking to her car. She made a mental note of the car's license plate number, its make, and its model. In her mind, she thought, Yeah, I see you. This is not over. If I catch you in my husband's space again…she let the rest of that train of thought trail off into the distance. Talaitha straightens and turns to sit next to Jevonte.

"I know that this whole ordeal has been incredibly hard on you. I really do. I know I haven't been here for you, but I want you to know it wasn't because I didn't want to be. I couldn't leave my clients alone because so much has happened with their treatment protocols. Their lives are literally in my hands, and I have an obligation to them as my patients. Please forgive me, King," Talaitha says as she takes Jevonte's hand in hers.

"I understand. It was just so difficult, and I felt completely alone. I know your work is important, as are your patients, but I also think I should be higher up on your list of priorities," replies Jevonte, surprised at the appearance of his backbone.

"King, why don't you lie back and let me show you how important you are to me? I never meant to neglect you.

Occasionally, I get so caught up in my work that I get tunnel vision, and when I saw that hoe… I mean, Melanie," Talaitha says, rolling her eyes. "I just saw red. Now let me take care of you. I know how to make you feel better," and she stands to help Jevonte lie down. She lifts his hospital gown and begins to rub his stomach, briefly but masterfully running her fingers through his pubic hair. She wraps her lips around his appendage and takes him deep into her mouth.

"Talaitha, no, you can't, not here. The nurses are right outside my door…"

Talaitha ignores Jevonte's pleas and continues her work. No one interrupts them, and Jevonte's moans echo harmlessly, his heart monitor bearing witness to the effect of endorphins dancing through his brain.

Melanie sits with the files the nurse slid to her when she left Jevonte's hospital room. As a nurse herself, Melanie was well aware of the legal repercussions of what her peer did and how much trouble the nurse could be in for sharing the file. Both Melanie and her newly acquainted nurse-friend knew that something was amiss with Jevonte's condition. When Melanie asked about Jevonte's condition on her way out, the charge nurse and nurse on duty refused to disclose any information, and they were correct not to do so; Melanie knew. However, it was the certified nursing assistant, known as a CNA, whom Talaitha had despised and ridiculed during Jevonte's first emergency room visit, who found Melanie before she reached the elevator and informed her of a problem. The CNA quickly handed Melanie copies of Jevonte's file and said, "I'm not very knowledgeable about what's in this, but you need to have a real doctor look at it. I think he was poisoned."

Melanie scanned the files, taking her time to review the blood work results. One of the pages read:

----

1. Complete Blood Count (CBC):
    o If there are secondary complications, the individual's overall health may reveal potential anemia or signs of infection.
2. Electrolyte Imbalance:
    o Hyponatremia (low sodium levels) occurs due to the increased secretion of bodily fluids, including saliva, sweat, and tears.
3. Renal Function Tests:
    o Possible mild elevations in blood urea nitrogen (BUN) and creatinine if there is dehydration or kidney impairment due to excessive fluid loss.

4. Blood Glucose Levels:

   o Hypoglycemia (low blood glucose levels): Due to increased metabolic demands and reduced food intake, gastrointestinal symptoms such as nausea and vomiting may occur.

5. Liver Function Tests (LFTs):

   o Dangerously low; co-ingestion of hepatotoxic substances suspected.

6. Coagulation Profile:

   o The coagulation profile is typically normal, with significant alterations unlikely unless there are complications.

7. Specific Tests:

   o While there is no standard blood test for muscarine levels, a urine toxicology screen should be performed to detect muscarine or other co-ingested substances.

Symptoms of chronic muscarine exposure include excessive salivation, sweating, lacrimation, gastrointestinal distress (cramping, diarrhea), bradycardia (slow heart rate), hypotension (low blood pressure), and miosis (constriction of the pupils). These symptoms highlight the systemic overstimulation of muscarinic acetylcholine receptors.

"Muscarine exposure? Jevonte doesn't even like mushrooms. He wouldn't eat those if his life depended on it," Melanie said to herself. Something is out of order, and the doctors should have seen this; they should know these signs, Melanie thought to herself in disgust. Melanie continues reviewing Jevonte's file and locates his current address. I need some proof. I can't go to the medical board or even the police without something tangible, she thinks.

Melanie types in the address, and within twenty-five minutes, she is outside of Jevonte and Talaitha's home. Jevonte's Jeep is still parked on the side of the house. Dust and pollen have coated the vehicle, and Melanie just shakes her head, knowing that the man she loved in college would never let his ride get that filthy. After parking down the street and around the corner, she exits her car and walks to Jevonte's home. Nervously, Melanie looks around to scan the homes nearby. It's quiet, and no one is about. That's all I need. Not for someone to see this Black girl peering into someone's home and mistake me for a burglar.

Still, Melanie isn't quite sure what she hopes to find. I need to get inside the house because this is ridiculous, and a whole lot isn't making sense to me. "Argh," Melanie huffs and walks around to the rear of the home. The trash bins are lined up neatly next to the side of the house. Melanie takes a peek inside each, not sure what she is looking for, but hoping something will be there that she can use. There is no loose garbage in the bins. Everything is in bags and tied off securely—except for one bag. Inside the bag, near its open mouth, is some charred refuse and debris that looks like blackened mussels and vegetable matter. The odor is foul, and Melanie has to close the lid.

Continuing her walk along the side of the house, Melanie can see basement windows spaced every five feet or so along the bottom of the side of the house. Most are clouded and obscured by dirt, except for one. Through the windowpane, Melanie spies a barren floor, upturned dirt, and scattered bits of concrete. It looks like the floor has been cracked open and partially filled with what appears to be trash, mostly compost material. Odd, Melanie thinks.

When Melanie crosses into the backyard space, she pauses at the greenhouse Jevonte built. She doesn't need to guess; Jevonte's craftsmanship is all over the structure. Melanie muses to herself about how good Jevonte has always been with his hands. She starts toward the greenhouse to peer inside when she notices a walk-in to the basement, and the door is slightly ajar. The temptation is too much, and she reasons this won't require her to force entry, so she heads inside to the basement. "Lord, please forgive me for this, but you know I have a good reason," Melanie says under her breath.

The basement is completely dark, with no lights on, so Melanie pauses to let her eyes adjust. Inside, Melanie uses her hand to trace the inside wall, hoping to find a light switch. Finding none, she proceeds cautiously, extending one foot and then another as she inches her way into the darkness. Something creases her forehead, and Melanie lets out a muffled scream. She reaches out into the dark, trying to fend off whatever touched her forehead, and then feels the space in front of her face. Her flailing hand finds a lanyard and a drawstring dangling in the space. She grasps it in her hand and tugs at it. Flickering light floods the basement, sending shadows fleeing to all corners.

Melanie gathers herself and looks around the room. Most of the basement is finished, so the broken concrete in the flooring is oddly misplaced. The soil seems very rich, dark brown, almost black. The unearthed flooring is nearly eight feet long and four feet wide. Melanie thinks that it must be a composting pit of some kind, but she wonders, "Now why on earth would anyone put a composting pit in the basement?"

There is a workbench crowded with an assortment of tools on the opposite side of the room. The workbench is backed by a wall-mounted corkboard where various saws and jigs are hung. Melanie reasons that this must be Jevonte's work area. She doesn't know why his things are down in the basement like this. A long stairway leading to the upstairs draws her attention, and so Melanie makes her way up the stairs. She pauses at the top and listens just in case there might be someone at home after all. After a few silent moments, Melanie opens the door and walks out into the kitchen.

An odd sensation comes over her. Melanie begins to feel nervous and a little afraid. She's trespassing, and she knows she would be furious if someone violated her privacy in this way. After a brief walk through the house, Melanie concludes she's had enough. This accomplished nothing, and judging by how Talaitha reacted to her presence in Jevonte's hospital room, if she were caught, Melanie shakes her head. Let me get my Black ass out of this crazy woman's house before she comes home, Melanie muses.

Melanie turns and heads back toward the basement, anxious to get out of the house, when a whirling, humming sound startles her. The desktop printer begins printing a page and stops after three pages have been printed. Melanie stares at the workstation, debating within herself as to whether she should take a look at the papers in the tray. "Of course I should," Melanie thinks out loud. Melanie picks up the papers and begins to scan them. It's a fax from Intrepid Pharmaceutical Labs. Melanie skips the cover page and reads the main pages:

Intrepid Pharmaceutical Labs, White Marsh, Maryland

Controlled Substances Usage and Safety Information

1. Scopolamine

- Description: Scopolamine is an anticholinergic drug used primarily to treat motion sickness and postoperative nausea and vomiting.

- Usage: Typically administered via transdermal patch for motion sickness or as an injection for severe cases.

- Dosage:
    - Transdermal Patch: Apply one patch (1.5 mg) behind the ear every 72 hours.
    - Injection: 0.3 to 0.65 mg subcutaneously or intravenously as needed.

- Warnings:

- o Adverse Effects: Can cause dry mouth, dizziness, urinary retention, and blurred vision. Higher doses may result in severe hallucinations, delirium, and memory impairment.
- o Contraindications: Not recommended for individuals with narrow-angle glaucoma, obstructive diseases of the gastrointestinal tract, or myasthenia gravis.
- o Cautions: Use with caution in elderly patients and those with cardiovascular disease.

2. 3-Quinuclidinyl Benzilate (BZ)

- Description: BZ is a potent anticholinergic agent that can cause incapacitating delirium and hallucinations.
- Usage: BZ is primarily used in research settings to study the effects of anticholinergic toxicity and to conduct pharmacological studies.
- Dosage:
  - o Research Use: Dosage typically ranges from micrograms to milligrams per kilogram of body weight, depending on the study parameters.
- Warnings:

- o Adverse Effects: Causes severe central nervous system disturbances, including confusion, hallucinations, prolonged delirium, and potentially dangerous behavior.
- o Contraindications: Should not be used in medical treatment due to its severe psychotropic effects and high risk of toxicity.
- o Cautions: Handling requires extreme care in controlled environments with appropriate protective measures.

3. Lysergic Acid Diethylamide (LSD)-25

- Description: LSD is a powerful hallucinogen that affects serotonin receptors in the brain, leading to altered perceptions and mood.
- Usage: Used in controlled research settings to study psychiatric disorders, brain function, and consciousness.
- Dosage:
  - o Research Use: Micrograms to low milligrams, typically administered orally or intravenously. Common research doses range from 50 to 200 micrograms.
- Warnings:

- o Adverse Effects: Can cause significant psychological effects, including visual hallucinations, euphoria, anxiety, and paranoia. High doses may result in severe psychological distress and long-lasting psychiatric effects.
- o Contraindications: Not suitable for individuals with a history of severe mental illness, epilepsy, or cardiovascular problems.
- o Cautions: Strictly controlled usage with close monitoring under ethical research protocols to prevent abuse and adverse events.

Safety Notice:

All personnel handling these substances must follow appropriate safety protocols, wear protective equipment, and ensure secure storage to prevent unauthorized access or accidental exposure.

For more detailed information, please refer to the Material Safety Data Sheets (MSDS) and follow institutional guidelines for handling controlled substances.

Intrepid Pharmaceutical Labs, White Marsh, Maryland

Contact: (410) 574-4578

Melanie starts to panic. She saw some of these drugs listed on Jevonte's blood screening results. She doesn't recall what the trace amounts were, but she swears she saw 3-Quinuclidinyl Benzilate in the file, or one of these substances. Her pulse starts racing, and she looks around for something to write with. Melanie curses because her phone is charging in her car. The silence of the moment is broken by the sound of a car door closing just outside the house, and Melanie is terror-stricken, frozen in place.

Melanie hears the sound of keys jangling just outside the front door, prompting her to dash to the basement! Racing down the stairs, Melanie crosses the open flooring, her foot sliding through the upturned soil. She reaches the walk-out and pauses, listening for any sound from upstairs. When she hears the front door close, Melanie makes a beeline to her car, crossing through the adjacent neighbor's backyard, hoping to avoid being seen from Jevonte's home. Sitting in her car, Melanie looks at Jevonte's file, her breathing finally slowing down and her pulse almost returning to normal. She reviews the blood panel results and closes the file. In her mind, Melanie believes she has all she needs to make a case, then her energy wanes, and her hope crashes swiftly. In her haste, she left the pharmaceutical company's fax behind! "Damnit!" Melanie cries. "Still,"

Melanie reasons out loud, "My suspicions are confirmed. I need to figure out how to expose that witch for what she is and what she's doing."

Talaitha begins sorting some of the mail that she had been carrying in her car. Once inside, she places the mail on the kitchen countertop and then freezes. Her eyes lock on the papers on the floor in front of the fax machine. Talaitha walks over and picks up the papers, noting that the fax machine's catchment is still in place and empty. How did these end up on the floor? she wonders. After reviewing the contents of the fax, she places them back in the fax machine bin and turns to find the basement door ajar. "What in the hell," Talaitha's voice trails off while her body tenses, alert to a possible intruder. Her eyes narrow, and she slows her breathing, listening for movement of any kind in the house. Talaitha walks to one of the cabinet drawers near the pantry and retrieves a carving knife. She holds the knife in a hammer grip, blade point facing up, and cautiously walks to the basement door. The light is on. Talaitha knew she didn't leave it like that. She starts down the stairs and hears the tweet of birds and sees rays of sunlight pouring through the open walk-out door.

Talaitha's anger flares as she traces a path of mud and dirt marking the intruder's departure. She crosses the distance and walks out into the yard. Talaitha scans the nearby woods and the surrounding homes. No one is around, and she can spot nothing amiss on the property. "The cameras!" Talaitha fumes and slams the door behind her as she heads back inside the house.

Sitting at her desk inside the home office, Talaitha launches the monitoring system. "That bitch!" growls Talaitha and hurls the lone crystal snowball perched on her desk at the door of her office. The globe shatters into tiny shards that spray against the door and adjacent wall in a flecked display of rage. She sits back in her chair, her temper pulsating and consuming her thoughts as she watches Melanie walk through her house. She watches until the end and sees the interloper exit the house and move through the neighboring backyard.

Talaitha picks up the phone and dials a number quickly. As she converses with the listener, her nerves begin to calm, and her body releases the tension that had been boiling just under the surface. The tremor that paced her voice when she began the call has vanished, and her vision is clear again. The call lasts thirty minutes, and when it concludes, Talaitha is relaxed and reclines in her office chair.

She stares up at the ceiling and then turns her attention to the picture frame on her bookshelf. It's just an empty frame, a silver and wooden frame that used to embrace the picture of a young girl, someone Talaitha once knew as family. It stands empty now, a reminder of a time in her past she can't bear to think of anymore.

It's discharge day, and the nurses carefully maneuver Jevonte's wheelchair into position. Two orderlies help Jevonte to stand and get him into the wheelchair. Dr. Plemmings hands Jevonte a folder containing paper instructions and aftercare guides.

"Mr. Greene, I know you don't feel as strong as you'd like, but you've made positive progress, and I feel confident that the worst of it is over. Now I want you to go home and get some rest. I've listed some foods I'd like you to include in your diet, along with what I feel you should avoid. If you have any questions or if you start to feel like you're relapsing, don't hesitate to give us a call. Do you have any questions before the nurses help you to the pick-up area?"

"He's fine, and I can take it from here," says Talaitha. "Sorry, I was late," and bends to kiss Jevonte on the cheek.

"Mrs. Greene, hello and good morning. It's hospital policy that the medical staff assist our patients from the point of discharge to the waiting area and ensure that appropriate transportation is waiting for them. I'm sure you agree that Jevonte's well-being is what's most important right now," responds Dr. Plemmings. He was briefed about Talaitha by the discharge nurse and the nurse on duty.

Talaitha smiles, "Why, of course. I understand completely. Ladies, lead the way. King, I'll be right behind you."

Jevonte sits quietly, silently observing the nurses, orderlies, and Dr. Plemmings. He is especially aware of the shift in Talaitha's tone and energy. He says nothing as the nurse wheels him out of the hospital room and down the hallway towards the elevator. Talaitha stands dutifully beside him as they wait on the elevator to reach their floor.

Before the elevator arrives, Dr. Plemmings rushes to catch up with the trio. "Hello, Mrs. Greene, I almost forgot to mention that we have assigned a home health aide to visit Jevonte in a few days."

"We don't need a home health aide. I can take excellent care of my husband, thank you," says Talaitha firmly.

"I apologize. I should have explained this requirement earlier. This requirement is actually a state mandate. Because Mr. Greene's illness is, or might be, linked to possible environmental toxins, state law requires a review and inspection of the home three days after discharge. We really have no choice, and if you refuse the visit, we are obligated to notify the authorities."

Talaitha says nothing at first, and Jevonte begins to tense slightly in the wheelchair, but to his surprise, she says, "Of course, we'll be glad to receive the home health aide."

Jevonte breathes a sigh of relief just as the elevator arrives.

As the orderlies wheel Jevonte to the pick-up area and he signs his discharge papers, Jevonte takes a deep breath and reminisces about the last week he's had at the hospital. It was one of the best weeks he's had in a very long time, even though he was deathly ill. The orderlies wheel Jevonte out of the elevator and park him in the reception area while Talaitha leaves to get her car. His mind, curiously, is on Melanie and her smile. He almost wishes that his hospital stay were longer so that he'd have another chance to spend some time with her. He chuckles within himself and then sags in his chair when he sees Talaitha's car pull up to the hospital entrance.

He watches as Talaitha exits her car and walks around the passenger side. Jevonte's thoughts drift, and a slight melancholy starts to set in as he realizes that what he really has been missing is the one person who's not here right now.

Each morning since being discharged from the hospital, Talaitha has been at Jevonte's beck and call, waiting on him hand and foot. The behavior throws Jevonte off balance, but it feels like a pattern, a dance he should know by now. He's eating everything Talaitha has prepared for him, and he's avoided straining himself moving about the house. The condition of his legs has improved very little, and the doctors informed him that because of the damage caused by whatever he ingested, their recovery would take longer. His interminable weakness is still the same. He hasn't regained much of his strength. He counts his blessings anyhow, seeing as no more fingernails have fallen off, and he looks very human again.

At the breakfast table, Jevonte asks Talaitha, "I need to get in touch with my family. I need to talk to my dad and find out more about my mom's accident. Plus, I have to go to the cemetery once I find out where they've buried her."

"King, I understand. I don't think they have very much information on the accident yet. How about you just let me nurse you back to health, and then we can visit your folks? I'm sure they would rather not see you like this."

"I need to call my dad at least. Do they even know what happened to me? Have you spoken with them?" Jevonte asks pointedly.

"Yes, King, yes. I explained everything to him, and I told him that you would be in contact as soon as it was medically possible. Just eat now. You still have a long road to recovery."

The front doorbell rang, and Jevonte watched as Talaitha rose to answer the door. "Oh my, has it been three days already?" asked Talaitha.

"Hello, Mrs. Greene. "Yes, my name is Ms. Farmington, and I am here for Jevonte's aftercare visit and environmental review," said the home health aide as she handed Talaitha a business card.

"I see. Well, come right in, then. Can I get you anything to drink, some coffee, or water?" asked Talaitha in her clinical, office voice.

"No, thank you. I had some coffee before arriving here. Thank you for offering. I don't think this will take very long at all. Shall we get started?"

The trio sits together in the living room, and the home health aide begins asking questions and jotting down notes. She asks Jevonte questions about what he's been eating, how much rest he's getting, and whether he's been able to get outside or exercise. All of the questions are perfunctory, and once completed, the actual home inspection begins. Talaitha takes the home health aide throughout the home, garage, and backyard. They spend extra time in the greenhouse. The aide admires the building's craftsmanship and what Talaitha has cultivated inside. Finding nothing that would constitute an environmental concern, the pair returns inside, where the aide begins to review the contents of the bathrooms and their medicine cabinets.

While Talaitha and the aide are finishing up in the guest bedroom, Jevonte rises weakly and begins clearing the breakfast dishes. Walking into the kitchen to deposit dishes into the sink, Jevonte's foot swipes something on the floor, just underneath the kitchen counter. He bends down to see what it was. An empty pill bottle lies on its side, and Jevonte retrieves it, examining it closely. It's not one of his prescriptions. The printed label reads, 'Lysergic Acid Diethylamide (LSD)-25.'

Talaitha and the aide return to the kitchen, and Jevonte asks her, "Is this yours, babe? I found it on the kitchen floor, and I know it's not mine."

Talaitha takes the pill bottle from Jevonte and reviews it. "Oh, yes. It is. I must have dropped it the other day after I got home from the office."

The home health aide asked, "What is it?"

"Nothing. I sometimes employ controlled substances in my work as a psychiatrist. LSD is therapeutic in the treatment of some psychological malformations," replies Talaitha, and she quickly stows the bottle in her purse.

"I see," says the aide, and then jots down a few more notes in her binder. "I think I have all I need for now."

"For now?" asks Talaitha.

"Yes. I need to make one more visit before I can close out this case. So far, everything looks in order, and I see nothing that would contribute to Jevonte's illness from an environmental standpoint."

Talaitha starts ushering the home health aide to the front door when the aide stops at the basement door. "Do you all have a basement here?" asks the aide while looking at the closed door.

Jevonte says, "Yes, we do. I completed most of the remodeling down there just before I fell ill."

"I'd like to see it if that's alright," replied the aide.

Talaitha says nothing, but the energy in the room becomes noticeably uncomfortable. "Sure," says Talaitha and opens the door to the basement. "Please watch your step. It's dark down there, and these stairs are a bit steep. I can't have you breaking your neck on your first visit to our home now, can I?" jests Talaitha.

"I'll wait here for you ladies," says Jevonte, still too weak to take a chance on the stairs. Jevonte returns to his task of clearing the dishes and the kitchen table. The effort exhausts him completely, and he shuffles into the living room to try to rest. As he sits, the drapes covering the living room window partially obscure the amber pinprick of light that catches his eye. He nearly missed the blinking light. Jevonte rises gingerly and walks over to the window, where he sees the blinking light. It's so faint, he can hardly find it even though he's standing right in front of it. He pulls back the drapes to find a small microminiature camera. The camera lens is the size of his thumbnail. The little beacon of light is faint, but Jevonte can see it within the center of the lens's eye.

Cautiously, Jevonte scans the rest of the living room. He finds two more cameras, but they are dark and have no blinking lights. Curious now, he begins walking around the house and finds additional cameras placed in odd locations, locations that have nothing to do with monitoring intruders. He even finds cameras in the bathrooms, although those are even smaller and harder to see. "What the hell is going on here?" he muses. Then Jevonte recalls the visits by the satellite technician who installed their home Internet system last month. Why didn't Talaitha tell me she was having these installed? Where do the feeds go?

Jevonte walks toward Talaitha's home office. He wants to see whether cameras have also been installed in there, but the door is locked. Jevonte can almost picture Talaitha monitoring activities from inside her office, but he's bemused as to why she would do that. Jevonte wonders silently and returns to the kitchen just in time to see Talaitha and the aide come from the basement.

"I really need to reexamine that area in the basement. I'll need some equipment from my car first. I'll be right back," says the home health aide and leaves to retrieve her gear from her car.

Talaitha and Jevonte watch her leave, and Jevonte takes note of Talaitha's face. She looks—he struggles to come up with a description—like she's seen a ghost. "Babe, are you alright?"

At first, Talaitha ignores him, but then she seems to come out of a stupor and says, "I'm fine. Why do you ask?"

"You look different, that's all. Was everything ok down in the basement? Did she find something harmful down there?

"Stop with all of these fucking questions. Go lie down somewhere. You know you shouldn't be up on your feet like this anyway. Remember what the doctor said?"

"Love, I was just asking…" Talaitha interrupts him mid-sentence by grabbing his arm and forcefully pulling him down the hallway and into the bedroom.

"Here, take two of these, and please, just lie down. I don't have time to coddle you now." Talaitha hands Jevonte two pills she pulls from a container inside one of the nightstands in the room.

"Wait, what are these? Jevonte asks in protest.

"They're sedatives and will help you get some sleep. You need these. They're safe. I use them with my patients all the time, so take them, and I'll get you water."

Jevonte is too weak and worn out to argue or ask any more questions, so when Talaitha returns with the water, he takes the pills and lies down on the bed. In minutes, Jevonte is fast asleep.

The home health aide returns with a small soil sampler and some other equipment. Talaitha opens the basement door for her and starts heading down to the basement behind the aide.

"Mrs. Greene, you don't need to be here. I'm just going to take a small air and soil sample and swab a few surfaces and be done."

Talaitha doesn't respond and closes the basement door behind her. The aide positions her equipment along the open pit on the basement floor and starts prepping the other instruments she brought. The aide withdraws a small spade from her bag, scoops out a small bit of soil, and then deposits it into several vials. She begins working the soil over, then scrapes off some of the topsoil and places the samples inside the sampler. She presses a button on the sampler, and it lights up and starts humming. The sampler's front panel has several small indicator lights that rotate through green, yellow, and red. After flashing intermittently, all three indicator lights begin flashing red, and the sampler's alarm begins to sound.

"Oh dear," muttered the aide. "This is not good. I think we need to…" Talaitha's hands clamp around her neck with such force that the sound of cracking bone pierces her voice. The aide's eyes bulge with fear and horror, and she struggles to pry Talaitha's hands from her neck. Talaitha shoves the aide face down into the soil of the open pit and bears down on her neck and spine. After several minutes, the aide stops moving; her mouth becomes packed with the black soil of the tainted earth.

Talaitha rises and brushes the dirt from her pants and knees. She stares down at the little aide, her head buried to her ears in the dirt, her body and legs sprayed. She looks like she's drinking from a pool of water, face-first. She surveys the basement and locates some of Jevonte's tools. The bow and chainsaw he has hanging on the wall should suffice nicely, and Talaitha sets her mind to work while Jevonte is asleep.

In the cool of the basement, as she begins pulling the chainsaw from its spot on the wall, a strange memory intrudes upon her. She's been here before. Pushed and prodded, made to obey and cower, she remembers a time when she promised herself never, ever to allow anyone or anything to control her. Talaitha stands with the chainsaw in her hand, and a flood of memories assails her mind; she has to sit; the weight of so much pain is too much to bear. Twenty-four years ago, things were different. Twenty-four years ago was the first time she had to kill someone. Twenty-four years ago, she experienced freedom for the first time in her life.

14

Talaitha's Story

I am seething with anger right now. I feel like a caged tiger, pacing back and forth, waiting to pounce on the first idiot who comes too close. I have nearly reached my limit with him. I work hard, have worked hard, and I am not about to let some fat cow come in here and take everything from me. I can't, and I won't. I know the nurses think I'm being stubborn, and that quack of a doctor thinks I'm stupid. I'm sure they all did at first, but I'll fix them. I'll fix them all.

I review the assortment of tools Jevonte has stored in the basement. "It's a good thing that my king keeps his tools in excellent working order," I say to myself, walking to this workbench. I doubt he'll hear any of this with the number of sedatives I gave him. Still, I know I need to work fast and find someplace else to discard the remains. I glance over at the freshly dug-up soil, "My babies won't like all this blood. But first, it's time to minimize and reduce!"

As I set about the gruesome task of disposing of the home health aide's body, my thoughts are of another time, early in my life, a place and time that taught me who I needed to be. I can't dwell on the past for too long, but my training informs me that it's often necessary. I know this. I do, but even now, after all of these years, I can barely bring myself to do it. I know that I wasn't allowed to become the woman I needed to be, and I also realize that my past traumas have shaped me in ways people won't understand. I know Jevonte won't, but perhaps one day, I will find a way to show him who I really am. As much as I wish I could forget everything, I can't. Some of these ghosts have refused to leave me alone.

I remember so clearly; it was a frigid night in December, twenty-six years ago. Christmas was only a week away. There was no tree. There were no presents to be found. We had no expectations. There were just us, two little girls sharing a room at 215 East Mary Street in Cumberland, Maryland. We never expected anything anymore. However, on that cold December night, I remember that something did change, and from that night on, I learned to expect pain, especially at night.

I was only eleven, but I knew the difference between good adult conversations and bad ones. I can remember lying still and silent in my bed, listening to my parents argue and fight. My twin sister, Noelle, was as quiet as a church mouse in the bed across from me. To call what we slept on beds was way too generous. The rusted metal frames of our beds were connected by springs, and the wire was wrapped so poorly that it could barely support pallets of blankets and sheets. There were no mattresses. As long as we lay still, we could hear the argument as though it were happening in our room.

"You have got to be out of your goddamn mind, woman. How in the hell is Charlie giving us twenty tonight? Didn't I tell you to make sure he paid fifty or one hundred for both?" You must be either crazy or stupid, or perhaps both."

I quietly crept out of my bed to peep through the side of the door. Noelle didn't move, but I could tell she was watching me. I could feel her eyes on me.

"Fuck you. If you wanted more money, you should have set it up yourself. I'm not your slave, Rufus," and before Momma could say another word, Daddy backhanded her across the face. Latriece crashed backwards and bounced off the stove, almost spilling the pot of greens that had been cooking on top. She lay there, cowering, her hands raised to fend off more strikes, but Rufus turned and walked away, mumbling, "If you want something done right, you have to do it yourself."

I just about jumped out of my skin trying to get back under my covers when Daddy started for our room. It felt like forever before he got to our door. The bedroom door swung open, and I lifted my head to see who had opened it, but I knew.

"Get up, girl. We're going out, so hurry," remarked Rufus.

"Where are we going, Daddy?" I asked, my voice tiny and barely audible over the pounding in my chest.

"Don't worry about that; just get dressed. There's work to be done."

"What about Noelle?" I remember asking. My voice trembled, and I don't know why I asked about Noelle. I think I was hoping she would stand with me so I wouldn't feel so scared.

Rufus paused and looked over at Noelle's bed. Noelle remained motionless. "I'm talking to you, not her; now get going. I'll be back in three minutes, and you better be dressed." I can remember the biting cold of the car ride that night and the silence and fear that gripped my every thought. Most of all, I remember how helpless I felt.

I shake myself and come back to the present. The chainsaw is stubborn to start at first, but with a few determined yanks, the small engine fires up and the chained blades whirl in near-invisible rolls of instant destruction. The exhaust begins to fill the basement, so I crack open the walk-out door to let some of the fumes out. Turning back to the open pit and the home health aide's lifeless body, I start to stare into the darkness of the black upturned soil in the pit. My cleanup effort has triggered so many memories. I can't stop thinking about that cold December night two decades ago. The task at hand is gruesome enough, but that night, nothing could come close to that night.

I remember that Rufus didn't have to drive very far. In fact, I knew where we were going by the houses we passed. Some of my friends and I used to play outside the nearby church grounds every Saturday. The same elder had been pastoring the church, First Baptist Assembly of Joy, for almost twenty years. My parents called him 'Bishop,' although he had never been ordained as such. The church's playground was the only fun place for Black kids in Cumberland, and we loved it. Friendships formed around the monkey bars and ended on the swing set. There were so many pleasant memories—until they weren't.

Damn, I can still see the church and the playground in my mind. I remember thinking it was too late and too cold to have playtime out here, and that the other kids were where? Rufus pulled into the church parking lot, drove to the back, and parked next to a dark-colored van. Both vehicles were shielded from the main street by the church, but it was late at night, and the streetlights hadn't worked along that stretch of the street for years, so the area the van occupied was very dark. I didn't recognize the van that night, but I never forgot about it after. My daddy turned off the car and said, "Stay here. I will be right back."

Rufus got out of the car and walked over to the driver's side window. I remember straining to see who was inside. I thought I saw Mr. Dandrich, but I was so sleepy, and the cold air was blurring my vision. Daddy took an envelope from the man, and the man rolled up his window. Daddy returned to the passenger side of the car and opened it. The cold wind made me shudder terribly.

"Let's go, girl," Rufus said.

"Daddy, I'm cold. I want to go home."

Rufus reached into the car, grabbed me by the arm and began dragging me towards the van. "Listen, child," Rufus growled. "Stand up and get in the van. Do what I tell you, and I don't want to hear any back talk," Rufus said and shook me like a discarded rag doll.

The van's sliding door opened, and the darkness inside made me recoil. In my mind, the open door was a vast emptiness and darkness. It looked solid, impenetrable, until a man's voice called me to come in, and then Mr. Dandrich's face pierced the veil of shadows cloaking the inside of the van. I was trembling, but not from the bone-chilling air.

"Daddy, please. I want to go home," I cried. I strained against my father's grip, but to no avail. I was just too little.

Mr. Dandrich's burly hands grabbed me by the arm and pulled me into the van. I thought he was a demon of some kind, and I was petrified. As the van door slid closed, I remember seeing my daddy's back as he walked slowly to his car. He didn't even look back at me when I screamed his name.

Something deep inside me broke that night. It wasn't just the hours of terror and pain my little body endured that night that changed me. I think my soul died. When the van's side door finally opened two hours later, what spilled out was not just a horribly torn human being but a battered, shattered prologue to a new world of disordered psychic pain that would remain my constant dark companion for life.

I remember how, on some nights, a series of cars and trucks would pull into the church's parking lot, each at a designated time. Despite my cries, no matter how I fought, and regardless of how big, filthy, and disgusting the men were, Daddy always turned a deaf ear and a blind eye to the hell I suffered. Two hundred and fifty dollars in the first week, then nine hundred the next, and by week four, Rufus counted fifteen hundred dollars and some change for the 'service' his daughter provided. I remember him bragging to Momma about how much money I was making him.

I need to snap out of all this, this trip down memory lane. Time to take a deep breath and put this chainsaw to work. It's going to be messy, but it should go fast. By the time I finish, the home health aide will be gone.

A few hours later, my body was drenched in sweat, and I had to take some breaks to stretch my back. I'm in great shape, but there are some things you can never really prepare your body for—like dismembering a human being. I didn't mind. The ache felt good; besides, the soil needed to be tilled and turned. The excavation was good work, and I knew my home garden needed it. Once I separate and reduce the body parts so that they can be submerged and buried deep enough to feed the microorganisms, the darkened, rich soil will serve my babies very well.

Then it hit me: there is a lot of DNA evidence around the pit now, shit. What was I thinking? I should have put something down around the edges to soak up all of this blood. I'm getting careless. What's done is done. I'll come back down and clean up more thoroughly once I check in on Mr. Sleepyhead.

I need to get some of her brain matter off of me now, though. I know how I must look. Jevonte would freak out if he saw me like this, so I walked over to the deep sink abutting the workbench and turned on the hot water. The hand cleaner feels good, and it's strong. I begin massaging the soap into my hands, turning them over and over, being careful to get under the nails. I let the hot water flow over my hands, and more memories begin to distract me—luckily—from the discomfort of the hot water.

Standing at the deep sink, I can remember, as though it were yesterday, how, as a little girl, I would curl up into a tight ball at night, hoping that Rufus would let me be, that maybe, just maybe, he would drag my sister out of her bed instead for a change. It never happened, but eventually, things did change—for the worse. On that night, it wasn't Rufus that opened our bedroom door. It was Latriece who visited us. She was worse than Rufus because she was supposed to be our mom, but she was never a mother to us. We, no, I, were just commodities to be sold and traded on our living room floor. She was so bold and cruel. She walked into our room like she was getting us for school, like it was just another day, except it wasn't. She sat on my bed, and the pallet of springs and blankets almost collapsed onto the floor.

In her mommy voice, she said, "Sweetheart, wake up. I have some friends I want you to meet," and I tried to ignore her. I begged her with all my heart. I told her it was too cold, that I was freezing, and that my stomach hurt really badly. She didn't care.

"Nooo, child. You are not going outside. Come on, get up," she said, and she started pulling back my blankets. The warmth of the covers evaporated quickly, and I started shivering as soon as I got out of bed. Latriece took me by the hand gently, almost lovingly, and led me out into the dimmed light of the living room. I could barely see, and I had to squint at first, but as my eyes adjusted to the light, I remember seeing two men seated on the couch. I didn't recognize either man, but neither looked old or young. They reminded me of Rufus.

I pleaded with Latriece, but my words fell on deaf ears. "Momma, I'm sleepy," I said, and I even tried to pull her back towards my room.

"Now, now, there, Talaitha, these two fine gentlemen came all this way to see you. They're good men, and they want to help us, so you do what they ask. Do you understand?" she told me. She was lying to my face, and it was so easy for her. I hated her.

"Momma, where is Daddy?" I asked. I wanted to do something even if it meant appealing to a far harsher monster.

"Rufus is working; your daddy isn't here right now, but these men are going to help us get away from this place, ya hear me?" and she walked me over to where the two men were sitting.

The man on her right said, "Hey, little lady, how are you? You're such a pretty little thing, aren't you? Now, don't be afraid; my cousin and I want to help you and your momma. Is that alright?"

I remember feeling sick. I wanted to throw up all over the man's shiny shoes. I almost did until the other man seemed to come to life. He got up, walked over to Latriece, and handed her something. I couldn't see what it was. I was so tired and sleepy. The man followed my mom to the back room, but then my mom came back out. Without even looking at me, she just walked out the front door. The man who first spoke to me stood and began guiding me towards the back room.

I shake myself and splash water on my face. The memories are so vivid and—to me, surprise—new. I've had glimpses and flashes of the past before, but right now, here in the dank gloom of the basement, deep, buried psychic traumas have started emerging as never before. I resume drying her face, then turn back to the pit to assess the work I was going to have to do to eliminate any DNA left behind, when I am suddenly assaulted by searing, stabbing pain across the front of my head. The pain is so intense that I fall to my knees and have to lie on my back.

My vision is chaotic and scattered, and I lie on the cold basement floor, trying to control my breathing. I close her eyes, and to my relief, the throbbing spike of pain pushing through my temple begins to ease.

What just happened? I've never felt pain of that magnitude since the night those two men visited, and Rufus came home the next day. Talaitha's recall is instant, and again, she finds herself reliving that horrible day in the living room.

I remember now. I remember that morning well. I hurt so bad—and the blood, now cold and plastered to the sheets, was everywhere. I fell out of bed, my little body battered and bruised. I tried walking out of the room but couldn't, and I collapsed in a heap. I wanted to die, right there, in the middle of the room, so that I could escape into nothingness and be free.

When Rufus came home and found me lying on the floor, he first went in search of Latriece, but she was gone. Coming to me, he just stared at me, this ruined ball of blood and bruises, at first not recognizing who I was. Then I moaned and started crying, and a spark of recognition entered his eyes. His next words raked my soul raw. "You stupid hoe, get your dumb ass up off the floor! What the fuck do you think this is?" and he stepped over my little body. When Rufus walked into the bedroom, he became enraged, not because of what he saw—the blood and brown-stained sheets—but because of what was missing. "Where's your bitch momma, girl?" Rufus yelled from the bedroom. I could only lie there in a sobbing heap of pain and sorrow. My throat hurt, and my bottom was throbbing with pain. I tried crawling toward my room, but Rufus grabbed me by the leg and hauled me into the air until I hung upside down, one leg in his iron grip, the other limb dangling lifeless. In his free hand, Rufus swung his belt, and after the second strike, I lost consciousness.

The memory ends, and I gather myself and stand on my feet. The distant recollections of a harrowing time in my young life cause my hair to bristle on my neck. I shake my head, clearing my mind of the painful thoughts, and start up the basement stairs.

He's still asleep. Damn, did I overdo it again? I can't worry about that now. I need to do something about the aides' car. I spotted her purse and prayed her keys were inside. After rooting around inside the aide's purse and finding her car keys, I headed out the front door. My head is clear. Hopefully, I don't experience any more headaches. I need my wits now. I can't make any more mistakes. There is too much at stake.

I hadn't planned on this, but I have to think on my feet now. I knew this place was going to be a good place to buy a house. My idiot neighbors are spread out, so I don't think anyone has seen this car in my driveway. I'll drive the car into Baltimore and just leave it. I'm positive someone will take care of it there.

I pull out my cell phone and launch the monitoring application. It's still a little buggy, but video footage of the house's interior and the room Jevonte is in comes into view. I relax and start heading for the interstate. But I changed my mind before getting to the on-ramp. The EZ Pass monitors capture video images of the cars, and, thinking ahead, I don't want any future investigation into the aide's whereabouts to center on why I am driving her vehicle.

Circumventing the highway cameras and EZ Pass monitors will add an extra hour of drive time, but it will allow me to relax and think more about my next move. My time alone also allows past experiences and memories to slip past my mental guards. The bouncing monotony of the endless country roads lulls me into a heightened awareness of how far I've come. My thoughts again begin to drift, tracing long-buried experiences that nearly ended my life so many years ago.

I think about the first kindness shown to me when I was in middle school. Ms. Gladys Topeeka was my science teacher, my favorite teacher, in fact. She was the only Black teacher in my grade. Until Ms. Topeeka's class, little me had never been recognized for my schoolwork. I loved to come to Ms. Topeeka's classroom. It always felt safe and warm. I thrived in that learning space—until one day before the Thanksgiving break.

All of the pain and suffering I endured in the back seats of cars, the floors of vans, and even in my own home allowed Latriece to bring home groceries and all kinds of Thanksgiving place settings and decorations for the home. I was a cash cow for my parents. This is how they justified what they made me do. I remember how the mood in the house was better than it had been in a long time. Noelle and I were in our room, cleaning it and getting ready for the day. Rufus had not come home from work yet, and for a moment, we were both relieved, me more so than Noelle.

I always had to get on Noelle because, well, she was stupid. She did things that would provoke Daddy, and I'd be the one he would discipline. She would leave her clothes on the floor or forget to flush the toilet. "Don't leave that on the floor," I would tell her. "You know how Daddy gets when we leave stuff on the floor like that," I warned her.

For once, my stupid sister did what I told her and picked up the towel and tossed it into the dirty clothes hamper. "When do you think he's going to be home?" asked Noelle, her face holding a weak but gentle smile.

Her stupid smile made me mad, so I said, "I don't care. I hope he never comes home. I hate him!" I replied with every bit of acrid vinegar my voice could muster.

"Don't let Momma hear you say that, Talaitha."

"Who cares? I don't! I hate her too!" I said.

"You hate Momma? Talaitha, she's our mom…"

She triggered me so badly at times. I exploded. "Why is it always me? It's always me who has to do the work! How come they never pick you? You never have to go with the big men, ever. I hate you, too, Noelle," I remember saying so clearly. We locked eyes, and I was ready to punch her dead in the face if she kept pushing me, but she started staring at the floor like she usually did when she caved. I could always read her like a book. Maybe that's why I loathed her so much. She never fought back, and she never stood up for me when Daddy was selling me to the men in the neighborhood.

"I don't hate you, Talaitha. You're my sister. I could never hate you. Please don't hate me," she pleaded.

"Just shut up and clean up the rest of the room. I'm going outside," I said.

"But we can't. We have to finish our chores first and…"

I was done. I hauled off and slapped her across the face, sending her into a state of sudden shock and surprise.

Using the words of our father, I told her, "I don't want to hear any back talk. Just get this room cleaned up, you hear me?" And then I stormed out of the room, but I didn't get far because guess who nearly crashed into me when I left the room? Latriece. She was standing in the living room, her arms full of two bags, her eyes focused on me.

I remember starting to turn and run in the opposite direction. "Where do you think you're going, heifer?" Latriece asked me as she walked to the kitchen counter to set the bags down.

I changed my mind about running. I knew it would only make things worse, so I tried to be polite and obedient. "Nowhere, ma'am," I said meekly. "I was just coming out to see if you needed any help," I lied. "Is Daddy home too?"

"Well, you're out here now, and yes, he's in the garage. He wants to see you out there now. See what he wants and make it quick. This chicken won't cook itself."

Oh God. I don't want to see him, but I know I have no choice. I remember that walk. It was like the walk of death. I walked through the kitchen and opened the door to the garage, and I could hear Rufus and a few other men laughing and bickering. The laughter stopped when the men noticed me entering the garage. All eyes were on me, and I tried to make myself small and invisible.

"Come here, girl," one of the men said. I saw him pass a roll of bills to Rufus, who pocketed the money, then walked out of the garage. Before the door could close behind Rufus, I bolted for the kitchen. I ran past Rufus and headed for the front door, but Latriece snatched my thick braided ponytail as I was passing by. A yelp of pain escaped my mouth, and I fell on my butt.

"Turn that bitch loose, Latriece. She's messing with my money now; turn her loose," I heard Rufus rage, and he cleared the distance between the garage door and me in almost a single bound. I fought hard this time. I remember kicking and screaming, but he slapped me so hard I thought he broke my face. I went limp with compliance. The rest was a blur. When I woke, I was lying on the garage floor. The men were all gone, but my private parts were hurting, and there was blood in my panties. My face felt bruised, and my neck was very sore to the touch.

After I managed to stand, the garage door swung open, and Rufus stood in its frame, leather belt swaying in his hand. "This is the last time you embarrass me; do you hear me?" and he closed the door. At the dinner table, Latriece sat, cigarette in hand, scrolling through her text messages. Noelle sat stone-like, but she flinched with each strike and cry from inside the garage. She couldn't taste her food, and tears began to form in her eyes.

"Do you want some of that, too?" asks Latriece, staring intently at Noelle.

Noelle shakes her head slowly, feeling defeated and terrified for Talaitha.

"No, well then, straighten your face and be quick about it."

The monsters that gave birth to me were cruel. I will never forget that about them, but one other thing I won't forget is how stupid they were. After my beating and rape, they thought it would be ok to send me to school the next day. They dressed me in long sleeves and a long dress and told me not to say anything to anyone at school. I went to school looking like a homeless child auditioning for Little House on the Prairie—as a runaway slave, of course. It was the last day before the holiday break. The only thing that got me through the day was the knowledge that I would get to see Ms. Topeeka one more time.

Ms. Topeeka stood at the entrance of her classroom. She had bags of goodies for all of her students. "Listen, everyone. Make sure you save some of these for later. I don't want you ruining your appetite before turkey day," and she hugged each child after giving them their own ribbon-wrapped bag with their name on it. I remember limping up to Ms. Topeeka and gingerly reaching for a bag. Ms. Topeeka noticed that I couldn't fully extend my arm.

"Honey, what's the matter? Are you alright?" she asked, and she wrapped her arms around my petite frame.

I couldn't help it, and I flinched and drew back. "I'm ok, Ms. Topeeka," I said. I wanted to tell her I wasn't ok, but I was warned not to say anything.

"Now, sweetheart, come here for a minute, please," Ms. Topeeka asked me with so much kindness. I hesitated. I stood still, frozen in the middle of Ms. Topeeka's doorway. Ms. Topeeka made a space next to her where she wanted me to stand while she finished passing out the remaining goody bags. After the last child received their bag, Ms. Topeeka closed the classroom door and turned to face me. She knelt in front of me and looked me in the eye. I just started crying.

"Am I in trouble, Ms. Topeeka?" My little voice was barely audible over the sobbing and tears.

"Oh, honey, no. No, sweetheart. You're not in any trouble. I just want to make sure you are alright, ok? I promise you. You are not in trouble. Now, tell me where it hurts, ok. I pointed at my back and buttocks. "Turn around for me, love," asked Ms. Topeeka gently. I turned around slowly, and my favorite teacher lifted my dingy, hem-tattered dress. For the space of 20 seconds, Ms. Topeeka said nothing. She stared in horror at the deep wounds crisscrossing my buttocks; some marks were scabbed over, and others were still swollen red. She lowered the dress and began examining my back and sides, pressing softly and gently along my stomach and ribs. Everything hurt, and I flinched with every touch, no matter how softly she touched me.

Her eyes filled with tears, and Ms. Topeeka said, "Baby, who did this to you? Who hurt you like this?" Our eyes met, but I couldn't get the words out. All I could do was cry and nod my head. Ms. Topeeka let her own tears fall, and she stretched her arms wide to let me fall into them, however I could. She gently, slowly embraced me until we were both crying and sobbing together in the middle of an empty classroom.

Christmas came a month early for my sister and me back then. I will never forget the look on Rufus and Latriece's faces as the cops handcuffed them both and walked them to the police car. It was probably the only time my sister and I ever embraced. I remember how we held each other tightly in the middle of our living room as child protective services and the police talked in our kitchen. Plans were made, and then we were removed from that house of horrors. I remembered being told that we would no longer have to live in that house and that a new home would be found for us, someplace safe, somewhere no one would hurt us again.

Although this city often receives a negative reputation, it's ideal for certain tasks, such as disposing of this car. If I leave it in the right place, the denizens will strip it for parts in no time. Ah, here we go. I see a spot no one will pay much attention to in the Cherry Hill Urban Community Garden.

After removing the license plates, I quickly walk to the corner and call for an Uber to take me back home.

"Before we get started, I need to modify the trip. I need to go to my office; can you do that?" I ask the Uber driver, who nods. "I'll need you to wait once I get there. Don't worry, I will make it worth your time."

I need to make this appointment quickly. Jevonte is not going to stay asleep much longer, and I still need to get the basement straight before he wakes and gets curious. I arrive at the office in time to see a new patient in my waiting room. My receptionist greets me and follows me into my office.

"Dr. Mercedes, I apologize for not alerting you sooner. The gentleman in the waiting area said that you scheduled an off-book appointment for him. Do you still want to see him?"

This child is as dense as they come. I really don't have time to see anyone today, not today, of all days. Still, why do I get the sense that I know him, or I've seen him before? "It's ok. Give me a few minutes to get some of my files in order, and I'll notify you when to see him in," I respond.

I take a seat at my desk and place a call to my Uber driver, releasing him. I can hear him cursing me as he hangs up. I open my desktop monitoring program and watch Jevonte turn in his sleep. Good, he's still under, but probably not for too much longer. I'll take care of this quick appointment and head back home.

I begin scanning my appointments and patient files, but there is no entry for an off-book patient appointment. I grab a legal pad and buzz the receptionist. The receptionist walks through the door, trailed by the new patient.

"Hello, sir. My name is Dr. Talaitha Mercedes. How are you today?" I motion for the new patient to take a seat on the couch in my office.

"Hi. Please, you can call me Nolan. Pleased to meet you finally."

That's a strange thing to say. Has this joker been to this office before? I don't recognize him, but, hmmm, I can't put my finger on it, but he does seem familiar. Apparently, he seems to think he's met me before. Let's see where the conversation goes.

"Well, Nolan, I am glad you found your way here. Tell me what I can do for you. My receptionist told me this was an off-book appointment, but I have no records of this in my personal files or calendar. Have we spoken previously?"

"We have met before, doctor. It was a very long time ago, and I'm sure you will remember in a little while. You see, I haven't always been this way, like I am now. I don't like to share the truth about myself because, well, you know, I'm sure, once you tell people certain things about yourself, they start acting weird. They stop seeing you, the real you, I mean. Most people simply cannot handle the truth, regardless of how gently you present it to them; do you understand what I mean?"

A brief silence ensues between us before I say, "I have to be honest, Nolan, I don't think we've ever met, but you do seem familiar to me. I'm not sure how yet, so for now, please tell me a little bit about yourself and why you sought me out. Let's start there, ok?"

"Of course. I was born and raised in Cumberland, Maryland. Are you familiar with it?"

Cumberland. He did say Cumberland. I wonder silently, What the hell is this, and who is this guy? I don't think I've ever met anyone from that God-forsaken place. "Cumberland, huh? I don't think I've heard of that place. What part of Maryland is it in?" I lie while staring at the blank legal pad in my lap.

"Are you sure you've never heard of Cumberland, Dr. Mercedes? I would think you are very familiar with that town, seeing as you were born there too," Nolan replied coolly.

I stop writing on my legal pad and lay the pen down. Who is this man, and how does he know that I'm from Cumberland? No one in this office knows that. Perhaps I need to move back to my desk just in case he tries something. I could take him from here, but I need an advantage, just in case.

"Listen, Nolan. I believe you are misinformed, but it's ok. You came here for a reason, right? You need my help, so what can I help you with?" I reengage Nolan's gaze with a firm, commanding glare while positioning my feet and posture for a quick response if necessary.

"How's old Rufus doing these days, Talaitha? Heard from Latriece lately?" asks Nolan in a deadpan, eerie voice.

My mouth parts slightly in shock and simmering anger, but before I can find a response, my office door suddenly swings open, and Melanie—with the receptionist in tow—steps into my office.

"Ma'am! Ma'am, please stop. You can't go in there! Dr. Mercedes, shall I call security?"

Melanie stops just feet away from me. We lock eyes, and I stand; my legal pad slides off my lap to the floor. Nolan remains seated, his face a stone, absent of surprise or concern at the sudden intrusion.

"It's ok. I can handle her. Please see Mr. Nolan out and reschedule something official with him," I instruct my receptionist.

Nolan remains seated and slowly uncrosses his legs. He looks between the two women who appear locked in a mental struggle for control of the room, neither breaking eye contact to acknowledge him. Finally, Nolan rises and turns to follow the receptionist as she heads for the door. Nolan pauses briefly before exiting and looking back over his shoulder, says, "We will speak again soon, my sister," and leaves the office. With that, I break eye contact with Melanie, my eyes now burning a hole through the office door.

I don't know who he thinks he is, but none of my patients are familiar enough with me to speak to me like this. I'll have to set Mr. Nolan straight, but first, let me deal with this sow.

"Melanie!" I effuse insincerely. "What, pray tell, brings you to my office?"

"Cut the shit, Talaitha. I think you know why I'm here."

"No, my dear. Please, enlighten me."

"I know what you've been doing to Jevonte. I saw the blood work and the lab results. And don't try to bullshit me because I'm a nurse, and I can read medical charts. I know what I'm seeing in Jevonte's charts and blood work."

This bitch! Let me sit down before I have to send her on a one-way trip to the pavement outside. She obviously doesn't know who she is dealing with, but let's play the game out a little.

"Honey, listen to me carefully because I'm only going to say this one time. There is no way you could have passed your clinicals and the state board if you surmised from Jevonte's charts and lab work that he was poisoned. If you believe that, based on his file, which begs the question of how they came into your possession in the first place, then every patient you've ever come in contact with is in grave danger because you're either grossly incompetent or too stupid to breathe. You shouldn't have any contact with patients, period," and I move to the side of my desk so I can keep an eye on the monitoring software. Jevonte is not in the bed!

What the hell. Damn it all. I don't have time for this bitch, not now anyway. I need to get rid of her. Why is she staring at me like that? I may have hit a nerve. Wait, she doesn't know that I saw her break into my house. I have this heifer on video!

Melanie stands stock-still, her arms folded across her ample bosom. She looks at Talaitha's office window, and a plan begins to form in her thoughts. "Oh, I know what I saw, and trust me when I say this because I will not repeat myself either; you are done. I will expose you for the fraud you are, Talaitha."

"Go ahead and try. Go right ahead and make a fool of yourself. Show everyone Jevonte's file and his blood work. Do that, and I promise you'll never work in the healthcare field again. Indeed, you will be as old as dust and as useful as fertilizer by the time you emerge from prison after violating my husband's privacy and HIPAA rights. Go ahead and try me, heifer."

"Talaitha, you don't scare me. You don't matter here; Jevonte does. I'm going to see to it that he leaves you if it's the last thing I do. Once I tell him what you've been doing, nothing else will matter. You will have loss, and you can twist that into a knot and spin on it!"

"Hoe, Jevonte, will never leave me. He may have been infatuated with your fat ass at one time in his life, but he has a real woman now. We're solid, but listen, you're welcome to try if you'd like to," I say, grinning gleefully.

"Is that all you've got? I feel sorry for you, Talaitha. You can call me names and make fun of my weight all you want; it just shows me how weak and insecure you are."

Sensing an opening in Melanie's psyche from the guarded way she is standing, holding herself, and covering her midsection with her folded arms, I continue my assault.

"I hate to have to be the one to tell you, but Jevonte isn't into jelly rolls like that. Blubber like that turns him off. He likes his pussy wrapped tight because he wants to feel safe and held in place, locked down and secure. He needs someone who won't abandon him during his most vulnerable moments, such as when he was in college."

I bet you felt that one, didn't you? I think to myself.

"You're a monster. You are a horrible person. I don't know what Jevonte ever saw in you. I…"

"And you wouldn't know because all Jevonte ever saw in you was the pitiful fat girl that everyone made fun of. He took pity on you and hung out with you while you guys were in school, but the real reason he left was that he couldn't take the weight anymore. It just got to be too much to bear!" I laugh derisively.

"Laugh all you want, Talaitha, but remember this: I will make sure you pay for what you've done, and when I do, I will be the one laughing. You don't fool me, and now I know exactly who you are," responded Melanie defiantly.

"Get the fuck out of my office before I call a U-Haul to transport your fat, sloppy ass out of here. The next time you come here or break into my house, I will have you arrested and won't lose a minute of sleep over it."

Melanie doesn't say a word. She looks into Talaitha's eyes, understanding now dawning over what she meant by 'breaking in.' She turns, walks out of the office, and glances at Nolan, the lone patient who is still sitting in the waiting area. After a few minutes, Nolan decides to leave too, having gathered an earful of the confrontation in Talaitha's office. He has a plan now, one that makes sense to him and will soon make sense to Talaitha as well.

After Melanie's departure, I took a few minutes to reset and practiced slowing my breathing. During my days as a patient and then as a student-employee, I learned various breathing techniques that helped me stay calm and lower my heart rate. I could not afford to lose control now.

That fat girl gets on my nerves, and now I'd better hurry and grab my things, but let me check one more time to see where that husband of mine went. I paid too much for this system, and if it can't track where he has run off to, a certain technician I paid handsomely will rue the day he failed me.

I meticulously examine each camera strategically placed throughout the home, only to find Jevonte absent. I meditate, wondering where he could have gone, then one of the motion sensors triggers the camera in the rear of the house.

There he is, whew. Gotcha.

Now that I have eyes on him again, I can shut the system down and head home. My mind is abuzz with questions, and I can feel the early threads of anxiety creeping in. "Get ahold of yourself, girl," Talaitha said out loud.

Once inside the elevator, I opened my cell phone and logged in to my home system. There, on the couch, lay Jevonte, a pillow and sheet wrapped around his frail-looking body.

He never listens. This is the problem, and this is why I must become the other person, the person I don't want to be. People don't understand. After all I have done for them, and they still try to disobey me. They try, but rules exist for a reason. I don't know why people won't follow my instructions.

Once downstairs, it dawned on me that I needed a ride home. I didn't want to sign out of my phone's monitoring app, so I told the front desk to call me an Uber. They made the call, and I sat in the lobby, waiting. I watched my husband sleep. He looked so small. I felt sorry for him at that moment, but that quickly passed. My creation was almost ready. I just needed to shape him a bit more, and he would be perfect. He would be the last man I ever loved, and he would never be able to leave me, ever.

Once in the Uber, I drifted off to sleep. I know they tell you not to do that because, well, it can be dangerous, but I didn't care. I let myself sink into a peaceful slumber, one that revealed more memories in my dreams.

15

Between Breath and Surrender

It's late in the afternoon, and Jevonte can finally move around better. He shifts on the couch, then sits upright. He feels like he's hungover. Ignoring it, he swings his feet to the floor and tries to stand. He's unsteady but manages to reach the full upright position. Yay me! He thought. But the room starts to spin, so he lets himself fall back down on the couch. The effort makes him feel queasy, so he sits still for a few minutes until the urge to barf subsides.

Jevonte feels like death warmed over. He can't stay on this couch all night, and God, he needs a shower. Let me try this one more time. He thinks to himself.

Jevonte bends forward, and using his right hand and arm, he manages to gain a little momentum to stand. Listening to the sudden quietness that eerily permeates the house, he carefully starts to shuffle his way back to the bedroom. The floor feels slanted, and he leans in the opposite direction to counter the imbalance, but since the floor is anything but slanted, he careens into the wall leading to the hallway. He faceplants into the wall, his arms and hands too slow to cushion the impact. He crashes in a heap, dazed but too stunned to care.

Jevonte just lay there; a small knot began to form on his forehead. If he weren't feeling awful, he would have started laughing, but he couldn't; even that hurt. As he lay on the floor, he wondered where Talaitha was. He couldn't remember how he even got to their bed, but the last thing he remembered was the nursing aide. Everyone is gone now. Wait, Jevonte thought to himself—didn't I see them go into the basement to do something or look for something?

Jevonte saw that the basement door was closed, and no sounds were coming from that area. He still found it difficult to stand and didn't want to attempt another nosedive into any other walls, so he started crawling—more like slithering—across the floor towards the basement door. The coolness of the kitchen floor soothed Jevonte. He took his time, pausing between humps and pumps. He looked like an overgrown inchworm, alternating between molesting the floor and elbow shuffles. He wasn't making much progress, but he was determined, and after a few minutes of effort, he finally reached the door.

Jevonte stopped and maneuvered his body so that he could sit upright and lean against the door. From this position, after he gained his wind, he would be able to open the door and see what was happening in the basement.

"King, what in the world are you doing on the floor?" Talaitha shouted from the front door.

Jevonte turned to see his wife walking towards him, and he smiled. "Babe, I just needed to get out of bed. I was trying to get down into the basement, but I could barely stand. I feel so weak and drugged out," Jevonte said, his eyes taking her in weakly. "I thought maybe you and the aide were still down there, doing things," he smiled jokingly.

Talaitha doesn't respond immediately. She continues into the house and walks past where Jevonte is sitting. She places her work tote on the desk chair and then walks to the kitchen cabinet to get a glass of water. After filling her glass, she drinks standing at the kitchen sink, the cold water temporarily distracting her thoughts.

Jevonte blinks slowly and begins shaking his head. "What's going on, Tal? Why aren't you speaking to me? Did I do something wrong?"

"Are you going to lie on the floor all day? Get back in bed and rest. I have work to do, and I can't be babysitting your grown ass all day," she responds gruffly.

"Well, excuse me for living. I'll drag myself out of the way then so you can do whatever work you have to do," Jevonte replied with sarcasm.

Jevonte, legs trembling, rolls back onto his stomach and begins to drag and hump his way back to the bedroom. Talaitha stands at the kitchen counter, observing his progress, a glass of water in hand. She makes no move to assist him but glances at her watch, marking the time.

His condition is pitiful. As sporting as it may be to watch him struggle like this, I can't be here all day. I need to follow up with that new patient, Nolan. Talaitha wonders, Why did he call me 'sister'? Talaitha contemplates silently, the focus of her attention shifting from her husband's plight in front of her until she spots something behind him on the floor.

"What is that?" Talaitha barked. "Dammit, Jevonte, you're leaving a trail. Did you piss on yourself again?" Talaitha mocks.

Jevonte pauses and turns to see what has happened. A small wound has opened in his leg, and pus-smeared blood lines his pajama pants. His movement across the floor must have ruptured a vein in his leg. He stops moving and rests his aching forehead against the cold of the floor. His thoughts in that moment are of his mom, Ruby, and his dad,

Jedidiah. Melanie's wide and beautiful smile fills his thoughts as well. Before he can use the power of those memories to help propel him further along the floor, an iron grip fixes around his neck suddenly and violently, and he's nearly hauled to his feet.

Talaitha swiftly walks—drags Jevonte to the bedroom, his legs and arms swinging helplessly at his side—releasing him to fall across the bed. Jevonte weighs less than Talaitha now. She grabs his thin legs and swings them around into the bed. The sheets smell, and spots of dingy brown, caked with peeled skin and dried pus, stain the area where Jevonte had previously lain.

Jevonte pushes up on his elbows and twists his body to face Talaitha. "Tal, that was unnecessary. I would rather not rest right now. I need a shower, some water, and food."

"What you need to do is stop whining and stop messing up my floors. The bathroom is right there. If you want to shower, get your ass up and take one. Did I marry a man or a boy? I'm so sick of you right now," and she slams the door with a thunderous boom.

The situation can't be real; it just can't be. I need some help, dear God, please. Jevonte cries to himself. I know she can be mean sometimes, but the way she is treating me feels more like hate, like she literally can't stand the sight of me.

He lets his face sink into his pillow, hoping that he will find relief in suffocating himself. He already knows he can't do that, but the pain and hopelessness are crushing, and all he wants to do now is die.

It's been a few weeks since Ruby's funeral. There were so many families and friends in attendance. Ruby's pastor, Elder Cecil, has been checking up on Jedidiah and the rest of the family almost weekly. On the day of the repast, he arrived in the evening; Ruby and Jedidiah's home was still packed with family and visitors. Plates of food had been dropped off, and there was nowhere to sit. Every available chair had been arranged throughout the living room, kitchen, and even on the backyard patio deck, and every seat was occupied.

The Elder was greeted at the door and began making his rounds, shaking hands, exchanging hugs, and whispering gentle prayers. There were so many people in the house, but Elder Cecil wasn't surprised. Ruby's ministry was always demonstrated by compassionate action for her community, especially the young mothers. She was everyone's momma or GiGi, as they called her. One matter did concern him deeply that day, and that was the absence of his friend, Jedidiah. Elder Cecil questioned several family members, but no one seemed to know where he was. His truck was gone, and no one remembered when he had even left the house. He didn't learn more about Jedidiah's absence until the next day, when Melanie welcomed him back to the family's home.

"Hi, Elder Cecil, won't you come in?" Melanie greeted the pastor as she stepped aside to let him enter.

"Hi there, Melanie, thank you. Is anyone else here? I don't mean to intrude."

"Oh no, sir. I came over early to help get things put back in order and clean up a little. Ms. Maybelle and her sister, Shaunda, had to run a quick errand. Jedidiah's brother, Roscoe, is supposed to be here soon as well. Can I get you anything? Some coffee, maybe?"

"Thank you, sweetheart. I appreciate the offer, but I was hoping to speak with Jedidiah. Is he here now?"

"Let's talk in the study, ok? Uncle hasn't been here since the funeral," says Melanie, her eyes beginning to well with emotion. The pair moved into the study, and Melanie prepared her mind for a difficult conversation.

"Daughter, listen," Elder Cecil said, using a familiar and calming voice. He addressed all of the young people at his church as "son" or "daughter." "If the subject is too hard to talk about, it's ok. We don't have to. I am just worried about him."

"No, I don't mind. I know, or at least I think I know, what happened to Uncle Jedidiah. After the funeral, he went to his and Ruby's bedroom and stayed there a very long time. I went to check on him and knocked on their door. When he didn't respond, I opened the door. I was so scared and worried that I was going to find him lying on the floor—dead—but he was alright. He was sitting on the floor underneath the bedroom window. He was holding Ruby's head wrap in his hands," and Melanie had to pause to collect herself.

"I'm so sorry you had to see that, daughter," said Elder Cecil as he passed her a handkerchief.

"I don't mean to be so emotional, but seeing him like that really hurt my heart. When he saw me, the look in his eyes expressed so much heartache and pain that I started crying right there and then. He got up when he saw me and hugged me. We had a wonderful long talk, and he handed me an envelope. He had written a letter that he wanted me to read to the family. Basically, he said he doesn't feel like he can live without Ruby, that he needed to get away before he did something that would hurt the family even more than it has already been hurt."

"I know my friend is hurting, but this just doesn't sound like him at all. I mean, the Jedidiah I know would never take his life, nor would he leave his family in a crisis like this. I don't understand," said Elder Cecil.

"Pastor, I don't know if you knew this, but Ruby and Jedidiah weren't always this close. I think that over the last five years or so, they have healed a deep rift that once existed. Not many people knew or remembered this, but one of the reasons Jevonte would never come home during college was because of what was going on between them. Jevonte never really went into depth about it, but I know it bothered him a lot, and he didn't want to be around them much at that time."

"Yes. I do know something about that period in their lives. I helped counsel them both and saw them through that rough patch. It was touch-and-go there for a while. I remember Jevonte telling me once that he felt deceived by both of them. I couldn't help him sort through those feelings at the time, but I do know that it affected him deeply," replied Elder Cecil.

"I'm going to have a good, long talk with Uncle Roscoe when he gets here. For some reason, he and Jedidiah haven't spoken much at all over these last few years. Neither said why, but I believe Ruby knew. Whenever I brought it up with her, she would say that everything is forgiven and that I should let sleeping dogs lie. Well, today, I need to hear more from Uncle Roscoe because this family is drifting, and we need an anchor," said Melanie, sounding exhausted.

"Child, Jesus is our anchor. Don't forget that. He will never leave us or forsake us," replied Elder Cecil with joy and encouragement in his voice.

"Oh, I know, Elder. I know, but this family needs a head, a leader, someone to step in and help guide us back to some kind of peace and healing. I know we have God on our side, but I don't think a sermon is going to fix what's broken," Melanie said, her voice tender and nonjudgmental.

"No, I understand, and I take no offense, either. I will be in prayer for Brother Jedidiah. I hope he reaches out to me soon. What about Jevonte? I hear he's married now. He didn't come to the funeral or the repast. Have you heard from him lately?"

"Yes and no. Jevonte recently fell ill. The hospital where he was admitted mistakenly sent a letter to Ruby and Jedidiah's home. Ruby let me see it, and apparently, Jevonte was exposed to MRSA after being poisoned."

"Poisoned!" cried Elder Cecil.

"Yes. It's a long story, and I'm still gathering information, but I think his wife poisoned him."

"Are you sure? I mean, that's quite the accusation. Have you told the authorities?"

"No, not yet. I wanted to confront her with what I knew and get her reaction first. I wanted to see how she'd react. Of course, she denied it, and we almost came to blows right there in her office! I wish I had recorded the meeting too, so that when I go to the police, I'd have an even stronger case. In fact, I intend to travel to Baltimore, to her office again, this week to see if I can trick a confession out of her or beat one out of her! I feel like something is wrong with her, like her mind isn't right, and she's a psychiatrist too!"

"Child, listen. Do be extra careful. Such individuals are extremely dangerous and skilled at manipulating people's thoughts—after all, that is their line of work," Elder Cecil says with a smile. "Maybe you should take someone with you just in case."

"I'll be fine, Pastor. I'll give you a call after I meet with her. Just keep me in your prayers and pray for Jevonte, too. When I visited him in the hospital, he looked so bad. He has lost significant weight, making it difficult for him to stand independently. Anyhow, I need to finish up around here and get ready for Roscoe. I have a feeling it's going to be a very long night."

"Of course. I'll see myself out; just know that I'm here if you need me. The entire church is here for you, so don't hesitate to lean on us as much or as little as you need," Elder Cecil offered before walking out of the house, humming a familiar hymn that warmed Melanie's heart even though she couldn't quite remember it.

It's 9 pm, and Roscoe's flight has been delayed. Melanie relays the update to the family and takes a seat in the living room with some of Jevonte's cousins, Kim, Rickea, and James. Melanie's brother, RhaShawn, is also there. Ruby's two older sisters, Rachelle and Bethany, are still there. They've been cooking and cleaning and doing what they can to nurse the family through the loss of their sister Ruby. It's a tall order. Ruby was the family's principal matriarch. So much of their lives revolved around her. With Ruby gone and Jedidiah absent, with no return date, one of her sisters or Roscoe would have to take on the task of gathering the family during this time of crisis.

"Where is Jevonte?" asked Rickea, loud and snarky.

Melanie took a deep breath before responding. Rickea was going to be Rickea, and she would not change for anyone or at any moment. "Jevonte has been sick…"

"Sick? What's so wrong with him that he can't even be bothered to see his mom put in the ground?" Rickea shot back. "No, I don't care what's wrong with him; he needs to be here."

"I know what you're saying, but…" Melanie started to answer.

"Melanie, what can you tell us about his situation? I mean, this is not like him. His mom was killed, and we don't hear a word from him? C'mon now, what's the problem?" asked James.

"Furthermore, has the police department released any additional details regarding Auntie's murder?" Kim piped in.

"I thought they said it was just an accident, or something like that?" asked Rickea

"Kim, where did you hear that from? Murder? What the hell are you talking about? " Ain't nobody said anything about a murder," responded James in rebuke.

"Please, everyone. Calm down. I really don't know any more than you all do right now. The police have not officially classified it as a homicide, so Kim, I don't know where you're getting that information from." Kim rolled her eyes at Melanie and sat back in her seat.

"What about Jevonte, then? What's going on with him, and where the hell is Uncle Jedidiah?" asked Rickea.

"Jevonte is in a situation…"

"Situation!" barked Kim. "What situation?"

"He's been seriously ill. He really only found out about Auntie's death well after the fact. He was in a coma and…"

"For crying out loud, Melanie! He was in a coma? How long? What was wrong with him? Why wasn't the family told anything? This is fucked up, and I don't know…"

Melanie cuts off Kim in mid-sentence. "Look, none of us knew about his health scare, and we only learned of it by accident. He's not in a coma anymore, thank goodness, but his condition is still serious. He physically can't even travel, so even if he knew about Auntie's funeral, he wouldn't have been able to attend."

The room settles down and grows quiet. No one makes eye contact, and the cousins begin looking at RhaShawn, Melanie's older brother.

As if on cue, RhaShawn asks Melanie, "Have you visited Jevonte?"

Melanie shakes her head. "I visited him at the hospital and gave him the news about his mom. He took it very hard."

"That's good, for now. What about Uncle Jedidiah? When was the last time you spoke with him?"

RhaShawn and Melanie were not blood relatives to the Greenes, but they were so close they might as well have been counted as family. The Descartes and Greene families became very close during Jevonte and Melanie's time at Howard University. Both families seemed destined to become one after graduation, but Jevonte changed all of that.

"All I can say about Uncle Jedidiah is that he needed to take some time away. Ruby's passing was just too much for him. He couldn't bear it. I don't think I've ever seen him this low, ever," said Melanie. "Uncle Roscoe will be here tomorrow. His flight was delayed, and the only flight he could get was early in the morning."

"Where is he staying?" asked Kim. "Ricky and I are here tonight, so where is he staying?"

"Girl, this is his brother's house. He's staying here. You and Rickea can come to my house if you like, or you can get a room at the Holiday Express," answered Melanie, her face set to put Kim in her place.

"Uncle Roscoe is going to stay with me," said RhaShawn. "I already discussed it with him. It's done."

Kim and Rickea stood, and Melanie stood with them. There was a brief moment of tension, but it vanished quickly. The women walked off to the kitchen and started packing a few things to take with them. James remained sitting with RhaShawn. The two men sat in silence, neither offering to exchange any further pleasantries.

After a few moments, James said, "Let's go outside and grab a smoke. I need to get out of this house."

The two men moved outside and sat on their uncle's porch rockers. There were two of them, with a small round table separating them. Ruby and Jedidiah were common fixtures on their porch. You rarely saw Ruby sitting out on the porch without Jedidiah, and vice versa.

"RhaShawn, nothing feels right about this. I know what the police are saying, but my gut is saying something else, you know what I mean?" said James.

RhaShawn sat in silence for a moment, then he said, "I don't know what to believe. It was raining badly that night. It could have been an accident, you know."

"Nah, son. I don't feel that at all. I can't say why, but it just feels wrong to me on so many levels. Like, Auntie wasn't a cripple. The water in that ditch wasn't even that deep. Like, how did she drown, man? How? I can't deal with that. I could accept a car accident, a collision, or something, but drowning in a shallow ditch? There's no way, sorry, cuz. I'm not buying that one."

"I feel you, James, I do. Freakier things have happened, though. I think all we can do for now is to let it all unfold and see what the police come up with. I think…"

"Fuck the police," spat James. "They aren't trying to solve Auntie's accident. They could care less, because you and I both know they're going to go with the easiest explanation possible, and they won't explore any other possibilities."

RhaShawn took a deep drag on his cigarette and held the smoke, then he released it through his nose, and two powdery streams of smoke engulfed the space between the two men.

"I understand. Let's just give it some time and see what they come up with. I'm not totally convinced they are being honest with us either. Jevonte is another matter. Something definitely isn't clean in the milk with him."

The next day, RhaShawn and Roscoe arrive at the house, and Melanie arrives later in the day after she hears that Jedidiah's brother has arrived. Rachelle is clearing the morning's breakfast dishes, and Bethany is putting the finishing touches on the guest bedroom. The home is quiet now with Jevonte's cousins gone, and there is an air of humility and peace hanging in the air.

Roscoe sets his bags down near the chaise and scans the living room and hearth. Ruby's touches are everywhere. Her spirit feels embedded in all the little knick-knacks adorning the space. Her knitted blankets drape the living room sofa, and some of the handmade pillows she created over the years fill the vacant seats throughout. Above the fireplace mantle is a portrait of Ruby and Jedidiah, with the husband standing just behind his wife, who is seated like royalty. In their eyes, there are so many stories of triumph and failure, love and sacrifice, and joy sprinkled with small doses of pain. She's everywhere, and Roscoe's heart can barely withstand the fact of her death.

"Uncle Roscoe, hello," greets Melanie as she walks to embrace the big man. Roscoe is two years younger than his brother, Jedidiah, but, aside from their height and weight, they could have been mistaken for twins. Roscoe was younger, but he was always taller and more muscular. Even after he retired from the Marine Corps after 22 years, Roscoe maintained a strict workout and exercise routine. During his military service, he earned a reputation for bravery under fire and precision under pressure. But his personal life was far messier. When he returned to Baltimore after retirement, he launched a thriving independent contracting business restoring historic properties—a solitary trade that mirrored his interior world: build, fix, remain unseen.

His relationship with his older brother, Jedidiah Greene, was fractured. Jedidiah was the more stable, family-oriented of the two, a devoted carpenter and husband. But beneath that domestic image simmered unresolved suspicions—Jedidiah always believed Roscoe and Ruby had a deeper bond than they admitted. Whether or not that affair ever happened, the accusation itself created a rift that never fully healed.

Roscoe loved Ruby—but from a distance, with a Marine's restraint. When Jevonte was born, Roscoe stepped back, limiting contact. Rumors persisted, and eventually staying connected to the family became too difficult. So Roscoe stepped back into the shadow. But quietly, he watched Jevonte grow, recognizing in him the gentleness and artistry that mirrored Ruby and, perhaps, something of himself. He and Jevonte became very close, even though that relationship was under constant strain due to Jedidiah's demands that Roscoe steer clear of his family.

"It's so good to see you, Melanie. You really look good. How have you been?" asked Roscoe, his smile as big as the sky.

"I'm good, Uncle, and now that you're here, I feel so much better. There is so much to share, so much that has gone on, even before Auntie was taken from us."

"Unc. Do you want anything? I'm grabbing a beer out of the kitchen," said RhaShawn.

"I'm fine, RhaShawn!" chided Melanie in jest.

"My bad, Mel," he laughed. "Do you want anything, ma'am?"

"No, sir. I'm good, thanks for asking," Melanie grinned.

"Thank you, Ray. I'm good, for now," offered Roscoe and sat on the sofa.

Rachelle and Bethany found their way into the living room just as RhaShawn returned with his beer.

"Start from the beginning, Melanie, and tell me everything you know about Ruby's death. Furthermore, Jevonte seems to have dropped off the face of the earth, so what do we know about that?" asked Roscoe.

Over the next hour, Melanie recounted her interaction with Talaitha at the hospital and the hospital letter detailing Jevonte's condition, and she shared the preliminary police report on Ruby's accident. After she finished, all eyes pivoted to Roscoe, but he sat stone-faced, deep in thought. After a few moments, he rose and walked to the mantle to look up at the portrait of Ruby and Jedidiah.

With his back still facing the family, he said, "I never wanted to see a day like today. I never wanted to believe this kind of thing would ever touch the people I love. It has." Under his breath, he mutters, "Ruby, I'm sorry I wasn't here for you and our relationship..." Roscoe's voice trailed off. Turning to face his people, his family, Roscoe continued, "I have a friend I can contact. He's a licensed private investigator, and he owes me a few favors. He can help us get to the bottom of Ruby's accident. I can also point him at Talaitha and get us some real background on her."

"Thank you, Roscoe," responded Bethany. "The police really haven't been helpful or forthcoming."

"Such situations are often problematic, particularly in our community; however, at this moment, I am very concerned about Jevonte's health and the potential issues occurring in his home. Have any of you been to see him there?" asked Roscoe.

"No, not yet, but I believe Melanie said something about confronting Talaitha sometime this week," responded RhaShawn.

"Sweetheart, I don't think that is a very good idea. Maybe just wait until my P.I. gives us a full report on her so that we know what we're dealing with?" interjected Roscoe.

"No, I hear what you're saying, Uncle, but you guys didn't see what I saw at the hospital. Jevonte is nothing but breath and britches now. He appears very frail, and during my visit with him, an important moment occurred between us. I have to do something, and I don't think we have the time to wait on the P.I. to dig something up. I'll be careful. I've already been to her office, so I know what to expect when I drop in a second time. Besides, it's not like I'm going to her house or anything—yet," exclaimed Melanie.

"Unc. How soon do you think you can get this P.I. on the job?" asked RhaShawn. "I'd like to meet with him, too, if you don't mind."

"I will arrange everything and include you in my emails to him." I'll also inform my brother about our plan. I know he's hurting, and he probably doesn't want to see anyone right now, but if any of you do happen to talk to him, let him know I've got him. He can take whatever time he needs."

"I appreciate this, Roscoe. There are a few matters that we still need to handle. Ruby's funeral costs…"

Roscoe cut Rachelle off. "It's handled. Paid in full."

"We still have to pick out a headstone and…"

"Prepaid. You and Bethany can pick out what you want at Mr. Perrymen's funeral parlor. He's expecting you this week," Roscoe said. "Focus on this house and Ruby's things. I don't think she left a will, so there will be plenty to do until Jedidiah gets back.

"Yeah, we need to square that away quickly because we already know there will be vultures circling the block named Rickea and Kim. I hate to be down on my kin, but they aren't anything like James," said Rachelle.

"C'mon, Rachelle, those are my nieces you're talking about. They aren't that bad," laughs Bethany. "James is no saint, may I remind you."

"At least your son has more sense than a bullfrog on that juice!" laughed Rachelle. My girls, God knows I tried with those two, I really did."

"Now, now, ladies. Haven't we all fallen a little short of the glory of God before?" asked Melanie, a short grin lining her ample cheeks.

The family enjoys a few more laughs together, and when the sun finally begins to set, everyone has departed for their homes, leaving Roscoe alone with his thoughts in the house. He makes good use of the dresser space and unpacks his things, setting his shower kit and toiletries in the guest bathroom. After getting his things squared away, Roscoe pulls out his phone and dials his friend.

"Marcus, it's time. I need everything you can get me on Talaitha Greene, maiden name Mercedes. Spare no expense this time.

16

Truth Inked in Darkness

Talaitha cleared her calendar for the rest of the week. After the scene with Melanie at her office, she decided to take a few extra precautions for her practice. I'll hire a new receptionist before the end of the month. I can't have people barging into my office the way Melanie did, Talaitha muses. How did she find my office in the first place? I'm not listed, and wait, there is only one hospital where I have privileges. Looks like I'm going to have to visit the good people at Sable Ridge soon.

Talaitha pulls out a tablet and begins taking notes for her meetings with her patients in the coming weeks. In the background, she can hear the shower running and smiles. He was really beginning to smell like death warmed over. "Good thing we have the spare bedroom because there is no way he's sleeping in my bed smelling like that," she thinks.

Let me get started on this grocery list. I believe the basement is clean, so I have nothing to worry about there, but my little garden needs some additional ingredients, so while I'm out, I might as well stop by the Garden Supply. I know I need to deal with this Nolan character, too. I've treated psychopaths and sociopaths before, but he was different. He's an unknown variable, and I don't need another one right now.

"Hey," said Jevonte, his thin body leaning against the hallway wall. "You were right. The shower was helpful."

Dammit, I was hoping to be gone by the time he finished, Talaitha thinks.

"I knew it would. I fixed you a fruit salad since you claim to be starving. It's in the fridge, and you should eat that now while you can. While I was preparing that, it reminded me that I needed to pick up a few things from the grocery store. I won't be gone long, so rest after you finish the salad. I just got the streaks off the floor, so please stay in bed until I get back," Melanie said.

"No worries there. I need to go online for a few hours anyway, but after that, I'll get right to bed," replied Jevonte weakly.

Talaitha paused before grabbing her car keys. "I know that I have been harsh with you lately. I want you to understand that," and she paused again. "It's not anything you did. I am under enormous strain because of the clinical trials I'm coordinating. There is a lot at stake for my patients, and occasionally, my attitude is, well, less than optimal. I apologize for that," Talaitha said, her voice sounding earnest and open, more genuine than Jevonte had experienced in a while.

"I appreciate you saying that, love. Maybe tonight we can have a relaxing dinner and have a little reset. It feels like we haven't been very intimate in a long time. I may not have my strength back, but I wouldn't mind just having some me time with you tonight." Jevonte's legs started to tremble slightly, and he sat down so he wouldn't collapse.

"One thing at a time, King. Just eat and get your strength back. I put a little extra herbal seasoning on the salad, and I think that will help flush and detox your body faster. Just make sure you eat it all."

After that, Talaitha approaches Jevonte, caresses his head, and gently kisses his cheek. Jevonte is invigorated by her touch and attempts to stand so that he can wrap his arms around her, but she places a calming hand on his shoulder, and he stops.

Talaitha grabs her satchel and heads out the front door.

It's an early Tuesday morning, but most of the rush hour crowd has thinned on this side of White Marsh. Only a handful of cars now occupy Prestin Middle School's drop-off lanes. The slightly cloudy day is typical for this time of year in Maryland. Autumn is making an early appearance, and the air is decidedly cooler than usual for late August. After parking, Roscoe and RhaShawn walk into Mike's Bully Bean Coffee shop, and after ordering two coffees and breakfast sandwiches, they grab a table at the far side of the shop. Mike's is the only Black-owned local coffee shop in White Marsh and is a favorite of the after-school crowd from the Community College of Baltimore.

"Marcus agreed to meet us here. He's a little paranoid about meeting in the city of Baltimore," said Roscoe.

"Why? Wasn't he on the force some years ago?" asked RhaShawn.

"He was, but he parted ways with them and decided to do his own thing. He never said why exactly, but what I remember about him from when we were in the Corps together is that he does not suffer fools or compromise his integrity. I think the force was putting him into too many positions where he was asked to cross a line, and he just wouldn't do that. I have always respected his code of ethics."

"So, you guys served together? Were you in the same unit?"

"Not exactly," Roscoe smiles before testing his coffee. "Marcus was part of an investigative team working alongside NCIS at Pendleton. You know who they are?" asked Roscoe.

"I've heard of them, but I don't know what they do exactly."

"The Naval Criminal Investigative Service is like the FBI, and their focus is defeating criminal, terrorist, and foreign intelligence threats to the Navy and Marine Corps. They are like the special forces of criminal investigative units, and they look into all kinds of crimes involving military members or crimes perpetrated against uniformed members."

"So pretty, badass, and pretty white, I'm guessing."

"Yes and no. I knew more than a few of our people working on their team or with them in one capacity or another. They were still pretty vanilla but more open and fairer than your typical law enforcement unit. Anyway, NCIS started a case involving my unit and a human trafficking ring operating in San Jacinto County. There was one gang there that had recruited a few sailors in my command, and they were transporting young captives across state lines, down into Juarez, Mexico. Marcus was, at the time, working with the 1st Marine Expeditionary Force's Inspector General's Office, and that's where I crossed paths with him. The sailors in question were part of the medical service in 9th Communications Battalion, my unit at the time."

"So, he has experience with looking into people like this Talaitha, huh?" asked RhaShawn.

"Yes, and he doesn't back down once he gets his hooks into something or someone. He's tenacious, and I saw that firsthand when he helped collapse that trafficking ring. It got messy, and the brass did not want the public exposure the investigation would create. I mean, he had one and two stars calling for his head, but Marcus didn't flinch even though his career was at risk. Over the rest of our careers in the Corps, we would come into contact here and there, and he never wavered in his commitment to finding the truth, no matter where the trail led him."

"Well, I look forward to meeting him. I hope he can shake a few things loose with the local five-O, because they aren't being helpful whatsoever," remarked RhaShawn.

"Looks like you'll get your chance right about now," said Roscoe, and he stood to greet the tall, lanky man headed toward their table.

"Master Guns, how the hell are you, old man?" Marcus said, extending his meaty hand to Roscoe.

"If that's not the pot calling the kettle black! Master Sergeant, you're looking good, receding hairline and all!"

Roscoe laughed. "This is RhaShawn, a very close friend of the family."

The group sat, and after some light banter and storytelling about the good old days, Roscoe began filling Marcus in on everything that had happened to Ruby and Jevonte. RhaShawn relayed Melanie's concerns and her plan to confront Talaitha at her and Jevonte's home. Marcus stiffened a bit after hearing that plan.

"Guys, I doubt that's a good idea. Can Melanie be talked out of that course of action? It could go very wrong," stated Marcus.

"Melanie is not going to budge. I've already tried, but she's very concerned about Jevonte and doesn't feel she can wait any longer. She's already been to Talaitha's office, and they almost came to blows," said RhaShawn in response.

"So, she and Jevonte are a thing, or what?" asked Marcus.

"They used to be hot and heavy back in college, but it didn't work out. I think seeing Jevonte in his current state has sparked something in her, or both of them. Regardless of what is happening between Jevonte and Melanie, Roscoe believes that Melanie is on a collision course with Talaitha."

"Well, one thing experience has taught me in cases like this, and I speak from years of investigative experience with shady characters, is that it never ends well when individuals take on investigations like this by themselves."

Roscoe, taking another swig of his coffee, said, "Melanie is a big girl, and I think she can handle herself. For now, let's focus on Ruby's death. When can you get started?"

The group continues to discuss and plan a way forward. Coffee cups are filled twice more, and when Roscoe and RhaShawn depart, Marcus lingers a few minutes more. His keen sense for the out-of-place alerts him, and the hairs on his neck begin to tingle. He exits the coffee shop and scans the street. At the NW end, he spots someone standing on the street corner. Not too unusual given the constant flow of foot traffic in and around the street shops on Hollins Avenue, but what does strike Marcus as strange is the way the individual is dressed. A trench coat in late October or maybe November wouldn't be a problem, but it's still summer. As soon as the stranger notices Marcus watching him, he darts around the corner and disappears.

"Ok, so we have a spy on deck, gotcha, partner," Marcus remarks to himself and pulls out a little notepad to mark the date, time, and a description.

In the weeks that followed, Jevonte's condition continued to worsen. He stayed faithful to the diet Talaitha set for him, but his weight did not stabilize, and his clothes hung off him as though he were nothing more than bones. He was unable to work around the house because of severe fatigue and brain fog. The weekend arrived, and Talaitha suggested that they do a little shopping in Baltimore.

"Let's take a trip to the Inner Harbor and grab some blue crabs. I think the air will do you some good," Talaitha said as she rose from bed.

Jevonte sat up in bed and gathered his thoughts. "I think that would be lovely, but honestly, babe, I don't believe I can. I don't have the strength to do it, and I feel awful about my appearance. Let me rest a bit more. You go ahead and enjoy the harbor for me," Jevonte replied, but he hoped that she would decline and instead opt to remain at home with him. Talaitha walked into the master bathroom and closed the door without responding. While Talaitha is in the shower, Jevonte lies back and begins planning his day.

With Talaitha out of the house—she's been working from home almost every day—I'll be able to look into these cameras she's installed all over the house. I don't think Talaitha is aware that I discovered the cameras, and honestly, I would prefer to avoid discussing them with her. She doesn't seem too concerned about leaving me here alone. She doesn't seem concerned about me at all, for that matter. Plus, there is something wrong with the home computer. I can log in, but the system won't let me reach my Gmail account or any messaging site. It's like all websites I might use to reach the outside world have been blocked.

The shower stops, and Jevonte makes plans to figure out the cameras without Talaitha finding out. While his wife is preparing herself in the bathroom, Jevonte struggles to get out of bed. He can feel the weight of depression starting to crowd his thoughts, and his mood is getting despondent. His arms and legs feel like they weigh a ton. As he sits up and scoots to the edge of the bed, his stomach begins to cramp, and he can feel his bowels constricting and rumbling. I haven't gone to the bathroom in a few days. My butt feels like it's about to explode, and that's the last thing I need while she's here, Jevonte thinks.

Jevonte focuses and tries to divert his attention toward anything else besides the griping he's feeling down below. They have more than one bathroom in the house, but Jevonte doesn't think he'll make it to any of the others in time. Finally, Talaitha opens the bathroom door and walks over to her dresser, bereft of towels save for the one wrapped around her head. Jevonte takes in her form and her perfect shape. Talaitha has the body of an Olympic gymnast; only her breasts are larger than those of today's Olympians. He's mesmerized by her. Her skin is flawless. Her beautiful brown skin almost glows. Jevonte tracks the droplets of water racing down her back and buttocks, wishing he could drink from her. She is all the distraction he needed.

Talaitha pulls out a few garments and pauses, finally noticing Jevonte's rapt attention. She smiles and lingers a bit longer at her bureau. She teases out a pair of panties, holding them, inspecting them so that Jevonte can see. She then puts them back and slips on her sundress. It's not quite sheer, but when the light hits it just right, Jevonte can see the few dainty pubic hairs she has peering from between her thigh gap. She's not going to wear any underwear in THAT dress, Jevonte thinks lustfully.

Talaitha walks into her closet and returns with one of the necklaces Jevonte bought her after they first met. She walks over to Jevonte and hands it to him. "King, help me with this," Talaitha purrs. She turns around, and her butt is practically in Jevonte's face. He can see her skin through the dress. He wants to kiss her back and trace every line of her, marking the powerful curves of her muscles until he can taste everything. He inhales, and her scent quickly fills his soul with fire. He no longer feels any pain. His body is rigid, and all his earlier discomforts have vanished—save one. His penis is throbbing, the sudden rush of blood making him feel faint. He can feel his scrotum swelling; a little knot is forming, and his balls are beginning to draw up inside him. He places a hand on Talaitha's hip and tries to pull her into his lap. He just wants to impale her, merge with her, and bind her body to his, but his arms are too weak. He's shaking and quickly tires of the effort. Talaitha shifts her body forward, resisting his attempt to couple with her, and says, "Never mind, I'll do it myself," and walks out of the bedroom.

Jevonte's spirit crashes, and he bows his head in shame. Before long, he hears the front door close, and soon Talaitha pulls out of the garage and heads off to do some shopping in Baltimore—wearing a sun dress and nothing else. After the pounding in his head subsides and he regains some composure, Jevonte gets out of bed and heads to the bathroom, his bowels once again rumbling and threatening to unleash hell.

Over the next few hours, Jevonte has cleaned himself up and is feeling a bit more human.

I still don't have much of an appetite, and if I eat another of Tal's fruit concoctions, I'll go batshit crazy. I'll grab something later. For now, let's see if we can get into the system and find out where these cameras are storing their footage. I don't want to piss Tal off, but I need to know what's happening here, Jevonte thinks.

Jevonte takes a seat at the home desktop computer and tries to log in. The system won't accept his PIN, so he tries using his password instead. Again, his credentials are rejected.

"Well, that's great. I can't even get into the system!" Jevonte grumbles.

As Jevonte rises from his seat, he notices a sliver of light coming from Talaitha's office. The door is not closed all of the way, something he's never seen since Talaitha protects the privacy of her office space with extreme vigilance.

Nah, I'd better not, but then again, the door is open, and I can close it later. I've always wanted to see what she's done with the space since the refurbishment, he thinks to himself.

Jevonte shuffles over to the door and pushes it open to peer inside. Talaitha's workspace is immaculate. Her desk is well-organized, with everything perfectly aligned. Looking at her office, it reminds Jevonte of a staged room, a showroom for office decor, bright, clean, and antiseptic. I suppose this is what a psychiatrist's office would look like, he thinks.

Jevonte starts exploring the room. He's impressed with how orderly everything is, and he's careful not to touch or move anything out of its place. He sits at Talaitha's desk and relaxes. He immediately feels a sense of command as he surveys the rest of the office. The desk is placed strategically to overlook the office entry and the lounge area. He never understood why she wanted the lounge area since she doesn't see clients at the home, but she demanded it, and he built it.

Her library is expansive. Jevonte rises and walks over to the floor-to-ceiling built-ins he created for the library. He's never heard of many of the titles and authors lining the shelves. He runs his fingertips over some of the titles. He reads them aloud: "Diagnostic and Statistical Manual of Mental Disorders," "Kaplan & Sadock's Synopsis of Psychiatry," and "Long-Term Psychodynamic Psychotherapy." There are so many, and then he finds one four-volume work by Samuel Robinson, Ph.D., called "Chronology of Transformation and the Mutilation of Self: A Narrative Study of Sibling Loathing and Gender Sacrifice." Samuel Robinson, Doctor Samuel Robinson, Jevonte queries within himself. The name is familiar. He's heard it before, but where?

Jevonte pulls the first book in the volume from the bookshelf, and when he does, he spots a journal tucked neatly behind the volume, lying vertically on its spine. Jevonte sets Dr. Robinson's book down and removes the hidden journal. His gut is telling him to leave it alone, but he can't resist the temptation. The writing is certainly Talaitha's. Her penmanship is perfect, elegant, and professional. It looks almost like a machine wrote it.

Jevonte sits on one of the lounge sofas and begins to read Talaitha's journal. Her words are cryptic, alien, and terrifying all at once.

November 17, 2000

I would have buried the whore myself had I been able to find her body. No one ever did. Noelle thought she was better than me, but she was never chosen. They didn't want her. They wanted me. I think that's why Daddy loved me best. She left, and she left me behind. When I needed her, she stayed in her bed, all warm and cozy. When they tore me, did she help? No, that bitch closed her eyes and ignored me. She left, and she never said a word to me, so if I ever find her, I will destroy her the way they destroyed me.

Who is Noelle? Jevonte wondered. I don't think I've heard that name before.

November 22, 2000

She should have been my brother. I hate that she never was. She just left me at the prom. She just left without saying a word. Now they blame me because she never came home. I hope wherever she is, she's getting her brains fucked out the way they did me. I can't even feel things. My thoughts are weird. Voices inside my head are telling me to do things, but I don't want to. My foster mom thinks I need therapy. She said that because of all the rapes, I must be broken inside. Well, fuck her. I'm not broken inside. I will break her inside; see how she likes that. Life sucks, and I can't wait to leave. I have to leave before the voices make me do something. They never shut up. I just want to make them stop.

December 12, 2000

Noelle, where are you, sister? Please come back home. I am all alone now. Rufus wrote me. He told me he didn't mean to let all those men do that to me, but the family had to eat, he said. I feel so sad right now.

"Sister? Damn," said Jevonte out loud. "All the rapes?" What the hell. My God, what has my baby been through? She never talks about her sister or her family, for that matter. I've asked dozens of times, but she always found a way to change the conversation. I should have pushed, he muses, but I think I understand some things now.

Jevonte continues reading through the journal, passing through the months until he stops on April 5, 2001; a red blotch of dried ink marks the page.

April 5, 2001

I tried to tell them. I warned them, but they wouldn't listen, so I put her in the garden where she can do some good. They can lock me up forever for all I care. I don't. I told that bitch of a foster mom that if she mentioned my sister one more time, I'd feed her the blades. She's not laughing now. I don't suppose she can laugh with the shears lodged in her throat. Noelle, you're next. I don't care where you are; you can't hide from me forever. I will find you.

There is a large time gap in the journal. Jevonte notices that three years pass with no entries, and when there is, the tone is decidedly different. It is not that of a sixteen-year-old.

May 7, 2004

Finally, my letter of acceptance has arrived. I wasn't sure what to expect, but Dr. Robinson assured me that the committee would support my application for the psychiatry and pharmacological internship program. They'd better accept me because I know what they have been doing to the patients here. It's going to happen; besides, I have them all fooled. They all think I'm this reformed young lady who suffered tremendous trauma growing up, and now I'm ready to rejoin society. I am alright. I will leave this place and never again be anyone's plaything. No, I will be the player. I will have control over my world. When that moment comes,

Noelle, be prepared because I will make you pay for what you did to me, I promise.

Jevonte closes the journal. His thoughts are a swirl of confusion and deep concern. The depth of anguish and pain described in Talaitha's journal is staggering. Who is this person I am married to, wonders Jevonte.

The next couple of years recorded in the journal documented Talaitha's acceptance into college and eventual graduation from medical school. She impressed the medical board so much that despite her stay at Sable Ridge State Hospital, her academic acumen and intelligence compelled them to approve and license her as a psychiatrist. She's always been impressive; that much is clear, Jevonte reminds himself.

Jevonte reopens the journal and skips ahead to last year's entries. His eyes go slack, and his mouth drops open in disbelief as he begins reading the entry marked, "My King, Found."

My King, Found – February 12, 2017

I watched him. No one is paying him any attention, and this is his so-called friend's party. They don't see him, but I do. It's taken a while, but ever since that day in the park, when he roamed around looking lost, I have not been able to get this close to him. I can make him mine. I can remake

Jevonte. I can show everyone that Noelle faked her death. I can finally uncover the truth.

February 15, 2017

I know they thought you were dead and gone. Wishful thinking. Nobody knows you like me, sister. You may have changed, and now you walk around making people believe you are a carpenter living alone, appearing as pitiful as possible, but I know the truth. I know who you are and what you've become. You walked away and left me on prom night, and now here you are. I found you, Nolla, or Jevonte. It doesn't matter what you call yourself, sister. Your days are numbered.

"My God. What is she talking about? Does she think that somehow, I am her sister? I don't understand. Before Jevonte can finish the sentence, the garage door begins lifting to let Talaitha's car enter. Jevonte panics and slams the journal shut. He rises quickly—too fast—and the office begins spinning in his head. Jevonte struggles against the sudden vertigo and pushes with all his might to stand. He gains his feet and lurches forward, aiming for the bookshelves and hoping to somehow fall in the right direction. Thankfully, he only staggers and keeps his feet. He reaches the bookshelf and places the journal back on the shelf, and hurriedly turns to get to the office door. Moving as if he were one of the walkers on The Walking Dead, Jevonte manages to miss the sitting table in the lounge area and shuffles his way out of the office. He closes the door behind him and starts toward the master bedroom when the front door opens.

Talaitha enters and pauses briefly. The hallway and the closing master bedroom door immediately capture her attention. So what have we been up to, Mr. Greene? she thinks. Talaitha places her keys and satchel down by the front door and walks into the kitchen. She doesn't announce herself or call for Jevonte. After pouring herself a drink, she enters her office and finds book one of Dr. Samuel Robinson's four-volume work lying on the floor next to her bookshelf. Talaitha stares intently at the book lying on the floor of her office. She appears statuesque, frozen in space. A look of recognition adorns her face as she realizes that her privacy has been compromised.

Walking over to the fallen book, she picks it up from the floor to return it to the bookshelf, and her eyes lock on her journal. It's facing the back wall of the shelf, and it is not lying on the spine, as she always leaves it. Talaitha moves to her desk and launches the monitoring application. Bitter disdain and anger begin to infest her thoughts as she watches Jevonte enter her office. She watches him sit at her desk and peruse the book volumes lining her shelves. Then, when he pulls out her journal and begins to read it, the violation and sense of betrayal she feels cause her eyes to water with rage.

As quickly as the storm inside her rose, her feelings soon changed, and she shuts down the monitoring system and leaves her office. Talaitha thinks to herself that she now needs to change the formulation of her special treats for Mr. Greene, since he likes to snoop around so much.

Later that night, Talaitha prepares an Italian meal of deep-fried risotto balls stuffed with ragù and cheese. The table is set with a new bottle of Barbera red wine she brought home from Baltimore the week prior. She's added a side dish of tiramisu to top off the meal.

Jevonte slowly shambles into the kitchen. The meal is fragrant and makes his mouth water. His appetite is nowhere to be found, but the meal and the setting look too inviting to pass up. He takes a seat and drapes a napkin across his lap. He wants to make conversation, but ever since he came across Talaitha's journal, he hasn't found the words. He knows that there may still be deep scars and trauma in memories of the past that Talaitha might want to avoid. So, he's been waiting for her to open that door for discussion.

Talaitha pours them both some wine and eats in silence. She doesn't even look at Jevonte. He knows she knows he's read her journal, but she hasn't said a word about it since that day.

They eat in complete silence, and when Talaitha finishes, she picks up her plate and walks into the kitchen to clean it. When she finishes, she heads to the bedroom, closing the door behind her. Jevonte sits in the dimly lit dining room alone with just his thoughts. The meal was good, and even though he didn't feel hungry, he finished it all, including the tiramisu too. The risotto balls were delicious. His stomach felt like it was going to burst, so he finished his wine and leaned back in his chair, too full to rise.

Tal has always been a good cook, but she put her toe in this meal tonight, Jevonte thought. She was on the silent treatment train this evening. Seems worse than usual. She wouldn't even look at me. I'll take the face shot and approach her. I have so many questions, but how do I…

Suddenly, Jevonte doubles over in pain, his gut retching, bile suddenly scorching his throat, and he falls out of his chair. His whole body is contorted. His voice was gone, scalded by the stomach acid percolating up from his stomach. He is curled up into a tight ball, but the pain is too intense, so he rolls over to his back, praying for relief. His throat begins constricting, and his vision is nothing but a blur of gray shapes and shadows. He stretches his hand towards the bedroom and begins slapping the hardwood floor, hoping to get Talaitha's attention, but he's too weak to generate enough force to make much more than padded sounds against the floor. She's not going to hear me. She's going to find me dead on the kitchen floor. Oh God, please, please, don't let her find me like this, Jevonte prays silently as he begins to lose consciousness. The last image he sees is that of a woman's silhouette in the hall, arms folded, unmoving and silent.

Morning comes for Jevonte. He's in bed. A sickening acidic taste fills his mouth. He can't move, but he's not paralyzed. His arms and legs feel like they're weighted down with tons of iron. Breathing hurts too much, so he takes his time and doesn't try to call for Talaitha. There is light streaming through the bedroom window, and that means he's been lying up for most of the morning. The light gives him hope.

My stomach feels like it's been someone's punching bag. If I'd thrown up a thousand times all at once, I wouldn't feel as bad as I do now, he thinks.

After ten minutes, Jevonte tries to sit up and take stock of his body, but he can't. He can feel his hands and feet, and he's trying to move and wiggle on the bed, but it's like struggling against a straitjacket. Straitjacket. Jevonte looks down the side of his body and chest, and he can see the outline of two folded arm sleeves coiled around and under his armpits. His feet are immobilized, but he can feel his ankles pressed together. He tries to draw his knees up, but his knees are bound together as well. Jevonte's heart begins to pound in earnest as he looks around the room for some sign that he must be dreaming, having the worst nightmare of his life. He opens his mouth in an attempt to call for Talaitha, but he can only make hollow, dry sounds that will reach nowhere.

"Good morning, King. I'm glad you're awake. You've been a very naughty boy, haven't you?" asks Talaitha as she strolls into the room and sits on the edge of the bed beside him.

Jevonte's eyes grow wide and pleading. He opens his mouth wide, trying to coax some words out of his body, but he can only produce dry, hacking coughs. Talaitha looks at him with pity, to Jevonte's surprise. Her expression is compassionate, sorrowful, and confusing. She sits next to Jevonte, seemingly blind to his struggle, his bonds, and his anguish.

"I have to run into the city for a while. You took a nasty tumble last night, and you made quite the mess. It took me a while to clean up. I actually didn't think your bowels could still produce so much shit. You may not feel well these days, but I am here to support you. You should be fine, so if you feel like you're getting sick, at least you won't fall and hurt yourself. I should be back in a few hours. Don't go anywhere," Talaitha laughs and walks out of the room.

Jevonte lies still. He stops trying to move against his bonds. He begins to sob, wishing that he could end it all in the blink of an eye. Eventually, he cries himself to sleep. Before slumber fully claims him, his last thoughts are of Melanie and her smile. He finds peace in the memory and gives himself over to hope for another chance at life.

17

Deception and Desperation

It's been weeks since Roscoe arranged a meeting with his friend and private investigator, Marcus Drummonds. Marcus made good use of the time, so when he called Melanie to request a meeting, he had plenty of information to share. Turns out, so did Melanie when they met at his office in Sparrows Point, Maryland. After a brief introduction and some case file creations, Marcus and Melanie took lunch across the street at the Atlantis Marina Bar & Grill. Business was slow for this time of day, and the two parties were able to hold a fairly private conversation.

"Ms. Decartes, pleased to finally get some time with you. I have heard so much about you from your brother, RhaShawn," Marcus said.

"Mr. Big Head, you mean," Melanie laughed. "Uncle Roscoe had nothing but good things to say about you," she smiled.

"All lies, I bet," Marcus replied.

"I was impressed because Uncle Roscoe rarely gives glowing reports about anyone. He said you were the real deal and that we could trust you with anything."

"Roscoe and I go way back. I truly owe that man my life. More than once, he's pulled my fat out of the fire. He's more than a brother to me."

"I've never dealt with a private eye, and I'm not sure how this arrangement is supposed to work. What do we do?" Melanie asked and motioned for the waitress.

"Well, it's not what 'we do'; it's what 'I' do. All I need from you, Roscoe, or anyone else in the family is information, whether factual or not. There will never be enough information. Rarely is there in most cases, so the more I get, the better. Now, RhaShawn told me when I met with him and your uncle that you were going to confront this Talaitha person. They informed me that you had already made up your mind, despite my advice to the contrary. So, how did things go?" Marcus asked.

The waitress finally arrives and takes their order. She's slow and dismissive, and her energy is decidedly not Black-friendly. Melanie has to repeat her order several times. Marcus is radiating his displeasure, and the waitress gets the hint and completes their order. After she walks away, the pair shakes their heads, knowing exactly what they just encountered.

"We'd better inspect the food when it returns," Melanie jested.

"You mean if it returns before our meeting is done?" said Marcus, shaking his head in disappointment.

Over the next thirty minutes, Melanie recalls her office visit with Talaitha. She recounts her visit to see Jevonte in the hospital and presents copies of the lab reports that the CNA at Sable Ridge State Hospital shared with her.

"That was brave of her, so I'll be sure to leave her out of my reporting," offered Marcus. "You mentioned a strange man sitting in Talaitha's office when you arrived. What can you tell me about him? How did he strike you?"

"I think he was a patient. He was Black and light-skinned, and I believe he had green eyes, maybe hazel or a variation. I don't know how tall he was, but he had to be at least 5'7" or 5'8" because when he stood up, he was taller than me."

"If you had to guess, what would you say he weighed?" inquired Marcus.

"Best guess, maybe 140 lbs, maybe 145 lbs, give or take. I don't remember everything he was wearing, but when

I walked out of Talaitha's office, he had a coat of some kind folded across his lap."

Investigator Drummond began writing in his pocket notepad. When he finished, he told Melanie about the man he had seen after meeting with her uncle and brother. "I can't be certain, but I believe these may be the same persons. Is there anything else you care to share?"

"Not really. It all happened so fast. The way Talaitha spoke to me made me want to beat her ass, for real. She was so smug, confident, and cold. I mean, she did not flinch when I told her I had evidence that she poisoned my man—my friend, I mean. All I know is that I get the sense that something is wrong with her upstairs, like some wires are seriously loose." Melanie looked around for the waitress; her stomach was growling.

"Listen to me carefully, ok. Do not confront that woman again. I don't know enough about her, and if what you shared with me about Jevonte's labs is true, and I do believe you, she is not someone you want to play with," said Marcus.

"I don't intend to play with her, believe me. When I see her again, let her front with me; I will knock that stupid grin of hers into her momma's womb."

"Melanie, no. Let me be very clear. This case is serious. Please refrain from contacting her until I can gather more information about her. At this point, she doesn't know we're looking into her, and I want to keep it that way. Trust me, we will get a chance to bring all of her and her past into the present. I will deal with her, but I also need you to stay away from her for now. Can you do that for me, please?" asks Marcus, his big brown eyes and furrowed brows centered on Melanie.

"I will not make any promises. I can't because I truly believe Jevonte's life is in danger, but I won't do anything without letting you and Uncle Roscoe know."

Less than satisfied with her answer, Marcus decides to let it go. "I have uncovered a few things about Talaitha, things I wonder if Jevonte knows about. Her records are incomplete, and some have been sealed. This situation usually means that there was something in her past where she was in the system, either under juvenile detention or possibly the foster care system. I'm still working on getting clarity on that, as well as troubling inconsistencies in her employment record. I'll know more in another week or so. Please keep in touch with my office until then, and if you find out where Ruby's husband is or how to reach him, please let me know."

The meeting ends, and Marcus and Melanie rise to leave when the waitress finally arrives with their food.

Roscoe has been cruising some of his and Jedidiah's old haunts. He has spent the last few days retracing the routes he and his brother frequently traveled when they needed to regroup and take a break from everything and everyone. Roscoe points his Electra Glide Ultra Classic towards Garrett County, seeking US 40 until he arrives at Keysers Ridge. He motors around the periphery, taking his time to scope out some of the fishing holes the two of them used to stop by. It's not the season for fishing in this area, so he isn't disappointed, but didn't really expect to find Jedidiah here. Roscoe continues to ride the National Road, following US 40 Alternate until he reaches the Savage River State Forest. He passes through Grantsville until he reaches one of their favorite stops, the Casselman Bridge. In the autumn, this area was always the place to be for its tranquil sunsets and perfect sunrises. The state has not kept up with the roads in the area, and Roscoe has to tease the big bike carefully around the potholes that greet newcomers to the bridge. He starts making his way back, using the Historic National Scenic Byway that runs through Henderson Avenue and Baltimore Street. Traffic starts to get heavier in and around

Baltimore City, so Roscoe pulls into the Urban Oyster on 36th Street to let his Black Beauty—as she is affectionately called—cool down and the traffic to ease. The trip has stirred his appetite, and for Roscoe, there is nothing like chef and owner Jasmine Norton's short rib pappardelle, which is "slap yo momma good," as Jedidiah used to say.

Roscoe walks inside, and the maître d' greets him with a smile. She informs him that the wait time will be fifteen minutes, but that he can be seated at the bar until then. Roscoe thanks her and walks over and grabs an empty bar seat. He orders his usual gin and tonic and thinks to himself, Brother, I have literally searched all of Maryland for you, so where are you?" The family needs you right now.

"Roscoe! I'll be damned. What in the hell are you doing here, dude?" asks Jedidiah from behind.

Roscoe turns in his seat and, with surprise and joy, reaches for his brother in an enormous bear hug. "Brother, I have been searching high and low for you. Everyone has."

Jedidiah drops his arms from around his brother and hangs his head. He takes a seat next to Roscoe and motions for the bartender. The two men settle into place at the bar, and silence ensues between them. For several long moments, neither man says a word, nor do they make eye contact. SportsCenter is playing on the television in front of them and offers a brief distraction from the awkwardness they're both feeling. Jedidiah finally breaks the peace. "Brother, I don't want to be here anymore, not without her," says Jedidiah. He continues to stare blankly at the television, and then the drinks arrive.

"Big brother, I don't blame you for missing her. We all do, but…"

"But what, Roscoe? Do you miss her as I do?" Jedidiah asks and then turns to face Roscoe.

"Yo, we all miss Ruby. She was our center, the family's rock, and you know this. We just…"

"We just what, brother? Are you telling me that you still need her like I do, like I always have?" A single tear begins to form in Jedidiah's right eye.

"Jedidiah, please. Don't do this, not now," pleads Roscoe.

"I don't even know why you're here, Roscoe. Haven't you done enough damage to the family, to me?" responds Jedidiah angrily.

Roscoe pauses and sips his gin. Now he understands. He knows what Jedidiah is hurting over. "My God, Jedidiah, is that what's eating at you right now? Really? We've been over this a hundred times before. That horse ain't never gonna rise again; we've beat it into the ground so many times, it's puree now. Jevonte is your son, full stop, man," exclaims Roscoe in exasperation.

"She told me she didn't know for sure, Roscoe," Jedidiah said, his voice trembling. "We used to fight a lot before we got our act together. Everybody thought we were this perfect couple. We were seen as the exception to the rule among Black couples. Ruby's church used to hold us up as models of what the Bible meant when it said that Christ loved the church and that husbands should love their wives the way Christ loved the church, sacrificially, but it was all a lie. It was my fault. I was neglecting her at home, I guess. I just wasn't there for her. I believe that was the time she became involved with you. I think she wanted to hurt me, make me see her, and what I was missing. I don't know." Roscoe remains silent, neither affirming nor denying Jedidiah's accusation. He stares into his glass, swirling the ice cubes around inside it.

The bartender makes another round and asks the two men if they want seconds. They both nod.

"I always knew, brother. I think I always knew. When she told me that she was pregnant with Jevonte, I did the math, man. I was driving my rig across Pennsylvania, carrying a load earmarked for Niagara Falls. I didn't get back home for weeks, so I know I couldn't be the father. I'm not Jevonte's dad."

"Brother, don't be ridiculous. Of course, you're Jevonte's father. You're the man he knows, the man that he grew up calling father…"

"But you are the one he's always leaned on. You're the one he always confided in and shared his secrets with, and you're the one he looked to for guidance with the women. It wasn't me, that's for sure," said Jedidiah.

"Jevonte is my nephew, and yes, we have always been super close, but not because I'm his father. We just always clicked. I don't know how to explain it, but we always vibed on the same level. I won't lie; if I ever had a son, I would want him to be just like Jevonte."

"So are you telling me that you and Ruby were never intimate, never?" asked Jedidiah, and his eyes fixed on Roscoe's face for an answer.

"Brother, I loved Ruby. I did, but I loved her like a sister, and that's all. There was a shared intimacy between us, but I never crossed the line with her. When you left, she reached out to me, and we talked until she felt better. We did that many nights when she had no idea where you were. She never knew whether you were dead or alive sometimes. You wouldn't call her or write to her. She had nothing to go on, and some months she was barely getting by. She had no one else to share her pain with, at least no one who wasn't going to put all of her business out on the street, and I won't apologize for being that listening ear," answered Roscoe, returning Jedidiah's glare. "She was my family too."

"I'm sorry, bro. I just feel lost and useless now. She was my everything. I can't even be in that house anymore. Her things, her clothes, she's everywhere, and it hurts, man," says Jedidiah through tears.

Roscoe stands and hugs his brother tightly. The embrace muffles Jedidiah's heart-wrenching cries as his soul is poured out on the strength of his brother's arms. The other bar patrons look on with sympathy, giving both men space to work through the moment. A waitress approaches the men carefully and respectfully and informs them that their table is ready. Roscoe wipes his brother's face with a napkin, and Jedidiah gathers himself.

"I'm sorry, brother. I didn't think it through. I should have known you weren't Jevonte's father. I'm sorry," said Jedidiah meekly.

"Listen, no harm, no foul, ok. Let's get these short ribs handled. Then we can talk about handling the rest of Ruby's affairs, and you need to know what's been happening with Jevonte, your son."

"Roscoe, I just don't think I can do that right now. If you're not Jevonte's father, who got Ruby pregnant then?"

It's the weekend, and Talaitha has been outside most of the morning clearing weeds from around the outside of the house. Her colony of mushrooms was moved inside just in time for the changing fall weather. Inside the home, Jevonte is still bedridden, free of the straitjacket. It's no longer needed since he can barely move his frail frame. He lies in bed, uncovered and emaciated. His mind is a fog on most days, but today, he is more alert than usual. He can hear Talaitha outside tending to her garden.

Alone with only his thoughts, Jevonte allows himself to daydream. He is a million miles away, surrounded by his mom and dad, his family, and Melanie is there. He's strong again and vibrant, bringing new life to old homes and structures across Baltimore. He's traveling and meeting new people. He's confident, and his friends seek him out and want his company. Occasionally, he dons a cape and flies around the world delivering justice to the victimized and oppressed. He's in space, visiting new worlds and discovering planets teeming with life. In all of his adventures, there is one common theme—there is no Talaitha, no cruise, no wedding, and no straitjacket. He is free in his thoughts, and the peace lasts until he hears the doorbell at the front of the house. There is no response, but he can hear that Talaitha has stopped working in the backyard. The doorbell is followed by pounding—incessant pounding, urgent, open-this-door-right-now kind of pounding.

Talaitha appears at the bedroom door and gives Jevonte a death stare, then she closes the door, confident that Jevonte's condition has fully immobilized him.

Talaitha walks to the front door and looks through the peephole. She expels an air of disgust as Melanie's brilliant smile fills her view. She takes a deep breath and opens the door, her smile now matching Melanie's.

"Ms. Decartes, how delightful to see you again! How have you been, ma'am?" says Talaitha, her voice laced with sarcasm.

"Where's Jevonte, Talaitha?" Melanie shot back.

"Jevonte is in his skin, right where he's always been and right where he needs to be."

"Look, I don't have time to fool around with you, Talaitha. I just need to see Jevonte and speak with him. Please go and get him."

"No," replied Talaitha, and she leaned against one side of the doorframe, her arms crossed in defiance.

"Talaitha, look, this is urgent. I have a message from his family for him. No one has been able to reach him, and everyone is worried. If I can just get…"

"I said no. You can't see him right now," Talaitha says, her voice now loud and assertive. "He is currently resting, and I will not interrupt his peace for trivial matters. Give me the message, and I will see that he gets it."

"What's the matter with you, Talaitha? You have him isolated from his entire family. Just give me a few minutes, and I'll leave and be out of your hair."

"You're not his family. I'm his family. I'm all the family he needs—or wants. Now get the hell off of my property before I have you dealt with," sneers Talaitha.

Through the door, Jevonte can hear Talaitha's voice, and as he strains to listen, he can hear another familiar voice, a woman's voice. Melanie? he thinks. Jevonte concentrates and begins rolling to one side, his hand reaching for the bedpost for leverage. With all his waning strength, Jevonte manages to swing his legs out of the bed and sits, hunched over, his arms resting on his thighs. He's winded from the effort, but he doesn't stop. With his eyes on the bedroom window, he leans forward, hoping to gain enough momentum to fall towards it. He starts rocking forward. His thighs shake, and his knees creak and pop from the strain; with one final effort, he falls out of bed toward the window.

Jevonte closes his eyes and attempts to relax as he lies there, his heart thumping like a jackhammer. He starts breathing deeply and slowly until his pulse slows. The women have stopped talking. Oh no, please no, Jevonte thinks. With renewed urgency, Jevonte begins dragging his limp, frail body across the bedroom floor. He reaches the bottom of the window, but the sash is too high to reach from the floor. He's going to have to stand somehow and gain purchase on the windowsill.

There is a menacing silence between the two women. Neither has surrendered ground to the other, but Talaitha breaks eye contact when she hears something crash to the floor from one of the bedrooms.

"I have work to do, Ms. Decartes. Do not come back to our home, or I will have you arrested for trespassing. Do I make myself clear?"

Melanie begins to push past Talaitha but decides against it, recalling the investigator's words. "I'll be back, Talaitha. Rest assured that this is not over, and when I come back, nothing you do will keep me from seeing Jevonte, I promise you that," says Melanie with confidence. "You are not fooling me. I know who you are!"

"I'm sure you do know who I am. I'm the woman who's mounting your man on the regular. Now get the fuck off my property," and Talaitha slams the door in Melanie's face.

For the briefest of seconds, Melanie stands staring at the door. Her hair is up, and her fists are balled in fury, but she turns and starts back towards her car. I'll be back, bitch, Melanie thinks to herself. Got me wanting to hit somebody today. I can't stand that psycho!

Jevonte has managed to get one hand on top of the windowsill, and he begins pulling with everything he has. Luckily, his weight has dropped so much that, even though he's diminished in size, he's able to pull himself up to almost eye level with the window's bottom sill. Peering just over the edge, he spots Melanie walking toward her car. His shoulders are trembling from the effort of holding on to the window ledge. Undeterred, Jevonte begins banging on the window, hoping to get Melanie's attention. He can feel his position shifting and sliding down the windowsill. He knows he can't stand much longer before gravity and his weakness push him back to the ground. He bangs as hard as he can and watches as Melanie stops at her car door—keys in hand. Did she hear me? Please, Mel, turn around, Jevonte prays.

Melanie stops short of unlocking the car door. She's standing at the door, and she's thinking about her next move. She would rather not leave without seeing Jevonte. Her instincts are screaming that something is wrong, that Talaitha is the problem, and, deep down, she knows she has to take action. When she looks back over her shoulder at Jevonte and Talaitha's home, there is movement at one of the side windows, or what she thinks is movement. There is nothing there now, and just as she begins to turn back to the car door, the curtains at the window close swiftly.

Jevonte saw Melanie begin to turn, and his heart started rejoicing. Then Talaitha burst through the bedroom door and rushed Jevonte; he braced for the impact. She moved like lightning, and her hands clamped onto the back of his neck. With a simple shrug, Talaitha tossed Jevonte to the floor and closed the curtains, casting the room into semi-darkness. Jevonte lay sprawled on the floor, his hope now dashed to the ground as well.

"See, you've kissed the floor again. This is why I have to keep you in the jacket. I can't have my little king falling out of bed and hurting his little self," Talaitha mocked him using a baby-like voice. "And don't be too disappointed about little Miss Peggy. She will be taken care of, so you don't have to fret about not seeing her."

As Talaitha lifted Jevonte from the floor, he tried to speak her name, but could only squeal and mouth a few words. She threw him onto the bed, and he lay there, his eyes pleading, begging her for compassion. She opened the closet door and withdrew the jacket, and Jevonte's eyes went wide with fear and agonized horror. "Don't worry, King. This is for your own good. Now be still like a good little boy," Talaitha purred as she unfurled the heavy-duty straightjacket.

The last of her clients has finished their session with Talaitha, and she completes the notes and annotations that were past due. Briefly, she launches the monitoring application to check on Jevonte. He's resting. The sedative she gave him before leaving for work has him calm and compliant. Today's dose will wear off in another thirty minutes, and he'll be able to remove the jacket. She stopped locking it since she started using the sedatives. He hasn't had very much bladder control, which Talaitha believes is a side effect of the psychotropic enhancer she's been adding to his meals. The lorazepam was easy to get since she prescribes it to over half her patients.

Talaitha closes the monitoring application and starts organizing her desk, making sure everything is back in its assigned place. She's about to walk out of her office when the door swings open. Nolan is standing before her. He's wearing his trench coat this time.

"Hello, sister. May I come in?"

"Nolan! What are you doing here? I don't have you on my schedule, and I'm closing for the day," Talaitha exclaimed.

"No, you're not," replied Nolan calmly as he pushed past Talaitha to take a seat in her office. "You have a problem, my dear sister, and I'm here to solve it for you."

Talaitha was taken aback for a moment by his brash entry, but she eventually closed the door slowly and settled into the therapist's seat across from Nolan. "So you think I have a problem, do you?"

"Yes, her name is Melanie.

18

Dead Man's Bluff

It's still early in the autumn season, but the change in the weather does not go unnoticed. In and around the town of Accident, evidence of change is almost everywhere. Mr. Randolph is hurriedly sweeping the front of his small convenience store of all the leaves that have been crowding the entryway. Mrs. O'Neill is setting fresh pastries in her bakery window, a sure sign that fall is soon to come. Tungsten's Coffee shop is buzzing with early morning patrons, many seated inside sharing the latest juicy tidbits about Mr. Henry and Mrs. Drysdale's ongoing illicit affair. Nothing is very private or secret in Accident—not for very long. Not surprisingly, the topic of the new homeowners on 52 Riverrun Drive was on nearly everyone's list of new things to talk about.

"I hear they have orgies happening almost every night," Janice Tickelton whispered to her friend Mary Barkington.

"Now, how do you know that? Have you been to one of them?" Mary replied with a raised eyebrow.

"No, that's not it. I hear they've been practicing some kind of Hoodoo there late at night," interjected Marybelle Crooks as she took a sip of coffee.

"That's right. I heard that too. Those Blacks are doing all kinds of wickedness and then calling it their religious freedoms. It's all evil if you ask me," exclaimed Susan Harrison.

Gerald Harper Jefferson couldn't take it anymore and stood up at the table adjacent to where the four women were sitting. He'd been trying to read his paper and ignore all of the silly talk, but the women were not the least bit bothered by his meal or need for peace, so he let them have it.

"If you four crows don't stop talking that willy-whack nonsense, I'm going to turn the hose on the lot of you. You don't know those people from Adam, and yet you sit here making up all kinds of shit about them. You all should be ashamed of yourselves," thundered Gerald.

The coffee shop went silent, and all eyes turned to see the faces of all four women turn as red as turnips.

"Well, excuse me! Who made you the Almighty judge and jury of the town all of a sudden?" barked Susan Harrison.

"The lot of you disgust me. They are good people; well, it seems the husband is, anyway. I haven't met the wife, but they keep to themselves and keep their home clean, which is better than I can say for you old, broken-down, dried-up chicken cacklers," he replied, his voice dripping with disdain. Gerald grabbed his coffee and paper and walked out of the coffee shop. The women resumed their shop talk without missing a beat.

On his way home, Gerald started to pay a visit to Jevonte. He hadn't seen him out of the house in months. Maybe not. The wife's car is there, and I don't know what she's like. She might not like uninvited guests. I'll come by at another time to see if I can catch Jevonte outside, he thought to himself, and resumed his walk home.

Inside the home, Jevonte was busying himself thinking about ways to contact his family. He hadn't eaten very much all week and was purposely avoiding Talaitha's juices. He felt stronger for it. As he lay in bed, he could hear the sounds of the season's change happening all around him. The squirrels were particularly active this morning, running back and forth between the trees in the yard and the roof. Jevonte marveled at their energy, but the noise inspired him, so on this Saturday morning, he decided to put his plan into action. He had a theory, and he was going to test it today.

Talaitha came into the master bedroom and began gathering some of her things for the office. It was Saturday, so why was she acting like she was going to work, Jevonte thought to himself.

"Listen, are you going to be alright by yourself this morning? I need to go into the Baltimore office, but I won't be long," said Talaitha.

Perfect, Jevonte thought. "Yes, my love. I'll be fine. I still feel out of it, though, so I'll just rest some more. I thought I could get out of the house a little bit today, but that's not happening."

"I see you haven't been drinking the juices I make for you. I think you need to continue with those. I'm not putting all that effort into making those for you just to see them go to waste," she said and walked over to the bedroom closet where the straitjacket was—her hand rested on the doorknob.

Jevonte's eyes got big, and his breathing momentarily stopped. "I—I hear you, love. I was just taking a break because I was going to the bathroom too much. My butt is sore, and I…"

"I'll take some of the ginger out; that should help. I'll make a new batch for you this evening when I get home. Just get back on schedule, and you'll be back on your feet in no time."

I've been taking that junk for months now, and it feels like I'm just getting worse, Jevonte thought to himself before responding. "Ok, babe. I'll get back on schedule. Hey, why are you going in on a Saturday anyway?" Jevonte didn't want to appear too eager for her to leave.

"I've agreed to co-author a paper for the American Psychological Association. I need some files from work to get started."

"Oh, ok. Congratulations on that. I know it will be good. By the way, I need to get on the computer, but something is still wrong with my access."

Talaitha paused before leaving the room. Then, turning to face Jevonte, she said, "I'll have someone come over to look at the system. And just so you know, my office is locked. I'll be back later this afternoon."

Talaitha walked out without looking back at Jevonte. Jevonte's apprehension was rising, but he felt confident that while she was gone, he would be able to test his theory fully. So, she knows I was in her office. If my prediction is correct, I think I'll have a window to discuss what she wrote in the journal. We have to talk about what happened to her, Jevonte thought. "And we need to talk about what's happening to us," Jevonte concluded.

Jevonte waited a good twenty minutes after Talaitha left the house to begin pooling his strength to get out of bed. It wasn't as hard as he thought it would be, but he was still winded and had to stand still for a minute after rising from the bed. With careful and deliberate steps, Jevonte made his way to the bedroom door and opened it. The house was silent, and he chuckled to himself, wondering why it wouldn't be. He shuffled down the hall and entered the kitchen. The coolness of the floor was invigorating.

He sat at the desktop computer and tried to turn it on. Nothing happened. It was plugged in, and all of the wires and accessories were connected. He examined the UPS, and its green power light glowed dimly beneath the desk. Everything looked right, but the computer monitor remained blank and unresponsive. Whatever Talaitha has done, she has rendered the desktop useless, so Jevonte decides to examine a few of the interior cameras around the house. It's not like they are hidden, but their placement makes no sense unless you were expecting to monitor traffic inside the house.

Time to test our little theory, Jevonte thinks to himself. He walks around the house, making sure he is in plain sight of the camera. Although he avoids direct eye contact with any of the units, he makes sure the camera captures him engaged in a purposeful activity. He is rummaging through drawers, examining magazines left on the coffee table, and sitting in the kitchen, seemingly deep in thought. After a few moments of thought, Jevonte stands and starts walking toward the basement door. Suddenly, he stops dead in his tracks and grabs forcefully at his chest. He staggers and leans heavily into the basement door. His legs are visibly trembling, and he sags to the floor, still clutching at his chest. Jevonte rolls to his back and begins straining to breathe, to draw air into his lungs. With one hand holding desperately to his chest, he extends his free hand towards space. The look of panic and fear crisscrosses his face, and then suddenly, he stops moving, and his arms fall to the floor in a lifeless heap.

Alerted to movement inside the house, Talaitha launches her monitoring app on her phone. She's watching Jevonte walk around the home. "It's about time you got your lazy ass up out of bed," Talaitha says to herself. As she merges onto the highway, she takes a last glance at the app and sees Jevonte begin to stagger and fall to the floor. "What the hell?" Talaitha says in nervous panic. She continues watching, and when Jevonte stops moving, she swerves back onto the state road and begins looking for a place to make a U-turn. In her haste, she nearly collides with another car before fishtailing. Talaitha manages to avoid the shoulder ditch and gets her car pointed in the right direction. She guns the A8 and heads back down the road towards Accident. She's not five minutes into the return trip when a set of blue lights and sirens captures her attention in her rearview mirror.

"Fuck, fuck, fuck!" blurts Talaitha as she begins pulling the Audi onto the side of the road. Talaitha turns the car off and looks at the monitoring app intently. Jevonte is still on the kitchen floor and not breathing. Her mind is racing. "I was extra careful this time. This can't be happening," she fumes. As she watches the deputy emerge from his vehicle, she hatches a plan to exploit the situation. She rolls down her window in preparation for the officer's arrival.

"Hello, officer," Talaitha says cordially.

"Good afternoon, ma'am. You're in quite a hurry today; where's the fire?" asks the deputy.

"Well, officer, there is a medical emergency at my home, and I need to get there right now," replies Talaitha.

"What kind of medical emergency?"

Talaitha launches her app and pulls up the video of Jevonte's collapse. She shows it to the deputy and says, "He isn't moving now, and it doesn't look like he's breathing. He's been sick a lot lately, and I was on my way to pick up some prescriptions when I got the alert," she lied. She upped the level of concern and panic in her voice and said, "It looks awful, and I just want to get home as quickly as possible. I am a doctor, and my husband looks to be in crisis. Can you help me get home, please?"

"Ma'am, give me your address, and I can dispatch an ambulance to your residence right now."

"It's too far. Sable Ridge State Hospital is about thirty minutes away from my home. From here, we can make it in under 10 minutes. Please, can you just escort me to my home so I can provide care for my husband? We have no time to waste. You can write me a ticket when we get to my house. All I am asking is some professional courtesy, one first responder to another."

The deputy says nothing and then turns to head back to his vehicle. Over his shoulder, he says, "Let me take the lead, and follow me." He then stops and asks, "I need the address!"

"Just follow me," yells Talaitha, and pulls onto the roadway.

The two cars arrive at Talaitha's home in less than 10 minutes. Talaitha rushes from her car; the deputy is not far behind her. Opening her front door, Talaitha and the deputy walk into the living room and approach the kitchen area, where Talaitha had seen Jevonte on the floor. He's gone. The dishwasher's start of its rinse cycle briefly breaks the silence.

Talaitha strolls through the kitchen followed by the living room. She walks into the sitting room and then to her office. The door is still locked. She then walks to the basement door, opens it, and calls out Jevonte's name. No response.

"The video showed him right here on the floor. You saw that, right?" Talaitha asks the deputy.

"Yes, ma'am. Have you checked the bedrooms? Shall I..."

"No, that's alright. I'll check them," and Talaitha walks down the hallway, opening the two guest rooms before reaching the master bedroom. There, lying comfortably on his stomach and breathing easily, was Jevonte. His face was turned away from the door, and had Talaitha seen the grin on his face, she would have flown into a blind rage, for sure. Talaitha closed the door and started to head back to the kitchen. When she turned around, she almost bowled over the deputy; he was standing right behind her.

"Oops, sorry," said the deputy. "Is your husband alright? Does he need medical attention?"

Talaitha gathered herself. "No. He's resting, and I saw that he was breathing just fine. He managed to make it back to bed, which is where he needs to be anyway. I'll take care of him as soon as he wakes."

After issuing a warning, the deputy leaves, and Talaitha eyes the bedroom area. She sits at the desktop computer and enters a keyboard command. The monitor lights up, and she completes her login. She immediately launches the monitoring software. She replays the morning video and watches Jevonte make his rounds until he starts clutching his chest and collapses. She continues watching for a few more minutes, then notices that Jevonte rises and, to her astonishment, flips her the bird! He rolls to his knees and stands. The hallway cameras catch him walking weakly towards the master bedroom, where he climbs back into bed and pulls the covers up over his shoulders.

Talaitha leaps from the computer desk and rushes toward the master bedroom. She halts in the middle of the hall, turns around, and heads back toward the basement. Opening the basement door, she rushes down into the darkness. Talaitha is furious. Cursing, stomping her feet, and hurling tools around the room, her anger is unhinged, and she is seeing red. "So you think this is all a game? You think you can just manipulate me like this? How fucking dare you?" She screams at her garden pit from the depths of her soul. "Ok, Mr. I got you. I will make you wish you had never left me alone on prom night; just watch." Talaitha grabs some of her rags and the solvent from the workbench. She then storms back up the stairs with violence in her heart.

Jevonte heard her. His heart begins racing. He didn't anticipate such an extreme reaction. He begins throwing off the sheets and comforter to rise from the bed. If he can lock the bedroom door, it might give Talaitha enough time to cool off, and then they can have a real conversation. Just then, the bedroom door slams open, and Jevonte freezes. He does not recognize the woman standing in the doorway. Talaitha's visage is alien to him. Her face is filled with an intense rage, unlike anything he has ever seen before. He is afraid of her. He is afraid of what he is seeing. Her chest is tight, barely moving when she growls, "You're going to pay for what you've done! You left me all alone at the prom, you bitch."

"Tal. Tal, wait. Please try to calm down," Jevonte begs, his eyes focused on the rags and can of solvent that Talaitha is holding. "I can explain. We need to talk, please, babe."

Her eyes are nearly bloodshot red, but her advance across the bedroom floor is like greased lightning. Jevonte doesn't even register her movement; it's so sudden and unexpected, but when her fist connects with his face, the realization of the assault explodes in his mind. The face punch throws his body into complete shock, and Jevonte falls backward with such violence that his head strikes the bedpost with a vicious snap and crack. Jevonte's chin digs into his chest, and he rolls unconscious to the bedroom floor.

Talaitha stands motionless. She watches Jevonte carefully, just as a cat watches its captured prey. Her head is pounding, but she bends down to feel for a pulse. She's holding out hope that he's okay after hearing the crack when his head struck the bedpost. Finding none, Talaitha rises slowly and heads toward the front door. She wears no expression on her face, but a single tear escapes down her cheek as she leaves the house. Her face is a stone, expressionless and devoid of any emotion. She pulls out of her driveway and heads toward Sable Ridge State Hospital.

Melanie arrived at Jedidiah and Ruby's home early Saturday. She was hoping that Jedidiah had finally come home. His brother, Roscoe, met her at the front door. She was happy to see him, but also disappointed that it was the wrong brother.

"Good morning, Uncle," greeted Melanie.

"Hey, young lady, come on in," replied Roscoe. "Can I get you some coffee? I just made a fresh pot."

"I'm good. I had my cup for the day before I left my house. Any news about Uncle Jedidiah yet?"

"I found him, but he still can't handle Ruby's death. It took a lot of talking to convince him to stay above ground, if you know what I mean. He's just very broken, and he is not coping with the pain of her death very well. I haven't been too active with this Talaitha situation because my brother needs me. At least twice in the last week, I had to stop him from ending it all. Things are very volatile right now, and I can't take my eyes off of him for too long." Melanie hugs Roscoe, and the pair moves into the living room.

RhaShawn walks out of the kitchen to greet his sister. "Hey sis, what brings you out of your bat cave today?" He jests.

"Same as usual. I just wanted to know whether you guys have heard anything yet. It's just been too long. The police still aren't providing much information. I don't think they've even assigned a detective to the case."

"No, sweetheart, we haven't heard a thing, but I'm not surprised by that. We weren't going to be a priority to them anyhow, so I am not surprised. However, I did hear back from Marcus. He has been very busy," said Roscoe.

"Oh my God, that is good news. What has he learned? Maybe we should have him over so he can share with the family all that he has." Said Melanie, her eyes brimming with hope.

"I believe we will get there soon, but for now, let's just keep this between the three of us, ok?" Roscoe begins sharing what the private investigator shared with him. According to the records Marcus was able to obtain, Talaitha was removed from her parents' care when the parents were sent to prison for human trafficking.

"The records are not clear, but Talaitha may have been pimped out by her parents at an early age to men throughout the area where she lived." Roscoe pauses to allow Melanie and RhaShawn to process what he had shared.

"Dear God," said Melanie, finally breaking the silence. "How old was she at the time?"

Roscoe doesn't immediately respond. He rubs his temple and says, "She was eleven, almost twelve."

"The hell?" gasps RhaShawn.

Marcus also told me that he was able to find her records in the foster system, which is normally next to impossible, but there was a breach of some kind, and he was able to take a look at the records. Talaitha and her sister…"

"She had a sister? I don't think any of us knew that," interrupted Melanie.

"She did, her name was Noelle. They both went into the foster care system at the same time and were taken into the same family. This is where the situation takes a dark turn—documents obtained by Marcus suggest that Talaitha killed her foster mom."

"Jesus!" mouthed Melanie. "She murdered her foster mother?"

"Well, Marcus mentioned that the details about her foster mother's murder were unclear. The police report copies he got his hands on only say that the foster mom was found in the backyard by their neighbors. When the police arrived, they found Talaitha babbling incoherently near the body, covered in blood from the garden shears sticking out of the neck of the foster mom."

"Uncle, when did that happen?" asked RhaShawn, his face still in shock from this revelation.

"Marcus didn't have an exact date, but there was information in the report about her sister, Noelle, and her disappearance sometime after their senior prom that year. The foster parents—the mom at least—were still around at that time because she filed a police report on the missing sister. So, the foster mom probably died sometime after this, if I were to hazard a guess," answers Roscoe.

"What happened to Talaitha then? Did the police charge her with the foster mom's death?" asked Melanie.

"Marcus stated that he did not come across any documents that indicated her arrest. He mentioned that there was some information about a state hospital, which he believes is called Sable Ridge. In fact, he's on his way to interview staff there. He said he'd update me as soon as he wrapped that up."

"Mr. Drummond has been very busy, and I'm impressed, too. Most of that kind of information is protected and hard to get at without court orders," Melanie said.

"I told you that Mr. Drummond is very good at what he does, but now I think I need to take a few matters into my own hands," Roscoe said, his tone becoming decidedly foreboding. "You weren't able to get in to see Jevonte, correct, Melanie?"

"No, sir. I'm telling you, it almost came to blows after I arrived at their house. She claimed that Jevonte was resting, but she wouldn't let me in and said she'd call the cops on me the next time I came there."

"I told you that you shouldn't go there and provoke that woman." Judging by what the investigator found, it's a good thing you didn't push it either," said RhaShawn.

"I agree, and your brother has a valid point. Please, just lay low until we get a full picture of what we're dealing with. I'm going to wait until Marcus finishes his interviews at Sable Ridge, then I'm going to visit this woman, and I won't get turned away without seeing Jevonte. What's their address, sweetheart?"

What have I done? Fuck, my temper just… What do I do now? I didn't think I hit him that hard, my God! I need to see Dr. Robinson. He'll know what to do. Wait, I can't tell him what I've done, not after the last time. Damn it to hell, Jevonte! Why?

Talaitha continues ranting to herself. She slows before hitting the Interstate and calms as she merges into traffic and heads west. Her nerves are frayed, but she manages to get her breathing under control. Her thoughts begin to settle, and some clarity starts to take hold in her mind. The drive to Sable Ridge will take her 20 minutes, giving her plenty of time to plan and craft a story to explain Jevonte's death.

I was in such a freaking rush, I left my phone at home. It doesn't matter. Who am I going to call now anyway?

Talaitha begins retracing the events and actions of the day.

Why in the hell did Jevonte do that? No, the question is, why did I let him bait me like that? That's the question. If I could go back, if I could just, I don't know. I hope Dr. Robinson is available on call today.

Nolan— I need to contact him. There's no need to go down that path anymore. I hope he hasn't kept his promise yet. Shit, why am I so unlucky these days?

Talaitha arrives at Sable Ridge State Hospital and pulls into the medical staff-only parking area. She makes a beeline for the mental health ward. She blows past the reception area, ignoring the pleas from the nurse on duty. Dr. Robinson's office door is closed, but she tries it anyway and, finding it locked, begins knocking forcefully. There is no movement inside and no answer. The nurse on duty reaches her and demands, "Ma'am, what do you think you're doing? You can't just waltz in here without checking in with the nurses' desk."

"Listen, cunt, I don't need to check in with you or anyone else at the hospital. I have visiting privileges, and I need to see Dr. Robinson right away," Talaitha shot back.

The nurse on duty was stunned into silence. She stood motionless, trying to process the unmitigated gall and utter disrespect coming from this stranger. Her eyes narrowed and focused hard on Talaitha. "I don't know where you practice or what they do at whatever hospital you work at, but let me tell you this: you will not be seeing Dr. Robinson today, I promise you. I'm calling security now, and if you would rather not end up in lockdown at County, I suggest you get the fuck off my ward now!"

Now this is a bold bitch. It's about time I ran into someone with some real stones. Maybe I should have been a lesbian, as if!

"Ok, ok, I have received the message. Please allow me to first apologize for how I spoke to you. I am in the midst of an impending medical emergency, and I have to see Dr. Robinson. It's a matter of utmost importance. I know I should have handled this a lot more professionally, but I am pressed, and the matter is very, very urgent," Talaitha said, her eyes feigning sincerity.

The nurse on duty said nothing at first. Talaitha could see that she was trying to calm herself and slow her breathing. "Dr. Robinson is with a patient right now, and he cannot be disturbed for any reason. I could get a message to him in the meantime, and he will respond as soon as he comes up from the lower wing."

"Wait, the lower wing? I thought that area of the hospital had been shut down over ten years ago. Is it still operational?" Talaitha asked, her voice betraying small tremors of concern and anxiety.

"It's been open now for at least the last three, maybe four, years. I take it you're familiar with the stories about the lower wing?"

"Yes, who hasn't? I assumed that after the investigation and the discovery of the bodies, they would have permanently closed that area. I didn't think the state would ever allow the hospital to reopen the wing."

"Well, they did. I think that's why Dr. Robinson has stayed on for as long as he has. He worked so hard to bring reform, but the abuses, the missing patients, and the cover-ups were just too much to fix."

Talaitha moderated her tone, subtly manipulating the conversation and further winning the nurse to her cause. "I feel so bad now for how I spoke to you. I realize you are safeguarding Dr. Robinson's peace here, and I admire that. It can't be easy, and my rudeness made your job all the harder. Sister, again, I am so truly sorry."

"Thank you. I appreciate that. It's not easy by a long shot," she chuckled. Talaitha smiled with her. "Listen, I'll let you into Dr. Robinson's office, and you can wait on him there. I'll just need your hospital credentials."

"Oh yes, sure, that's no problem," offered Talaitha, and she fished out her medical ID badge.

The nurse on duty took the credentials and headed back to her desk to scan the badge. Talaitha leaned against the wall and began counting silently in her head. Her nerves were beginning to grate within her, and she wanted to hit something. The counting helped, and she became distracted by the oval-painted designs lining the hallways. The color choices made her laugh within herself because they reminded her of the day Ms. Topeeka, her middle school science teacher, helped set her free. She was the only one who ever believed in her. She was the only one to see her scars, the ones that were hidden from people's eyes. She saved her that day. Ms. Topeeka saved her. Where was Ms. Topeeka now?

I killed my sister, and now I have no one to save me anymore. What? Jevonte is dead, not Noelle. Wait, what is going on here? Talaitha, girl, you are losing it right now. This heifer needs to hurry. If I can't see Dr. Robinson now, I need access to a file from the hospital database that is only available on his desktop.

Almost on cue, the nurse on duty returns with Talaitha's credentials. "Sorry that took so long. Here you go," and she opens the door to let Talaitha in. "Have a seat, and Dr. Robinson will probably be right in after his first break. I'll make sure he gets this message."

"Thank you," says Talaitha, and she takes a seat on the loveseat facing Dr. Robinson's desk. After the nurse leaves and the door closes, Talaitha is immediately at Dr. Robinson's desk. Using her credentials, she scans herself in the system portal. She doesn't try to get into Dr. Robinson's directory because she would be flagged immediately. Instead, she navigates to the Internet browser and types in the URL for her monitoring application server. The application launches from the browser, and she watches as the screen clears to reveal the body of her king, sprawled out and lifeless on the bedroom floor. The image is more than she can bear, and she shuts down the application. Panic once again rises from her stomach, and her head begins to feel dizzy.

Rising from behind Dr. Robinson's desk, Talaitha walks to the loveseat and sits. She places her head between her knees and begins to tremble. All the planning. All the effort she put into building, crafting, and assembling this new world—this new life—and now it's all over. The room is blistering and stuffy. She can barely breathe.

I can't lose it in here, not now. Buckle up, bitch. I've been here before. I can handle this. I'll start over, no problem. My garden has room for one more.

Talaitha leaves Dr. Robinson's office, and before she can reach the nurse on duty, a small figure walks out of an empty patient room.

Well, if it isn't the CNA, the little CNA piece of trash who gave Melanie that file on Jevonte. "Excuse me, nurse," Talaitha calls after her.

The CNA turns to face Talaitha, and before recognition can set in, Talaitha pushes her back into the patient room she just exited. There are no words. Talaitha's grip is a vise around the CNA's neck. In that moment, Talaitha exercises all her fears, all of her anxiety, and all of her panicked energy into her hands and forearms. She bears down on the CNA, and her little body slams quietly against the tiled hospital floor. The hatred, anger, and disdain in Talaitha's eyes are evident as she straddles the small CNA. The little CNA cannot scream. She cannot breathe, and soon her little body stops moving, all its life gone in a frenzy.

Talaitha does not move. She remains on top of the lifeless form, squeezing. She is barely breathing from the effort, yet she feels a rush of excitement. Her body reacts to the rush in waves of intense pleasure. Endorphins flood her brain as she lies on the cold hospital floor. Her mind is reeling from the explosive pleasure gripping her body. After a few moments, she stops squeezing the neck of the CNA and rolls to the floor beside her—her thoughts now subdued into peaceful spasms of semi-conscious bliss and relief. She lay next to the dead CNA's little body for the next few minutes. Her hands and legs are trembling from the intensity of the encounter. She doesn't care whether anyone walks into the room. She is happy again—and she knows what she needs to do, at last.

19

Confessional of Blood and Chains

Jevonte moans. His face is swollen and numb. He can barely feel his face, and his neck is bent at a terrible angle. His eyes flutter, and he begins focusing on his surroundings.

Am I dead? No, I'm in too much pain. I don't think I've ever been hit that hard, ever. My jaw feels broken, maybe dislocated. Did I bite my tongue off?

Jevonte rolls to his side and rests on one elbow. Sensation is returning to the inside of his mouth, and he can taste the blood. With his tongue, he tests to see if he lost any teeth. Everything is where it's supposed to be, and Jevonte breathes a sigh of relief.

How long have I been out? Lord, please have mercy. I think Tal wants to kill me, and if I don't get out of here, she just might.

Jevonte is too weak to stand, so he lies on his side and closes his eyes. Reaching behind his neck, he begins slowly rubbing his neck and jaw. The ache is hard and deep, but the rubbing seems to be helping. After resting a bit, Jevonte manages to turn over and push up enough to crawl.

He attempts to stand, but a wave of nausea overwhelms him, and he stops.

I might have a concussion. Everything is spinning. Now, where did she go? It doesn't matter, as long as she's gone. I have to find a way out of this place, even if I have to crawl into the street.

With a great deal of effort, Jevonte begins crawling out of his bedroom. The hallway looks a mile long; its walls are dark in his vision and seem ready to collapse on him. He falls to his side and rests—the ceiling mocking him from above.

C'mon, man. You can do this. If I can just get to the door, I can get somebody's attention. Maybe Mr. Jefferson will be passing by. Let's go, Jevonte; just keep it moving.

The medical staff and nurses on duty at Sable Ridge State Hospital are in a full-blown panic. Orderlies are escorting patients on the mental health ward towards the B and C wards to keep them away from the room with the murdered CNA. Some of the nurses are in tears. The head nurse and charge nurse both arrive around the same time. The on-duty nurse alerts them to the police's arrival. Questions fly at the nurse on duty, but no answers are forthcoming. The head nurse turns to Talaitha, noticing her for the first time since arriving.

After brief introductions, the head nurse asks her, "Did you see anything?"

"I'm so shocked," lies Talaitha. I think I saw her briefly while I was waiting on Dr. Robinson, but I can't be certain. Were any of you close to her? I'm a psychiatrist with privileges here. If any of the staff need to talk to someone, I'm available."

The nurse on duty nods her head in agreement and says, "This is bad. The cameras in that hall are not working, so we can't see when she went into that room. She wasn't even supposed to be here since it's her birthday. She only came in to lend a hand with these files because I asked her to," and she breaks down in tears.

As her fellow nurses begin comforting the nurse on duty, Talaitha fades into the background and walks to the exit sign adjacent to the elevators. She makes her way down the stairs and enters the lobby in time to see two state troopers enter the hospital. She smiles to herself as she gets into her car.

Before they figure anything out, I will pack up and leave this state. All I need to do is make a brief stop at the office in Baltimore, and I'll be ready.

Talaitha starts the car and, before she can shift out of park, decides to check her monitoring application one last time. There, as clear as day, is an empty bedroom—Jevonte is gone. Her pulse begins racing, and Talaitha starts scanning through the rest of the house—nothing. Jevonte is gone, but how, she thinks to herself. She searches the entire house again but finds nothing. All at once, her panic turns to relief as she realizes that maybe, just maybe, she doesn't have to leave. He's still mine. I don't have to start over again, she thinks.

Talaitha pulls out of the parking lot, careful not to invite too much attention, and hurries down the road toward the Interstate. She's moving fast, but she manages to be careful enough and arrives at the house without getting a ticket—or warning. She darts up the walkway to the front door. The door is still locked.

Good, so maybe he's still inside. Perhaps he's hiding from me again.

She opens the door carefully and steps inside the house, listening intently. "Jevonte, I'm home," she announces. There is no response. She begins walking through the kitchen, looking throughout the den and kitchen area. Her office is still locked, but she opens it anyway to peer inside. Finding it as expected, she walks down the hallway towards the bedrooms, and Jevonte is not where he was, collapsed on the floor. Talaitha is pleased and angry at the same time.

He's not dead, and that's good, but where could he have gotten off to? She turns and walks out of the bedroom and heads for the basement door. He may have opened it and fallen down the steps. Damn, he might still be dead then.

Before Talaitha can reach the basement door, she spies some light pushing its way into the back of the den. The back door is open, and she never leaves it open. Investigating, she walks out into the backyard and sees the greenhouse door ajar. Inside, Talaitha finds Jevonte sprawled out on the earthen floor. He's covered in sweat. His body is shaking from the cold. She walks over to his side and gently places a hand underneath him to turn him onto his back. His eyes are closed, but she can see that he is attempting to open them and speak.

"Shhhh, King. Don't say a word. I got you, baby. I got you," Talaitha purrs. She lifts Jevonte's ninety-two-pound frame from the greenhouse floor with seeming ease. Jevonte's frail body jangles helplessly in Talaitha's arms. The effort to get out of the house has left Jevonte depleted and wasted. As Talaitha begins walking back to the house, Jevonte's head lolls limply over her arm, and she takes care not to jostle him as she navigates the stairs back into the house. She looks down into his eyes with compassion and tenderness. Jevonte's eyes begin rolling up into his head, and Talaitha hurries to get him to the bathroom. She places him gently on the bathroom floor and begins filling the bathtub with warm water. She removes his tattered pajamas and places him into the rising warm water. After propping up his head on a rolled bath towel, Talaitha removes her clothing and gets into the tub behind him.

Talaitha embraces Jevonte in a warm, sensuous bear hug. She doesn't squeeze too tight and makes just enough contact with her hands and arms to keep him from shivering. The warm water begins to do its work, and the tension in Jevonte's body eases. She pours some of her bath oil into the water and starts massaging his chest and stomach. She traces slow circles through the curled hairs of his chest and abdomen. Jevonte starts to waken, and his breathing keeps pace with Talaitha's hand motions. After the water level has risen to his midchest, she shuts it off and leans forward to reach into his pubic hair.

"King, I thought I had lost you. I was afraid I'd never get to hold you again," Talaitha coos.

"What are you doing, Tal?" Jevonte said, his voice raspy and weak. "You almost killed me. What did I do to deserve that?"

There was only silence and the gentle sloshing of water in the tub, but Talaitha kept her hand moving, never pausing or stopping. When she finally responded, her voice was choked, and tears joined the warm water of the bath. "I didn't mean to, Jevonte."

It was very rare for her to say his name, and the act struck him because of the depth of her sincerity. "Tal, but you did. What do you mean that you didn't mean to? You almost broke my neck," he whispered.

"I have a past, King. There are things about me that I have never told you, or anyone, for that matter."

"Babe," said Jevonte weakly. "We all do. We all have scars and skeletons in our closets, things we want to keep buried. But babe, there is something else going on with you, something that I've wanted to talk to you about for a very long time. I just never did because I would rather not provoke you or run you off."

Silence envelops them, and for long moments, neither speaks a word. Talaitha reaches for some bath soap and turns on the hot water. She rolls the bath soap between her hands and begins to move her hands all over Jevonte's body. The heated water relaxes Jevonte even more, and his pores begin to open, his skin softens, and his blood begins to flow in earnest. Talaitha grabs his manhood in soapy hands and begins massaging and stroking him gently.

"Tal, babe, don't. I want to talk. We have to talk, love," Jevonte pleads.

"Hush, King. I am talking to you now," and she reaches down further to caress his balls. She rolls the first one, then the other smoothly with her fingers, before extending her middle finger to rub his scrotum. "I'm going to tell you everything tonight, ok. I'm going to tell you about my childhood rapes. I'm going to tell you about the way grown men would put themselves into my ass when I was only eleven. I'm going to tell you about the money my father made off of selling me to old men who would pound me unconscious in the back of their cars and vans."

Talaitha begins stroking Jevonte's hardness with increased pace and pressure. Her grip was smooth and sure. Jevonte attempted to reach for her hand to push her away, but he was too weak, and his will to resist was quickly fading. "Tal, that's not what I'm talking about," moaned Jevonte.

"I'm going to tell you all about the way my mother would watch the men take turns with me in our house. I'm going to tell you how the men would beat me senseless if I gagged while sucking their cocks. I'm going to paint a whole picture for you so that you fully understand what it feels like to be so torn that you bleed for days. I'm going to tell you about the strangers who would show up at the house and mount me while I was asleep in bed, how they would pass cash off to my father, and how they tried to make me do it with their dogs. Oh yes, you'll want to hear all about that," Talaitha growled in his ear as she ran her hands up and down the length of Jevonte's dick, pausing at the head, teasing it with warm, soapy water.

"Oh God, Tal, I didn't..." Jevonte stuttered before Talaitha cut him off.

"You wanted to know everything, right? There is so much more, so much more. I need to explain that my father would beat me with his belt while holding me upside down until I passed out. He never touched me in any other way. No, he let the other men fuck me and abuse me, but he didn't want me. He wouldn't give me love. He just let all the other men love me!" Talaitha spoke with gut-wrenching sorrow that overwhelmed Jevonte's senses.

Jevonte starts thrusting involuntarily. Talaitha maintains her pace, her hand gliding effortlessly up and down his shaft. Jevonte tried to turn in the tub; he wants to feel her inside, but he can't. "Talaitha, I can't hold it, please," he begs.

"No, we're not done, King. You like this, right? You like hearing about how those men filled me, stretched me, and hurt me. I can't have any kids now because of what they did to my body!" Talaitha cried in anguish as she pushed Jevonte around under her body until he was lying on his back in the tub. She quickly swung her leg over and around him until she straddled him. The water in the tub splashed and spilled onto the floor as Jevonte's head remained submerged. He struggled vainly to break the surface and gasp for air. Talaitha pulled his head forward to keep him from drowning.

"Tal, Talaitha," Jevonte sputtered, choking on the water that almost filled his mouth.

"Shhhh, and listen to me real good," Talaitha demanded, pausing to sit firmly on his throbbing appendage. She began grinding slowly, carefully guiding him into her body. Jevonte's mouth went wide, and his eyes rolled up into his head as he entered her. "They thought they could break me. They thought that I deserved what they did to me. They thought I was just going to die like some street dog, some castaway, nobody, but they were mistaken. They were all wrong. I survived," she said and started moving her pelvis harder, increasing the rhythm of every stroke and thrust. "No one, ever again, will ever control me. I will never be a plaything, a toy, or a freak show for anyone," she exclaimed and plunged Jevonte's head back under the bathwater.

Talaitha's thighs pinned Jevonte's arms, immobilizing him. She began humping him harder and harder, the water spilling out everywhere, drenching the bathroom floor. Jevonte was almost out of breath when he started cumming. He couldn't ask for permission this time; he would surely drown. As quickly as it all began, Talaitha dislodged Jevonte from her body and stood up in the tub. Jevonte broke the surface, gasping, wheezing, and choking for air. Talaitha stepped out of the water and sat on the toilet facing him in the tub. Her eyes were languid. Her body was covered in goosebumps and an oily sheen. She stared at Jevonte as he struggled to sit up. Almost all the water had drained from the tub, causing Jevonte to shiver again. Talaitha tossed a towel at him, then stood and left the bathroom.

Jevonte sat in the nearly empty tub, unmoving, as stunned silence gripped his mind.

As the evening descends on the town of Accident, and Jevonte pulls himself out of the tub, he reviews all that Talaitha said to him. Was she serious? Was she telling me the truth? I don't know what to believe. Jevonte looks at the bathroom door and whispers, "I didn't know. My God, how did you survive all of that horror?" I look at my wasted body. I'm a wreck. "Tal, all of this time, and you've been shouldering this pain and trauma all by yourself. I can see why she became a psychiatrist now."

Jevonte lies back on the bathroom floor and stares up at the ceiling, and utters a prayer, "Father in Heaven, help me to find a way to support my wife and love her even if it kills me. I know I sound ridiculous, but I've never loved anyone like this. Now that I know what's behind her anger and hurt, I can adjust; please help me. She's in crisis and in a lot of pain. I have to be the husband that she really needs."

A week has passed since Talaitha found Jevonte in the greenhouse. Jevonte has since started eating and drinking the food and juices Talaitha prepares for him. During that time, Talaitha has worked from her home office. Jevonte is following her instructions, and while Jevonte's strength has not returned in any measurable way, he can join with her at night for lovemaking that reminds him of their early days as a bonded couple. She has been patient with him, and he has not asked her any more questions about her past. They are taking meals together, and the atmosphere in the home is gentle, quiet, and more hopeful than it has been in many months. Jevonte is buoyed by this change, and in the mornings before he rises, he has started praying the way his momma taught him when he was a boy.

One early Wednesday morning, he wakes to find Talaitha is already out of bed, sitting at her vanity, and dressed for work. Even when she is working from home, she dresses for business, so this doesn't surprise Jevonte. What creates despair and panic in Jevonte this morning is the chain he finds around his ankle! In shock and surprise, he moves his leg and discovers that the chain is tied to the footboard of the bed. The rattle of the chain gets Talaitha's attention, and she turns to face Jevonte.

"Good morning, King. How are we feeling this morning?" She asks with sincerity.

"Tal, what is this?" Jevonte asks, lifting the chain in his hand.

"I'm going into Baltimore today and will probably work there most of the week."

"Okay, but what is this, and why am I chained to the bed?" Jevonte asks, his voice firm but not too demanding.

"You are making improvements, but you're still not well, and I don't want anything happening to you. I don't want to come home and find you've fallen down the stairs or something like that. It's only until I get home, and I can watch after you," Talaitha smiles.

"Tal, come on. Don't do this. I'm fine, and as you said, I am getting better. If I start feeling dizzy or sick, I'll just get in bed and wait until you come home. This really isn't necessary, babe," he pleads.

"Would you prefer the jacket?" and Talaitha walks over to the bedroom closet.

Jevonte goes silent. His mouth becomes dry, and he has no other response than to shake his head. He thinks to himself, Where in the hell did she get these chains, and how did I not feel her locking me down like this?

"I knew you would understand, wonderful. Now you just rest. I'm going to bring you some breakfast, and I will have your lunch prepared and sealed. It will be in the cooler next to the bed."

Jevonte looked to the side of the bed to see the blue-and-white cooler. Damn, she has thought of everything, he thought. "Tal, what if I have to go to the bathroom while you're gone? I can't just lie here in filth."

"There's enough length in that chain to reach the bathroom. You will be fine. Besides, if something happens to you, I'll see you and come home," Talaitha remarks sarcastically. Talaitha walks over to Jevonte and kisses his forehead gently, and cups his face in her hand. "I just need you to stay put and don't do anything stupid, ok?"

Jevonte says nothing. He lies back on his pillow and closes his eyes. He begins a silent prayer as Talaitha walks out to the kitchen to prepare his breakfast.

Dear God, maybe it would be better if you just took me right now. I want to be a good man. I want to be a good husband, but I don't think I can do this anymore. I just want to be gone. Please, Lord, hear my prayer and take me out of this situation. I want to see my mom again. I know she is with you now. I know she is happy. Please, don't let her see me like this. I beg of you, Father.

Mentally and emotionally drained, he eats the meal Talaitha has prepared for him and soon falls into a deep sleep. He dreams. He is a boy again, and he's with his uncle Roscoe. His uncle is preparing his tobacco store for the Saturday afternoon crowd. Roscoe established the store not long after he retired from the Marine Corps, and it was one of little Jevonte's favorite hangouts. Roscoe was a casual smoker, mostly cigars and some pipes. Jevonte would sometimes cough when the shop's smoke hit his nose, but he loved the smell inside the store. His uncle would let him help stock the tobacco and arrange the collection of pipes he sold at the store. Most of all, he just liked hearing his uncle's war stories from when he was in the Marines, and he'd get a kick out of some of the men who would come into the shop to swap stories and make up lies.

Jevonte's dream shifts to an incident in which three white men entered his uncle's store. It wasn't unusual because they were white, but their tone and disrespect towards his uncle surprised him. He recalls a heated exchange in which the three men started hurling insults at his uncle, with one of them even calling him a nigger. He couldn't remember why the three white men were being so hateful, but he will never forget the beatdown his uncle gave all three of those men. It wasn't even fair, Jevonte remembered thinking. Uncle may have been retired from the Marines, but he could still lay hands, and he did on that day. Jevonte never saw those men again, and from that day on, he knew which path he wanted to take. He saw a Black man stand up for himself, protect what was his, defend his own, and tolerate no disrespect, none.

Jevonte's dream landscape changes, and he and his uncle are at the comic book store. There were days when Roscoe would close his shop just to take Jevonte downtown to Book'ems Comic Shop. It was like going to Disneyland for Jevonte. His uncle was a DC fan, but Jevonte was Marvel all day, every day. He and his uncle would spend hours debating who was the strongest between Superman and the Hulk. They discuss each character's strengths and weaknesses, but never reach a consensus on which is the strongest. Roscoe would say, "My dude can move a whole planet, and he's smart." Jevonte would counter with, "So, the madder the Hulk gets, the stronger he gets. He has no limits. If he were mad enough, he could move a planet too, plus he doesn't get whack weak because of some green stuff!"

Comics helped Jevonte learn to read, and his uncle always bought him the latest issues of the Incredible Hulk when they hit the bookshelves. His uncle was always there for him. He never really had this kind of relationship with his dad. He didn't grow up aspiring to be like his dad. He respected him, but he often remembered how things were at home, how there was a time when his mom and dad would argue and exchange harsh, hurtful words. Some days, Jevonte would get scared and call his uncle. His uncle would come to the house, pick him up, and they would get ice cream or hit the comic book store.

It was his uncle who came to visit him while he was at Howard. His uncle made sure his meal card always had enough credits. He called his uncle when exam time rolled around, and the stress became overwhelming. His uncle would find the time to visit him and get him off campus for a breather. Jevonte's mom would sometimes come with his uncle, and the three of them would spend time together during spring break. His days always seemed to be on the road or away from work. He didn't think anything of the connection between his uncle and his mom, but there were times he'd catch them whispering together, or he'd notice their hugs lingered a little too long. He didn't care. His momma was happy, and so was he.

When Jevonte woke from his dreamy slumber, he felt drugged and hazy. *She probably put something in my breakfast this morning,* he thought. He swung his legs out of the bed, and the chains rattled on the floor, reminding him of his bondage. The chains weren't too heavy, but he was certainly in no condition to attempt breaking free from them. He stood and started shuffling to the bathroom, his bladder full and pressing for urgent deliverance. True to her word, Jevonte was able to reach the toilet and moaned with relief as the urine streamed from his body.

While Jevonte washed his hands and began brushing his teeth, he heard a beeping sound coming from a few houses away. It sounded like a truck backing up, but Jevonte couldn't see exactly what it was. He finished up in the bathroom and shuffled over to his bedroom window. Pulling back the curtains, he could just see a UPS truck attempting to use one of the neighbor's driveways to do a U-turn. The driver was successful and started heading toward Jevonte's house. Jevonte got an idea.

If I can get the driver's attention, maybe I can get him to come to the window. Jevonte started waving his arms from the window, but the driver never saw him and passed by the house on his way to his next delivery. Despondent, Jevonte walked back to sit on the edge of his bed.

I need someone to just come to the house. If I can get their attention, I can get a message out to someone, anyone. God, I know you see me. Please, send someone soon.

Jevonte grew depressed and lay back down on the bed. He knew he had the right idea, and even though there was a huge part of him that wanted to be here for Talaitha, to find a way to love her like a good and faithful husband, he knew that this kind of treatment was not something his uncle would put up with. Jevonte resolved within himself not to put up with this anymore. So he decided to skip the lunch Talaitha had prepared. He didn't trust that the food wasn't also drugged with something.

Songs he remembered his mother singing at church helped him kill time. He let his imagination carry him far from his bed of bondage, and he imagined her leading the praise team or taking the minutes during board meetings. She was always so active in the church. Jevonte wasn't a strong or practicing believer, and he wished he had paid more attention during Sunday school, but he understood the power of prayer. He got that gift from Ruby. Then, out of nowhere, Melanie's beautiful, joyous, round face appeared in his thoughts. Her face reminded him of so many things he had taken for granted, things he wished he could do over again, and regrets he didn't know if he would ever live down. He always knew Melanie was something special. She actually fought for him and fought for them, and he let her get away.

He thought, If I get out of this situation, Father, please help me make things right with her.

From outside, Jevonte heard the sound of another truck on the street. He heard the brakes squeal as the truck approached his house. Jevonte got out of bed as quickly as he could and shuffled over to the window. It was an Amazon truck. The driver was sitting in the vehicle, looking down at something Jevonte couldn't make out. Jevonte's hopes were climbing. He started waving, hoping to get the driver's attention. It did. The driver looked directly at Jevonte. Their eyes met, and Jevonte started bouncing lightly on the balls of his feet, doing a little praise dance in front of the window.

The driver exited the vehicle with two packages in his arms. He started up the driveway, but Jevonte started yelling and screaming, trying to get the driver to come to the window instead. The driver didn't hear Jevonte; his voice was just too weak to pierce the window of his bedroom. The driver reached the front door and rang the doorbell. He rang the doorbell once, then tried again before leaving the packages at the front door. He looked a little pissed, like he was expecting the man at the window to come to the door to receive his packages, but was ignored. So, the driver started walking over to the window. Jevonte smiled a huge smile of relief until he saw Talaitha's car pull up into the driveway. Talaitha got out of her car and walked towards the Amazon driver.

"Sir, what do you think you're doing looking through my home like this?" Talaitha said with such authority that the driver was speechless. "I'm talking to you, Mr. Amazon driver. Do I need to call the police?"

The driver finally regained his tongue. "No, ma'am. My apologies. After I dropped off your packages, I saw the gentleman in the window waving at me, like he wanted to get my attention. I thought maybe that he was in trouble or something."

"I see. Well, my husband is going to be in trouble because he's supposed to be resting in bed. I appreciate your concern. Now, have a lovely day and get off my property,"

Talaitha ordered. Without another word, the driver hopped back in his truck and vanished down the street. Jevonte was no longer at the window when Talaitha glanced in that direction. Inside, Jevonte had stooped to grab his ankle chain in the hopes of raising it to the window so that the driver could see what was going on with him, but he could not gain enough leverage and balance to lift his leg to the window. When Jevonte stood up again to look out of the window, the driver was gone, and Talaitha was opening the front door. Jevonte lowered his head in despair. He shuffled back to the bed to await his punishment. He knew there was going to be an explosion of some kind, so he just lay in bed waiting, his arms behind his head and his fingers interlaced.

"My goodness, you have been a busy little bee, haven't you?" asked Talaitha as she entered the bedroom.

Jevonte didn't answer. He was defeated now. He just wanted to get it all over with, so he said nothing.

"Cat got your tongue, King? I'm not mad. I'm disappointed, but don't worry. I'm going to fix this little lapse for you."

Talaitha left the bedroom and went down into the basement. Jevonte could hear her moving things, her chains clanging, and finally walking back up the stairs. She came back into the bedroom with a new set of shorter, heavier chains swinging from her hands.

"Talaitha, no! Just let me out of these, please," begged Jevonte.

"No. Now be still, or so help me, God, I will pull out the jacket and leave you in it all week long," Talaitha shot back as she placed her shoulder bag on the floor next to the bed and sat next to Jevonte. She unlocked the chain around his ankle and put the new set around both ankles. She fashioned them securely around the footboard and legs of the bed. When she finished, she grabbed up the former set of chains and her shoulder bag. The chains knocked over the bag, and Talaitha quickly gathered the contents off the floor without paying them much attention.

"I am going to write up a few notes from my office. I'll start dinner in about an hour. Until then, I want you to think about what you've done, and I want you to carefully consider how you'll act from now on when I am gone from this house. Are we clear, King?"

"But why do I have to be stuck here while you're home? I thought this was only going to happen when you were gone," whimpered Jevonte.

"Stop whining. Consider this a dry run of sorts. I need to make sure you understand my instructions clearly. Now, are we clear?"

Jevonte didn't even look at Talaitha. "Sure, we're clear," and he turned his face away from her.

"Excellent. I'll be back in an hour or so. Don't go anywhere," mocked Talaitha, and she left the room.

Jevonte could feel his mind slipping into the darkness. He remembered all too well the crushing weight of his depression, and that beast was threatening to bear him down to hell. Although the chains were heavier this time, Jevonte got out of bed and began to kneel. It was time to pray like he hadn't before. He wasn't going to take this abuse lying down, nonchalantly passing the time while chained like an animal. He wasn't anticipating how the weight would affect his balance, and he fell over on his side. There, underneath the bed, was Talaitha's cell phone. Jevonte couldn't believe what he was seeing. He quickly retrieved it and whispered a quick prayer that it wasn't locked. It was. Crestfallen, Jevonte sat back in bed, the phone in his hand. He had no idea what PIN Talaitha may have used for the phone. He tried his name, combinations of his and her initials, and his birthday, but nothing worked. He didn't know Talaitha's birthday or her parents' birthdays, so he couldn't use them.

But he did remember one name, and he keyed it in: Noelle. The phone unlocked to reveal the image of a man sitting on a park bench. His back is to the camera, but Jevonte recognizes the park. It's Canton Waterfront Park, and the camera is capturing his back.

Jevonte files the image away for another time. He has no time to waste. Talaitha is sure to notice it missing soon. He listens carefully to place her location. She must still be in her office because he can't hear anything from the kitchen area. He pauses for a moment. His first instinct is to call his mom, then he remembers, and a small tear streaks down his face. With a deep sigh, he starts to call his Uncle Roscoe, but his voicemail box is full, and Jevonte can't leave a message.

Wait, what am I doing? I should just call the police. No, I can't do that. I don't trust them to handle this the right way anyway. If I call someone, she'll hear it and probably murder me for sure.

Jevonte thinks hard, and then he starts texting Melanie.

"Melanie, hi. This is Jevonte, and I'm using Talaitha's cell. I don't have much time, but I need your help."

She responded immediately.

"JEVONTE!! We've been so worried about you! How have you been? What's going on? Tell me what you need."

"Talaitha has me chained to the bed, and she won't let me out. I'm too weak from whatever she's been giving me. But I don't want the police involved. Promise me you won't call the police."

"I promise, but we have to do something. I came to your house once. That woman is crazy. She wouldn't let me in. Uncle Roscoe hired a private investigator to look into her. We're all worried sick over you."

"I'm so sorry. I made a huge mistake, and I have so much to tell you, but I don't have much time. Just let Uncle know I'm alive but need help. Honestly, I don't know how much more of this I can take."

"I'm coming for you. We're all coming for you, ok. Don't worry. Just hold on and pray. God's got you, and so do I."

"I have been praying. Listen, don't text back because Talaitha will get this phone back. I don't want her to know I made contact with anyone. I'll delete these messages as soon as we finish. I don't know when or if I will be able to contact you again. Thank you for always being there for me."

"I understand. Just know that we all care about you and love you still."

Before Jevonte can send another text, he hears Talaitha pulling out a few pans in the kitchen.

"I gotta run. I think I hear her coming. I thank God for you, Mel. I really do. Don't reply."

Jevonte begins deleting his texts and Melanie's. He erases the call he made to his uncle and then slides the phone back where he found it. Thirty minutes later, Talaitha opens the bedroom door, and she's carrying a tray of food. She sets the tray down across Jevonte's lap and sits next to him on the bed.

"I made spaghetti, one of your favorites."

"Thanks," says Jevonte, melancholy heavy in his voice. "Aren't you eating?"

"I will, but I wanted to take care of you first," she grins, and then, from underneath the bed, a ringtone buzzes loudly. Earth, Wind, and Fire's 'Reasons' blares from underneath the bed. Talaitha looks at Jevonte, who stares blankly back at her. She reaches under the bed and pulls out her cell phone. "Wow, it must have fallen out of my bag."

She doesn't recognize the number but answers it anyway. "Hello, this is Dr. Talaitha Mercedes. Who is this, and how can I help you?"

The line goes silent for a few moments, and then a deep basso male voice responds, "This is Roscoe Greene. What the fuck have you done to my nephew?

20

The Devil's Daughter

The drive took longer than P.I. Drummond anticipated. Based on information he received from a confidant in the Baltimore Metro Police Department, he felt he had little choice but to follow up and take a trip to the Patuxent Institution in Jessup, Maryland. The documents he purchased indicated that two prisoners there might be able to shed light on Talaitha Mercedes. If he was going to do a proper investigation and build a case against her, he needed to know more about who she was and where she came from. The profile he was developing would not be complete without this necessary background information. Of course, Marcus knew that at some point he would have to meet Talaitha face-to-face, and only then would he get a real sense of the woman and her spirit.

Marcus arrived on time and presented his credentials before taking a seat in the visiting room. It wasn't long before an older gentleman, slightly built and limping, walked over to where Marcus was seated. The man sat at the table and said nothing. Marcus scanned the table number and asked, "Are you at the right table, sir?"

"I am, but are you?" the prisoner asked.

"Yes, I am. My name is Marcus Drummond, and I'm here to meet Rufus Mercedes. Is that you?"

"I'm here, ain't I, shit. What do you want?" Rufus asked gruffly.

"I'm doing a little background on your daughter."

"Fuck, Noelle's been gone. I ain't seen her since," and Rufus pauses, straining to think. "I ain't seen her since those people took her from my house."

"Mr. Mercedes, no. I mean Talaitha. I'm doing some research, and I need some information about her."

"Oh, her. I don't know what to tell you, except that bitch is a liar. She lied on me, and that's why I'm locked up like this."

"Sir, can I call you Rufus? Would that be alright?"

"That's my name, ain't it, shit. I don't care, man. I don't. Look, can you put some money on my commissary?"

Rufus started shifting around at the table, nervous, and Marcus could see that the man was not well. Despite the comfortable temperature in the room, Rufus was sweating, and he kept looking over his shoulder, scanning the room as though he were expecting an attack.

"Rufus, I'm not here to do all of that, but I might be able to speak to someone in the Warden's office about you if you're willing to help me out here."

"As I said, that bitch is a liar, straight up. I never did anything to her, but she told the cops that I raped her or some shit like that. She even had the school reporting on my wife and me for no fucking reason."

"Rufus, there were photos and all kinds of physical evidence of the abuse she went through. Are you saying that all of that was made up, that she fabricated her injuries?"

"I don't know how she did it, but she lied. She was always defying Latriece and me. She was always sneaking out, screwing around in the streets with all those boys. We couldn't control her."

"Rufus, the abuse started when she was only eleven. Do you mean to tell me that she was whoring around the streets at eleven years old?" Marcus said forcefully.

"She wasn't eleven—well, I'm not sure how old she was actually."

"Sir, please. You don't know how old your daughter was when all of this started?"

"She wasn't mine," Rufus stated. He stopped fidgeting and looked directly at Marcus. "My bitch-ass wife just brought her home one day as a baby."

Marcus said nothing. He started writing on his notepad while slowly shaking his head. He hadn't actually seen any birth records, so maybe, just maybe, Rufus was speaking the truth. "Ok, say that's true, and your wife just brought home a baby. You didn't question that at all? That was normal to you, and you just assumed your wife's stomach started expanding of its own accord for nine months? So, when she started gaining weight and getting sick in the mornings, what did you think was happening?"

"I wasn't paying attention to all of that shit. The bitch was just getting fat."

Marcus clinched one fist and took a deep breath. He wanted to throttle Rufus for the asshole he was being. "Again, all of these changes happening to your wife and the new child showing up was all normal to you?" Marcus said, exasperated.

"No. It wasn't normal, but I had a lot of shit going on back then. I didn't question it because I couldn't afford to. An opportunity presented itself, and I had to make some money, so I did. Don't judge me. I bet you don't walk on no water either," said Rufus, sitting back in his seat with his arms crossed.

"We all have stuff, Rufus. We just don't rape our way out of it," shot back Marcus.

"I didn't rape anyone, asshole. Aren't you listening?"

"Got it. You just let other men rape her," Marcus said with derision and scorn in his voice. "What else can you tell me about Talaitha besides your earlier statement about her lying?"

"She is smarter than people give her credit for. I know you don't believe me, but she staged everything. She concocted a whole story about being abused, and the police bought it all, hook, line, and sinker. She is a master manipulator. Everybody be playin' checkers, and she's into that chess shit. I'm telling you, she is always ten steps ahead of everyone. She probably got you up here, too, as part of whatever she's up to."

"I suppose you're right, because she successfully influenced a jury to find both you and your wife guilty of multiple counts of child abuse, sexual assault, and human trafficking."

"Fuck you, man! I don't care whether you don't believe me or not. I'm done here. You'd better watch your back if you're going to keep dealing with that crazy psycho bitch," Rufus said, and he left the visitation room without a single glance back at Marcus.

Marcus made a few additional notes and scheduled an appointment to return the next day to interview Latriece.

He wasn't getting anywhere now, but Rufus had planted a seed that he intended to cultivate once he met with Rufus' wife, Latriece.

Talaitha sat stunned on the bed next to Jevonte. She stared down at the handset, incredulous at the gruff-sounding, authoritarian voice on the other end of the call she had just answered. At first, she felt as if someone had slapped her face with a cold, wet towel, leaving her unsure of how to respond.

"Umm, Mr. Greene. I don't know what you mean," said Talaitha; her confidence was momentarily shaken.

"It's a straightforward question, but in case you're daft and dumb, I'll ask again. What have you done to my nephew, Jevonte?"

Talaitha sat up quickly, regaining her composure and leaving the bedroom. She saw how Jevonte was about to make noise, and she didn't want Roscoe to hear anything. Jevonte struggled to move, to grab something to toss towards Talaitha. He heard her say his uncle's name, and now he was energized like never before. His uncle knew that something was wrong. Finally, someone would come for him, and it would be his uncle. Talaitha looked back at Jevonte and registered the look of hope on his face before closing the door behind her.

"Mr. Greene, may I call you Roscoe?" Talaitha asked.

"No," responded Roscoe. "Stop fucking around and tell me what's going on? What are you doing to my nephew?"

"Mr. Greene, I am not doing 'anything' to my husband. Perhaps you weren't aware, but he has been very sick, and I am managing his care. I don't ..." and Roscoe cut her off.

"I'll be coming to see him tomorrow. I will personally assess whether he has received proper care, and I pray to God that he has. If he hasn't, God help you. Do you hear me?" Roscoe said, his voice cold and menacing.

Talaitha's tone transformed instantly. A calculated calm descended over her. She took a deep breath and stepped into her role as a psychiatrist. "I understand that you are concerned about your nephew, and let me assure you that he is recovering nicely. He is under the care of medical staff at Sable Ridge State Hospital, and they have been coordinating with me almost every other day. As his wife, I am as concerned, if not more so, than anyone with Jevonte's health situation. After the initial misdiagnosis at the hospital, his care team and I feel we have an excellent handle on his treatment plan. I don't know what information has gotten back to you. Still, as a medical professional, I can tell you that all of the melodrama and turmoil surrounding the accidental death of your wife is detrimental to Jevonte's treatment plan. Ruby's passing was truly heartbreaking, wouldn't you agree?"

Roscoe was silent. This bitch is good, he thought. "What do you think?" he replied. "Jevonte didn't even get to say goodbye to his mother, so of course that was going to be painful, but that is also the time when family needs to pull together, support one another, and show love in a time of crisis."

"I could not agree more, Mr. Greene. Look, we are family now, too, right? I wouldn't lie to you about this. I'm not hiding Jevonte or keeping him from his family. In fact, he had just finished renovating our home, and we were getting ready to host you. We were planning a big family get-together before he took ill—and we still want to do that as soon as he is fully recovered. It is one of the things that keeps him working hard on his recovery. He just needs some time and patience on the part of the family."

"Well, if he is as sick as you say, why isn't he in a hospital now? Why isn't his care under the direct supervision of a doctor?" asked Roscoe impatiently.

"I am a doctor, and as I said, I am in constant communication with hospital staff. He is receiving the very best care possible. Now, let me be clear, Mr. Greene. When I deem it suitable, I will open my doors wide so that you and everybody else can come see your precious Jevonte. No one is coming here until I say so. I am his wife, but if you feel like testing the boundaries a bit, go right ahead. I promise you won't get the reception you plan on."

Roscoe laughed. "Bitch, please. Don't worry. When I come, I will see my nephew, and nothing you do will stop me." In fact, I guarantee you won't even see me coming," he said before disconnecting the call. Talaitha tossed her cell phone against the wall in anger. She took a few deep breaths and walked back into the bedroom, where Jevonte was chained to the bed.

"So that's your uncle, huh. I wouldn't get any ideas or raise your hopes. You are never going to see him or any of your stupid family again, I promise." Talaitha stood for several minutes next to Jevonte's bed, looking down at his chain. Jevonte said nothing, but he started grinning and closed his eyes. Talaitha turned and then stopped at the doorway. "Perhaps we need to break out the jacket anyway."

Later in the day, Roscoe starts unloading some of his gear in the garage of Ruby and Jedidiah. His footlocker looks like it's been through three wars, and his seabag bears the faded stencil marks of his military unit and ID. He sets the footlocker on top of the workbench and unlocks it. The M4A1 sits snugly in its cutouts; magazines are loaded and stored in two rows alongside the carbine. The weapon's sling assembly is coiled tightly in a neat roll and tucked away in a side compartment. Non-standard military adapters are bundled in the corners of the footlocker, containing scopes, cameras, range finders, and other accessories Roscoe has collected since retirement. "Tiger-Paw," as he calls his weapon, has seen him through more than a few tight scrapes, especially since his work in the Marines garnered him more than a few enemies. He hoped that there would be no need to break her out for this occasion, but just in case, he decided to give her a thorough cleaning.

"Hi, Uncle," said Melanie as she walked into the garage. Melanie's appearance startled Roscoe, catching him off guard. "You're slipping, sir. What are you up to?"

Roscoe grinned. "I heard you coming, but my mind was focused elsewhere."

"Yeah, ok, if you say so."

"I'm just making sure Tiger-Paw is ready for action. I take care of her, and she takes care of me."

"Whatever, sir. I need to talk to you about Talaitha. I recently got a text from Jevonte," Melanie said excitedly.

"I called her," Roscoe said flatly.

"What? You did? How?"

"I have my resources," he grinned. "She is not some random psycho. Things will get messy. I think they have to get this predicament straightened out."

"Uncle, Jevonte sounded desperate in his text. I mean, seriously, he is in a bad way. I think we need to just go to the house in force and demand to see Jevonte. We can't give her a choice in this."

"That's what we're going to do, but first, I'm going there alone."

"No, Uncle. I'm going with you," Melanie shot back.

"I understand. I do, and you will be going with me, but not on this visit. I'm not going to walk up to the door and knock. If I enter the house and the police come, I'll be the one arrested, not you. Additionally, if I enter and discover that something is seriously wrong or that she has done something harmful, I want the police to be notified. If all is well, and I'm overreacting, I can explain all of that to the police and let the chips fall. I have a feeling, though, that

Talaitha won't want the police to know what we know about Jevonte's tests. So, she'll keep her mouth shut, and we will get eyes on the nephew.

"I suppose you're right, but I don't like it at all. I feel like I'm failing him. He reached out in a desperate cry for help. I feel so helpless, Uncle."

"I think that boy knows that you care about him, that you still love him—we all know that," Roscoe says, and Melanie closes her eyes in a quiet blush. "He knows that you wouldn't abandon him. I think he knows that I wouldn't either. Just hold on for him and be patient. We're going to figure this thing out soon, really soon."

Roscoe walks over to Melanie and embraces her in a warm bear hug.

"Oh, have you heard from Marcus lately? Has he made any progress on Ruby's murder?" asks Melanie, and she walks over to the workbench.

"He's been radio silent for the last week or so, but I know him, and that's not unusual, especially if he's gotten onto some evidence. He's like a bloodhound that's hot on the trail. I suspect we will hear something soon. Have you ever fired a gun?" asks Roscoe as he walks up beside her and lifts the M4A1 out of its cradle.

The two continue to talk, and Roscoe takes Melanie through the various components of the weapon, showing her how to hold it, load a magazine, and sight down the barrel. He places her in several stances, letting her get a feel for the weight and balance of the weapon. After about thirty minutes, the pair goes inside, and Melanie offers to whip up some dinner. She's in constant motion, wanting to stay busy and her mind occupied so she can stop worrying about Jevonte, but it doesn't work. Her thoughts continually review his text, and she can hear the messages now in his voice. Her heart aches deeply, but for now, she can only follow Roscoe's lead; however, she silently promises herself that she will not wait much longer, come hell or high water.

It took Marcus three days to make a return visit to interview Latriece. The prison could not confirm his follow-up visit, so he had to wait a few extra days. He was ok with that because he had a feeling that talking to Latriece, Talaitha's mom, was going to be a whole different experience than he had with Rufus. The backstory he had on Mrs. Greene was complicated and baffling. Mrs. Greene was college-educated and had a master's in finance and accounting. Her undergrad was in business and technology. She had all the markings of a successful Black businesswoman, but she ended up married to Rufus, a two-time felon and former pimp. Rufus had been in and out of lock-up dozens of times since he turned eighteen. Latriece's story was the complete opposite. She didn't come from a broken home. She had advantages that Rufus lacked, so how and why did they end up together?

Marcus was directed to an entirely different section in Patuxent Institution for his meeting with prisoner Latriece Greene. The women, while housed in the same institution, were kept in holding areas on the opposite side of the men. When Marcus arrived at the conference room, Latriece was already there, seated and ready. Unlike Rufus, Latriece looked healthy. She looked like a woman on her way to work—except for the orange jumpsuit. Her hair was neatly pulled back into a bob, and while she wore no makeup, her facial features were clean, strong, and unmarked. As Marcus pulled out his notepad and pen, he couldn't help but get the impression that he wasn't interviewing a convicted criminal but a Don, a mastermind-type boss, or someone in charge of or used to running things. She gave off an air of confidence that Rufus lacked.

"Hello, Mrs. Greene. My name is Marcus Drummond, and I'm here to ask you some questions about your daughter, Talaitha. Do you mind if I record this?" Marcus asked, his hand starting to pull out the mini-recorder.

"Not at all, and hello," Latriece said as she relaxed her shoulders and crossed her legs. "I've been looking forward to this for a long time now."

"Oh, why is that?"

"I have a story to tell, and I need to set the record straight because I shouldn't be in here," she said with deadly seriousness.

That's what they all say, Marcus thought to himself. "Well, I'm here to listen, so let's get started with whatever you can tell me about how Talaitha came into your family. Did you give birth to her?" No use beating around the bush, Marcus thought to himself.

"That's a strange question. Why would you ask me that?"

"Your husband, Rufus, told me you weren't Talaitha's mother, that you just brought her home one day."

Latriece paused for a few moments, reflecting before responding. She didn't look at Marcus, and she averted his eyes. When she spoke, it was with deep regret and heavy anguish. "I just needed something. I needed a baby, and I couldn't have one. I tried for a very long time, but I was infertile. I went to so many doctors, and they all said the same thing. They all showed me the same test results, but I felt like I was supposed to be a mother. It wasn't fair."

"So, you took Talaitha from someone, from another mother and family?"

"Yes. I did what I felt I needed to do. I needed to do it." Latriece began staring at the wall, refusing to meet Marcus' eyes.

"Where did you find her? Who are the birth parents?" asked Marcus.

"I don't know. I saw her in her playpen with her sister at the park. She was such a beautiful child. I think she wanted to go with me, so I took her."

"In broad daylight? You just grabbed the child, and no one said anything to you? No one tried to stop you?" asked Marcus incredulously.

"They were all too busy running after some other kids. They weren't paying attention or anything. That's how I knew they didn't want her, because why would they leave her all alone like that?"

Marcus scribbled a few notes down and held his emotions in check. He would make sure she paid for this new crime, this new horrific tragedy she created in the lives of those parents. He returned to the moment, looking at this woman who, judging by her outward appearance and demeanor, was a normal person, well adjusted, and perfectly sane—until she spoke her truth out loud.

"You understand that I have to notify the authorities about what you just shared? All of your statements are on the record," said Marcus.

"Yes, I know that, and I will deal with the consequences. I just want to get all of this out in the open and tell my story once and for all."

"Your Husband implied that he either didn't notice your pregnancy, which, if what you are saying is true, he wouldn't have seen you as a pregnant woman, so when you just came home one day with a child, how did you explain that?"

"Rufus is an idiot. This should not be a surprise to you now that you've spoken with him. He knows what I did when I came home with Talaitha. It wasn't long after that he started looking for ways to make money and that's when he decided to abduct Talaitha's twin, Noelle."

"Wait, are you saying that Noelle was also stolen from the parents?" Marcus asked.

"My genius husband wanted to take the child and use them both for ransom, but I wouldn't go along with it. I had my babies and that's all that mattered," explained Latriece.

Marcus' blank stare hid the revulsion he was feeling inside, and he couldn't recall the last time he felt this level of disgust for another person. Marcus continued. "What can you tell me about the abuse? When did it start, and why did you let it go on for so long?"

"I didn't—at first. I lost everything when my father left us alone when I was little, and when my mother died of an overdose, I had no one. My brothers and I moved in with my grandma, and she raised us, but it was hard because Nana didn't have much money. We were always just barely scraping by on nothing. We were always hungry, and we never got new clothes; everything was a hand-me-down. But when I got to high school, I learned how to make money on the streets. My body kept me in new clothes and put food on the table for my brothers and me. I did what I had to do, and when I got into college, my body paid my way. The currency of lust is real, and I learned how to use it for my purposes."

"I see," said Marcus, his voice non-judgmental. "But what about Talaitha? From the court trial records, she was made to have sex with men at the age of eleven, and you facilitated many of those transactions."

"See, now that's what I need to clear up," shot back Latriece, her eyes now fixed on Marcus. "I didn't facilitate anything; that was all Rufus and his stupid, hateful ass. In the beginning, when we got married, things were all good. I had my master's degree, and several headhunters were interested in me. I was on my way, and then Rufus fucked up. He got involved in this gambling ring outside of Baltimore and landed in a giant hole of debt. The bastards he was running around with threatened to kill him unless he came up with nearly $57,000. Yeah, I know, lots of money, and we didn't have it. We didn't even have enough assets to sell to settle that debt. So I made a decision. I went to this group and tried to strike a deal to work off the debt plus interest. They agreed, and I thought, Cool, I'll just do what I did in college and earn our way out of the debt with my body. But they wouldn't accept that deal. They wanted something else," and Latriece's voice grew somber.

"They wanted Talaitha?" asked Marcus.

"Yes, but I said no because they wanted to sell her to these Russian guys overseas. I was not going to do that; however, Rufus suggested we could still proceed with the deal if we kept everything within the house. We would have control and pay off the debt, and he said we could pay it off faster since she was a young girl."

"She was eleven, Latriece, eleven!" said Marcus.

"Talaitha was advanced for her age, and she wasn't as innocent as you might think."

"She was a child—a child!" Marcus sat back in his chair. A wave of nausea threatened to overwhelm him for a moment, but his stomach eventually settled down. His temper did not.

"I know I should have done more to protect her, but Rufus was overwhelming for me, and the gangsters had us cornered." We just did the best we could. Talaitha was grown for her age, and we didn't think it would go on for as long as it did. I mean, we paid the debt off in almost a year. After that, I tried to leave, wanting to take her and Noelle with me. I wanted to get out of that place and start again, someplace new, just the three of us. But…"

"But what?"

"She killed a man," Latriece said flatly.

Marcus leaned forward and said, "She killed someone?"

"There was this one man who ordered her for an 8 pm service. Rufus drove Talaitha to the spot, but he didn't stay there. He usually stays to bring Talaitha back home, but on that night, he left early. I think he went to run some of his other whores or gamble; whatever it was, he left. When he got back to the spot, the man was gone, and Talaitha was on the playground swinging on the playset. When he went over to her, he said that she had a blank look on her face and wasn't talking. The man's truck was still in the parking lot, but the dude was gone. Rufus told me that there was blood on the front seat, but it wasn't Talaitha's," said Latriece.

"What makes you think Talaitha killed him? Did he turn up later?"

"Three days later, we see police officers at the location, and they have placed police tape around the playset and the parking lot. Cop cars are all over the place, and then on the news, we see that the dude's body was recovered at the scene. His neck had been slit, and his body was stuffed in the bushes that lined the parking lot. I know it was Talaitha because there was no one else there, and that spot is well concealed."

"You mean to tell me that an eleven-year-old slit a man's throat and then dragged his big old body into the bushes by herself?" asked Marcus with doubt in his voice.

"It's the only logical explanation, and I asked her directly about what happened that night. What she told me convinced me that she was demonic or had some kind of darkness inside of her. She said to me, "This is what I needed to do. I needed to get ready for what's coming.""

Marcus stared at Latriece and decided within himself that the only person who had some kind of darkness inside them was Latriece. "So, let's move on from here, ok. What was her relationship like with Noelle? So they were twins but you and Rufus never used Noelle the way you did Talaitha. Why?"

"They weren't really twins. I gave birth to Noelle and…"

"Wait, didn't you say you were infertile earlier?" interjected Marcus.

"You're confusing me. I didn't say that; what I meant was that I became infertile after the girls were born, and I…"

"Mrs. Mercedes, did you have more than two children? If you took Talaitha and Noelle from another family, and you said you didn't become infertile until after you had your 'girls,' where is the third child? What happened to her?"

Latriece grew quiet, and she stared at her hands. Her face looked strained, her brows knitted in troubled consternation. "I don't want to talk anymore. My head is hurting. You keep mixing up my words. Can I go now?" Latriece asks, her voice now small, almost childlike.

"Ok, just one more question, please. Has Talaitha come to visit you since you were convicted and sent here?"

"No, she has not, but the other one has."

"Noelle has come to see you, really?" Marcus said in surprise.

"No. It wasn't Noelle. At least she didn't look like my Noelle. It was like she had some kind of cosmetic surgery done. She looked more like a man to me than a woman. Same sounding voice, but a different face. It was spooky."

"What did Noelle say? I have some notes that said she disappeared as a teen, and the foster parents and authorities were never able to determine what happened that night."

"She just wanted to know about Talaitha. She didn't say anything about prom, but she did tell me that she was never far from Talaitha and that she would make sure nothing ever happened to her again, like it did when they were just girls. She only came once to see me, and I don't know if she visited Rufus."

"Interestingly, she was never sold or traded for profit, unlike Talaitha. Why was that?" asked Marcus.

"Talaitha wanted to be the one. It was her choice. I believe she was trying to protect Noelle, but their fierce arguments made it seem like they hated each other. Watching them interact, you would have thought they despised each other."

Marcus made additional notes and told Latriece that he would put a little something on her commissary account. He wasn't going to report the disclosure about the kidnapping. He didn't believe that part of the story, and he would confirm the validity of her statement once he got his hands on Talaitha's birth records. For now, Marcus was convinced that Latriece was not well and was still withholding information, and much of what she said could probably be discounted. The interview wasn't a total waste, as he saw it. He had a new lead to follow, and her name was Noelle.

21

The Deep

Since resuming his oversight of the mental health ward and psychiatric programs at Sable Ridge State Hospital, Dr. Samuel Robinson has all but made the hospital his second home. He is a fixture in the infamous lower ward and regularly screens all incoming residents to the mental health department, even if they aren't assigned to him. He has spent the last decade working hard to reverse the disastrous outcomes associated with some of the inhumane and horrendous mental health practices of the facility from its early days.

The legacy of Sable Ridge is dark. The hospital was often used to house the enslaved population following the end of the Civil War. The facility's staff at that time helped transition the enslaved into indentured servitude, which was supported by racist local ordinances characterized as Black Codes and vagrancy laws. Routinely, victims of these laws were declared mentally incompetent and subsequently committed to confinement in the hospital's lower ward, known as "The Deep."

In the lower ward, patients were subjected to experiments and disappeared from society. The iron-barred cells and crumbling stone masonry of the damp corridors have since been replaced, but the lower ward never lost the insipid dark energy that brushes the consciousness of most who walk its halls. Sable Ridge State Hospital received state funding and private donations from benefactors who supported the eugenics movement. Special conferences frequently took place at the facility, conducting live, experimental neurological surgeries and behavioral modifications without the patient's consent. One of the hospital's most telling legacies is that most, if not all, of its patient-prisoners were poor and Black.

Despite his initial hiring in 1990, Dr. Robinson was unable to fully dismantle some of the hospital's practices, much to his dismay. After the Civil Rights movement orchestrated the elimination of Black Codes and vagrancy laws in many states and localities, the hospital continued to accept children from state-run orphanages, where they were subjected to unsanctioned and nonclinical procedures. The children who survived this period of horror often emerged as mentally unstable and psychotic and needed to be confined for the safety of the community. Dr. Robinson was successful in removing most of the medical staff that worked in "The Deep," but he couldn't repair the damage that was already done to the children. Most of these children were placed at other, modern, sanctioned mental health facilities where their care continues to this day—but there were a few that slipped through the cracks.

One child in particular caught his attention early, and he intervened in her case and had her reassigned to him personally. He spent years providing counseling and therapy to help mitigate her diagnosis of borderline personality disorder. He watched her grow from being labeled by the state as violent and considered unstable by her doctors to being described as remarkable, high-functioning, and ready for reintegration in her file notes. His work with this young girl brought him comfort, knowing that mental health treatment can reverse the effects of years of trauma in her life. Dr. Robinson became deeply concerned when he saw Talaitha on his monitor outside his office on the day of the CNA's murder. It wasn't the fact that the young lady was murdered, although he felt sorrow over her death, but it was the cause of death that troubled him even more. The CNA had her throat crushed and died from a brutal strangulation. Law enforcement was operating under the assumption that the CNA's killer had to be a man because of the force applied to the victim's throat; however, Dr. Robinson recalled several video interviews he conducted with Talaitha while she was in his care. Most of his recorded interview data was archived in the lower ward, so he would need to make a trip down below to actually review the videos. He had a troubling suspicion that he might need to remove some of those files to protect one of his former patients.

Dr. Robinson could only take the service elevator to the B3 level. He would have to walk down two additional stairwells to reach the lower ward. The Deep was aptly named. The corridor connecting the stairwell to the reception area was dark and cold. The halls glistened with condensation, and the wooden panels bulged in some places. They were horribly dated and reeked of mold and mildew. The dank aura of the space felt heavy, and Dr. Robinson always wore his medical mask when moving through the area.

Some improvements to the lower ward made it possible to work for longer periods during Dr. Robinson's off-clinic hours. The recirculatory air cleaners and industrial dehumidifiers extended the lifespan of files and archives, especially VHS and 8mm video materials. The footage he had amassed and stored in the archives helped build cases against many of his former colleagues and was crucial to their removal. In their hubris, they recorded everything they did; every bit of wickedness and torture was captured on video and ultimately served to condemn and bring to light the many crimes against the community of Black and indigent people that took place in the name of science.

Dr. Robinson cleared some boxes from the shelving along one wall in the archival storage room. He knew what box he needed to see. After locating the box he sought, Dr. Robinson retreated to one of the offices he used while he was in the lower ward. He unsealed the box and examined the chronologically dated row of VHS tapes. He decided to start with 2001, the year Talaitha would have been 18. He loads the VHS into the player and watches his TV display the scratched, blurred images of someone sitting on a stool, facing the camera. Once the VHS tape stabilizes, the image on the TV becomes clearer, and Dr. Robinson can make out the features of a young adult woman. Talaitha isn't smiling, but her eyes are intense and focused. She's alert and appears to be watching the camera, anticipating. There is a long pause in the recording, and no one is speaking. Dr. Robinson sits back in his chair and marvels at the specimen in front of his eyes. She's young, as the video shows, but she projects power and strength even at this age. She sits calmly, relaxed, and confident. She's wearing a simple pullover tank top and jeans, but Dr. Robinson notes how chiseled her physique is, how taut her arms are. She is lean, and there are no hard edges, but lines of grace and power are traced in the contours of her neck and shoulders. Observing her on video now, it is easy to understand how and why none of the girls on the ward ever messed with Talaitha. Dr. Robinson also recalled that her demeanor and bearing, as displayed on the tape, seemed to project high intellect and confidence. He went to great pains to get her into his program and later into a special college program for gifted students because he saw her untapped potential and acuity.

The doctor scans several tapes until he comes across one with the date smudged and a bold red X in the corner of the label. He loads it and pushes play. The video opens with Talaitha yelling and pacing back and forth on the tape like a caged tigress. Her hair is blown out and wild. She is enraged and verbally abusive, and begins to hurl chairs while directly throwing an object at the interviewer. Dr. Robinson stops the tape and rewinds it to the beginning. When the tape starts playing again, Talaitha is sitting calmly, facing the interviewer, her expression blank and hard to read—until the questions start.

A man's voice can be heard on the tape, and Dr. Robinson doesn't immediately recognize it. "Talaitha, I don't think it's helpful to skip over everything that happened. In fact, it is vitally important that we reconstruct everything to piece together an appropriate action plan. It won't be easy, but we have to drag these things out into the open. We need to lay out the worst of it, no matter how awful it may appear. I promise you, once we do, and you face it head-on, the nightmares will stop."

Then Dr. Robinson recognizes the interviewer as Dr. Richard Gross, who should not be speaking. He didn't have authorization to touch any of his patient files, let alone treat any of them. Dr. Robinson looked at the date stamp and then remembered that it was during this time that they had him removed from the hospital and placed on administrative leave at home. It was the beginning of his whistleblowing campaign and getting him sacked was part of their retribution.

Talaitha's soft, sure voice can be heard in reply to Dr. Gross. "Sir, I've already talked about all of that with Dr. Robinson, and I don't care to rehash all of it again—not with you, anyway."

"Well, young lady, that is unfortunate because we are going to proceed with this discussion regardless. If you ever want to leave this place, you need to participate in the session. All I have to do is make a few notes and say how uncooperative and hostile you've been, and your chances of leaving any time soon disappear. Am I clear?"

Talaitha says nothing, and Dr. Robinson can see her energy beginning to change. He knew this look. He knew what it meant. She was communicating and conveying a very specific message, but Dr. Gross was oblivious to it.

"I will take your silence as consent," and when Dr. Gross said that, Talaitha flinched where she sat. "At what point did the sex start feeling different for you? I mean, when did you start to see it as pleasurable rather than something to dread?"

Talaitha ignored the question, but Dr. Robinson saw her clench her hands into fists.

"These questions may sound very crude, Talaitha, but they are important questions, and we have to probe this topic deeply," said Dr. Gross; a demented eagerness was evident in his voice. "You know, there are other ways that we can work to uncover some of the memories trapped in your psyche; there are medications we can employ to help jog the memories free."

Now Dr. Robinson could see Talaitha's shoulders rise and fall, tighten, her breathing change, and her eyes grow incredibly distant. She was blowing air slowly in and out of her mouth, the way he had taught her to do when she needed to calm herself. It wasn't helping her calm down during Dr. Grosses' questioning. He could see that something was about to blow in Talaitha.

"Listen, girl. You can either cooperate, or I can call the orderlies in here, and we can dress you in a straitjacket until you feel like talking. What's it going to be?"

Talaitha finally looked directly into the camera, and after a few seconds, she was a blur. Talaitha locked her hands around Dr. Grosses' neck, causing the video image to shake violently as her sudden attack brushed against the camera. Off camera, Dr. Robinson could hear gurgling, choking, and gasps for air. Amidst the terrible sounds of chaos, the clamor of struggle, the rumble of wingtips slapping the tiled floor, furniture suddenly shoved and moved, scraping along the linoleum floor, and the constrained, small voice of a man desperately pleading for his life, the last gave Dr. Robinson the most satisfaction.

With these final video frames, Dr. Robinson knew what had befallen the little CNA, and he now knew why Talaitha had come to see him. It was time for him to find her before someone else paid the ultimate price for pushing Talaitha too far.

Two weeks have passed, and Marcus' schedule has cleared, giving him time to meet with Melanie and Roscoe at the Greenes' home. Melanie is feeling somber and hopeful that Marcus can tell them something positive about the investigation into Ruby's death and Jevonte's situation. Roscoe is unreadable, sitting at the dining room table. His cigar isn't lit, and his whisky hasn't been touched. Marcus begins by sharing his findings from the interviews with Rufus and Latriece. Both Roscoe and Melanie were shocked that he actually paid them a visit at the prison and were eager to hear what he learned.

After sharing his findings and reviewing the subsequent birth records he could find about Talaitha, the trio was convinced that a pair of cruel, demented sociopaths undoubtedly abducted and raised Talaitha and Noelle. Marcus went on to discuss his newest lead, Talaitha's sister.

"We were shocked before to learn that she had a sister, but why do you think she's important to what we're looking into?" asked Melanie, deflated.

"Well, now that we know her sister is not dead, and I have proof from the prison visitation logs that she visited her mother, Latriece, at least once since she's been locked up, it begs the question of whether Talaitha knows the truth as well. They purportedly hated one another growing up, even though they were twins. My investigative mind is itching, and I feel like there is more to their relationship than meets the eye," answered Marcus as he left the table to grab some more coffee from the kitchen.

Melanie looked across the table at Roscoe and asked, "I still think we're going down the wrong direction here. None of that gets at what happened to Ruby. Like, why is Marcus wasting time on this?" she whispered discreetly. "You've been mighty quiet, too, Uncle. What gives?"

Roscoe took a deep breath and set his cigar down in the tray holder. He took a slow sip of Uncle Nearest and savored its warmth in his mouth before swallowing. He waited a few more moments for Marcus to return, and then he shared what happened when he went to Jevonte's home.

"When I arrived at their house, I decided to leave Tiger-Paw…"

Melanie interrupted, turning to Marcus, and said, "That's what he calls his rifle," then laughed lightheartedly.

"He knows, young lady; now let me finish, please. He's seen the old girl in action. He knows her well," grinned Roscoe as he took another sip of his whisky. "Anyway, I would rather not leave Tiger-Paw in the car. Other houses didn't crowd the house, but it wasn't isolated enough to assume there were no prying eyes. So, I played it straight and walked up to the house and rang the doorbell. No one answered, so I took a look around the outside of the house and the backyard. Jevonte's Jeep—I could barely recognize it because of all the debris and overgrowth from the trees and hedges. It looked like an abandoned vehicle and obviously hadn't been driven in a very long time."

"I saw that too," said Melanie. "Did you see the greenhouse in the back of the house?"

"Signature Jevonte, for sure. I'd know his handiwork anywhere," responded Roscoe. "After I finished looking around, I went back to the front door and started banging on it. No one answered, and I started yelling, hoping that someone inside would hear me and come to the door."

"Was there any other car there? I think Talaitha drives an Audi or something like that," Melanie remarked.

"No, there was no other car either in the front or along the curb. No one may have been home, but I had a sense that there was someone there. I mean, I couldn't hear anything, and it took everything within me to keep from breaking in to have a look around…"

Marcus interrupted, "Be glad that you didn't, brother. Had you entered unlawfully, our progress in making any further discoveries and our efforts to establish a link to Ruby's death would have been snuffed out. You would have become the target of the police, and anything we tried to offer in defense or in hope for further investigation would be out the window."

"And that's why I didn't. This isn't my first rodeo, my man," Roscoe said.

"Uncle, so you've done this whole breaking thing before?" asked Melanie with humor.

"As I was saying, after no one came to the door, I rang the doorbell again; only this time a message started playing through the doorbell system. It took me by surprise because it was her voice."

"What did that psycho say?" asked Melanie.

"It was a standard, prerecorded message in her voice, you know, like, 'Hello, we can't come to the door right now. Please leave a message after the tone, that kind of thing. So that's just what I did on the off chance that Jevonte would hear it later."

"What did you say, uncle?" asked Melanie, her attention instantly revived.

"I said, Jevonte, I'm here for you. Melanie is here for you. Your family is here for you. No matter what you're going through right now, we love you. I love you, and I don't want you to ever forget how much you mean to your family or me. I won't ever stop. Your mom wouldn't want me to, and she wouldn't want you to ever give up on yourself. She and your dad always believed in you. I still do. I am unsure whether you will ever hear this message. And then I ran out of time."

Roscoe sat back in his chair. He sipped some more of his whisky and exhaled slowly. "I don't know if he will hear the message, but I have to believe that somehow, it will find him."

"I hope so, too, uncle. I know it was not a good idea, but I kind of wish you could have broken a window or something, anything to see inside the house," Melanie said.

"I noticed something else, too, while I was there. They have cameras everywhere in the house, and most of them are hard to see. They aren't exactly hidden, but unless you know what to look for, you'd miss them, and I don't think they were Jevonte's doing. My nephew is excellent with the wood, but electronics isn't exactly his forte. They had to be Talaitha's doing," said Roscoe.

"Ok, so what about Aunt Ruby, Marcus? Are the authorities sharing any information on what happened in the accident?" Melanie asked, pivoting the discussion. Before Marcus can answer, the doorbell chimes. Melanie walks to the front door and opens it to an elderly, bespectacled gentleman she's never seen before, dressed in a white overcoat. The older man extended his hand and introduced himself.

"Hello, my name is Doctor Samuel Robinson with Sable Ridge State Hospital, and I need to speak with someone about Mr. Jevonte Greene. Would that be possible?"

Melanie stood transfixed at the front door. She was nearly speechless, but remembered her manners, took Dr. Robinson by the hand, and returned the greeting. "Oh my goodness, where are my manners? Please come in. Uncle Roscoe, Marcus, come here, please," Melanie called from the dining room. "Come in and have a seat, Dr. Robinson. Can I get you anything, sir?"

"I would like a coffee if that's possible," responded Dr. Robinson.

"Of course. We have a fresh pot on. How do you take it?" asked Melanie.

"Black will be fine, thank you."

Marcus and Roscoe soon joined Dr. Robinson in the living room. As Melanie returned with the coffee, the three men exchanged greetings. While they waited, Marcus introduced himself and talked about his interviews with Rufus and Latriece.

"I know very little about Talaitha's parents. I do know that she emerged from a toxic, abusive environment, one that certainly shaped her life demonstrably. But I am here today to speak to warn her husband, Jevonte. I need to share some things with him for his safety," warned Dr. Robinson. Melanie returned with a tray and a carafe of hot coffee and placed them on the table in front of Dr. Robinson.

Melanie sat down and said, "Dr. Robinson, Jevonte isn't here. We haven't seen him in almost four months. The last time I laid eyes on him was when he was hospitalized at Sable Ridge. None of the other family has seen him either since before he got married to Talaitha."

"We have tried but have not yet made it past his wife. It's like he's in some kind of prison living with her," Roscoe said.

"I did get a text from him a few weeks ago, so we know, or we believe, he's alive, but he's in trouble and wants us to help him," Melanie added, her tone serious and alarming.

"I see," said Dr. Robinson. "I wasn't expecting that. I mean, I met him by accident when a prior neighbor reached out to me about some questions concerning a former residence of mine. I didn't know Mr. Greene's home was the one my previous neighbor had questions about. When Mr.

Greene invited me into his home, there was Talaitha, a former patient of mine. I was stunned, but I didn't disclose to Mr. Greene that I had history with Talaitha. She was aware that I knew who she was, but I thought it was best to act as if I didn't know her because I wasn't sure what the situation was like in that house. I wanted to come here instead to see if I could find a way to share some information with his family so that you could then advise him confidentially. I saw that the hospital sent a letter to this address some time ago and took a chance that I'd find his family here."

"Yes, they messed up and sent some mail here; that's the only way we knew anything was wrong because Talaitha didn't reach out to any of us," replied Melanie. "Additionally, I am unsure if you are aware, Dr. Robinson, but Talaitha's sister, who was long thought to be dead, is actually alive. Noelle is alive."

"Oh, dear. This has become more serious than I thought," said Dr. Robinson. "It appears that Talaitha has begun to sequester her own intimate reality, and she may be creating what I have termed in my research as an effective symbiotic transference movement, or EST-M. This condition generally remains benign in twins, but in one out of 1.2 million cases, there's a psychotic fixation where one twin becomes irrationally consumed by anger because of the mere existence of the other twin. Their actions are characterized by attempts to snuff out the life of the other twin. Twins with this condition assume that their twin is an imposter who is intent on not just eliminating them but also destroying all evidence of their existence. The reality they share is marred by violence, and we have found that the best way to treat them is to separate them permanently."

"We do know that Noelle disappeared from Talaitha's life in their teen years, and the foster parents could never account for her whereabouts. Noelle was presumed dead, prematurely, by local law enforcement twenty years ago when they could not find any trace of her," offered Marcus.

"This may explain Talaitha's relative calm over the intervening years—Noelle's absence. Now that her sister has re-emerged, Talaitha's personality disorder, coupled with the EST-M, is creating a mentally unstable and hazardous condition for Talaitha as well as anyone else in her proximity. If you can't reach Jevonte, well, that's intentional because she is creating a new state of reality that allows her to exercise dominance and complete control over her surroundings. She had no such control as a child and was continuously victimized and subjected to abuse."

"Dr. Robinson, I know you have to be delicate and professional, and you have to say all of the right things, but

I don't give a shit, pardon my French. She may have mental health issues, and there could be factors in her life that contributed to her situation, but you are overlooking an important point here. She is an evil bitch, plain and simple. That's just a fact, scientific or not, it is," Melanie stated, her voice rising a few octaves.

The doctor said nothing in reply and sat quietly, deep in thought, for a few moments. "I recognize your passion, but the way you understand the concept of evil is a fabricated idea that originated during the European colonization period. The European powers labelled many of the religious practices they came across, especially in the continent of Africa, as evil pagan practices. It was how they stigmatized the spiritual practices of the dark races. This label has been used to describe most things that are not white or European."

"I hear what you're saying, Doctor, but you didn't see what I saw when I paid her a visit at her office and at her home..."

Dr. Robinson interrupted, "You went to her office?"

"I certainly did. Why? What's wrong with that? I needed that psycho to answer some questions about what I saw in Jevonte's charts."

"Please, please, do not ever try that again. People in the throes of an EST-M event can become confused and mistake any kind of interaction as an attack. They see basic questions and inquiries as something akin to slurs. They think their twin is taunting, pushing, and hurting them, which angers them. It's like when some people have an extreme negative self-image or when they suffer from body dysmorphic disorder. BDD, as it's called, is a mental health disorder characterized by obsessive focus on a perceived flaw in appearance, which to others may seem minor or not observable. The twin with EST-M becomes so focused on their perception of the other twin that they see it as a caricature of themselves. Maybe the best way to help you understand this condition is to imagine looking at a funny mirror at the carnival. Now, envision the distorted image moving in sync with you, mimicking your words and actions, but doing so in a twisted mockery of your behavior."

"Damn," said Roscoe. "That's really bizarre and twisted. I've never heard of this kind of mental illness."

"Nor have I," added Melanie. "But, hell, I don't feel sorry for her, and I still believe there is something dark inside that woman."

"I understand. I'm still in the early stages of my research, but for now, I caution you: please steer clear of Talaitha. I intend to make contact with her again soon, and when I do, I will also check on Jevonte, ok?" said Dr. Robinson.

"Thank you, Dr. Robinson. We appreciate this information, and I appreciate the time you took out of your schedule to stop by and share it with us. I don't know what I'm going to do, but I feel forewarned now at least. I can't make any promises, but your warning is understood, thank you," said Melanie graciously as she stood to escort the doctor to the front door.

"Yes, of course. Here, let me give you my card. If you all have any questions, don't hesitate to call me. I practically live at the hospital. If you can't reach me at my cell, call the admitting desk. They will know how to reach me. One more thing. It's possible that Talaitha may even confuse Jevonte for her sister Noelle. The condition EST-M manifests is sometimes known as the transference effect. The hatred for her twin may become so extreme that she transfers the persona of her twin onto someone else, someone she can control and manipulate. My research is not clear on the trigger point for transference, but my data over the last ten years is very thorough."

After the doctor leaves, Melanie turns to Roscoe and Marcus. "I know what the doctor said, but to hell with that.

I'm not going to wait around much longer. I'm going to have it out with that woman and bring Jevonte out of that hell."

Days pass, and the chill deepens throughout the rolling hills of western Maryland. A surprise cold front prompts some residents of Accident to fire up their furnaces in an attempt to beat back the early cold. Inside the Greene home, a kind of détente has settled between the married couple. Jevonte is dangerously emaciated and underweight, but he's found a balance and harmony in his daily meditations. He doesn't fight Talaitha when she carries him to and from the bath, and he allows her to feed him as she wants, with whatever she wants. He reasons that the less he resists, the better her mood, and he won't have to worry about seeing the straitjacket. In fact, and Jevonte is rather proud of this, he has learned a new way to speak to her, to negotiate with her, and to nudge her in a direction he wants to go. He's become a little manipulator himself.

"I really like this, my love. I haven't had any problems keeping it down, and the taste is pleasing. I can taste a hint of something that I can't quite identify. What's the secret sauce, Tal?" he asks as he forks another mouthful of leafy green and brown mash into his mouth.

Talaitha says nothing at first, but a small smile begins to creep around the edges of her face. "I know you like my herbs, so I added some to my garden kale and mushrooms. I cold-pressed them to remove some of the bitterness," Talaitha finally replied softly.

"It's working, my love. They're not bitter at all. Can I have a second helping, if you don't mind?"

Jevonte's exchanges with Talaitha continue in this same vein. He is apologetic, demure, non-aggressive, and deferential in all things. He waits for her to signal him when she's ready to change topics, move differently, and speak his mind. He is careful not to oppose her viewpoints and is always encouraging. His strategy is proving effective. Talaitha hasn't threatened to pull out the straitjacket once, and she has started leaving him unchained while she works in her home office.

Some mornings, Talaitha carries Jevonte out into the backyard so that he can watch her in the greenhouse he built. He doesn't complain. The fresh air, while chilly, feels good on his chafed brown skin. While he sits and watches, he's thinking and planning. He has Talaitha's routine and schedule down. He is now familiar with some of her work in her practice. He has been paying attention during dinner table talk. When Talaitha lets her guard down, she's expressive, and Jevonte can hear the passion in her voice as she talks about her patients. All the while, Jevonte is cautious not to open any discussions involving Talaitha's past or this Noelle person. The last time he asked a question about Noelle, he ended up in the straitjacket for a whole week, nonstop. He learned.

With each passing day, Talaitha's controls begin to ease. Jevonte is now sleeping in the master bedroom with her. His lithe, frail body can't offer her much warmth, but she seems to enjoy listening to him breathe. Some nights, he's woken to find her staring at him, watching him, unmoving, and deadly silent. When she notices that he's awake, she curls up into a tight ball and falls asleep. It's unnerving, but Jevonte doesn't mind. There are no chains in the master bedroom, and for that, Jevonte is thankful. He just absorbs this new behavior and locks it away in his brain housing group—as his Uncle Roscoe calls it—for later.

Then, on one particular morning, Talaitha decided to go to the clinic in Baltimore to work. She didn't explain why, and Jevonte didn't question it. She packed up her things and reminded him that his juices and salads were prepared in the refrigerator. Jevonte sat at the breakfast table and nodded with understanding. When she walked out the door, he sat stock-still, staring at his scrambled eggs and kale salad in disbelief. He didn't want to move. He slowed his breathing as much as he could and listened for the sound of the Audi as it backed out of the driveway. He strained carefully, listening for the crunch of the tires as the luxury vehicle turned and headed down the street away from the house. He wasn't chained. The jacket was locked away. A silly joy started flooding over him in that moment. She was gone, and he was free. I'm free, he thought. Now what?

The cameras, dang it, I almost screwed up this chance. I can't forget about those. Gotta watch myself. I don't want to look directly at them. I want her to think I've forgotten about them. She thinks I can't get around the house because of my condition, and I don't want her to know that I can walk. What she doesn't know will work to my advantage. I've got to take advantage of the time I have free. I know she's got appointments with three patients today, and those generally run about an hour each. It takes an hour and thirty minutes to get to the office, and that's three hours round trip, so I should have almost six hours and change alone to figure out how I'm going to get a signal back out to my family.

Jevonte decides to act. He pushed his plate away slowly and leaned sideways until he fell out of the chair. The fall is soft and controlled; he braced himself for the impact. He begins slithering across the floor. The act isn't as painful as it used to be, and the wounds on his legs have been bandaged—so no blood trails. He has time, so he doesn't exhaust himself inching towards the back door. On camera, he imagines that he must look like he's headed towards the bedroom, but when he arrives at the hallway entry, he rolls to his side and arches in the direction of the back door. He's hoping the cameras have a blind spot there and can't see the bottom of the hallway entryway or the bottom of the back door.

Jevonte lies flat on his stomach; the top of his bald head barely touches the foot of the back door. He rolls over onto his back and stares at the doorknob. He won't be able to reach the doorknob while lying on his back, so he will need to sit up and expose himself to the cameras, if he hasn't done so already.

Well, here goes nothing. What do I have to lose? If she sees me, she sees me. I still have plenty of time to get someone's attention before she can get back to the house, so fuck it!

Jevonte bunches his knees up close to his chest and pushes his back flat against the door. Little by little, he starts rising against the length of the door until his hand can grip the doorknob. He struggles to pull himself up but finally manages to stand upright, leaning heavily against the doorframe. He unlocks the door and twists. Nothing happens, and the door remains closed. He twists harder, and still the door won't open. The knob is turning as it should, but the door is still locked and secure. Jevonte peers through one of the quarter-panel windowpanes and finds another bolt holding the door in place. Jevonte is perplexed. He starts replaying the last few times Talaitha carried him out into the backyard. He didn't remember seeing anything new on the door, but then again, he wasn't looking either. He gives the door another twist and weak shoulder shove, but he might as well have been pushing against a steel door.

The situation makes no sense. Why would she do this? There is no point in hiding the fact that I can walk now. Let me check the rest of these doors.

Jevonte ambles to the front door. It's also somehow locked from the inside. Wait, she left out the front door, so how is she supposed to get back inside the house when she gets home? Jevonte wonders to himself.

He wanders over to the interior garage door; it, too, is locked, and this time the doorknob won't even turn. Then the realization sinks in; he's in a prison, a homemade prison, and he helped build it with his hands. He returns to the kitchen table and places his head in his hands, and begins to weep softly.

22

Love in the Dark Soil

After a challenging week with a few clients, Talaitha makes her way down to the basement of her and Jevonte's home. She had been planning to feed and care for some of her garden babies—as she called them—for a few weeks, but she had to adjust her schedule to take care of Jevonte. Getting her hands into the dark soil was therapeutic, helping her release some stress. Her garden babies didn't need too much hands-on, but she always made sure to check on them, speak to them, and let them know that they were not alone in the dark. In many ways, Talaitha felt a deep kinship with the mushrooms that thrived in the warm, moist soil in the basement. Most forest dwellers and passersby misunderstood and ignored the wild mushrooms. They were feared but fragile. They needed very little light and grew without external interaction. The best part, she thought, was that they shared a vast network with extended communities and could, when under duress, share critical information and resources. They were microcosms of twin plants, clustered in vegetative energy that could sustain each other under harsh conditions. Likewise, Talaitha could still feel her sister Noelle, even though she had vanished from her life over twenty years ago. What she felt now wasn't healthy, but it was there, under her nails and skin, crawling over her scalp and around her neck; an urgent need to eradicate her from everything thrived and flourished.

In one of the work cabinets she had Jevonte build for her were rows and rows of tinctures, unlabeled, but each was filled with very specific combinations of weak and strong cultures of false morel, destroying angel, and fool's funnel, freeze-dried and crushed into very fine powder. They were not labeled, but Talaitha knew, from the row order, how deadly or severe the collection was. Over the years, Talaitha had experimented with several varieties of webcap and sweating mushrooms to work out the exact combinations that, when combined with concentrated doses of dandelion root, astragalus, ginger, and parsley, would produce the desired cooperative effect, paralysis, or worse for the consumer. She also had one row, a last and final row of tinctures that contained highly efficient remedies and antidotes for each of the deadly concoctions she created. Not every creation of hers had a counter; thus, she called them remedies. Through trial and error, she discovered the optimum exposure rate and load values needed to bring someone under her complete control or eliminate them. The amount of time and exposure required to achieve her goal depended on the individual's sex, size, and weight.

After inventorying her vials and tinctures, Talaitha walked over to the deep sink to wash her hands. Standing in front of the deep sink's mirror, Talaitha reflected on how far she'd come with her special garden. She smiled as she recalled Jimmy Foles, the graduate assistant who believed he could manipulate her into having sex with him during her time in grad school. She experimented with various combos of Fool's Funnel and False Morel, liberally sprinkling them into his soup container in the teacher's lounge. Still, the onset of kidney failure was too rapid, and the young man expired after only a few meals. She had intended to stretch out his agony over several months. Then there was the Alpha Kappa Alpha sorority, Nneka Ogumakey, who tried to force Talaitha to join her sorority using blackmail. She planned to accuse Talaitha of cheating on the final comprehensive exam and get her expelled. Nneka needed one more high-academic-scoring student to finalize her chapter's standing on campus. Talaitha's grades consistently landed her on the Dean's list every year. Talaitha's experiment with nettle and horsetail taught her that without an inhibitor, the toxins in the mushroom cocktail were too potent and too obvious to detect. An autopsy of Nneka's body showed severe kidney and liver damage, the kind only possible after exposure to toxic mushrooms. Fortunately for Talaitha, the authorities attributed Nneka's death to accidental poisoning of the food supply, and the cafeteria was shut down for four months. Lessons learned, Talaitha remembered thinking.

After drying her hands, she returned to her workbench to sort and put away her equipment and look over her garden babies one last time. She pulled out her phone to check on Jevonte. Talaitha's brow immediately furrowed into a line of fury and unbelief. There was Jevonte, straining to push a kitchen chair across the floor. He was attempting to wedge the chair against the door underneath the doorknob. He was not making good progress. She can see him trembling and straining to wedge the chair against the door. He's sweating and looks like he's about to pass out from the effort, but before he does, Talaitha launches herself up the stairs and aggressively pushes the door open. The chair and Jevonte go sprawling backwards, with both tumbling across the kitchen floor.

"What the hell do you think you're doing, Jevonte?" Talaitha yelled, furious over what it appeared he was attempting to do. "I saw you. I know you can walk now. I know you tried to leave me," she said, emotion heavy in her voice. Talaitha's right hand has a slight tremor, and Jevonte eyes her cautiously before responding.

She called me by my first name, Jevonte thinks to himself, and he proceeds to answer her carefully. "My love, please don't be angry," Jevonte says before rubbing the elbow and shoulder he landed on. She thinks I was trying to leave her. Let's focus on that, he thinks. "My dear, you are doing everything for me, and I truly appreciate it. I just wanted to try doing a little for myself. I just wanted to get outside for some air, but when I saw the doors were locked and I couldn't get out, I panicked a little. What if the house caught on fire? How would I get out?"

"You just want to abandon me as all the other men have done before. I saw you, King. I saw what you did. You are just like the other men, and I believed you wanted to be my husband and spend eternity with me. That's what you promised me, Jevonte. Well, you're not leaving me, ever," Talaitha said and started down the hallway to the master bedroom.

"Talaitha," Jevonte yelled after her. "Please don't do this." Jevonte knew where she was going and what she was going to come back with, so he started scrambling, moving as fast as his diminished body would allow, into one of the corners of the living room. He pressed his back firmly against the corner, pulled his skeletal-looking legs close to his chest, and waited. He bowed his head and began praying.

"Our Father, who art in..."

Talaitha was upon him before the word "heaven" could escape his lips. The blows were immediate and swift. Jevonte was battered out of his protective corner, and in a blind rage, Talaitha tossed Jevonte into the dishwasher door so hard it left a slight dent. Like pooled molasses, Jevonte slid down the dishwasher into a heap of pummeled agony. He couldn't see clearly, but he heard her as she started shrieking and cursing his name.

"You're never leaving me! I won't let you. You left me before, and they kept on fucking me. They didn't care. Nobody cared. You were supposed to protect me, but you left; you just left me on the dance floor. You knew what they were doing to me, and you never tried to stop them. I hate you, and by god, I will make you pay for what you did!" Screamed Talaitha.

As Jevonte slipped into unconsciousness, he saw the kitchen ceiling fade from view. He noticed the lower cabinets disappearing from his peripheral vision while Talaitha dragged him by one leg toward the bedroom. He could no longer feel the carpet burn under his head as he was hauled down the hallway. He welcomed the bliss of the coming darkness and yielded his mind to dreams of other times, places, and people.

Two days later, Talaitha relented and removed the ankle restraints from Jevonte. He said nothing and just lay in bed, unmoving. He stared blankly at the ceiling fan above the bed, wishing its blades would somehow come loose and find themselves embedded in Talaitha's head. Talaitha ignored him and went about her day as though it were just like any other. She prepared breakfast for Jevonte, bathed him, and dressed him before leaving for Baltimore. She didn't warn him or threaten him about leaving. A distinct melancholy permeated the air, and Jevonte had now become accustomed to the de facto state of affairs between him and Talaitha. He resigned himself to the fact that he would not hope anymore for anything save a quiet, gentle death.

His body weight was down another few pounds, or so he guessed. He had no way to weigh himself, but each time he looked in the mirror, he could see the curvature of each rib. He saw how gaunt his arms looked and how shallow and collapsed his abdomen was, as well as his knees—he cringed looking at them. They looked like two round balls sitting on top of sticks. Nothing fit his body. His underwear sagged and almost always fell off him when he stood up. Looking up at his face, Jevonte wanted to cry, but he couldn't—his body couldn't spare the moisture. His eyes were a yellow hue, sunken deep, recessed in his head. His cheekbones, though bruised from his beating, were puffy and swollen. He wondered if his jaw was broken because he found it difficult to open his mouth fully. His once smooth, brown bald head now bore scarring and healed-over scabs that marked different areas along his scalp and neck. I am a mess, he thought to himself.

Jevonte managed to make it back to his bed, where he collapsed into an exhausted state of despair. He knew it was just a matter of time before his body stopped living altogether. He didn't believe he could endure much more. He welcomed the thought and surrendered to sleep that would bring him into the evening when Talaitha would get home. What a gift it would be if she came home and found that I had escaped through death, he thought. Jevonte smiled and closed his eyes, knowing that for the next five hours he would be safe from her.

When Talaitha arrived home that evening, Jevonte was so deep in slumber that he never heard the garage door open or her entry into the house. Talaitha came into the bedroom and began changing. She walked over to Jevonte and felt his forehead. No fever, though his skin was clammy.

She stood over him, watching him, taking in each of his breaths. A look of concern spread across her face. It was as though she were seeing him in this condition for the very first time, helpless and vulnerable. She bent down and kissed him lightly on the cheek and caressed his chapped lips softly. The look of regret and heartache was an alien mask, and Talaitha felt uncomfortable in that moment. She straightened and began walking out of the bedroom, but halted as she approached the door. She turned to look back at Jevonte's corpse-like body and began to weep. She turned to face the wall, struggling to regain her composure, then returned to his bedside. She sat beside him and took his frail hand in hers.

"King, can you hear me? Please, King, wake up," she pleaded softly. She ran her fingers lightly over his rib cage and started rubbing his hollowed-out belly, making circular motions with her fingertips. She left and went into her boudoir to retrieve some of the specially blended arnica and frankincense oils she created. She warmed her hands by rubbing them together and applied the oils to his chest, neck, and arms. She layered some eucalyptus oil behind his ears and under his jawline. Last, she massaged his feet with lavender and chamomile oil, then wrapped both in plastic wrap.

Thirty minutes later, Jevonte woke up to find Talaitha rubbing warmed shea butter into his hands and forearms. His spirit broke, and he wept dry tears from the relief his body was experiencing. He trembled from the intense stimulation, and when his vision fully cleared, he saw his wife, Talaitha, smiling into his face with a joy he didn't recognize. His tongue would not obey his mind, and he couldn't speak. He only stared longingly at her, his heart feeling whole. His mind, however, was still screaming objections.

Talaitha said nothing. Jevonte could not understand the shamefacedness he beheld in her face. Who is this, he thought quietly. She gently pulled back the sheets from his emaciated form and began to pour out a small measure of what smelled to Jevonte like rosemary oil upon his genitals. The fragrance of it all soon overwhelmed him, and he closed his eyes. This has to be a dream. I'm dreaming, Jevonte thought to himself.

Most of Jevonte's pubic hair was gone, so Talaitha gently rubbed the oil across his pelvis and around his penis. She massaged him gently, carefully holding his testicles away from her probing fingertips while she rimmed his scrotum with her index finger. She could feel his skin start to bunch up, and his testicles begin to tighten and draw back, so she pressed her probing finger into his body and began searching for his prostate. Jevonte cried weakly, but Talaitha spoke softly to him, hushing him with motherly coos and whispers. Jevonte relaxed under her gentle commands, and then she took him into her mouth. Jevonte's mind was reeling from the intensity of her index finger and the inferno of her mouth, saliva, and oil mixing in one as she guided him past her tonsils.

This time, Jevonte didn't ask for release; Talaitha demanded it. "Give me," she slurred while holding as much of him as she could in her mouth. Jevonte exploded. Talaitha emptied him and remained affixed, letting neither air nor fluid escape from her mouth. She breathed through her nose and waited for him to finish. When he was done, so was she. Talaitha let him slip gently from her mouth. She smiled up at him and said, "My King!" Both her eyes and his were wet with emotion. Talaitha lay down beside him and draped an arm across his frail body to warm him. Her body was a furnace, and combined with the oils she had applied earlier, Jevonte could feel himself slipping into a cocoon of love and safety. He wanted to live now, and thoughts otherwise could not penetrate his soul.

In the ensuing days, Jevonte was treated to more intense oiling and restorative interludes with Talaitha. He could feel the healing rising within him. Talaitha's attentiveness and care buoyed his spirits. He hadn't experienced the straitjacket once since the sessions began, and on a few occasions, he noticed that she would even leave the back door open when she went to work, with only the screen door closed—and unlocked. Talaitha had also stopped preparing juices and special salads for him. For the first time in a very long time, he felt like he was getting normal food again. Even though there were times when he tasted something odd, tangy, or strange in the food, it was better than what he had been getting. There was no denying that Talaitha could burn in the kitchen, and his meals were something he now started looking forward to again.

Jevonte ponders to himself, I know my gut is telling me to be wary of her, but she really seems to have changed. I believe she has transformed into this new person, but I don't know if I can trust her. I hope the transformation is real. I know one thing for sure: I feel a lot better. I think I'm gaining a little weight back, too. Let's not jinx it, though. My legs look so much better now. I can still see the bulging veins and all, but they don't look as severe, and pressing on them doesn't hurt.

Jevonte senses that dinner is almost ready, so he decides to get dressed and see what's cooking. Sure enough, the table is set, and Talaitha is bringing serving plates. It all looks delicious—and edible! There is even some meat on the menu—how about that! My goodness, she is a sight. I could stand here and watch her all day. I have never seen anyone move as she does, with such elegance and power. Observing her transports me to the day I first laid eyes on her. She is still the most beautiful woman I have ever seen.

"Is there anything I can help you with, sweetheart?"

Talaitha says nothing. Her back is toward Jevonte, and he can't see what she's doing at the counter. Maybe she didn't hear me, Jevonte thinks. Let's try the procedure again.

"Babe? Earth to Tal, earth to Tal, come in Tal," Jevonte broadcasts playfully.

Talaitha finally turns her head to the side so that her left ear is facing Jevonte. Her eyes are pointed straight ahead. To Jevonte, she looks as if she's listening to someone or something far in the distance, as if she's focusing on discerning its location or identity. Jevonte decides to sit. He doesn't know what's got her so preoccupied right now, but he just wants to have a quiet meal with her this evening.

Talaitha picks up the last serving plate and walks over to the dining table. The table is filled with dishes. Jevonte mistook them for meat dishes until he saw the labels Talaitha placed in front of each dish. There is a mushroom stroganoff to his left, a vegan chili dish, and some vegan mac and cheese in the middle of the table. To his left, there are two dishes: a dish Talaitha has labelled 'Lentil Shepherd's Pie' and a final dish labelled 'Lentil Bolognese'. Jevonte was leery. The food looked tasty, and some of it really looked like actual meat dishes, but he was a bit puzzled by the quantity and the presentation.

"Are we having guests over?" Jevonte asked. "This is a lot of food, my love."

Talaitha sat quietly, her hands folded in her lap. Her head was bowed as though she were praying, and she said nothing in response to Jevonte's question.

"Well, it all looks good. I've eaten vegan food a few times, and I always had mixed feelings about it. I didn't know you could prepare vegan-style dishes," Jevonte said. He was having doubts about the mushroom stroganoff, though. "I'll just skip the mushroom-looking stuff. I don't think my stomach could handle those right now."

Still, Talaitha remained quiet. Her head was bowed the whole time Jevonte was talking to her, then she lifted her head and turned to face the living room. There was no expression on her face that Jevonte could discern. She looks possessed, Jevonte thought. What has her attention in the living room?

"The mac and cheese looks like a definite winner. I'll try some of that. My heart, what's the matter? Are you gonna eat?"

Silence.

"Ok, then. So, we're not talking tonight? Are you mad at me for something? Is something bothering you?" Let me chill before I piss her off, Jevonte thinks. He takes a few mouthfuls of the mac and cheese but stops to spit it out onto a napkin.

"What are you doing?" demanded Talaitha across the table, startling Jevonte, and he dropped his fork and nearly knocked over his water.

"Oh, hey. I couldn't eat that; it didn't feel right in my mouth. I can't place it, but it doesn't taste like cheese…"

Talaitha cut Jevonte off when she stood up and walked over to where he was seated. "You don't like my food?" she said, towering over him.

Jevonte leaned away from her in surprise. "Love, I didn't say that. I…"

Talaitha grabbed a handful of mac and cheese and shoved it into Jevonte's mouth. She covered his mouth and pinched his nose, forcing him to swallow the food. "I worked all fucking day to fix this meal for you, and you mean to tell me it's nasty!"

Jevonte tried to swallow but gagged from the force of the food being shoved down his throat. He spat some of the mac and cheese out of his mouth, which triggered Talaitha, who grabbed another handful and stuffed it into his mouth. Jevonte started choking, and mac and cheese bits started spilling out of the sides of his mouth and through Talaitha's fingers. "How dare you!" she screamed. She grabbed the mushroom stroganoff and straddled Jevonte's lap. She began slapping whole handfuls of the stroganoff into his closed mouth. The mushroom dish was splattered all over his face. His eyes were coated in beige and brown, and his cheeks were packed with the mixed remnants of mac and cheese and mushroom stroganoff. He couldn't say a word in protest, and after another handful of the vegan chili, he couldn't breathe.

Jevonte's eyes grew wide with fear and panic. Talaitha did not care. She slapped him hard across the face, and his mouth exploded with its contents. "You make me sick. Why do I do all of this for your pussy-ass? All I do is slave for you," and she slapped him again; only this time she rocked him with her right hand, sending beige and brown particles flying against the wall. Jevonte's eyes rolled up, and his head reeled from the brutality of her strikes.

He tried to free one of his arms to help fend off the blows, but Talaitha had him pinned down in the chair. She twisted around and grabbed the bowl of lentil bolognese. She dumped it on Jevonte's head, and its heat made him scream. Talaitha stood up and shouted at him, "Shut up," and punched Jevonte in his face. His head rocked backward hard, and he toppled out of his seat. His food-plastered body struck the floor with a wicked-sounding thump. Two of Jevonte's teeth rolled across the kitchen floor, bouncing and dancing until the kitchen floorboard halted their clattering. Blood gathered around Jevonte's face. His nose was split, and his right eye was rapidly swelling shut.

Talaitha stood facing Jevonte's fallen body. She stood stock-still, showing no signs of exertion. The colors of mushrooms, yellows, and painted streaks of brown and chili red were splattered all across her dress and blouse. The dinner table was bedecked with all the platters she had prepared, with light sprinkles of blood scattered here and there. The cabinet doors looked like Jackson Pollock originals. The kitchen was the scene of a culinary horror show, and Jevonte was its centerpiece.

A few minutes passed, and Talaitha came to herself. She looked around the kitchen, genuinely shocked. She sat down hard on the kitchen floor. "Jevonte," she cried. "King, oh god, oh god," she wailed and started crawling towards his crippled, food-caked form. One of his eyes fluttered open, and he looked at her, but there was no recognition there. "King, please say something. Don't leave me," she cried and lay down next to him, her arm surrounding his neck and shoulders. Mushroom stroganoff dripped down his forehead and cheeks as she lifted him into a sitting position and rocked him gently in her arms.

The fall weather was becoming more winter-like as October arrived. On this Saturday morning, James was up early. Jevonte's oldest cousin wanted to take a little of the edge off the chill in the air and ignited the furnace. The rustic, burning smell of heated air began wafting throughout the home. Kim, Jevonte's youngest and precocious cousin, was busy in the kitchen, pulling out frying pans and bowls. She was the master pancake maker among the cousins. Kim switched on the radio, and Marvin Gaye's melodic voice echoed softly throughout the home, stirring the family to rise in rhythm.

"(Wake up, wake up, wake up, wake up)
'Cause you do it right

Baby, I got sick this mornin' (heal me my darling, heal me my darling)
A sea was stormin' inside of me
Baby, I think I'm capsizin' (heal me my darling, heal me my darling)
The waves are risin' and risin'
And when I get that feeling
I want sexual healing."

Melanie can hear the music as she walks up to the front door of Jevonte's parents' house. She smiles and unlocks the door with the key Roscoe gave her. James greets her from Jedidiah's chair, and Melanie rolls her eyes.

"Boy, why are you in Unc's chair? You know he doesn't like anyone sitting in his chair," Melanie exclaimed.

"Because he ain't even here. He won't know unless you tell him," James replied, a sly grin on his face.

"Well, you already know then, right? So get up out of his chair," Melanie shot back, standing her ground until James got up, cursing under his breath. Melanie watched him plop down on the loveseat next to Jedidiah's chair before she walked into the kitchen. As soon as she entered the kitchen, though, James jumped back into Jedidiah's chair.

"Hey, Kim, that smells delicious. Did you put some coffee on?" asked Melanie, her voice easy and nonthreatening. She and Kim didn't always get along, and she was not in the mood to start the day fighting this woman.

"What's wrong with your eyes? Mel, the pot is right over there where it usually is," said Kim as she flipped the hotcake over on the griddle.

This child, I swear before God, I'm going to hurt her badly one day, so help me Jesus, Melanie thought to herself. "Thank you," replied Melanie, feigning a smile. "I appreciate you guys coming over this morning…"

"Coming over?" said Rickea as she walked into the kitchen to join the two women. Jevonte's middle cousin, Rickea, was the same age as Melanie and the most distant and aloof of the crew. "We've been here all night, Mel."

"All night! You guys have your own homes; why were you here?" asked Melanie. She sensed that there was an alternative motive here. There always was, it seemed.

"Look, we just want to keep everything in order until Uncle Jedidiah decides to show up. I mean, we can't just leave the house empty," said Kim.

"How did you guys even get in?" replied Melanie.

"How did you get in, cousin?" shot back Rickea.

There is no use fighting through this mess, Melanie thought to herself. "I didn't come here to fight with you all. I just want to coordinate our actions and see if we can get the police to do a better job on Aunt Ruby's murder investigation. They haven't been very forthcoming with information."

James walked into the kitchen. He was hungry; otherwise, he wouldn't have bothered interfering with the womenfolk. "Are the pancakes done, Kim? I've been waiting for hours now, shoot," he jested.

"Don't even, sir. They will be ready when they are. Now excuse us, adults are talking," responded Kim.

"Adults? I don't see any. Where are they at?"

"Go sit down somewhere, James," instructed Rickea.

"James, have the police contacted you yet?" asked Rickea. Have they told you anything about Aunt Ruby's death?" asked Melanie.

"Naw, but I did get a text from one of my friends who works on the force. He's not involved in the investigation, but he did tell me that the case is at the bottom of the pile, and the detective assigned to it has been out for a long time on medical or something," replied James.

"What the hell," exclaimed Melanie. "It's been almost three months now, and no one is even working on it?"

"I don't know what to say to you, Cuz. My boy could be wrong. I mean, he's just a patrolman. He probably doesn't know what he's talking about, so I wouldn't take what he said with a grain of salt," said James.

"Look, y'all are in the way. Take all of that somewhere else so I can finish cooking. I'll call everyone when it's ready," instructed Kim.

Melanie grabbed her coffee and headed to the front porch. James remained seated, waiting for the first few hotcakes to get done. Rickea followed behind Melanie, and the two of them sat on the porch. The two women sat quietly, each in their own thoughts, neither wanting to intrude on the other's peace. After Rickea finished her coffee, she set her cup down and looked at Melanie. Melanie noticed and knew a serious conversation was coming.

"Mel, I need to ask you something. I have had this on my mind for quite some time, but there was just never a good time to mention it."

"Sure, Ricky, go right ahead." Melanie and the cousins started calling Rickea "Ricky" in the fourth grade. It was Jevonte who started calling her that. No one knew why the nickname stuck, but Rickea didn't mind; she understood that being called that name meant family discussions were about to begin. It was an invocation of sorts that the family business was underway.

"You have been a part of this family for as long as I can remember. Uncle Jedidiah and Uncle Roscoe treat you like their daughter. I'm fine with that. You're more like a sister to me than a cousin anyway. I know Kim talks out of her ass sometimes, and James is just, well, James." The women laughed, with Melanie shaking her head in agreement.

"I appreciate you saying that, Ricky."

"Of course, but one thing I have never really understood, and quite frankly, I wasn't concerned about it either, is why? I mean, there is no blood relation between you and any of us, or at least I don't think there is," Rickea continued with one eyebrow raised curiously. "So, why have you been so connected and invested in us, in Ruby and Jedidiah? I don't even know when or how that started."

Melanie reflected for a long moment. She finished her coffee and set the cup on the porch table beside Rickea's.

"My mother disappeared when I was a little girl. She didn't just leave us either. She was taken. The police ruled her death a homicide, but they could never find her body. However, they did capture several individuals involved in human trafficking and discovered DNA linked to my mom at a transfer point. Testimony from one of the traffickers pointed to my mom's death, but the police believed that several women, including my mom, were killed outside of the United States. My grandmother, Louise, took me in. Do you remember her?" asked Melanie.

"Yes, I do, Mel, and I'm sorry. I didn't know that about your mom," replied Rickea.

"No one does, really. Anyway, my grandma couldn't really support me, but she didn't want me to go into the system. My dad was not in the picture. I don't think he even knew about me, but I knew him. I know who he is, and Grandma refused to have anything to do with him. She didn't have the opportunity to explain that before her death, and I haven't been interested in learning more since then. I met Ruby and Jedidiah at the playground with Grandma. Grandma started taking me to Ruby's church, and then I'd have playdates with you guys and Jevonte. Aunt Ruby really showed up big for me. She instructed me on how to style my hair because Grandma's hands suffer from arthritis, and she was unable to do it herself. Uncle Jedidiah would take me on fishing trips whenever he took Jevonte. He taught me how to ride a bike and swim. I think they informally adopted me," laughed Melanie.

"I see. I had no idea, Mel."

"In Grandma's last year before she died, Uncle Jedidiah put me in his will. They have always loved me like their own, and I don't know where I would be without them. When all of this happened, it was like my own parents were attacked, my family, so I have no choice but to make sure Aunt Ruby gets justice."

After another long pause between the two women, Rickea sheepishly asks, "Um, well, doesn't that make what you and Jevonte are into... incestuous?" Melanie's eyes grow wide, and she almost chokes on her spit. The two of them look at each other and burst into riotous laughter on the porch. The women are laughing so hard they don't notice RhaShawn pull up in the driveway. He gets out of the car and approaches cautiously, watching two grown women laughing so hard they have tears in their eyes.

"Ok, what did I just miss?" RhaShawn asks.

"Don't worry about it, brother. This is just girl talk," and Melanie gathers herself and regains some composure.

"Hi, cousin. What brings you here this morning?" asks Rickea, rising to head back inside the house.

"Nothing, but I heard Kim was cooking, so here I am," laughed RhaShawn.

Both Rickea and Melanie looked at each other and said, "James."

"I'm headed over to the police department this morning. Want to come with?" asked Melanie as she too rose to take her coffee cup back inside the house.

"What, did Marcus say anything? Does he have some news?" responded RhaShawn.

"No, he didn't, but I intend to get some answers from them, and I'm not going to stop pestering them until I do."

Later that morning, Melanie arrived at the police headquarters in downtown Baltimore. Parking has always been problematic in Baltimore, but she manages to find a spot and goes inside. She checks in at the front desk, and the desk sergeant gets her information and instructs her to have a seat. Melanie is fortunate enough to be the only person waiting for her that morning. After about fifteen minutes, Detective Albright walks into the waiting area carrying several file folders and, seeing that Melanie is the only person there, walks over to greet her.

"Hello, I'm Detective Albright. You must be Ms. Decartes, correct?"

Melanie stands and extends her hand. "Yes, I am. Thank you for meeting with me."

"Of course. Please, right this way," and the detective leads Melanie to one of the interview rooms. Once inside and seated, the detective places the files in front of him and takes out his notepad. "I think I know why you are here. Ms. Decartes."

"Ok, so why am I here, detective?"

"I know the department has been slow in getting you answers about your aunt. I apologize for that. I want to assure you that we have not forgotten about Ms. Ruby. The Special Crash Investigations unit, or SCI, handled the crash investigation early on. All of their initial findings pointed towards negligence by the driver..."

"They were blaming my auntie?" interrupted Melanie, her anger rising.

"It appears that the case was about to conclude until private investigator Marcus Drummons contacted me regarding it. He told me that there was a strong possibility that foul play may have been involved in the accident and that I should take a closer look at Ruby's body, so I did."

"And?" asked Melanie, urgency now rising to replace the anger in her voice.

"I had the coroner take another look at the body before Ruby was let go to the funeral parlor, and he found traces of DNA under her nails—DNA that was not hers."

"Auntie fought back? Is that what you're saying, detective?" asked Melanie, her eyes now welling up with tears.

"Yes. Your aunt did not go easy. She gave the bastard 'what for' before she succumbed to drowning. Sorry to be so callous," he said.

Melanie sat with that for a few minutes. Her emotions were frayed, but she felt some pride knowing that her auntie fought back, as she suspected she would because that's who she was. "So did the DNA have a match?"

"Not in our criminal records. The databases we have access to, both statewide and federal, did not return a match. I reviewed military records as well, and we didn't receive any hits there either. Now that doesn't mean too much; it just tells me that this person has no criminal or military record, but they may have medical records. Unfortunately, those databases are harder to get at than military records. I'm still looking into that and won't stop until I get a chance to query them. It's just going to involve some major court interventions to get it done, and that just takes time. I am sorry."

"So, it's officially a homicide then?" asked Melanie.

"Yes, ma'am. The DA has backed a criminal investigation into your aunt's death. The DNA we found under Ruby's fingernails was from a female, so that will help us narrow down the search."

Female, could it be? Nah, let me not jump to conclusions here, Melanie thought. "You mentioned Mr. Drummond. I know him, and he's been helping us look into some other matters, possibly related to Aunt Ruby's murder, but I..."

The detective stopped her. "I am aware, and that's something I also wanted to discuss with you. I shared our lab results with Mr. Drummond. I owed him a favor or two. I don't have enough evidence to look into this Talaitha person, but he can go where I can't at the moment. So, I encourage you to support what he's doing and follow his lead. He communicated to me that he does believe this person could be dangerous, so don't confront her in person—not without backup or police presence. Also, and this may not mean anything, but the state reported one of their home health aides was missing. The employee was assigned to do a home site visit with Jevonte and Talaitha but since she was dispatched, no one has seen or heard from her. It's probably nothing, but I am aware that an incident report was filed and some follow up may happen soon. I will let you know whether that turns up anything related to what we are going to be investigating."

"Thank you, detective. I know what I need to do now. I appreciate getting this update. I think the family already knew that something wasn't right about Aunt Ruby's death, and now we have something concrete to focus on, and we will."

Late in the evening, after the cousins and Melanie had gone from the house, Jedidiah sat in his truck just out of eyeshot of the house he and Ruby called home. He watched as Melanie closed the front door and checked to make sure it was locked. He watched her start up her car and drive down the street away from one of the few places she felt at home. It was tough for Jedidiah to see. He felt like he was hiding from her. He was, and he knew that.

He got out of his truck and started walking to the house. For reasons he wasn't sure of, he couldn't bring himself to park in the driveway. Unlocking the front door and entering the home, Jedidiah felt like an intruder. He crept inside, expecting to startle someone. He passed through the kitchen, and the weight of her absence started pressing in on him. Everything was clean, spotless, and in its place, the way she always left the kitchen. He walked into the sitting room like a lost apparition seeking solace in the shadows. His recliner looked as it always did, inviting and beckoning for attention, but he ignored it. He passed by all the other spaces and went into the bedroom. He thought that he would lie down and get some rest before he started bringing his bags into the house. He was worn out, and his shoulders ached from the constant tension he'd been carrying.

He sat on the edge of the bed, once expansive and overflowing with her joy. The comforter looked as deflated as his spirit. Even the pillows looked lost without her, as though they no longer had a purpose. On the nightstand, the answering machine is blinking furiously. There is one message, and at first, Jedidiah struggles to remember how to play it. "The infernal machine had too many damn buttons," he would always say. Ruby was always the one who would end up playing it for him. Finally, he gets it right, fearful that he might have erased the message until he hears her voice:

"Hey Jeddy, please don't forget to defrost the chicken tonight. I know I said I'd fix your meatloaf tomorrow, but I still need some things to make it. Let's have it this Friday; that way, I'll have enough time to prepare everything. You missed a fantastic Bible class tonight. Elder was on it! Look, it's raining pretty hard now, and I can barely see these streets. I'll take my time, so I will probably be late this evening. Let me go; someone is riding my tail, and they have their brights on. What is wrong with…" and the message ended. Jedidiah looked at the recording and the display. This was her last moment, her last call, and the last time he would ever hear her voice. This was the night his cherry blossom was taken from him.

Jedidiah crumpled to the floor and began to weep from the deepest parts of his soul. He felt completely alone in this life, destined to remain so for the rest of his days. Every memory of her flooded over him, engulfed him, and surrounded him in anguish and travail. Her smile, her laugh, the way she would scold him, and the way she teased him because he couldn't dance; all of their memories together overwhelmed him. Jedidiah wept out loud and lay on the floor of the bedroom. Through his sobs, he almost missed the sound of the doorbell at the front of the house.

Jedidiah gathered himself up and went to the bathroom to dry his face and beard. His nose had been running, and his eyes were bloodshot, but he didn't care how he looked. By the time he reached the front door and opened it, the man was walking away, headed back to his car. When he hears the front door open, he turns to greet the homeowner.

"Can I help you?" asks Jedidiah, his voice a bit hoarse and scratchy.

"Good evening, sir. If you have a moment, I work for New Life Insurance out of New York. We recently received notice of the passing of one of our insureds, and I was hoping to complete some of the paperwork we need to finalize the claim."

Jedidiah says nothing at first, but he takes a deep breath and answers, hoping that he can contain his emotions long enough to speak. "Yes. My wife recently passed, but I haven't been handling very much of the insurance stuff. My daughter and a family friend have been helping us with all of that.

"I see. Well, that's ok. I can speak with her, too. Is she here?"

"No, not currently, but if you provide me with your information, I will have her contact you right away."

"That sounds fine, sir. What is her name, if I may ask?"

"Melanie Decartes. She's a longtime family friend. Who, may I say, wants to speak with her?"

The man pulls out a business card and hands it to Jedidiah. "Please tell Ms. Decartes that Nolan Ashcroft would like to speak with her at her earliest convenience, or I could drop by her home if you don't mind sharing her address with me."

23

Fractured Identity

It was the middle of the week, and Talaitha needed to meet with a client at her Baltimore office. She only had one client today, so she knew she wouldn't be there all day. She didn't think she could stand the sight of Jevonte's crumpled and broken body any longer. She was experiencing an emotion she was not familiar with—guilt. She felt bad for missing an appointment with Dr. Robinson that had been on the books for weeks. She knew she needed to see him and probably get new scripts, but Jevonte just couldn't be left alone for too long, and now her decision was costing her—and him. She had started seeing and hearing Noelle again. In her thoughts and nightmares, Noelle was showing up more and more, and Talaitha just couldn't silence the voices. She feared that she was losing her mind.

Entering her office, Talaitha fired up her desktop and launched the monitoring application. Jevonte was asleep. The ketamine she had given him had effectively put him into a deep slumber. He wouldn't wake until she finished at the office and returned home. So, Talaitha opened some of the files she had on her client. There wasn't much information there at all. She could not find any medical records in the electronic health system, which was highly unusual. There was no medical history whatsoever, and that troubled her. She would be flying blind for a bit until she got the patient talking and disclosing information. Her desk phone buzzed, and it was the receptionist informing Talaitha that her 10 o'clock had arrived. Talaitha told her aide to show the client in, and she rose, notepad in hand, to greet her patient.

Nolan walked in behind the aide and said nothing until the aide closed the door behind her on the way out.

"Mr. Ashcroft, good morning. Come, have a seat and get comfortable," Talaitha said, her face blank but accepting.

Nolan began walking toward the counselor's den. He wasn't wearing his usual London Fog trench coat, despite the chilling weather harassing the denizens of Baltimore. He was wearing black leather pants, a blue blazer, and a checkered olive-and-yellow tie. He had immaculately white sneakers on, and when he sat, Talaitha could see he wasn't wearing any socks. He wore his hair in evenly spaced cornrows that framed his head like a crown, not too long in the back and tapered neatly behind his ears. For the first time, Talaitha noticed how clear his skin was, and, interestingly, it almost matched her own bright caramelized hues.

Nolan removed his glasses and began cleaning them. When he put them back on, they were crystal clear, and the frames nearly blended in with his skin. "Good morning to you, Dr. Mercedes."

"I made some notes here from our last sessions…"

"But that's not what you want to talk about, is it?" he interrupted.

"Yes, you are correct about that, among other things. I have questions I'd like to ask you. Your file is very thin, and there isn't much medical history to go on. If you don't mind, I'd like to get some background information. It will help me formulate a proper treatment plan."

Nolan didn't respond. He sat perfectly still as though he were a statue in the park. "Are you sure, sister?" he finally responded.

"Mr. Ashcroft, it is vital for our work that you are forthcoming and transparent with me. If I am going to be able to help you, I need you to speak your truth and answer my questions. Can you do that? Otherwise, we're both wasting our time here."

"Truth is a funny thing, Dr. Mercedes. People think they want to know it, to hear it spoken, but when it comes, it changes everything, and people are rarely ready for the changes it demands. Besides, I like coming to your office. I like seeing and working with you. I don't want all of that to change. I don't want you to change, not yet," Nolan confided.

Talaitha made a few notes and returned her attention to Nolan. "Mr. Ashcroft, seriously, you must leave that decision to me as your therapist to decide whether what you're going to share is too much for me to handle. We all have dark secrets. We have all done things and are doing things that we don't want anyone to know about, but this place is a safe space, Mr. Ashcroft. You can tell me anything, and I will keep it in confidence. I am enjoined by professional standards and ethics to maintain the privacy and confidentiality of this treatment space. No matter what, I am bound by doctor-patient privilege."

Nolan considered Talaitha's words before he responded. "Very well, sister. We will let the chips fall where they may, but don't say I didn't try to warn you. Ask your questions."

"We were rudely interrupted during our first meeting. A deranged lady burst into my office, and I had to deal with her. Before that, you asked me about someone named Rufus and Latriece. I don't know those names. Should I?"

"Hmm, ok. I thought you wanted to be open and transparent, but I see we're still going to play the game. Very well," Nolan said, reaching for his glasses to begin wiping them again.

"I want to be open and transparent, but I need you to be that way with me even more than anything else."

"Still that girl, are you?" he interrupted again.

Talaitha was beginning to get agitated. She recrossed her legs and set her pad and pen on the end table beside her. "Please clarify, Mr. Ashcroft."

"You really have not changed much, Tally," Nolan answered.

Nolan's casual use of a nickname, unknown to anyone except her parents and possibly her teacher, Ms. Topeeka, shocked Talaitha. On hearing it, she was speechless, but she rose from her seat and walked to her kitchenette to boil some water for tea. Calmly, she gathered some lemons and one of her teacups from the cupboard, then she turned to face Nolan. "Would you like a cup of tea, Mr. Ashcroft?" Talaitha asked as she attempted to reassert an air of professionalism between them.

"I never really liked tea, not since it was thrown in my face in high school." Nolan rose and walked to Talaitha's office library. He traced several of the volumes with his fingertips, taking his time to capture all of the titles and authors.

"Oh my, Mr. Ashcroft, that sounds horrible. Your skin looks really good. Did the hot tea leave any lasting scars?"

"I had several excellent surgeons help me overcome any scarring that might have been there. The brutality I experienced as a child left some scars that were not reparable by the surgeon's scalpel, but I made do. I was in a very precarious position as a teenager. You see, the one person I loved most in the world hated me. She could never bring herself to love me back."

"Let's take our seats again; please go on," Talaitha asked, gently guiding and pointing towards the den area.

The pair sat back down. Nolan never took his eyes off Talaitha as they were getting seated again, which made her nervous. "Who was this person you're speaking of, sir, and why do you say she never loved you back?" Talaitha picked up her pen and started taking notes.

"She poisoned me," Nolan said flatly. "My own twin sister hated me so much that she tried to kill me when we were in high school."

The silence that descended on Talaitha's office became impenetrable. Time felt like it stopped, and with it, all of Talaitha's blood chilled. She couldn't write any more notes, and she didn't dare look up at Nolan. Her brain was scrambling to find something to say, anything, but her confusion had paralyzed her. After a few moments, she centered herself and attempted to regain control of their conversation.

"That sounds horrible, Nolan. I can imagine how that must have been a very traumatic experience for you. How did your parents handle the situation? Did they get you and your sister some help, some counseling?"

"Oh, no. My folks were in prison by the time that happened. No, it's probably a good thing that they were locked up. Rufus and lovely old Latriece were shit for parents, but of course, you already know that, don't you, sister?"

"I don't know what you're talking about. I had very loving parents. They would never have…"

"What, sold you to random men for pleasure? What is it they would not have done?"

"Nolan, you are here in my office because you're not well, and you need my help. We need to take some time to establish…"

"Establish what, Tally? Establish what, exactly, our father was: a son-of-a-bitch who got off on using the strap on you and loved listening to you get gangbanged by old men in the garage. What part do we need to establish?"

Nolan exclaimed and leaned forward, his eyes never leaving Talaitha's own. Do we need to clarify that Mr. Dandrich, if I remember correctly, was one of the few donors who returned every Thursday night to assault you in the church parking lot? Do you remember the playground at First Baptist Assembly of Joy? I bet you do, sister."

Talaitha wanted him to stop, but he wouldn't. Nolan continued to hammer away at her, and distant memories began coming back into her consciousness. All of the work she and Dr. Robinson had done came tumbling down in a torrent of suffering as a result of his unrelenting attacks. Her emotions were beginning to swirl, sending her mind reeling in confusion. The office suddenly felt hot, and the air was thick. She was sweating slightly and uncomfortable. Memories of strikes, slaps, and the pitiful sobbing of a broken little girl began flooding her thoughts. Flashbacks of blood and torn underwear caused her throat to feel closed, and she thought she was going to suffocate. She tried to gather some strength to stand, to get away from this person, this monstrous memory of torture and pain, but her feet would not obey.

Finally, Nolan ceased bombarding her with his words and sat back. The room felt like it was shrinking, pushing the pair closer together. Nolan removed his glasses and stared hard at Talaitha. In a small, feminine voice, he said, "What do you see, Tally?"

Talaitha swallowed and returned his gaze. "Noe, Noelle?" She whispered nervously.

"In the flesh, sister."

On the drive home, Talaitha is zoning out and misses her exit. The honking car behind her startles her, and she regains her focus.

How in the hell is this possible? That can't be my sister, but he looks like me now that I think about it. Nolan knows only what Noelle would have. I mean, he could be faking it, but how? I don't know how to process this, but for some reason, it feels true; it feels right somehow. But he, no, she, disappeared at prom and just vanished. That bitch just up and disappeared, forever. If she were trans, I never saw that when we were growing up, but I guess I wouldn't have anyway. I couldn't stand her. All I know is that when she left, I always felt better. Not having her around just made me feel better for some reason. I hated her, but Nolan is different. I feel a little connected to him, but I feel none of the anger when he is in my presence. So how can he be Noelle, fuck?

I'm a psychiatrist; I should be able to figure this out, but it feels like something is blocking me, hiding the truth from me. All I know is that something is going on with Mr. Ashcroft, and before I buy his or her story, I need to do some digging. If she had a sex change and plastic surgery, there is bound to be a paper trail. Medical records are necessary, given the exceptional quality of his treatment. But first, I need to get back to Jevonte. He's still in awful shape, and I still don't know what got into me that night. I don't understand, and I feel like things are getting worse. This reminds me, I am way overdue for my appointments with Dr. Robinson. I have to get my anger under control. I feel like I am losing my temper over the slightest things, even though I used to have a lot of control over my emotions. It's probably that fucking Nolan. I didn't start losing control of my emotions until he first came to see me.

The drive proceeds without further detour, and Talaitha pulls into her driveway just as the sun begins to set. The house is dark, with only the kitchen microwave light on. She does a quick scan of the rooms, and nothing appears out of place. She grabs a bottle of Merlot from the wine rack and a glass and sits at the kitchen counter. She pours a tall glass and drinks it in one swallow. She contemplates pouring another, but she hasn't checked in on Jevonte. She peers back toward the bedroom. All of the lights are off. She looks at her empty wine glass and decides to wait for the second glass.

She can't see very much in the bedroom, but she can hear Jevonte's raspy breathing. He sounds miserable. Through subtle moans, she can tell he is still in a lot of pain. Talaitha vanishes into her office, and when she returns to the bedroom, she has a syringe and a warm washcloth. Jevonte's eyes flutter when she turns the bedroom light on. His good eye finds her when she lets out a small gasp.

"Tal," groans Jevonte. His words are difficult to understand due to his swollen lips. He can't fully say the words because of his fractured jaw, but he continues. "I need. Could you take me to the hospital? I am having difficulty breathing. I need help, please, Talaitha."

"I know, King. I know, but we can't do that right now. Look, I am going to fix you right up. I can make this better, ok. Now just lie still. This will help with the pain and help you to sleep," says Talaitha, and she pulls back the sheet to uncover his little arm. Jevonte doesn't resist. He couldn't tell if he wanted to. The sedative has an almost immediate effect, and within ten minutes, he is fast asleep again.

The next day, Talaitha starts her day behind schedule. She was up most of the night watching over Jevonte. She was worried that she might have given him too high a dose of the sedative. In her haste, she left her phone on the kitchen counter. It wasn't until she was seated at her desk, preparing to welcome her first client of the day, that she realized that her phone was missing. She tried calling the phone, and after several rings, her voicemail picked up. I probably left the damn thing in the car. It will just have to wait until after my first session is done, she thought to herself.

Jevonte stirred. The loud ringing of Talaitha's phone pierced his morning daydreaming. The phone stopped, but by then, he was awake and struggling to get his body moving. Everything hurt all over, but he managed to get up and into the bathroom. He ignored the mirror. He would rather not see what he already knew his damage was. The depression was already descending upon him, and he didn't need any more visuals to aid in its landing. After a very painful shuffle into the kitchen, he was surprised to see Talaitha's phone perched on the countertop. How did she forget it? He mused.

Jevonte walked over to the counter and picked up the phone. There's no doubt she's realized by now that she left it, and I can bet she's flying to get back here to get it, so I don't have much time, he thought. Jevonte couldn't call Melanie or his Uncle Roscoe because the phone was locked, but he could still dial 911. Frantically, Jevonte tried to launch the dialer to call the police, but his grip on the phone was unsteady, and he dropped it. His hands were trembling, and the phone felt like it weighed a ton. He fumbled the phone again, and on his third try, he punched in the three digits he hoped would bring the cavalry.

"911, what is your emergency?"

"Yes, yes, hi. I need help, please."

"Ok, sir. Do you need police, or is this a medical emergency?"

"I need both, please."

"Sir, I can barely understand you. Can you tell me what the nature of your emergency is?"

"I am being held against my will, and I have been beaten. I need some help."

"Yes, sir. Can you provide your address, please? We'll get someone over to your loc…"

Jevonte dropped the phone again. Frustrated, he bent down as best as he could to retrieve the phone when Talaitha burst through the front door. Jevonte sat motionless on the floor, hoping and praying that she hadn't seen him—but she had. Talaitha walked over to the counter and peered over its edge at Jevonte, who sat cowering on the floor with her cell phone in his hand. With remarkable ease, Talaitha lifted Jevonte off the floor, and though he tried to maintain his hold on the phone, his feeble attempt was laughable, and she pried his fingers open to retrieve her phone. After she released him, Jevonte sagged to the floor like a worn-out rag doll.

"King, now who were you calling?" And when Talaitha looked at the screen, she saw the number 911.

The operator's distant voice cut through her momentary curiosity, snapping her to attention. Talaitha held her breath.

"This is the 911 operator. Hello, can you hear me? Are you still there?" The voice sounded tiny through the phone's speaker.

Talaitha hung up on the operator and saw red. Jevonte rolled to his side and started convulsing—no, he was laughing silently. Every time he laughed, his body seized with pain, but he didn't care. The laughter was a salve. He could barely breathe or catch his breath. His head started feeling dizzy from the lack of oxygen, but he beckoned for the bliss of unconsciousness.

"Operator, there's a meeting in the lady's room," mumbled Jevonte, his face flush against the cool kitchen floor and his mind overwhelmed with delirium. "You. You're cooked now, Tal. What are you gonna do now, huh? How are you going to fix..." And Talaitha cut Jevonte's words short as she grabbed him by the neck, slamming his face into the floor before hauling him down its length towards the bedrooms. Jevonte went limp and waited to be tossed into the bed per her usual. There was no tossing, and she let go of the grip on his neck when they entered the bedroom. Jevonte slid to an ignominious stop in the middle of the bedroom. Talaitha continued on her path to the closet. Jevonte knew what was coming and resigned himself to being locked down for the rest of the week.

When Talaitha emerged from the closet, the straitjacket was not in her hands. Jevonte looked at her in horror and disbelief as she lifted the baseball bat high in the air and brought it down on his stomach with sudden swiftness. Jevonte expelled all the air from his lungs as a shockwave of trauma and pain rolled through his midsection. She raised the bat again, and again, and again, pummeling him in the stomach and rib cage. Jevonte tried to intercept the blows with his arms, but it was no use. The bat blew past his defenses like paper. He tried to roll to expose a stronger part of his weakened body, but nothing helped; nowhere was safe from the beating. She struck him across his groin, and one of his testicles popped. She continued ravaging his lower body with blow after blow. Jevonte cried in agony and tried to crawl and snake his way underneath the bed.

Talaitha's wrath was out of control, and she grabbed Jevonte by his legs and dragged him away from the bed. She resumed beating him on his legs and feet until the tops of his feet split and the bones in his right foot shattered. Jevonte started to black out, and with what he believed was his final breath, he cried out, "Talaitha," and he pointed a small stick finger at her. "It doesn't matter now. I will be free, and your hateful ass is going to jail."

Talaitha stopped and tossed the bat across the room. She stepped over his mangled body and left the bedroom. Jevonte was not going to fight anymore. He pleaded with the angel of death to come, to come and whisk him away from the nightmare that never seemed to end. When Talaitha returned with a pair of shears in her hand, Jevonte's eyes rolled up in his head. Talaitha grabbed him by the wrist and held up his arm in a vicelike grip.

"You coward. You want to call the police on me?" Talaitha said in a blood-curdling growl, and she cut his index finger off. "Try that shit again, King, and I will take the whole hand next time. Jevonte passed out and never saw the finger fall to the carpeted floor.

Jevonte woke to a knock at the door, announcing Talaitha's return. He was delirious from the blood loss and feared that a new round of horror and dread was about to begin. Jevonte's thoughts became jumbled and scattered as he felt all reason and sanity start to slip from him. There was a time, not too long ago, when everything between them made sense. They used to be whole. They used to be in love, or so he thought. When Talaitha entered the room, Jevonte trembled in fear, and as she placed some bandages on the nightstand, he withdrew into his mind, where things were so good and so right, until they weren't. What was once solid was now based on nothing more than hollow vows.

It's Saturday, and the Accident Police Department is minimally staffed. So when Baltimore Police Detective Albright calls, no one answers. He is more fortunate on his third attempt.

"This is Corporal Hayes from the Accident Police Department." How may I direct your call?"

"Good morning. It seems like you might be experiencing a staffing shortage. This is Detective Albright with the Baltimore Police Department, and I need to speak with one of your on-call investigators or detectives if possible."

"Yeah, well, we don't have much crime in these parts, not like the jungle in other cities, if you catch my meaning," said the corporal.

The dog whistle did not go unnoticed by Detective Albright, but he needed a favor, so he pressed on. "I'm calling on important police business and need your cooperation. Is there a detective on duty, or do I need to work with your lieutenant?"

"The detectives are off on the weekend, and my lieutenant is out. It's just the Sergeant and me today, so what do you need help with, Detective Albright?" replied the corporal snidely.

Albright took a deep breath and then provided details. The corporal listened silently, permeating the conversation with "huh-uh," "I see," and "got it."

"I think we can accommodate your request. Is there a case number I can associate this with?" asked the corporal.

Detective Albright provided the case number and asked whether the department had been called upon to look into the disappearance of a state worker sent to a local address in Accident. The detective ended the call after the corporal assured him that he would handle it and that they had not yet been asked to look into any missing state workers. Nevertheless, the detective made a mental note to follow up with the Accident Police Department on Monday morning.

True to his word, a police unit pulled up to 52 Riverrun Drive later Saturday afternoon. Private Trigg and Private Hamerstein stepped out of the patrol unit and walked to the front door. They rang the doorbell and waited. Inside, Talaitha was in the kitchen, working on the bloodstains on the floor. She never noticed the patrol unit when it first arrived at the house. When the doorbell rang for a second time, her heart raced. Her car was in the driveway, and she didn't think it was a good idea to just ignore them. They would be back. "Damnit, Jevonte!" she cursed to herself. She quickly looked around to check whether the living room and kitchen looked presentable. She walked back to where Jevonte's badly beaten and bloodied body lay sprawled on the floor. She closed the door and started walking to the front. On her way, she quickly typed a brief message to Nolan.

"We will continue our conversation later, but for now, I need you to do something for me."

Nolan replied immediately. "And what is it you need from me, sister?"

"Cut it out. We haven't established that relationship yet, but if you do this, I promise we can work that out."

"Very well, but that's soon to be two favors you owe me."

"Look, whatever. I may need to call you in a few minutes. I just need you to play along as my husband."

"Ooh, that sounds kinky, sister."

"Just do it, Nolan."

Talaitha cleared the messages and announced to the visitors that she was on her way. She looked at herself in the guest parlor's mirror before she walked to the front door.

"Hello, what can I do for you, officers?" Talaitha asked politely.

"Hello, ma'am. I'm Private Trigg, and this is Private Hamerstein. We're with the Accident Police Department, and we wondered if we could speak with you for a few minutes."

"Speak with me about what, officers?" said Talaitha, her body partially blocking the patrolmen's view inside the home.

"Well, ma'am, it is a delicate situation, and it would be best if we discussed this inside, out of sight of your neighbors."

Talaitha hesitated. "Sure, why not. I understand, and thank you for your discretion. Please come in." Talaitha opened the door and gestured toward the sitting room. "Would either of you like something to drink? Coffee, or maybe water?"

"No, thank you, ma'am. We're fine. I'll get right to the point. Our department received a request from the Baltimore Police Department asking whether we could conduct a wellness check on one Jevonte Greene. Is that your husband, ma'am?" asked Private Trigg.

"Yes, he is my husband, but why would the authorities request such a thing? Has something happened to him, officers?" asked Talaitha, suddenly feigning concern and anguish.

"We have no report of anything amiss with Mr. Greene, but to support the request from Baltimore, can we speak with your husband, please? Is he here?" asked Private Trigg. Private Hamerstein began scanning the interior of the home.

"Well, I can understand that. Can you tell me specifically who it was from Baltimore that requested this in the first place?" said Talaitha, avoiding the question.

"We can't say, ma'am. All we can tell you is that Baltimore made the request, and we would like to honor it without involving the courts. If we could just look around and see for ourselves that your husband is not here, we can close this request and be on our way," replied Private Hamerstein.

Talaitha inhaled slowly and stood up. "But of course. If that's all you need, that's fine. I have a ton of work to do this morning before my husband gets home. So if you'll follow me…"

Private Trigg interrupted her. "Uh, ma'am, if you don't mind waiting here with my partner while I look around. It's protocol for us, and safer for us, if you remain here. And this wellness check is strictly voluntary, so if you don't feel comfortable doing that, we can withdraw and come back with some paperwork."

"No, like I said, I am fine with all of it. Take your time and be as thorough as needed." Talaitha sat down and pulled her phone out. She had previously typed up a message that read:

Call me in exactly five minutes.

Private Trigg began walking through the home. He looked in the garage, then went down into the basement. He spent an inordinate amount of time down there, and Talaitha got a little worried, but after a few brief minutes, he was back upstairs and headed to the dining room. He walked toward the back of the home and started opening bedroom doors. Both guest rooms were made up and immaculate. Just before Private Trigg started to open the door to the master bedroom, he noticed there was one more door he had missed. It was Talaitha's office. He tried the door, and it was locked.

"Excuse me, ma'am. Can you unlock this door, please?" Private Trigg asked in a loud enough tone to reach the front of the house.

From the sitting room, Talaitha yelled back, "That's my home office. I have sensitive patient files in there, and I must guard their privacy."

"Ma'am," said Private Trigg as he walked to the front of the house. "I don't need to see any patient files. A quick peek inside is all I need, please."

"Okay, just a second. I need to get my keys from the bedroom."

"Private Hamerstein, please accompany Mrs. Greene to the bedroom," instructed Private Trigg.

I told that man, exactly five minutes. It's almost been eight, Talaitha thought to herself. She started walking towards the bedroom. In her mind, she was formulating a plan to eliminate both of the officers. She wasn't sure how, but she knew that once they saw Jevonte—or heard him— she would be arrested, and she was not going to be locked up ever again. Almost on cue, her phone started ringing. She let it ring until she reached the kitchen.

"Hello, my love. What's up?" she asked, her heartbeat starting to slow with relief.

"Hey, sister," said the feminine voice on the other end of the call. Talaitha cringed.

"Did you forget something, love?"

"I certainly did. I forgot to tell you that I arranged to have Rufus shanked at his home away from home. I wanted to tell you sooner, but we were distracted by other news," Nolan purred.

"Ma'am, is that your husband? Can you let me speak with him, please? I think we can clear all of this up right now, if you allow me," said Private Trigg.

"I think that is a fantastic idea. Just a second. Honey, we have some friendly officers of the law in our living room, and they would like to have a word with you," said Talaitha, and she handed the phone to the officer.

"Hello, sir. This is Private Trigg with the Accident Police Department. The Baltimore Police Department called us to your home to conduct a wellness check on you. Your wife was kind enough to allow us to walk through the home and see that everything is in order. I just need you to confirm with me that you are well and not in any kind of danger."

"That little lady is the very best partner I could ask for. I do appreciate the checkup, but I assure you I am completely fine. I couldn't be better. I'm due home in about ten minutes if you guys want to hang around for some drinks. I have a bottle of Uncle Nearest I've been saving, and you guys can help me break it in. What do you say?" teased Nolan.

"We'll have to pass, sir. We're still on duty, but perhaps next time." Private Trigg handed the phone back to Talaitha.

"Honey, hold on while I walk these gentlemen to the door," said Talaitha. She walked the two officers to the front door and bid them farewell.

As they got into their patrol vehicle, Private Hamerstein asked, "What's an Uncle Nearest?"

"When you grow up and get a little more hair on your chest, I'll tell you. Let's head back to base. The game may still be on."

Inside the home, Talaitha walked back to the master bedroom and opened the door. Jevonte was beginning to wake, making restless moans and groans from where he lay on the floor. The temporary wrapping on his hand would need to be changed, and he would have to be sedated and locked down. Before she set to work on Jevonte, she whispered into her cell phone. "Ok, Nolan. You cut that too damn close, but I owe you one. We will meet to talk." She hung up the phone and began gathering medical supplies and carpet cleaners.

"I believe my brother has been by the house," says Roscoe as he removes the hinge from the barnyard door. The barn had long been in a dilapidated state, just waiting for someone to come to its rescue. Roscoe had promised Ruby that he would take care of it, but he never had the time until now.

Melanie swats at the flies gathering too close to the meat she intends to grill outside. "Why do you say that, Unc? I haven't seen hide nor hair of him in months. If you hadn't seen him that one time in Baltimore, I would have thought he had gone on to the upper room."

"It's Ruby's message. It's gone. There was one last message on the answering machine, from her. She left it the night she was killed."

"Oh my God, are you serious, Uncle? I didn't know Auntie left a message. What was it? What did she say?"

"It was typical of Ruby. She was calling my brother to check on him and ask him about dinner. It was her last message and the last time we could hear her voice, and now it's gone."

"But how do you know Uncle Jedidiah erased it?"

"He never could figure out how to play those messages. He would just hit all of the buttons until something happened—or so Ruby said. I saw the machine blinking just a week or so ago; now it's dead, nothing. There are no saved messages at all. I'm pretty sure it was my brother, and if he heard her voice, I bet it pushed him over the edge. Who knows when we'll see him again?"

Melanie wiped the tears from her eyes and started uncovering the meat for the grill. She started fanning the coals when Marcus Drummons walked through the side gate to the backyard. He joined Melanie and Roscoe at the picnic table and set some folders down in front of him. Roscoe stopped what he was doing and took a seat. Melanie finished placing the hot links on the grill and joined the two men.

"I hope you're hungry, Marcus. We have plenty," offered Melanie.

"Yes, indeed, but are they the 'for-real hot links' or those other make-believe hot links?" Marcus jested.

"They are the real deal, brother. Whatcha got for us?' asked Roscoe.

"I called in a favor with a friend at the BPD, and they managed to get the police in Accident to do a wellness check on Jevonte. You are not going to believe this, but it checked out, and Jevonte is fine."

"Wait, what do you mean by fine? What did they say?" demanded Melanie, suspicion rising with her voice.

"They went into the house and looked around. They found nothing, and they did speak with Jevonte himself. He reported nothing unusual and assured them of his well-being. In fact, the police officers stated here, and you can read it for yourselves, that they spoke with him directly."

"No way, Marcus. Something is not clean in the milk here. They said that they talked to Jevonte face-to-face, and he was fine?" Melanie shot back.

Marcus slid the file report over to Melanie so that she could read the statement for herself. "Now I'm not saying that there's still nothing fishy here, but all immediate indications are that Jevonte is not in as bad a shape as we once thought."

"Marcus, I respect your work. Always have and always will, but this is some bullshit. Those sloppy-ass police hoes couldn't find their way out the door if you put the knob in their hands. I believe they missed something. I don't believe they spoke to my nephew. Wait a minute," and Roscoe put his glasses on to look at the report again. "Uh, yep, right here! The idiots said that Jevonte called from work and spoke to them. How in the hell did they know it was

Jevonte and not someone else? How did they positively identify Jevonte?"

"You're right, and I thought about that too, and that's why I am going up there next Tuesday—unannounced," said Marcus. "This was sloppy, but I'm not surprised. From what I've heard, Accident is a small town, and its local law enforcement doesn't necessarily strive for excellence. I'll go and look into it myself."

Melanie was quiet. She wasn't really listening anymore. She was glad that Marcus was going to visit that she-devil. But she told herself that if he went next Tuesday, then he would be late to the party.

24

Tableau for a Black Madonna

Some nights, the crushing loneliness becomes too much, and he falls. He fails, and when he does, a new victim emerges to satiate his hunger. He isn't always filled, but he lives for the work. He revels in the triumph of his decision to make the change, to become what he needed to be, and he only lives in regret when he fails to capture what he needs for his masterpieces. He has long perfected his craft, and these days his greatest effort comes from doing the research, stalking, and planning the newest additions to his ever-changing tableaus.

It wasn't hard at first, though the process—cutting away and removing unnecessary pieces—cost him dearly. Walking away from her that night at prom was probably the bravest thing she had ever done up to that point, but she had to. She didn't have a choice. Had she stayed, she would have perished at the hands of her sister, and she knew, even then, that there was no way she could ever end her sister's life, even in self-defense. Thus, it was an act of self-preservation that led her to eliminate herself from a situation with only one possible outcome. She would have to transform, and knowing that the change was an act of true love, she steadied herself.

The cost was high, and she had no money, no resources, and no one to turn to for help. So, Noelle used what she had—her body. She peddled her body at truck stops, at fleabag motels, at dive bars, and at 24-hour restaurants where only the lonely and desperate congregated at midnight. She travelled and began to make a name for herself and the services she provided. For a young teenager, the world was overflowing with men who thirsted for the forbidden and unlawful. There were no boundaries, and she confirmed time and time again, over and over, without fail, that the greatest harvest of men came from within the halls of the so-called Church on Sundays. They could never get enough of her young flesh, and she obliged them every single time. They were without shame or guilt, and she was not their judge. She reaped bountiful harvests sufficient to remake herself.

Noelle saved up enough money over five years, filled with dark, painful work, hope, and many disappointments, to put her plan into action. She found that she could not effect her transformation as some do via medical plans, counseling, and innumerable sessions of hormone replacement therapies.

She didn't have the insurance anyway, nor did she have time to wait or to follow prescribed medical and psychological protocols before she could shed her painful existence. So, Noelle travelled and, for the right price, found physicians with worldviews like her own. Noelle was finally laid to rest on August 3, 2004, and Nolan was born.

Living authentically for the first time in his life was transformative in itself, but the surgeries and unsanctioned, illegal drugs he used had their cost—his sanity. For a few years, Nolan lost his way. His identity shifted, and he was not prepared for the demon that emerged in the mirror of his life. Clarity only seemed possible when he eliminated false reflections and faded counterfeits of what once was. He found that the noise in his head quieted when he erased and then properly installed women in the Artscape he created, a tableau of feminine subjugation. When the disappearances of women began to create too much attention, he would move on to other cities, but when he located Talaitha, he settled down. He tried to establish a new life and halt the work on his tableaus. He failed.

One day, his handiwork would reveal to Talaitha that her irrational hate and fears—of her womanhood and sisterhood—were misguided. His work would show her how beautiful Noelle was, and once Talaitha saw that, she would understand the depth of sacrifice in her sister's transformation. At least now, as Nolan, Talaitha could love him, accept him, and embrace him openly, but his tableaus would always be there to remind everyone of what was taken to make room for his new existence.

Nolan's home studio in Middleton, Delaware, reflected a mix of dark gothic colors with several pieces hung throughout the home that served as an ode to the late medieval and early Renaissance periods. He created his own interpretations of Dante's Inferno and infused them with Afrofuturistic imagery, which he suspended overhead, creating a celestial environment of observers in his work. His workspace was his sanctum, and once his guests expired and he fixed them in place, he knew that his true genius would rise like a phoenix in the night. Nolan understood that at last, his true genius would give birth to a new vision displayed before all the world on the dais he had carefully built in the center of his studio. He just needed one final piece—a Black Madonna—to ground his vision and free him from the abbess raging inside his mind.

Monday had arrived, and neither Roscoe nor Melanie had heard anything from Marcus. Today was the deadline, as far as Melanie was concerned. She didn't care what anyone said. She would be cautious, but too much time had gone by without concrete answers about Jevonte's situation.

As Melanie stands in the hallway gathering her thoughts, she takes a moment to consider what her coming actions might mean. I'd rather be wrong and embarrassed to find out that he's actually doing well than to find that he's hurt because I failed to act. She was going to give Marcus his time, but the more she thinks about it, the more she's convinced that now is the time to act.

I can see it on Unc's face, too. He knows we have to do something. I don't understand why he hasn't yet. It doesn't matter. I will, but I need to get home and clear my work schedule.

Melanie glances at her watch, reminding herself to be strategic in choosing a time to visit Jevonte's house. If I were certain about the demon lady's work hours, I would plan my visit accordingly. I'll just have to chance it, she thinks.

Melanie leaves Ruby and Jedidiah's home and notices that Roscoe's car is gone. When did he leave? I didn't even know he was gone, Melanie thought. She heads over to her townhome in White Marsh and checks her mail before heading inside. The home is only two years old, and it's already creaking like an old, lived-in home. Melanie didn't think she could afford to buy a house on her own, let alone a new construction model. Still, after she landed the position as a critical care nurse in the neonatal unit at John Hopkins Medical Center in Baltimore, everything seemed possible. She was thriving in her new role. Melanie attributed the good fit to all the love and care that Ruby had poured into her. Melanie's goal was to model Ruby and the way she loved people, carried them, and surrounded them with love. Melanie emulated the natural, homegrown "Mamma's love" that was Ruby's trademark, knowing that her affection was what the babies in her care truly responded to.

Melanie poured herself some juice and sat out on the balcony porch of her home. She thought about getting something a little stronger, but decided against it since she had a drive ahead of her. Townhomes didn't suit her when she was first in the market for a home, but she had come to enjoy her decision, and the balcony was one of her favorite places in the house to find peace. She was fortunate, too, because she was on the end and not sandwiched between two other townhomes. She only had one set of neighbors to worry about, and thankfully, hers were kind.

She sat on her plush outdoor lounge sofa and went through her mail. Before she could finish, it occurred to her that she probably should give Roscoe a call and let him know where she was going. She even considered borrowing one of his guns for security, but she didn't want to drive all that way only to turn around and drive up to Accident. "Now, where did I leave my phone?" She mused aloud. As if on cue, her phone began ringing from inside the house. Melanie rose and headed back inside to answer it. The ringing stopped, and when Melanie unlocked the phone, she saw it was a spam call, at least that was what she thought, since the number was blocked. She hated those things.

On her way to her bedroom, she started dialing Roscoe's number. He didn't answer, so she left him a voice message telling him where she was going and that she had made up her mind to see about Jevonte for herself. She told him that she would text him once she arrived in Accident. She ended the call and tossed the phone on her bed. She needed to shower all of the day's frustration off of her before she got on the road. The demon lady loved to make fun of her weight, so Melanie was damned if she would go in there smelling bad, too.

She let the hot water run for a minute or two, then stepped into its hot embrace. The steam and water released the tension in her neck and shoulders, and Melanie wanted to remain planted forever under the directed nozzle sprays of her shower, but like everything else, time was running out, and she would have to put off this luxury until another time. She stepped out of the enclosed shower and stood in front of the mirror alone with her thoughts.

Jevonte, you have to be alright. I don't know why I feel so responsible for you now, but I do. I should never have allowed anything, including your fear of commitment, to get in our way. I won't make that mistake again.

Melanie finishes oiling her body and walks out into her bedroom to dress. A man is sitting at her vanity. He's combing the tips of his braids and retwisting them. He is slow with his strokes and deliberate in lining them up behind his ears. He is completely calm when Melanie walks in on him. Melanie screams at him while securing her towel around her breasts and waist. "Who the fuck are you, and what are you doing in my house?" Then she moves toward the bed to retrieve her phone.

"They thought I disappeared on prom night. But you see, my sister needed me to come out so I could protect her, and that's what I did. I transformed, and now I am here to install you. You will be the centerpiece of my grand tableau. I will honor you as you deserve," Nolan said as he rose from the vanity.

"Look, you psycho bastard, I don't know who you think you are, but you have about two heartbeats to get the hell out of my house, or I'm calling my people," Melanie shot back.

"Your people? You mean Mr. Jedidiah? Or did you mean Ms. Rickea? How about Mr. James or Ms. Kim? No, you don't mean them; you mean someone else. They can't help you now since I'm pretty sure they're enjoying a group hug with Mrs. Ruby," Nolan grinned.

All of the life drained from Melanie's face. Her deep, beautiful brown skin appeared blanched and drained. Her knees felt like they were about to give out, and she started feeling lightheaded as though her blood sugar were crashing. She stared at Nolan; his countenance was blank, except for the clownish smile he wore. Before her light was snuffed out, she yelled towards her window in a voice that gave Nolan pause for an instant. "Bingo!" screamed Melanie, her last word puzzling Nolan but leaving him undeterred from the gruesome task he had in store for her.

Though Melanie's body is far heavier than that of his previous guests, Nolan can cart her dead form away and stuff her inside a large footlocker he brought just for this occasion. He doesn't drag the locker outside but waits in the new townhome until night has fully taken hold of the day. He takes his time in the home and finds a wall near the balcony to leave a calling card. In his mind, he knows that he's being careless by leaving his mark on the wall, but it has become a ritual for Nolan, and one mustn't break with tradition. When he's finished, Nolan lights the fireplace and relaxes on the sofa. He takes in his work and is pleased with himself. The glow of the fireplace highlights his features. The crackle of fire upon the wood and the rise of embers activate memories he thought long too dormant to recall, but he does, and they cause him to wince uncomfortably. Too many families, too many endings, and no time for her. Everyone brushed Noelle aside and forgot about her. No one would ever forget Nolan.

It's late in the evening, and the next day, Talaitha has completed her documentation for the presentation she is giving at the American Psychological Association's East Regional Convention next month. She reheated the dinner she had made earlier that day and brought Jevonte a plate. He was in no condition to walk or hold a fork, so she sat near the bed and dutifully prepared to feed him his dinner. Most of the swelling had not gone down, and his right eye was still closed. The dark black and blue coloring in and around the eye worried her that he might lose the eye. He couldn't open his mouth very much because of the fracture, so the food she prepared for him was soft and easy to slurp. Jevonte stared weakly at her with his one good eye. Talaitha could see the anger in his face. She almost felt bad.

Talaitha's phone buzzed. The text on her screen read, "For you, sister." She opened the message, smiled, then chuckled devilishly and pointed the phone at Jevonte's one good eye. Jevonte choked, and a weak, muffled scream began pouring from the depths of his soul. Jevonte let loose a sad, pitiful cry, like that of a horribly wounded animal, into the dark confines of the room. He wept loudly, openly, through broken, missing teeth, and screamed with all that his feeble body could manage. The image on Talaitha's phone of Melanie's death face, her tongue lolling out of the side of her mouth, her eyes empty and blank, and her repose corpselike and displayed on a dais bathed in spotlight, seared into his brain like hellfire.

Talaitha stood over him, holding her phone so he could see it all, and when Jevonte stopped wailing and lost consciousness from sheer exhaustion, she began to laugh. She laughed so hard that her stomach hurt. Her head was pounding from the joy Nolan just gave her. "What a gift it is to have a brother like you," she texted in reply.

The end of October is approaching, and Roscoe has not heard from or seen Melanie. He knows her work at the hospital can really keep her busy, but what seems particularly odd is the absence of his nieces and nephew, who have practically moved into his brother's house. No one is returning his phone calls either. He let it go for a few days, but now he was concerned.

This silence is highly unusual for these three. He chuckles, "If there's money in the mix, these three will be involved in some way. Let me give Marcus a call to check if he has been in contact with Melanie, Roscoe thinks. Before he can call Marcus, he decides to reach out to RhaShawn first. He might have received a message from Melanie. That woman was just bound and determined to have it out with Talaitha, so there's no telling what she may have done. Roscoe dials Melanie's brother, RhaShawn, and can hear a phone ringing at the front door.

"Hey, Uncle Roscoe. I'm at the front door," says RhaShawn.

"Good morning, nephew. Funny how I was just calling you and there you are," jokes Roscoe.

RhaShawn steps through the door and says, "I wanted to come by to see if Melanie was here. The hospital called me because she hadn't been to work in a couple of days and hadn't been heard from. I stopped by her house, and the car was parked in the driveway, but she wouldn't come to the door. She wasn't even answering her phone either. Have you heard from her?"

"No, that's why I called you. I can't find any of my nieces or James. No one except you is answering their phones. I tell you what, let's have Marcus meet us over at Melanie's house, and while we're driving over, I'll call Roxanne, Eugene, and Faith to see if they have been in contact with their kids. Surely they know where they are, or they've heard something. Let's go," said Roscoe, heading for the door, cell phone in hand and dialing.

When Roscoe and RhaShawn arrive at Melanie's home, police vehicles have cordoned off the block, and police tape is draped across the front door. Marcus and Detective Albright are standing in the front yard, and a uniformed officer is standing beside them, writing something down on a notepad.

"What's going on, Marcus? How did you get here so fast?" said Roscoe as he and RhaShawn rushed out of the car. "What's with the tape?"

"Mr. Greene, please, stand back," instructed the detective. "We are in the process of locking down this home because we suspect there has been some foul play here."

"Foul play? Sir, we're just here for my sister. Is she inside? What happened?" demanded RhaShawn.

"There is no one in the home. I understand that this residence is the address for your sister, Melanie; is that correct?" asked the detective.

"Marcus, I need to talk to you," said Roscoe as he looked Marcus directly in the face. The two men ambled over to one side of the yard, near the mailbox. RhaShawn and Detective Albright continue their discussion, RhaShawn providing details about his last known contact with Melanie.

"Roscoe, before you say anything, we don't know that Melanie is missing. The house showed no signs of struggle, blood, or burglary. Everything looked clean, the way she always kept her house," said Marcus, hoping to head off Roscoe's questions.

"So, can you explain why there is police tape and why Detective Dipshit mentioned foul play?" replied Roscoe.

Marcus paused and rubbed the gray hair on his head. "The department has been tracking a new development involving what they say is a possible serial killer on the loose in Maryland. Apparently, there have been at least twenty-five murders that they attribute to this killer."

"Well damn, man. What the fuck is going on? Has the incident been reported in the news? How do they know that this killer was here?" asked Roscoe, exasperated.

"Detective Albright told me that this killer leaves a calling card behind after each kill. He draws a symbol on the wall facing the home's front door. It's the same symbol or marking, and it's on one of Melanie's walls." Marcus opens his phone and shows Roscoe a picture.

Nolan's Calling Card

"What is that?" asks Roscoe.

"The authorities don't know exactly what it is, but the killer leaves it at the site of all their kills. They've been analyzing it for months now and haven't found a link between the image and the victims."

"But do they know if the missing people have been murdered rather than kidnapped or something else?"

At most of the sites, there were copious amounts of the victims' blood at the scene—too much blood loss for anyone to survive. This scene was the exception, so Melanie may have been merely taken and may still be alive."

The two men walk back over to where the detective and RhaShawn are standing. "Listen, Mr. Greene, I apologize for not having better information, but as I'm sure Marcus told you, we don't know that Ms. Decartes is in danger or that harm has befallen her. We will do everything we can to find her and make sure she is okay. Here is my card and contact information. You can call me if you have questions, or contact Marcus. He'll know how to reach me for any updates on this case."

Before the detective can walk away, Roscoe asks him, "Most of these homes have door cameras on them. I assume you guys will be speaking with the neighbors?"

"It's already in progress, sir. Don't worry, we've got this handled and will know something soon. Now, if you'll excuse me," Detective Albright said as he headed back to Melanie's open front door.

Roscoe and RhaShawn turn and start walking to their car when RhaShawn stops halfway down the driveway. Marcus almost runs him over because he stopped so suddenly. RhaShawn hurries back to the front of the house, calling for the detective. Detective Albight, his face agitated, emerges from the home. "My sister had cameras inside the house. They're hidden and might have caught what happened in the house. She told me that if she needed to turn them on, she could just use a voice command. I think she set it to activate when she said the word 'start' or something like that. No, maybe the command was 'engage,' like on Star Trek. She loved that TV series almost as much as she loved playing bingo."

"I understand that's possible, but unless she found a way to activate it, the interior cameras probably didn't capture any…"

"Sir, you've got to see this," interrupted one of the investigative officers from inside the house.

"Wait here," the detective ordered RhaShawn, and he stepped back inside the home. Roscoe and Marcus stood beside RhaShawn on the front step.

Marcus looked at his old friend; he knew what he was thinking. Roscoe's eyes were cold, and his posture was tight. He had been holding so much down inside that he was just about ready to explode. The two men didn't need to exchange words. No matter what the detective found inside, there was going to be but one reaction—payback. RhaShawn wore a look of worry and dismay. He was dreading whatever the detective was called back inside to see. As the moments ticked by, RhaShawn began to doubt himself and felt guilty for not spending more time with his family, especially his sister, leaving him without any excuses. She was always there for him. She practically raised him along with Grandma.

After several minutes, Detective Albright returned to the three men standing in front of the house.

"I don't know how she did it, but your sister managed to activate her interior cameras, and we can see what happened. Mr. Decartes, gentlemen, I'm sorry, but it looks like Ms. Decartes was murdered."

RhaShawn rushed to the front door to see inside, but the uniformed officer barred him from entering.

"No, that can't be right. Get out of my way," and RhaShawn tried to shove the officer out of the way, but another officer joined the policeman, and they wrestled RhaShawn out of the doorway. RhaShawn fell on the lawn and kneeled on all fours, his head hanging low between his shoulders and arms. He started crying and pounding the turf with his fists. Roscoe and Marcus rushed to his side and reached down beside him, and put their arms around him. All three men began rocking back and forth. RhaShawn's tears rained down on the lawn, and the three of them held on to one another tightly, hoping to squeeze some sense into the senseless. The uniformed officers backed away, giving them space to pour out their grief upon each other.

Inside the home, Detective Albright gave strict instructions on retrieving the captured video. "Get the CSI and data forensic team in here as soon as you get the chance. We just caught our first real break in this case because if my eyes don't deceive me, there is a big fat fucking clue staring right at us on the screen. Our suspect has just made his first mistake, and I hope it will be his last."

The large-screen TV in Melanie's living room displayed a scene of a man lounging on the sofa with his legs crossed and a pair of eyeglasses perched on a head full of cornrows. He looks pleased. Around his neck is a silver chain with a silver leaf medallion hanging from its end, embossed with interwoven leaflets of small emeralds. The craftsmanship of the medallion and its setting is the hallmark of only one marketplace located in Upper Marlboro, Maryland. Detective Albright instantly recognizes the piece because he has one just like it.

25

The Necklace in the Mezzanine

Detective Albright has been poring over the recovered video footage from Melanie's residence. The digital forensic technicians were thorough in recovering almost everything. Although the video clip began with a delay, it was evident that Melanie maintained her composure and remained fearless in the face of her attacker until the very end. He replays the scene over and over, looking for any identifying marks, tattoos, or scars on the assailant, but he is consistently drawn to how fierce Melanie was. She didn't go down easy. She kicked, punched, and clawed at the unknown attacker with everything she had, and at one point, it looked like she was going to come out on top. She looked bigger than the unknown person and probably outweighed him by at least twenty pounds, but he was quick. She managed to body slam him into the vanity, but he recovered too fast, and that may have caught her off guard because he rebounded from the fall and got behind her in a full nelson chokehold. After that, Detective Albright watched as the life drained out of Melanie's eyes in concert with her last breath. The attacker took her to the ground, and it was all over.

The detective watched the assailant move from room to room, clean up the wrecked vanity, and then disappear from the cameras. The murderer moved calmly and practiced, and didn't appear to be aware that he was under surveillance. When he came back into view, he was dragging an extremely oversized trunk. Detective Albright hadn't seen one that size before, and it dawned on him that the murderer must have been planning to abduct or kill Melanie because nothing else would have held her body securely. It demonstrated forethought and careful observation. Detective Albright jotted down a few notes next to those he had already made, wondering how the murderer got into the house since there was no sign of a break-in.

There was a knock at his office door, and after the detective waved him in, one of the data forensic technicians stepped inside. "Sir, we found something else on the security server that was uploading the video once the deceased activated it."

"Well, don't just stand there with your dick in your hands, what did you find?" Groused Albright.

"Sir, the server's programming caused it to send an email with a link to the footage to a third party."

"What third party? Where did the link go?"

"We're not exactly sure at this point. We only know that there was outbound traffic after the last recording was uploaded, but we should have more info soon.

"Damnit," cursed Albright. "I think I know where that footage link went," said Detective Albright. He reached for his desk phone and dialed a certain private investigator. While the phone was ringing, he instructed the technician to call one of the junior detectives into his office. While he waited, Albright continued reviewing the captured video, and once he found the frame he wanted, he froze the playback.

Junior Detective Mason walked into Albright's office. "You rang?"

Albright rose and walked over to his printer. "Get this screenshot out to all local and state media. We have a solid suspect for this killing, and I'm sure, given his artistry, we can link him to several others in the state," and he hands a full-color frontal face shot of Melanie's killer to the junior detective. "Activate the tip line and make sure it's manned 24/7. Someone knows this man."

The next day, after the photo makes the rounds among local news outlets, city and state law enforcement units are mobilized, and a full manhunt is underway. The streets in Baltimore are abuzz with talk of the murder and the lead made possible by Melanie's actions. Nolan is not amused. Sitting at Starbucks at 100 East Pratt Street in downtown Baltimore, Nolan is inundated with news stories flashing across the shop's television screens. There he is, his face as big as day, grinning for all the world to see. He watches in amusement as the reporter and lead anchors discuss the announcement by the police and speculate on what possible motives there might have been for what they called a senseless murder.

Senseless? How dare they? They have no appreciation for artists like me, none, Nolan thinks to himself. He knows what is coming next and decides to leave before someone gets lucky and recognizes him. Time to lay low and disappear for a little while, he thinks, and he vanishes into the bustling crowd outside the coffee shop.

The day ends finally at the station, and Detective Albright is shutting down his system and gathering some files to take home when his phone rings. He looks at the phone and his watch, then almost walks out of the office, but decides to answer the call instead.

"This is Detective Albright."

"Good evening, detective. My name is Dr. Samuel Robinson. I work at Sable Ridge State Hospital, overseeing the mental health ward."

"Hello, Dr. Robinson. I was just heading out the door for the day," Detective Albright said, hinting politely that it was quitting time for him.

"I apologize, detective, but I'm calling about the person of interest who has been all over the news media these last few days. I know who this person is, or at least I believe I do."

Detective Albright sits back down at his desk and takes out a notepad. "I see. Who is he, and how do you know him?"

"I believe your person of interest is, or once was, a woman named Noelle Mercedes. I treated her sister when she was a juvenile, and while I cannot say more about my patient, I do recognize some of the facial features of your person of interest."

"Wait, so you're saying that our suspect is a woman? I don't know about that, but the video footage we have definitely suggests this is the man we're looking for. Are you telling me she's trans, doctor?"

"No. This person, if it is who I believe it is, is not transgender. This person, whom I believe is Noelle

Mercedes, is the twin of my patient, and she is deeply troubled, so much so that she has surgically altered her appearance and possibly her sex to achieve harmony with my patient. I know it sounds bizarre, but Noelle's transformation was not the result of any gender dysphoria."

"Doctor, do you think you can meet me here in Baltimore and provide more background on this person? I have a lot of questions, and I think it's best if we meet in person to discuss this further."

"I understand. I have a fairly full schedule tomorrow, but I can make it to your office by the end of the week, for sure. Will that work?"

"Yes, I can make that work. I will have our office reach out to you for scheduling. Is this a suitable contact number for you?"

"Yes, this is my personal number."

"One last thing, if you don't mind, doctor. Just how dangerous is Noelle? What should my officers be prepared for when we encounter her?"

"Her twin, and therefore this probably applies to Noelle too, is highly intelligent, and most clinicians would diagnose them with antisocial personality disorder. Noelle, more than her twin, identifies with the sociopathic behavior scale. The fact that she underwent surgical modifications to adjust to her twin's needs indicates the level of conviction and desperation she operates. To answer your question, detective, tell your officers to be ready for anything. She is fully motivated and committed to one thing and will not let anyone or anything get in her way."

"And what is that, doctor?"

"Her twin. I believe Noelle has experienced a severe psychological break and may be operating in what we call a state of anosognosia. Noelle is completely unaware that her experiences are signs of mental illness. I'm really only speculating here since I have not treated her personally, but given what I know about her sister's case, I doubt my prognosis is far off."

The men exchange a few more thoughts, and the call ends. Detective Albright scribes one more note on his calendar, reminding him to contact the DA's office for a warrant to search Dr. Robinson's patient records.

Upon Marcus's arrival at Jedidiah and Ruby's home, Roscoe's truck is backed into the driveway, and the garage door is closing. Marcus parks his truck and makes his way to the front door. It takes a while for Roscoe to come to the door, and at first, Marcus thinks he may not be home, but then, who just entered the garage? Marcus wonders. His truck is here, so Roscoe should be inside. Marcus rings the doorbell one more time. Finally, Roscoe opens the door. His eyes are red, and his cheeks are wet.

"Hey, come on in. I just got in, and you're not going to believe what I just got in my email from RhaShawn," Roscoe said as he turned and headed back to the kitchen. The two men are seated in the kitchen, and Roscoe swivels his laptop so it faces Marcus.

"What is this?" asks Marcus.

"It's surveillance video from inside Melanie's home from the day she was murdered. Apparently, she set the system up to forward links to certain people. I didn't get it originally, but her brother did and forwarded the file to me. Everything is on there, including..." Roscoe pauses, not sure he wants to actually speak the words. "Her death. I just finished watching it when you got here."

"Sorry, brother. I've seen it already. This is why I'm here. Detective Albright gave me a heads-up and asked me to try to get to you before the link did. We didn't know exactly who might get the link, but we guessed it would be you or RhaShawn. I don't need to watch it."

Roscoe was quiet. Both men sat in silence for a full minute, then Roscoe got up and poured himself some coffee. He gestured to Marcus to help himself, then said, "I'm going to find that piece of shit and end him. I don't care how long it takes. I will find him no matter where he hides, and he'll never see me coming, I promise you that."

"She," remarked Marcus. "Albright told me that he had a conversation with a doctor from Sable Ridge State Hospital who claimed that he knows who the person is in the video."

"Sable Ridge? You mean the Sable Ridge Hospital that treated my nephew?" exclaimed Roscoe.

"Yes, sir, the one and only. And guess who the doctor was? Yes, you guessed it, Samuel Robinson."

"That bitch is in this? She's behind this?" said Roscoe in a fury.

"Dr. Robinson didn't name Talaitha, but he said the killer was a twin to one of his patients, and we all know who that had to be."

"What was Talaitha's sister's name again? Was it Noe or Noella?"

"Noelle Mercedes."

"You said 'she,' but the video showed a dude; it was a man who killed Mel," said Roscoe as he set his coffee down on the table and sat. He pulled the laptop back toward him and began replaying it.

"According to Dr. Robinson, Noelle had a sex change or had some kind of plastic surgery to alter her appearance. He said that she was not trans or anything and that she did all of that so that she could be accepted by Talaitha."

"So, we're dealing with a real sicko. I don't care. She can change herself into Minnie Mouse for all I care. Her days are numbered."

"Listen, brother, I am with you, but let's be smart about it. We can't go off half-cocked; we need to be sure this is our guy, or gal."

"Oh, I'm sure. I can feel it in my bones that she did this. Talaitha either put her sister up to it, or that crazy wig decided on her own to kill Mel just to please Talaitha. Either way, Talaitha is in it, and now so am I."

"Since I can't talk you out of this course of action, and to be honest, I don't want to, I know where we can start. Albright showed me the necklace Nolan was wearing in that video clip, and he said he thought he knew a place where they were made. Let's head over to Upper Marlboro and look around. If he bought that jewelry there, we can probably find clues about him when we arrive."

"Maybe you should just let me go alone. I know what I need to do, and I don't want my actions to fall on you. I would rather not jeopardize your state license, your livelihood."

"Brother, we have been down this road before, many times. I'm all right, so let's go while we have some daylight," Marcus said, and the pair loaded up Roscoe's truck and headed south towards Upper Marlboro.

The pair arrived in Upper Marlboro and toured several antique and craft shops, but found nothing. Most of the mom-and-pop stores don't sell anything remotely similar to the jewelry Noelle was wearing in the video clip. They show the shop owners a picture of Nolan, but none recognize him. They spend half the afternoon continuing to look, and after several more stops, decide to call it a day and head back to Baltimore. Roscoe pulls into a Shop Mart to fuel up, and Marcus heads inside to grab some water and some food. A gray Volvo sedan pulls into the gas station behind Roscoe's truck. The driver exits the car and walks up to where Roscoe is pumping gas. The driver is a young, blond, very tall white woman. She looks like a volleyball player: lengthy, angular, and with strong, well-defined legs. Roscoe stops pumping his gas and fixes her with his eyes.

"Hello, sir. I saw you and your friend at my mom's store and overheard that you were asking about the person in the news that the police are looking for."

Roscoe cautiously answered, "Yes, we are. Why? Do you know this person?"

"No, sir, but I think I know where you can find more information. I have a friend who works in Alexandria who told me that they saw this person buying stuff at the store where she works. She works at Dejan Studio Jewelry. They make customized jewelry and all sorts of artwork."

"Did your friend contact the police?" asked Roscoe.

"No, she said she was scared to report what she saw. I told her she could do it anonymously, but she said she just didn't want to get involved."

"I understand. Do you have an address for this place?" asked Roscoe. Marcus came out of the store and headed toward the pumps.

The tall blonde saw Marcus coming and smiled. "Yes. The shop is at the Torpedo Factory Art Center, 105 N Union St #23, Alexandria. I have her number, too, if you want to call her first."

"No, that won't be necessary. We'll just drive down and have a look around, but thank you for this information. Sorry, I didn't get your name," said Roscoe.

"Julia," she replied, and she perked up, pleased at the sound of her name.

"Roscoe, and this is Investigator Marcus. Thank you. You've been an enormous help."

The two men drive off and head further south, making good time, and arrive at the Torpedo Factory Art Center before the late-afternoon rush hour kicks in. They walk into Dejan's and begin asking questions and showing Noelle's picture around. The store's manager doesn't recognize Noelle and doesn't recall designing anything similar to the jewelry in question. While they are speaking, Marcus notices a teenage-looking girl behind one of the display cases. She's watching them wearily, trying to remain unnoticed. She, too, is blonde and tall—volleyball player tall. Marcus walks over to her.

"Ma'am, do you know someone named Julia? She told us that you might know who this man is or that you can confirm that he bought something from this shop."

The girl hesitated, then looked agitated that her friend would rat her out. "Yes, I've seen that man before, and he ordered something from us. I didn't take the order, but I saw the invoice. Fucking Julia," the girl muttered under her breath.

"Can I get a copy of that invoice, please? And don't be mad at your friend. The information is helpful and may help us stop this person from hurting anyone else," Marcus added.

The young girl retrieved the invoice and copied it. She handed it to Marcus as Roscoe walked over to where they were. "Is there any kind of reward for this?"

"I really can't say. I'm sure if you talk to the police, they will know more," answered Marcus.

"Oh, I thought you guys were the police," she replied, now concerned that she just gave the invoice to strangers.

"No, but we are working with them. Thanks again for your assistance, and thank you for your time."

Marcus and Roscoe sat in the truck and looked over the invoice. The bill-to line had a business name and address. Marcus read it out loud. "Chalice & Chimera Emporium at 1050 W. Industrial Blvd, Cumberland."

Roscoe entered the address in his GPS. "It's a two-hour drive from here. It'll be dark by the time we get there, but I'd rather check it out now than wait."

"Let's roll," replied Marcus, and he handed Roscoe a green Monster energy drink. "The dark will give a little cover, too, when we get there, although Nolan will probably be gone for the day."

"True, but if he's gone, I'll leave him a little calling card of my own," and Roscoe points the truck northwest and heads toward Cumberland.

It's 7:45 pm when Roscoe and Marcus arrive at the Chalice & Chimera Emporium. Most downtown shops are closed, but the Chalice is still open. Roscoe drives by the storefront twice, then locates parking at a nearby CVS pharmacy. Cumberland is predominantly white, and the two men stick out like sore thumbs as they exit the truck. There is nothing they can do about that, but they know how just their presence might attract undue attention, so they code-switch with their gait and bearing. They decide to split up: Marcus walks to the front of the store to try to enter, while Roscoe darts around the back of the store into the garbage pickup area.

Marcus enters the store. No one is there. No clerks or anyone to assist him. He scans the interior and finds no cameras. The owner may not even be aware that a customer has entered the shop, so Marcus walks to one of the art displays, his hands visible and his shopping intent obvious. The shop is impressive, occupying a narrow three-story converted townhouse with exposed timber beams and stone walls that seem to exhale centuries of history. A collection of

Gothic silverwork dominates the main floor, displayed in glass cases lined with midnight-blue velvet. The light from the diamond-paned windows shines on the ornate chalices, which bear Latin inscriptions and semiprecious stones. Medieval patens gleam beside Renaissance pyx boxes, while elaborate monstrances rise like silver forests of devotional art. Against the far wall stands a magnificent oak armoire housing illuminated manuscripts, their pages open to reveal marginalia where whimsical creatures frolic among sacred text. Marcus strolls over to the armoire to view a cobalt-blue dragon coiled around a capital letter. A golden griffin guards the opening verse of a psalm. The margins teem with rabbits playing trumpets, snails racing knights, and chimeras breathing flowers instead of fire.

In the alleyway, Roscoe notes how dark and deserted the area is, but his thoughts come to a halt when the back door of the Chalice & Chimera Emporium opens, and Nolan, appearing very masculine, walks out carrying two full trash bags. That cannot be Noelle, Roscoe thinks, and he steps out of the shadows and heads toward her. Nolan spots him, but continues to the dumpster and tosses both bags in. When he turns, Roscoe is almost standing behind him.

"Hey, good evening. Didn't mean to startle you..." started Roscoe.

"You didn't," interrupted Nolan. "May I help you with something?" Nolan recognized Roscoe right away. He knew who he was because he'd been stalking the whole Greene family for months.

"Yes, you can. You can tell me your name, please."

Nolan smiled. The game was about to begin, and he started feeling excited. "Why? Do I know you or something?"

Roscoe relaxed his stance before answering. He felt as though he was in the presence of a predator, and his gut told him to be wary and ready for anything. "I'm looking for a woman named Noelle. I was told she lives or works around here, and I'd like to have a word with her." The mention of her name seemed to trigger a reaction in the man, prompting Roscoe to continue his inquiry. "She may have had some plastic surgery in the past. I was told that she is trying to pass herself off as a man for some sad reason."

Nolan's demeanor changed, and his countenance became blank and lifeless. "I can't say I know anyone by the name. Now, if you'll excuse me, I need to return to my shop. Perhaps you should come back in the morning when there are more shops open and people to pester."

"No, I don't think so," Roscoe responded, moving to block Nolan's path. "I think I'm at the right place, and I have the right person, Noelle," Roscoe said, his voice cold and pointed.

"Sir, whoever Noelle is, she probably doesn't want to be found, and if I were you, I'd stop looking for her. People like that, who don't want to be found, can be mighty dangerous when cornered." Nolan leaned forward slightly on the balls of his feet.

"I'm not you, Noelle." Again, Nolan bristled at being called Noelle. Roscoe could see his control slipping, and he grinned in Nolan's face.

"You know, Roscoe, people like you really need to spend more time at home protecting the people who depend on you. Instead, here you are harassing an innocent businessman in a dark alley at night. I advise you to get on the road now and go back to wherever you came from. I hear a severe storm is coming, and record rainfall is in the forecast. Cars hydroplane in conditions like that, you know. Some people have even drowned in such conditions due to the poor engineering of these roads. You feel me?"

Roscoe's eyes narrowed. "How did you know my name?" asked Roscoe angrily.

"That old bitch told me before I made her kiss the dashboard," said Nolan, smiling.

Roscoe swung wide and missed Nolan's chin by a mile. His momentum carried him past Nolan, who kicked him in his back, shoving him headlong into the side of the dumpster. Roscoe recovered and stood to his feet, somewhat embarrassed, but he started to advance on Nolan again, this time cautious of the younger man's speed. Nolan stood stock-still and confident, waiting for the older man to come within reach. Roscoe lunged at him again, and Nolan sidestepped him and caught him with a vicious right behind his left ear. Roscoe hit the ground hard and dazed. He'd been hit plenty of times in hand-to-hand combat encounters and bar brawls, but he wasn't a spring chicken anymore. He knew Nolan was toying with him. Nolan was too fast, or he was just too slow; either way, he would have to outthink the younger man.

"Not bad for a woman. I expected you to fight like a girl," Roscoe mocked. Nolan advanced on Roscoe while he feigned struggling to rise. Nolan snarled and started to straddle Roscoe, and when he did, Roscoe rolled his hip and thrust, shoving Nolan over his body. Roscoe felt more at home in a ground fight, so he went on the offensive. Nolan's glasses flew off his face, which temporarily distracted him. Oddly, he began reaching for them when Roscoe dove on top of him and began working to gain a dominant position, using his elbows and forearms to pummel Nolan and wrapping his leg around the younger man. Roscoe was heavier, but Nolan was wiry and taut, and began to counter Roscoe's attack by pulling the older man closer, where his strikes were less effective.

Nolan, nearly cheek to cheek with Roscoe, whispered in his ear, "At least Jedidiah put up more of a fight. Ruby was too easy."

Roscoe hesitated, and Nolan thrust his palm into the older man's nose. As Roscoe fell away from the younger man, blood sprayed from his nose. Nolan rose to his feet and kicked Roscoe across the side of his head. Roscoe barely managed to get his hand up to parry, but still, the kick landed with enough force to spin him across the gravel road. He lay on the ground, his sight blurry and his head throbbing with pain.

Inside, Marcus noticed a sign just above a spiral staircase that read: The Mezzanine: Medals and Miniatures. The shop was bigger than it looked from the outside. Marcus started up the stairway and, upon arriving on the second floor, came into a room filled with shelves of Renaissance portrait medals in shallow drawers lined with cream silk. Bronze profiles of Medici princes shared space with silver commemorative pieces honoring papal jubilees. Opposite the wall of shelves were display cases of carved boxwood prayer nuts no larger than walnuts. Some of the boxed pieces were open to reveal entire Crucifixion scenes populated by figures the size of rice grains. One shrouded display stood alone toward the very rear of the room. It was covered from top to bottom in a dark blue velvety material and stood at least seven feet tall. He removed the shroud to reveal an intricate miniature dais, bathed in amber LED lighting. In the center of the small dais was a coiled silver chain with a silver leaf medallion hanging on its end, embossed with interwoven leaflets of small emeralds.

"Gotcha," Marcus exclaimed and pulled out his phone to take pictures and then call Detective Albright. He relayed the address and left to look for Roscoe.

Outside, Nolan walked over to where Roscoe lay, stunned. "I will enjoy watching your lights go out more than I did with the fat cow. It took a little while for her, but you, I'm just going to end quickly."

"Bring it, girly man. You're pathetic. Obviously, your mommy didn't show you enough love when you were a little girl. Or was it your father who showed you some of his special love? Is that it? Did Daddy rub you in all the wrong places?" Roscoe taunted.

Nolan charged at the fallen older man in a blind rage. Roscoe had been waiting for this moment. He tossed a handful of dirt and gravel into Nolan's face and mouth, and the younger man stumbled and fell. Nolan began spitting and choking on the debris, and Roscoe connected with a sweeping roundhouse punch to his face. Nolan collapsed backward and hit the ground like so much dead weight. Roscoe hauled the semi-conscious younger man to his feet and delivered a powerful uppercut to his chin. Nolan's head rolled back, but Roscoe kept his grip on him and started throwing body blow after body blow into Nolan's midsection. With every strike, Nolan was lifted slightly, but Roscoe would not let him fall to the ground. Backing Nolan up against the store's outside wall, Roscoe went to work, hammering Nolan's face and ribs. Nolan gasped between swollen lips and laughed, blood and spittle running down his split lips and cheeks. Roscoe was relentless and held Nolan up with his left hand and rained punch after punch into his face with the right.

Marcus opened the back door and rushed out into the alleyway in time to see the person they knew as Nolan slide down the wall and slump sideways unconscious. "Dude, did you kill him? Please tell me he's not dead? This is our guy. I found the necklace inside."

"If he's dead," Roscoe said quietly, "then so be it. I'm at peace with that."

Marcus bent over the unconscious form and felt for a pulse. "He's alive. He's beat to hell, but he's alive." Marcus paused, staring at Nolan's chest. His shirt was torn, and his chest was bare. "My God. What is that?" and he reached down to uncover more of her chest. The scarring was thick and unevenly spread across the top and bottom of where her breast would have been. The marks were ragged and haphazardly spaced across her chest. The front of her chest reminded him of the photograph he'd seen when he visited the National Gallery of Art in Washington, D.C., known as The Scourged Back. It was said to depict an enslaved man named Gordon. "No properly trained surgeon did that," Marcus commented, horrified.

Roscoe, too, appeared shocked and dismayed by what had happened to her, yet his anger remained unresolved, yearning for retribution. "He confessed, brother. Not only did he kill Melanie, but he said he killed Ruby, man, and Jedidiah!" he cried. He was gloating over it, too. I should kill him now. I just need to…"

Marcus interrupted him. "Hold on, brother. You can't. The police are on the way. I called Albright, so he knows we're here. We can connect him to Melanie's murder even if he doesn't confess. I know it won't be enough, but at least we'll know he's off the streets. He will pay for it all, I promise you he will."

The Cumberland police arrive and take Nolan into custody. Roscoe, too, is taken down to the station to give a statement while Marcus helps secure the evidence from the jewelry shop. Detective Albright arrives hours later and returns Nolan and the evidence to Baltimore. Nolan is placed in temporary confinement in the infirmary while police medics attend to his wounds. He is secured by handcuffs to a hospital gurney. He's in and out of consciousness, and Detective Albright informs the medical staff that he is to remain confined and will be questioned as soon as medical clears him.

Outside the infirmary, Roscoe and Marcus are sitting, waiting for the detective to update them on the case. "Gentlemen, I wish you had simply called me before engaging with our suspect. That beating you gave him, Roscoe, may end up costing us a case against her/him," Albright chastised.

"It was self-defense, detective. She's a killer, and I had no choice," Roscoe shot back.

"It won't matter, detective. Once your team analyzes the necklace, you'll have confirmation that this is Melanie's killer," added Marcus.

"Be that as it may, it will be up to the DA to decide whether you face charges, Mr. Greene. For now, don't leave town, and don't do anything else related to this case. Is that understood? The investigation is not over yet," said Albright.

"He killed my brother, and he killed my sister-in-law. He confessed to it, so when you question him, please keep that in mind," replied Roscoe.

"I will. Now, please, go home and wait for my call."

26

Goodnight, King

Talaitha is hard at work in the basement, expanding her garden. Several weeks have passed since Melanie was killed. As she breaks up more of the concrete floor, she feels elated that her brother responded to her need. Nolan understood what was needed and made it happen. With every swing of the pickaxe, she rejoiced that her prayers had been answered and Noelle was truly gone forever. Now that she had a brother, a protector, she laughed, knowing that no one would be able to hurt her again, especially that accursed Noelle. She had her doubts at first when Nolan proposed eliminating Melanie to prove his devotion and sincerity. He came through, and even though he'd gone silent for the last week, she wasn't worried. She saw the news reports and figured Nolan was lying low. When he was ready, she would have her brother over to the house to see all that she'd created and set in place. They would be a new family, but of course, Jevonte would need to be recycled. His change in attitude wasn't working for her, and she no longer believed that he loved her the way he used to. After all she'd done for him, and now he's showing his true colors, just as all the rest did.

Most of the soil has been richly prepared with organic matter, and when she widens the pit even more, she'll have twice the capacity to cultivate her garden babies. While Talaitha continues to bury the pickaxe deep into the concrete and chip away at the edges of the pit, Jevonte has awakened. The intermittent pounding and hammering of steel on concrete heighten his consciousness. He groans and curses under his breath. He's still alive, but everything hurts. The drugs Talaitha was giving him kept him from screaming in agony. He still has to take short, shallow breaths because his ribs are badly fractured. Twisting and turning in bed is impossible since his abdomen is still constricted with trauma. He flinches every time he sees the bat in his mind's eye, descending, crashing into his stomach and ribs. He relives the nightmare whenever he moves or his hands touch his waist. His catheter continues to fill with blood. He can't feel the contraption and refuses to examine his man parts. He's just numb from the waist down.

This morning, the constant banging in the basement won't let him drift back off to sleep. There are still enough painkillers and sedatives in his system that he manages to swing his stable leg onto the floor. His right leg is useless and no longer heeds any of his commands, so he reaches for the cane Talaitha set next to the bed. She told him that she would not take him to the bathroom anymore and that he would have to figure out how to use the cane. *I know how I want to use it, you horrible bitch; just come a little closer,* he remembered thinking. The memories give Jevonte comfort. His defiance, albeit silent, was remarkable to him. He didn't ever think he would feel so strong emotionally, even though his body couldn't win a fight with a paper bag. On more than a few occasions, he had flicked her off or rolled his eyes at her. Small acts, of course, but doing those things marked a shift for Jevonte, one he was becoming proud of.

It took Jevonte almost ten minutes to hobble down the hallway and reach the basement door. He sat in the closest kitchen chair, one facing the door. Beads of sweat punctuated his forehead, and he was feeling extremely lightheaded from the effort. Because he couldn't draw a full, complete breath—his ribs felt like they were about to puncture his lungs—he couldn't get enough oxygen. He remained in the chair, trying hard to manage his breathing and not collapse on the floor. He was concentrating so hard he didn't notice that whatever Talaitha was doing in the basement had stopped. It was too quiet, in fact, and Jevonte started to worry.

Rising on his one wrecked leg, Jevonte moves to the basement door and places his ear against it, straining to hear anything down in the dark space below. As he rested with his face against the door, it occurred to him that an opportunity had just presented itself to him. Could he trap Talaitha in the basement somehow? Jevonte reasoned that surely, she probably didn't consider him a threat because of his brokenness, but maybe, just maybe, he could do something. Maybe, he thought, I could fix the door long enough to get out or perish trying. The question is, how and with what? He turns to lean his back against the door and looks around for something he can use, but there is nothing. The basement door has a plain doorknob, and there is nothing around him to use to wedge the door securely. Then he spots the kitchen chair he was sitting on and smiles through broken teeth.

Jevonte hobbles back over to the chair and tries to slide it over to the basement door. The chair is heavy, and he struggles to maneuver it into place. He pauses to catch his breath when he hears the stairs into the basement creak with Talaitha's weight. Somewhat panicked, Jevonte shuffles back to the door to listen again. The door opens, and Talaitha begins to take a step onto the kitchen floor. Jevonte flings his body against her as hard as possible and drapes himself around her neck. Talaitha is taken completely off guard and is unbalanced as she attempts to step forward and catch Jevonte's withered body. The momentum of Jevonte's lunge forces Talaitha to lose her footing on the top step, and the pair falls awkwardly back down the stairs. Talaitha attempts to twist her body as they crash against the wall, but the pickaxe she had been carrying hits the wall too, and its weight compromises her balance further. She tries to regain her footing, but Jevonte's arms and legs are tangled around her waist and neck, and she overcompensates. The two tumble violently down the stairs. Talaitha's head smacks the support banister with an awful wet-sounding thud, and Jevonte's good leg bends the wrong way when it crashes through the handrail. At the bottom of the staircase, Talaitha lands on her back and is impaled by some of the rebar that she freed from the basement floor. The violence of the fall lands Jevonte on his face, his legs sprawled unnaturally.

Minutes pass, and the two remain unmoving and silent on the cold, dirty floor. Pieces of concrete are scattered everywhere, and dust, disturbed by the impact of their bodies, dances and floats in the air all around them. The basement is shrouded in darkness. Jevonte is startled suddenly by the sound of a lone wooden banister, jarred loose by the tumbling bodies, as it falls to the floor. The sound echoes across the basement, and Talaitha flinches.

Jevonte can't see her, but her moans reach his ears soon enough. His pain becomes evident as he writhes on the cold floor in maddening agony. He knows that he is bleeding again and in different areas. He can't see where, but he can feel the warm wetness of his blood seeping through bandaged legs. His hand reaches down the length of his useless left leg, and when his fingertips touch the bone protruding through his pant leg, he erupts in screams of agony and terror. Jevonte's pitiful cries nudge Talaitha into consciousness, and she begins to stir.

Several moments pass until Jevonte can steel himself against the pain in his leg. "Tal," Jevonte cries. "Can you hear me, Tal? Are you alright?"

Talaitha moans in reply. The basement becomes quiet again, and Jevonte strains to see where Talaitha is. He knows he's about to go into shock or will soon, so he tries to control his breathing, but his ribs feel like they are smashed, and every movement sends streaks of pain across his whole body. He lies completely still and starts to surrender to the gentle calls of depression beckoning him to let go. He fights against that tide of despair, but the effort costs him his consciousness, and he blacks out.

"King? Where are you? Can you hear me?" Talaitha's voice trails weakly through the dark of the basement. She cannot see, and she doesn't know whether it's the impenetrable blackness surrounding her or whether her eyes have stopped working altogether. Her head feels like a spike has been driven through it, and so she reaches one hand up to her temple. The whole left side of her face is swollen, and there is a deep gash along her scalp and forehead. She can feel something wet and hot running down her face and pooling in her ears as she lies on her back. She tries to sit up, but waves of intense nausea push her back to the floor. She attempts to roll to her side but is prevented by something pressing on her stomach. In the dark, she passes her hand over the spot to find a piece of metal sticking through her shirt. It's drenched in her blood. She traces the metal object back to its source and stops where it exits the right side of her abdomen. She lies flat on her back and uses one hand to stabilize the rebar, preventing it from causing more damage to her side. She considers pulling it out but decides against it when more blood begins oozing out of the wound. Jevonte groans a few feet away from her. "King?" Her voice is weak but soft as she attempts to reach him in the darkness of the basement.

"Tal? I'm here," Jevonte responds, his voice seeking hers.

"I, I can't move. There is a piece of rebar sticking out of my stomach."

"Rebar," Jevonte responded weakly. "How? Where did that come from?"

Talaitha said nothing in reply. As she lay on her back, she wheezed and spat blood. She was feeling dizzy from the concussion. After her head calmed from the thunderous pounding she was experiencing, she turned her face in the direction she thought Jevonte was. "I was going to set you free, my love. I prepared a special place just for you in my garden," she wheezed.

"Talaitha, why are we still doing this?" Jevonte asked, his voice small and trembling. "This can't be what you wanted. I know it's not what I wanted. This isn't how I wanted us to be."

"Everything was on track, King, but you had to go and ruin it. You had to bring that fat cow into our marriage. I. I could have handled that betrayal, but then you let my, my..." and her voice became garbled and addled. She spat more blood, and Jevonte could hear her hawking the spittle and phlegm up from her throat. She was choking on her blood.

"Talaitha, don't speak. Save your energy. I can't move either. I think I have a compound fracture or break in my leg.

It's serious, and if I don't get it treated, it could be fatal for me. We have to work together now to get out of this basement. Tal? Did you hear me?"

Suddenly, the concrete next to Jevonte's head exploded in a rain of concrete pieces as Talaitha's sledgehammer slammed violently into the basement floor. The strike sent a brief flash of sparks into the air around Jevonte's head. The impact of the hammer against the concrete floor momentarily deafened Jevonte in his right ear. Against every objection of his body, Jevonte rolled to his left side and began inching away from the location of the hammer strike. He could hear the sledgehammer scrape against the floor as Talaitha pulled it back.

"Ta…" Jevonte started to call her name, but he didn't want to give his position away. Where did she get the hammer from? Damn it, Jevonte. She has all of my tools, he thought. He listened intently, trying to fix her exact location on the floor. Hopefully her injuries are too severe and will keep her from reaching me, but I have got to find a way out of here, he thought to himself.

"Don't try to hide from me, lover. Come over here, please. You were right. This was not how our story was supposed to end. I thought I chose the right one, but I see that I didn't, so come here, darling, and let me make amends," Talaitha screeched. Jevonte just listened, and what he heard next horrified him to his soul. The sound of jagged metal scraping against concrete filled his ears, followed by the sound of ripping, tearing flesh. He could hear her grunting and growling low and guttural with the strain. Her cries grew in intensity and volume, as did the curses bellowing from her effort. Talaitha was pulling the rebar from her side—through the flesh of her side. She let out a desperate scream of anger and pain as her lateral abdominal wall gave way and the rebar came free from her. The bloody piece of rebar clanked to the basement floor and rolled to a stop at the edge of the pit. Jevonte covered his mouth to stifle his scream. He could hear her rolling on the floor, crying, shrieking, and slapping the hard, cold surface of the basement floor with her hand. When she finally stopped, Jevonte thought that she had passed out, but then he heard the sound of cloth tearing as Talaitha started wrapping her blouse around her midsection.

How is she still moving, Jevonte thought. He'd hoped that the rebar would have kept her pinned in one spot, but now she was free to roam and find him—sledgehammer and all. He started rolling to his left again until he rolled into the edge of the garden pit. The soil was cool to his touch and foul-smelling, but it muffled his movements, and he could drag himself more easily on it than on the basement floor. Talaitha finished wrapping her torn abdomen and lay still. Jevonte could hear her panting from the effort, and he had a good idea where she was on the basement floor. He started inchworming through the soft, dark soil until his hand came into contact with a large object just under the surface of the garden. He went absolutely still, listening to what Talaitha was doing, and then he let his fingers probe the area he had come into contact with. His fingers hit something squishy and firm, and, like a blind man reading the features of a stranger, Jevonte's hands and fingers searched across the surface of the object until they found the eye socket and the decayed skull of the home health aide. "Oh God, nooooo," recoiled Jevonte in terror as he yanked back his hand quickly. As he did so, he could feel the remnants of the aide's flesh cling to his fingers; the stench, once buried and hidden, was now exposed by his exploratory raking in the soil. Just as he was on the verge of vomiting, he heard a familiar sound. Talaitha knew where he was and started crawling towards the pit, hammer in tow.

"Why did you stop loving me, King?" and the hammer struck the concrete. "I wanted to give you the world, and I did." Hammer strike. "No one could love you as I did." Hammer strike. "I gave you all of my body. I gave you every inch and in every way you wanted." Hammer strike. "I just needed your protection. I needed you to stop, Noelle, but you lied to me. You brought her here, and she wants to kill me." Hammer strike. The last strike was almost on the edge of the pit and was too close for Jevonte's comfort. He didn't know if he was at the center of the garden, but he could hear and feel her getting closer with every clap of the hammer against the floor. Desperately, he tried to focus on how he had redesigned the basement and its layout. It had been so long since he was down here; it seemed strange to him, but he focused on the stairway and the deep sink. The workbench and the cabinets began to become clear in his mind, and he imagined the open pit and how it was originally planned to avoid blocking access or impeding traffic from the basement to the walkout. With those landmarks in his head, and now that he felt he had Talaitha's position fixed, all he had to do was get around her to get up the stairs. If I can just keep from blacking out, I might survive this hellhole, he thought.

Talaitha's eyes were not adjusting to the dark, and she reasoned that her concussion had something to do with that, so she focused on her hearing. She stopped at the edge of the open pit and listened. She could barely make out the whistling sound of air escaping through Jevonte's broken teeth, but the sound was low, and she couldn't place his exact position. Jevonte could feel her presence mere feet away from where he was in the dirt. His smashed ribcage prevented him from taking full, deep breaths, which helped conceal his location, but he was beginning to suffocate from the lack of oxygen. Talaitha began swinging the hammer in a wide, sweeping arch on the ground. Jevonte could feel the dirt thrown up by Talaitha hitting his face, and he knew it was only a matter of a few more swings before she either struck him or revealed his position. He had to do something, fast.

Jevonte slid his body in what he prayed was a perpendicular angle to where Talaitha was. He inched carefully forward and could feel the dirt from Talaitha's swinging hammer strike him along the side of his body. He stretched as much as his tortured ribs would allow until he started feeling the spray of dirt and debris strike him along his calf and ankle. Then, Talaitha stopped swinging her weapon along the ground, and she started scooping handfuls of dirt to toss in random directions. Jevonte could hear the dirt and small stones hit and bounce off the basement walls and the floor, then dampen as they hit the soil. Jevonte thought, She's not stupid; this is frustrating! She's trying to use echolocation or something like that to find me, damn it! Gotta keep moving.

Jevonte tried to inch his way further, but he could no longer get any traction in the dirt of the pit. He had no power left in his good leg, and the dead weight of his broken leg was creating too much drag. He was grateful the leg was dead now. If he could still feel anything in his left leg, the compound fracture would have paralyzed him in pain. He stretched himself out as far as he could and extended his right hand, hoping to grab the edge of the pit. When he did, his hand found the piece of rebar that Talaitha had separated from her waist. He became hopeful, but just as he pulled the piece of metal to him, it scraped along the edge of the pit, and Talaitha stopped tossing dirt. She heard him.

"There you are, my love. Come to me, King. Oh, right, you can't, so I'll come to you. Now don't go anywhere." Talaitha cackled, and she got to her hands and knees. She started crawling through the soil of the pit in the direction of the sound she had heard. Jevonte was worn out. He was so weary, he wanted to just quit and let her have him. Talaitha reached Jevonte's leg and gripped it hard. "King, you did good. I didn't think you would last this long. I didn't give you enough credit, but it's over now. Just close your eyes and let Momma put you to sleep."

Talaitha rose, and while kneeling, she raised the sledgehammer high over her head and paused while the hammer was suspended in the air behind her back. She started laughing, and as she started her forward swing, she yelled, "Goodnight, King." The arch of the hammer was unmerciful and swift but imprecise. Through the air, the hammer descended with power and struck the pit with a sickening, wet thud. The darkness surrounding the pair was penetrated by the sounds of choking and gagging as Talaitha was once again transfixed by rebar; only this time the metal had found her neck. The force of her swing had been so great that her whole upper body was cast forward onto the piece of rebar that Jevonte had wedged between the pit's edge and his shoulder. He had been trying to use the metal bar to lever his way out of the pit, but it was just too heavy. Now, as Talaitha fell kicking and screaming backwards, choking and grabbing at her throat, Jevonte was glad his weakness prevailed.

Talaitha writhes, choking violently, struggling to remove the rebar from her throat. She was lucky. The metal did not pierce her esophagus, but her throat was almost crushed. She couldn't get enough air and started screaming and thrashing around in the dirt. Jevonte, having reached the edge of the pit, redoubled his efforts to get out of the dirt. He reached the bottom of the staircase after what felt like forever. He was spent and exhausted and couldn't go any farther, so he tried to rest. Talaitha had stopped her thrashing. Maybe she's dead or passed out, Jevonte hoped.

"You coward of a man!" choked Talaitha from the pit. "I won't let you leave me, too," she screamed through a damaged windpipe. Though dazed and blind, Talaitha rose from the soil of her garden and began shambling toward the edge of the pit. She stumbled and fell flat on the basement floor. She lay disoriented and weak. She tried to rise but collapsed in an unconscious heap. Jevonte prayed silently and waited to see if she would get up again. Almost twenty minutes passed, and Talaitha was still unconscious on the floor, so Jevonte resumed his efforts to get up the stairs. His body started shaking, and he could barely breathe. Time was running out. He had lost too much blood, and he couldn't think straight from the lack of oxygen to his brain. He would make one last attempt.

Rolling onto his back, Jevonte managed to prop his left elbow on the first step of the staircase, and he pushed down as hard as he could. His body lifted up and over part of the first step, and he used his left heel to push himself up further. It worked, and he repeated the elbow jack, lift, and push maneuver with each step. He traversed four steps this way before resting. He gathered his energy to begin climbing the next few steps when Talaitha crashed into the staircase wall and collapsed at the foot of the stairs. She was unsteady, and her legs were uncoordinated, but she made concerted efforts to orient herself towards Jevonte's prone body. She picked herself up and began slithering up the stairs, blind, bloody, and raving mad.

"I said you won't ever leave me, King. Get back down here. Please, I need you. I need your help; just wait for me. I'm coming, King," Talaitha howled.

Jevonte started moving faster, but he wasn't going anywhere; he just didn't have any energy left. He struggled to get his arm up and positioned again to jack his body up the stairs, but his strength had become water, and he sagged in place. Talaitha slipped and pawed her way up the stairs, slowly crawling up one step at a time until she collapsed against Jevonte's broken leg, and he felt that. One hand at a time, hand over hand, Talaitha pulled herself up along Jevonte's helpless body. Her face slid up his torn and bandaged midsection, then her right hand found his collarbone, and she hauled herself up while he screamed in agony and pain. Finally, she reached his neck and nuzzled her face under his cheek. She rested her left hand on his dick and held him firmly.

Jevonte was crying, not from the pain his body was in, but because this was the position that first united them oh so long ago on the cruise ship where he almost ended his life. She had saved his life then, and now she was about to end it. He wept bitterly and openly as the memory filled his mind. Talaitha's bloody forehead smeared Jevonte's cheekbone, and her gravely wounded side, gashed and oozing, pressed tightly against Jevonte, so tight that he yelled out in excruciating pain. She pulled against his body more and more, increasing the pressure in a sideways bear hug, and then her wound stopped bleeding. She was using his body as a makeshift bandage to stop the life force from escaping her own wounds.

Talaitha slowly tilted her blood-smeared face so that her lips were inches from Jevonte's left ear. "My heart, and my King. I really do love you. It may not seem like it, but I do," she whispered gently. "Everything you read in my journal was only half of it. You don't know my full story. You are unaware of the extent of the damage they inflicted upon me. The men, the animals, and the videos they made—all of it made me, shaped me, and defined my existence. They broke me, King. They broke my soul from the inside and gave it back to me in tiny, filthy pieces," she said, and then started to cry, sobbing in fits. "I was made to be a receptacle for the pleasure of others, an object of men's lusts and desires, and no one ever tried to help me."

Talaitha squeezed Jevonte so hard that he passed out and stopped breathing, prompting her to smack him across the face in an attempt to revive him. He took a breath and said in a small, tiny voice, "Tal, please. You are killing me. Please let me go, please."

"King, I just need you to understand. I need you to see it this way, and I need you to understand why I have to plant you in my garden. Now, be still and listen. My demon is not a figment of my imagination. I didn't just conjure this thing. It has existed since I was born and always has. It first manifested when I was just two years old. Latriece and Rufus said it was my twin, but I knew better; even as a child, I knew that was a lie. It mocked me in everything I did. The entity assumed my appearance and likeness. It spoke in a different voice, but it tried to disguise itself as me. I was smarter, though. I saw it for what it was, a demon dressed to look like me," Talaitha moaned weakly.

Jevonte was losing consciousness, unable to comprehend most of Talaitha's words. He couldn't focus on what she was saying, and he tried to answer her, but his words blurred in a slur of incoherence. He tried to shift his body away from hers and reached for part of the banister to his right, but Talaitha threw her left leg over his torso, and the weight flattened him against the stairs, pinning him.

There was nothing more he could do physically, but he thought maybe he could get to her mind and appeal to the love they once had.

"I love you too, Tal. I do with all of my heart, and with everything that is within me, I swear. I believe you, honey. If I had been in your life back then, I would have protected you with mine. I wouldn't let anyone touch you; you're my world. You do know that, don't you?"

Talaitha loosened her grip slightly, and Jevonte drew a shallow breath of air. "I don't know, King. You're acting like you don't want to go into my garden, and that hurts," Talaitha whispered in reply.

"Babe, I just need some time, that's all. I'll go into your garden, I promise. Let's just get upstairs and start all over. There is so much I want to do for you and with you, but we need to heal and recover, and then we can explore the garden together. How's that sound?" Jevonte said, his voice genuine and pleading.

Talaitha relaxed a little and drifted off to sleep. Her grip on his manhood fell away, and his body felt light as hers sagged in relief. It had to be the loss of blood, he thought. I've never known anyone as strong as this woman, but even she has limits.

Jevonte tried to pry himself free from Talaitha's body. The blood from her body acted like a warm lubricant, and he inched his way carefully up the stairs, again taking one step at a time. Talaitha's body rolled lifelessly onto her back, and Jevonte started to gain momentum, moving closer to the door of the basement. He is one step away from freedom when Talaitha yanks his legs back toward her, forcing him down the stairs and dashing all of his hope against the banister. Reaching for broken pieces of the banister, she launches herself over him, causing his head to crash into the steps. She slaps his hand away, and he starts sliding down the staircase, his head bumping against the steps on his way down. She reaches the top step and turns to look at Jevonte.

"King, I hear what you're saying, but I swore to myself that I would never, ever, let that demon run my life again. I forced Noelle to expose herself at prom, and now that my brother has come into my life, together we will make sure that demon never shows itself again. Unfortunately, the price is your life," Talaitha finishes and then reaches for the door and twists. The light of the kitchen pours into the darkened stairwell, and Talaitha steps into the kitchen. Before she closes the door, she stares down into blackness and, holding her midsection tightly, says, "Rest now, King. I will be back

27

Bedlam in the Basement

I can barely move. Maybe I'm dead. No, I'm not dead. I'm in hell.

Jevonte is a bloody mess. Most of the bandages that bound his ribcage have come loose, so he used them to wrap his broken leg. There is still a piece of bone protruding through his shin. He can't feel his leg at all, and given its condition, that's a blessing. His abdomen is bloated and sore to the touch. Probably bleeding somewhere inside, he thinks. Breathing has become harder after Talaitha kicked him down the stairs, so he lies still, working hard not to move his body for fear of what his ribs might puncture. At least the ringing and throbbing inside his head have quieted, and he can hear himself think again. The adrenaline that probably saved his life during his struggle with Talaitha on the stairs has worn off, and his body has started crashing. He didn't fight it. He didn't care anymore. He reasoned that death would finally grant the escape he had been craving.

When Jevonte next opens his eyes, hours have passed, and the dank, mildewy smell of the basement floor immediately greets his nose. The aroma has settled, joined by the pungent smell of decay and wet soil. There is an eerie silence blanketing the room. It feels thick and menacing, and it's alive. Jevonte can finally see some of the features of the basement, but everything is still too dark. In one of the corners, he sees someone, someone squatting, watching him, and waiting on him with folded hands. He tries to focus intently on that corner, but he still can't make out what it is. Suddenly, it moves out of the dark embrace of the corner. It's huge, menacing, and exudes malevolence. Large leather-looking wings drape behind its back in dark, majestic splendor. The horns on its head almost touch the ceiling, and when it takes a step towards Jevonte, he can feel the concrete floor creak and break under ponderous hooves.

The beast looms over Jevonte, its fiery eyes locking onto his. From its side, the beast retrieves an enormous sledgehammer and raises it to the ceiling just above Jevonte's head. With terrifying speed, the hammer plummets toward Jevonte's skull, and he cries out in abject horror, knowing he cannot get out of its way.

Jevonte shudders and wakes trembling, his body wet with perspiration. His dream having ended, he cries in relief that it was only a dream. What the unholy hell was that? he thinks. My God, help me, please help me. I don't want to die in the dark like this. I won't. Strengthen me this last time; just help me, please.

Jevonte started praying and thinking about his family, his mom and dad, and his Uncle Roscoe's message. Talaitha forgot to erase it, but he heard it when he first left it on the door camera system. His uncle's words and their promise gave him life the first time, and now they lit a fire of hope in his spirit. More than just the words, it was his uncle's voice that transported Jevonte back to the days when he would visit his uncle at his shop, to the days when he would take Jevonte to the comic book store, and back to the day when his uncle beat the brakes off of some hate-filled men who tried to intimidate him. His uncle was a man of conviction and strength, and Jevonte aspired to live and walk in courage and hope as well.

The basement was getting colder, which Jevonte knew meant the sun was setting and the evening was approaching. He hadn't had any water in what felt like days, and he knew he needed to do something about that. His body was too damaged to sit up, and he had no leverage to get to his one working leg, but his left arm was still in good working order, and the bottom of the staircase abutted his head. Jevonte placed his hand against the step and pushed while using his left leg and heel to claw his way from where he lay. The concrete basement floor was smooth and offered little resistance to Jevonte's body. Combined with the sweat and blood on the floor, Jevonte could scoot and slide his way along without sitting up and risking a punctured lung. Using his good hand and leg, he made it to the deep sink. There was no way he was going to get himself up off the floor to drink from the faucet, and he lay his head back against the cool of the floor in exhaustion.

Then Jevonte spotted the shut-off valves under the deep sink, and he started smiling. One of the more difficult tasks during the basement remodel was determining what to do about the condition of the aged sink pipes and valves. They were ancient, and parts were difficult to find. For weeks, he could not get the water system in the basement to work until he got a tip from his neighbor, Mr. Jefferson. Good old Gerald; I will have to send him something special when I get out of this mess, Jevonte said to himself. He was able to find nearly exact replacements for the valves, and now they would be the source of his salvation.

Jevonte maneuvered under the sink and began loosening the valve and dislodging the PVC connecting the water source to the sink. The valve wouldn't budge under Jevonte's weakened state, but he kept twisting, putting all the strength that remained in his wrecked body into turning it and freeing the water supply hose. The hose and valve remained closed and tightly sealed, but moisture began to appear around the wall where the cold water line entered. Jevonte could get the valve to release its hold on the water pipe, but somewhere inside the wall, a leak was forming.

Encouraged by the sign of water but humbled that he may have missed something in his remodeling project, Jevonte claws at the drywall surrounding the water line. The pipe is fractured, and he can see a trail of water running down the middle of the line. He begins hammering at the waterline, trying to increase the pressure on the fracture. The hairline widens, and the water pressure wins the day as water starts spraying through the wall, showering Jevonte in the face and chest. The spray of the cold water is bracing, but Jevonte gulps as much as he can without drowning himself. The water rinses his face of blood and debris that had become caked and hardened on his skin. "I've never showered lying down," he thought to himself and laughed.

"Thank you, gentlemen, for coming back to my office this morning," Detective Albright said as he greeted Roscoe and Marcus. "Come on in and have a seat. Let me give you our overnight brief on the suspect."

"Suspect? She's guilty, detective; we have solid evidence on her, at least you do now," replied Roscoe.

"She?" remarked the detective, his eyebrow raised. "Would you care to elaborate on that, Mr. Greene?"

"She may look like a man, but only because she had herself altered to look that way. Nolan was born a female named Noelle," Marcus added.

"We haven't given him or her a physical, so I'll withhold that judgment until then. I have to list them as a suspect until I can fully verify the evidence and its source, so until that happens, they are innocent until proven guilty."

"I get that, I do, but she confessed everything to me, and I'd swear to that in a court of law. She is not well, Detective, and I know a doctor who can attest to that as fact," said Roscoe.

"Dr. Robinson, I presume?"

"Yes, how did you know?

"I spoke with him last week. He gave me a very detailed profile about the killer and warned me about their psychosis. We still don't know that the perpetrator is the same person he spoke about, so I still have some work to do, starting with an interrogation of the suspect."

"Can I speak to her first? I think she'll say things to me that she wouldn't say to the police," said Roscoe.

"Out of the question. I will allow you and Mr. Drummons here to sit in the viewing room. You can see and hear the interview, but I can't allow you further interaction with the suspect."

"I guess we have no choice then…"

"No, Mr. Greene, you don't. I hope, though, that this process will begin to give you and your family some closure."

"Just so you know, and I have it written down in my statement, he confessed to killing multiple members of my family, including my brother Jedidiah. He could have been lying to me, trying to get under my skin, but I haven't seen any of the family, and it's been almost a week now. None of them are answering my calls, and that's not random happenstance. "My brother might miss my calls, but those kids definitely would not," Roscoe finished before adding one more statement. "We believe this person didn't act alone."

"Since the serial killings began, we suspected that maybe there was more than one killer, that perhaps there were two of them working as a team, but we had no real evidence of that."

"No, she committed the murders on her own, but we believe she did it at the behest of my nephew's wife, Talaitha, her sister."

"Do you have any evidence that the suspect acted in collusion with this Talaitha person?" asked Detective Albright.

Roscoe was quiet. He had just about had enough of the doubt and naysaying regarding who was actually responsible. He knew Talaitha was behind it all, and he didn't need any further evidence or proof. "Well, detective, let's just see what your 'suspect' has to say about all of this, but I know in my heart that she did not act alone."

"We also do not know that the suspect is a woman. You keep using the pronoun 'she,' but they look very male to me," Albright interjected.

"Detective, the person you have under arrest was born female, but she is not transgender. She had her appearance altered. Her parents confirmed this when I interviewed them," Marcus said.

"Dr. Robinson said as much, but I still find it hard to believe, and without a full physical, I have my doubts," countered Albright.

"She did some of the cosmetic surgery herself. I can't explain it, and it blows my mind, but I saw scars on her chest that couldn't possibly be the work of a real surgeon; there's just no way," Roscoe responded.

"You would be surprised at what some people will do to achieve their goals. There are a lot of black market medical services in this country, but those are dwarfed by the number of illegal, unsanctioned, and privatized medical services available outside the United States." Detective Albright responded, "Anyone with a passport and sufficient funds can obtain nearly any medical procedure."

Albright led the two men to the observation room. There was a large one-way mirror separating the interrogation room and observation space. The trio watched as Nolan was brought into interview room number 1. Deputies cuffed him to the table and walked out. "Well, there's my cue."

The detective walked into the interview space and sat down across from Nolan. He placed a file on the desk and flipped a switch on the audio recorder at the end of the table. "My name is Detective Albright with the Baltimore Police Department. Have your rights been read to you?"

Nolan, his expression peaceful and contented, answered in the affirmative. Detective Albright continued with the interview.

Detective Albright stared at him, trying to read beyond the surface. He had dealt with cunning individuals before, but something was unnerving about Nolan. His calm demeanor and unwavering gaze—it all pointed to someone who felt they were always in control.

"Do you know why you're here, sir?" Albright began, his voice steady and professional.

Nolan's smirk widened slightly. "I'm sure you'll remind me," he said smoothly, his tone almost casual.

Albright leaned forward, opening a manila folder filled with crime scene photos, witness statements, and forensic reports. He laid out a photograph of the latest victim, Melanie DeCartes, in front of him. Nolan's eyes flickered to the image briefly before returning to Albright's face.

"Recognize her?" Albright asked.

Nolan shrugged. "Should I?"

"Her name was Melanie Decartes. She's missing, but her home bore the same calling card as a series of other murders in this state. And we've got physical evidence linking you to the scene."

Nolan's smirk faded slightly, but his demeanor remained relaxed. "Physical evidence, huh? Like what?"

Albright replied, tapping the photo, "We located a partial fingerprint on the vanity in the master bedroom, some DNA, and the necklace you wore when you killed her. Hair strands in the living room. Skin cells under her fingernails. We have lots of good stuff that points directly at you."

Nolan leaned forward, his face serious for the first time. "Maybe they got there after you did your fancy testing. Have you ever considered that?"

Albright raised an eyebrow, keeping his cool. "Oh, we've considered everything, Nolan. But you and I both know those aren't coincidences. "Besides," he said, leaning even closer, "we have more than just the physical evidence. We've got witnesses who saw you lugging a huge clothing trunk from Melanie's garage."

Nolan's smirk returned, though it was tinged with frustration. "Circumstantial. You know that won't hold up in court."

"Perhaps," Albright conceded with a nod. "But that's where you come in. You see, we don't need just enough to get you convicted. We need enough to stop you from hurting anyone else. You can make the situation easier on yourself. Tell us where Melanie is."

Nolan chuckled, a cold sound that sent chills down Albright's spine. "And why on earth would I do that?" he asked, his eyes glinting with a dangerous mix of amusement and cunning.

Albright paused for effect, then decided to play his ace. "You think you're the smartest person in the room, don't you, Nolan? Or is it Noelle? We've got someone to help us understand you—a profiler who's worked with people like you. They know your patterns, your habits, and even the way you think."

Nolan blinked, a flash of uncertainty in his eyes. "Profiler, huh? How fancy of you!"

"Oh, we're not being fancy," Albright retorted. "Dr. Samuel Robinson. Heard of him? He's very familiar with you, especially since he's treating someone you may be very close to. He is intimately familiar with your personality. In fact, he's already given us enough information to understand what it is that you're doing and why. He told us that you likely had a site set up where you were creating something of enormous significance, something you might want to show someone important in your life, a defining reveal, if you will."

Nolan's eyes narrowed. "You're full of shit, detective."

"Am I?" Albright took out another sheet of paper and slid it across the table. It was a detailed profile outlining

Nolan's past, tendencies, and predictive behaviors. Nolan glanced at it and scoffed, but the slight tension in his jaw betrayed him.

"We don't need you to confess because we have enough evidence to see you fried for your crimes," Albright pressed on. "However, if you want to save your life, you can help us find the other victims. Dr. Robinson believes they're somewhere significant to you. Somewhere you think they'd never be found."

Nolan seemed to consider the matter for a moment, then leaned back and crossed his arms. "Victims? There are no 'other' victims."

"Ok, so then it was just Melanie?" Albright maintained his composure, sensing he was close to something. "The one person who fought back and almost beat your ass."

Nolan's smirk returned, though his eyes seemed to betray a flicker of vexation. "She didn't beat my ass. I just wanted to…" Nolan went silent.

"What did you want to do, Nolan? Placate someone else? Follow someone else's instructions? We saw clearly in the video how she was manhandling you. She nearly stomped you into high-yellow paste, but the chokehold saved you. So why did you continue to fight her when clearly, she was out of your league? You were so persistent. Why?"

"It wasn't luck! It was a skill. I'm an artist, and an artist is only as good as the brush and canvas they use. I am a grandmaster and would never, ever dull my work using substandard materials. My inspiration has always come from where it all began."

Albright's heart raced, but he kept his expression neutral. "Where did it all begin?"

Nolan sighed dramatically. "Yes, but I grow tired of this discussion. You can't hold me much longer, and you don't have enough to charge me, so let me…"

"I'm tired too, Nolan, or is it Noelle?" And Detective Albright lifted a remote from his blazer and pointed it at the monitor on the wall. The screen came to life, and a still image appeared. Albright pressed play, and Melanie came into view as she body-slammed Nolan into the vanity. The entire struggle played out before Nolan and Detective Albright. When the video segments finished, Detective Albright said, "I think we have everything right there. All we need is a lovely velvet bow, so where did you take her body?"

"I want to speak with my lawyer," Nolan replied dryly.

With that, Detective Albright rose, switched off the monitor, and gathered his files, except for the photo of Melanie. He left that on the table in Nolan's full view.

"Detective, you forgot something," and he pushed the photo across the table.

"No, I have everything I need. I just thought I'd leave this photograph with you to remind you of the innocent life you snuffed out."

"I don't need a reminder. Ms. Melanie is right at home now," Nolan sneered.

"Now, I have what I need, so thank you, Noelle," Detective Albright beamed as he left the interview room.

Roscoe and Marcus stood to their feet when Detective Albright entered the observation room. "I assume you heard all of the discussion?"

"Is it enough? He didn't exactly confess," Marcus quipped.

"No, he didn't, but he gave himself away, and he also inadvertently told me where we could find Melanie's body. While we can't question him further without his lawyer present, I can get a search warrant based on what he said."

"So where do you think Melanie's body is, detective?" asked Roscoe.

"I'll just keep that close to the vest for now. I know how you two like to get out in front of things, and I can't have you contaminating the scene or compromising my investigation. I will keep you posted and up-to-date on whatever we find."

On their way out of the station, Roscoe pulls Marcus off to the side for a quiet chat. "I don't like this, not one bit."

"Albright is right, though; at this point, we have to step back a little and let him do his detective thing."

"And while he's doing that, what about my nephew? He didn't ask the question that needed answering concerning that situation or Noelle's ties to Talaitha."

"It's that little bugger called the Constitution. It tends to slow things down at the worst time, but I feel good. Noelle is off the table for now, so we can focus on Jevonte," replied Marcus.

Roscoe turned and headed for his truck with Marcus in tow. "Well, he's my sole focus now, and come hell or high water, I'm getting him out of that house."

Talaitha sits at the kitchen counter and plunges her face into the sink filled with ice water. Her mind is still scrambled, and she can't focus. As a doctor, she knows how dangerous concussions can be, and she knows she needs to seek medical attention, but she also knows that she can't. She managed to patch up the horrific gash in her side, but it's makeshift and won't hold for long. Though she packed the wound extensively, she's going to require stitches and a significant amount of cosmetic rebuilding. The amount of blood she's lost has left her barely able to stand, let alone function.

She stands, hovering over the sink's cold water. In the shimmering water's reflection, she becomes dismayed at her visage. She is saddened by how much damage the fall down the basement stairs did to her face. One side of her face is swollen, and the tear along her scalp is an ugly mess. Her vision has started clearing, but she still can't see details. She lifts her shirt and sees the purpling and blackening spreading from her wound. If left untreated, she will become septic, she thinks to herself.

For a brief moment, she starts to recollect everything that has happened over the last day or so. She really doesn't know how long they were down in the basement. The basement, she thinks, and she turns to look at the closed door. My king rose against me down there. Where did all of that come from? Her mind flashes to the fall, the rebar penetrating her, and Jevonte's near escape. I'm going to have to see a therapist when all of this is done, she thinks.

Her thoughts scrambled and incoherent, Talaitha reflects for a moment on the hurdles facing her. She thinks, He hasn't been that alive in months. He's in worse shape than I, though. I'll just leave him down there and let nature run its course. I've got to stabilize my injuries and make plans to start all over. Fuck, all of my efforts have been for nothing. Well, maybe not. "I have my brother now, at least," Talaitha whispers to the sink. With that, Talaitha wonders, why hasn't she heard from him? Let me give him a call. I could use his help in this basement.

A news alert causes her cell phone to vibrate from the opposite counter. She staggers across the kitchen floor to retrieve it and falls to the ground. Lying there, she feels like she wants to vomit, but she distracts herself from the deep nausea by focusing on the vibrating phone. She backs herself up against the counter and pulls the phone down into her lap. The phone has been buzzing almost nonstop, and when she opens it, she sees that she has missed several calls from Nolan. There are several messages from him, and she clicks on the first one to play it.

"Sister. It's done. She will never be a threat to you again. I hope this offering brings us some peace."

Talaitha clicks on the next message from Nolan, recorded almost a day later.

"Listen, I think the police are onto me now. They have my picture all over the news, shit. Your enemy had some kind of surveillance system in the house. I may not make it to your place, so I'll lie low at my spot in Delaware. If you don't hear from me today or the next, just assume that they got me."

Finally, Talaitha plays the last message from Nolan.

"Hey, I just want you to know that I did it all for you, for us, and for our family. I know I have been absent from your life for a long time, but I needed to cleanse myself of her existence so that I could become what you needed. It took a very long time to get it done, lots of pain, and many tears, but getting back to you was worth it. I don't regret any of the sacrifices. Besides, I know who I am now. I know my calling, and erasing her was the best thing for both of us. We will always be family, and nothing will ever separate us again, nothing."

Talaitha is barely able to close the message when she is overwhelmed by the need to close her eyes and sleep. She knows she shouldn't, that she needs to stay awake, but her body and mind just can't, and she slumps to one side and falls asleep on the kitchen floor, her cell phone now ringing from an unknown caller. Her voice service answers the incoming call.

"Hello, Mrs. Greene, this is Detective Albright. We have arrested your sister on several charges of murder in the first degree. Please come down to the station to speak with me at your earliest convenience. I advise you to do so as early as possible; if you cannot, I will be forced to send units to your home to retrieve you. Please return my call at the number provided, or you can reach me directly at (410) 396-2413.

28

Mausoleum

"Sir," one of the junior detectives knocks on Albright's door. "The warrant has come back, and it looks like we're cleared to search the suspect's residence in Delaware."

"Good. Get on the horn with the state's troopers, and let's get coordinating clearance to proceed as soon as the state's attorney's office confirms."

Nolan has been in conference with his attorney most of the morning. Now that they have a warrant to search Nolan's home, Detective Albright is in no real hurry to pry any more information out of the suspect, but he decides to see if Nolan has anything else to say before the warrant is executed. Heading to the interview room, Detective Albright almost runs over Nolan's lawyer in the hallway.

"Excuse me, ma'am, I'm sorry. You almost became a casualty; what's the rush?"

Nolan's attorney appears disheveled and visibly shaken. She readjusts her glasses and brushes back her braided locs from her eyes and face. "Detective, I was just on my way to come see you. Ah, we need to talk now," and she extended her hand. "My name is Angela Briscoe, but please, call me Angie."

"Of course, Angie. Does your client have anything more they want to offer in the way of defense?"

"Can we speak off the record in your office, please?" Her face is fearful, and her tone is not what one would expect from a defense attorney.

"We can use my office, but I can't promise it will be off the record. Right this way," and Detective Albright leads the attorney to his office, where he shuts the door and draws the window blinds. "Go ahead, Angie, what's wrong?"

"I have been a defense attorney for over fifteen years, and I have defended some really horrible people. I know how that sounds, and I know what some people think about defense attorneys. Everyone is entitled to a competent defense, everyone. I have always believed that, and I still do, but…" She hesitated.

"But what, Angie?"

"I don't think I can defend my client, not in good conscience. I could be disbarred if I continue. Now, I can't disclose anything my client told me, but based on what he shared, I might actually throw the case. I wanted you to know the truth because if I did, it would undermine the state's case, and he'd have to be retried."

"Ma'am, what are you telling me? You would lose the case deliberately? Why?" Albright said, a bit puzzled.

"I cannot clarify further without risking the state's case, and although I understand that my role is not to support the state's position, I cannot ethically defend my client given what I know."

"I don't know what to say, Angie. I'm just the investigating detective on this case. What you're telling me is probably something you need to discuss with the D.A.'s office. Is your client willing to speak with me further?"

"At this point, detective, I don't even want to speak with him anymore. I know how that sounds, but I don't think I can go back in there. In fact, I won't, so until Mr. Nolan can obtain new representation, I suggest you refrain from questioning him further."

"Well, I probably won't need to anyway. We're in the process of executing a warrant for his residence in Delaware. We already have sufficient evidence to put him or her behind bars for life. I hope to uncover sufficient evidence at his home, bringing closure to the numerous lives this individual has ruined. This will serve as the conclusive evidence I've been searching for since we apprehended your client."

Angie walked over to the water dispenser in Albright's office and poured some water. She drank it all and refilled the cup. When she finished that, she took a deep breath and turned back toward Albright. "There is something very diabolical and insidious about how my client thinks. You may have him on the ropes, and you may well get a conviction, but my every instinct is telling me that he is not done, not by a long shot."

Just then, there is a knock on Albright's door. One of the crime scene technicians hands him a vanilla envelope and leaves. Albright opens it and begins reading. "Well, we got a hit on your client's DNA in the state's database. We didn't find a match for them in our criminal database, but there is a sibling match in the healthcare affiliations database records. It seems the suspect was a 100% match to a juvenile who was once under the jurisdiction of the state's mental health division. The name of the juvenile is not provided, but the name of the treating physician is. Dr. Samuel Robinson treated the patient who has a familial connection to our suspect. Angie, can you just get me in with Nolan one last time, please?"

"I'm out as soon as you finish, and I won't be back," she replied.

"Fair enough, let's go."

Detective Albright took a seat across from Nolan, and Angie remained standing just to his left, opposed to her client. Nolan looked at her and smirked.

"Nolan, you still haven't said whether I should address you as Nolan or Noelle. Which name do you prefer?" Which will it be?" Albright asked.

"Noelle is dead," was his instant reply. His stare became glossy as he turned from Angie to focus on Albright. Angie glanced away in relief.

"Very well, Nolan, it is then. We are about to visit your home in Middletown, Delaware, warrant in hand. Care to tell us what we might find when we get there?

"As I said, detective, I am a master artist. I promise you that you will be wonder-struck when you see what I have created. There is nothing like it in all of the world."

"Yes, so you've said, but there is something that I have been bothered by for a while now, and I'm hoping you can just clear the matter up for me." Detective Albright leaned forward, resting his elbows on the table separating them. "Who commissioned your work?"

Nolan said nothing, but a small smile escaped across his face in response to the detective's question. After several moments, Nolan placed his elbows on the table and looked Albright in the eye. "My benefactor is an angel. She has been cast down and trapped on the plane of mortals for too long. What I do now, I do under the patronage of her divine majesty. She called me out of my misery and helped set me on a path of redemption. All of my sacrifices have been made to show her my worth and curry her favor."

"Did this angel instruct you to murder Melanie?" asked Albright, hoping that Angie would not act like his defense attorney and object. Angie remained quiet.

"You cannot understand the goddess. She doesn't have to instruct me at all because I live in her perfect will. I know what she wants, and I do what pleases her, always. I remove her obstacles and her enemies. I smite those who rise against her. I take her full revenge on any that defy her, and I always will."

"Is the name of this angel Talaitha? Is your sister the one who has commissioned you and set you on this path of redemption, as you call it?"

"Don't you dare speak her name," Nolan hissed. "You are not worthy. None of you are, and none of them were, so they have become part of my greatest gift to the angel. I have become the redeemed one. I have been engrafted into her, and the heavens have accepted me," he yells and stands to his feet. "Holy and swift shall my consuming fire continue until all of the chaff has been swept from her path." With a sudden burst of anger, Nolan jerked hard against the handcuffs to break free from the manacled braces holding his wrists securely to the table. The cuffs held, but the braces on the table snapped, and his wrists were free. Angie screamed, darted for the door, and began banging on it, crying in terror for help.

Albright, taken by surprise by the ferocity and swiftness of Nolan's aggression, fell over backwards in his chair and started scrambling to get to his sidearm. He was too slow, and Nolan pounced on him from across the table. Nolan's left knee pinned Albright's gun arm, while Angie continued to cry out in terror. Nolan stretched his handcuffs across Albright's neck and started choking the much older man to death. He bore the entirety of his weight on the detective's throat, and Albright's eyes popped wide and filled with fear. Nolan began laughing at the horrified look on the detective's face and started reproving him, rebuking him in a frenzy of madness.

"You thought wrong, sir," and he pressed against Albright's neck harder. "She didn't manhandle me. No one beat my ass. The goddess gave me all the power I needed to defeat her foes. I am her phoenix; do you hear me?" Albright's eyes rolled until nothing but the white showed in their sockets. His Adam's apple collapsed and disappeared under the weight of the handcuff chain across his neck. Nolan stopped pressing when he heard a convincing pop from the back of Albright's neck, then he looked up at Angie with menace and intent in his eyes.

Angie began screaming louder. She pounded and pounded on the door until two uniformed officers entered the room. As soon as they got the door open, Angie bolted out of the room. The officers dove on Nolan and wrestled him away from the detective, who was no longer breathing.

"Medic, we need a medic in here stat," one of the officers cried out.

Nolan refused to comply and fought the two officers until he almost got free, smashing the head of one of them into the wall and rendering the other unconscious with a pile-driving punch to the chin. By then, more officers began pouring into the room and, by sheer weight of numbers, brought Nolan under control. They restrained him and removed him from the interview room. Angie cowered at the far corner of the squad room and watched the medics as they started working on Detective Albright. As they covered his body with a white sheet and started to remove him from the room, she sobbed deeply.

Jevonte now had another problem. His thirst was quenched, but now he didn't have a way to shut the water off. In his mind, images of drowning pried at the edges of his worried thoughts. The water was cold, and he started to shiver under the spray. He would have to move away soon before he succumbed to shock. As the water started to flood the basement, moving around became a little easier. Patches of soil spread across the floor, making it slippery. Mixed in with the spreading water, the resultant slurry offered very little resistance to Jevonte's efforts to scoot and wiggle across the floor. The water revived him, and he started to feel the effects of the blood loss lessen. His vision brightened too, and he could now clearly make out the outline of the basement door. It still felt like driving to Mars would take less time than getting back up those stairs, but Jevonte pushed himself forward regardless. Climbing the mountain seemed like a better option than drowning in the valley, so he focused on gathering his strength to make a final push out of what had become a living hell.

To complicate matters, Jevonte started to gain sensation in his fractured leg. The shifts and movements he was making across the floor started to send thunderbolts of pain up his leg and back. The protruding bone in his leg was beginning to grind against his muscles and bones. He couldn't keep moving in the way he was. He was going to have to stabilize the bone or find a way to force it back into his leg. The thought almost made him faint.

My god, why couldn't the leg have stayed dead to the world? I have to find something I can use to splint the leg and keep the bone from moving. Think, man, all of my work tools are down here. There's got to be something a world-class carpenter can use to repair a compound fracture in his leg. All I need are a few tools, and I can MacGyver this thing back into working shape.

Jevonte turns his head to the right to better scan the room. His eyes find his workbench, and all of his hand tools are hanging neatly on the wall. I won't be using those, he thinks. But then he spots his minibox—his special box of tools he usually leaves in his Jeep. For some reason, they were in the basement now, and they were tucked conveniently under the workbench. All he needed to do was shift his direction in the back crawl and scoot to the workbench area. He would have to cut through Talaitha's garden pit to get there, which meant he would also need to find a way over or around the home health aide's decaying body.

What a revolting development this is, Jevonte thought. He started to angle his body back towards the pit, being extra careful not to aggravate his ribs along the way. When he came out of this situation, he imagined that his one healthy leg would be twice the size of the other, given the workout it was getting. In between sliding his body sideways and scooting on his back, Jevonte paused to listen for any activity upstairs. He hadn't heard anything from Talaitha since she left him down in the basement. It was too quiet up there. Maybe she left the house, or maybe she died from her injuries. He found the thought of her dying from all of this hell she had put him through satisfying.

The water had reached the pit and coated the surface to within a quarter inch. Jevonte tried to hurry, but the mud was turning sticky and became more challenging to push through. His shoulders were acting like plows pushing soil ahead of his direction of travel. It was getting harder and harder to scoot across the surface, and the mud was weighing him down. He was becoming too exhausted to continue sliding on his back. Again, he would have to change tactics if he was going to get out of the pit and secure the tools he needed to fix his leg and save his life. He didn't give up this time, and he refused to let despair and doom lock him into a silent killing room in his mind. No, this time, he would do whatever he had to. He would push through every barrier and obstacle to get free. He would have to take a chance and pray his ribs would hold and not puncture a lung. He would have to try to stand on his good leg.

Jevonte pushed his body forward, bending as much as he dared at the waist. The pain in his left side almost slammed him back into the mud, but he pressed on. He couldn't stand at all on the fractured leg, so he curled his left leg and pulled his heel as close to his groin as he could. He then leaned slightly to his left and pushed with his left hand until he managed to get to his left knee. He wobbled and almost fell over. He couldn't maintain the balance or hold the position for very long, and he hoped he wouldn't need to. Once he got on one knee, he left his right, fractured leg extended as a drag. In his mind, the maneuver seemed simple enough. He would get to one knee, rock back, and push with his good hand until he was standing on one leg, then he would hop his way across the pit. Simple, he thought. As soon as he pushed with his left hand off the surface of the muddy pit, it slipped, and he fell face-first into the pit's thick stickiness. His ribs caused him to cry out, and he received a mouthful of rot-tainted soil for his efforts. He gagged and choked on the foul mixture and spent five minutes trying to clear the mud and decay from his mouth and gums.

In frustration, Jevonte slapped the surface of the muddy pit and tossed the blackened substance around the room in anger. He started hurling more rotten soil when his hand caught on something beneath the surface. Jevonte grimaced, hoping that it wasn't more of the home health aide. It was indeed more of the home health aide, but this time it was her uniform. He thanked God there was nothing else left of her inside. The uniform and belt were under the surface, tied together. Jevonte unhooked the belt and wrapped parts of the uniform around his fractured leg. The pain was almost too much to bear, but Jevonte gritted his teeth and proceeded to use the belt to secure the leg, tying it tightly above the area where the bone was protruding from it. Successive waves of nausea bombarded him, and the room started spinning in the darkness. He lay back and was almost submerged; the water was rapidly filling the pit.

This is good, Jevonte thought. I don't have to stand. I can let the water lift and float me toward my workbench. He could feel his torso get lighter with the rising water, and he started sloshing his way toward the edge of the pit closest to his minibox. The movement became effortless with the cold water supporting his body. He reached the edge of the pit and crawled on his back until he reached the minibox. He turned it over so he could see what he had on hand. The water had spilled over the pit's edges, and it wouldn't be long before the entire basement was under a foot or two of frigid water.

He located one of his vise grips and one of his panel wedges. The wedges were thick and sturdy. He used them often when he needed to establish a good right angle on doors that were out of tolerance. There were three in his minibox. He placed one on each side of the fracture and the third on top of the break. He took the aide's belt off and coiled it around the outside of the wedges until they pressed snugly against his leg. Once the belt was stable, he pulled some twine out of the minibox and, using one of his long screwdrivers, slipped the tool through a loop in the twine and started twisting slowly. When the top wedge began pressing the bone back into the leg, Jevonte almost fainted from the agony and lay back in the cold water. The cool of the water shocked him back into full consciousness, and he sat up. He had to get the bone back inside the leg, and it was obvious that he wasn't going to be able to twist the twine and force it back slowly. So, he took a deep breath and counted to three before slamming the wedge down on the bone.

When the investigators arrived at Nolan's residence in Middletown, Delaware, state troopers were already on the scene. No one entered the residence until the Baltimore team arrived. Upon their arrival, the team members encountered scenes that would necessitate numerous counseling sessions and extensive therapy. The immediate interior of the ranch-style home was immaculate and well-decorated. The kitchen and sitting rooms looked professionally designed and furnished. Beyond this facade lay an entirely different world, something that challenged the team to find the right words to describe their horror and disgust, yet at the same time struck them with the beauty and harmony of the various scenes that assaulted their senses.

As the team moved through the home, cautiously traversing the dining room. Then, into the open spaces at the back of the residence, the atmosphere and mood shifted in a decidedly darker direction, and they found the first body. The body of a white woman, naked and posed on a chaise lounge chair, introduced the team to Nolan's macabre tableau. The woman, her face frozen like stone, her eyes and mouth sewn shut, lay on her side with her left leg bent at the knee, her head resting on her right hand. Her left hand rested on her elevated knee, and she was pointing at a door shrouded by a black curtain. The dark, deep bruising and purpling around her neck indicated how she was murdered. All around the chaise, rose petals and blue orchids were scattered. As the investigators moved toward the black, shrouded door, pressure panels under their feet triggered water streams to descend from the ceiling, forming a shimmering liquid wall behind the chase. Neon lights and LEDs began flashing and strobing throughout the room, while a red laser painted the shrouded door.

The team moved through the door cautiously. Once inside, they found two dozen human forms spread out across the open living space. Some were naked, but most had hospital gowns and nursing uniforms on. A couple was dressed as teachers. Some pairs were posed in the act of violent lovemaking. A mixed couple was posed sitting on a park bench facing one another; their eyes and lips were joined together in a permanent kiss of sewing thread and staples. Other victims completed a circle around a raised dais in the center of the room. Pairs of lifeless figures lay prostrate in front of the steps of the dais, their arms outstretched as though they were in unholy supplication and worship of the lone brown figure on the top. A giant chair, dressed in green velvet, sat at the center, and its occupant was posed inelegantly, naked. One leg was draped over the right arm of the chair, her legs spread wide, with nearly a dozen roses protruding from her belly button. The ghastly scene caused some of the investigators to fall back, racing from the room to find somewhere to vomit.

A gold collar adorned Melanie's neck, containing numerous sparkling gems, and streaks of silver beads ran down her swollen, pendulous breasts. Her right hand held a long, gold-plated rod with a large crystalline ball affixed to its top. Her left hand was propped underneath her left breast with the nipple pinched between her thumb and forefinger. Melanie's face—her once full-of-life smile and joy-filled eyes—was now the antithesis of happiness. Her eyes were gone, replaced by red marbles the size of jawbreakers. Her mouth was pulled back into a grotesque parody of laughter and joy. Her lips were stapled to her gums, and her tongue was pulled forward so that the tip almost touched her chin. A large tiara rested on top of Melanie's head. It was slightly skewed to the right, but the investigators could see the large-lettered inscription on its front that read, "Black Madonna."

The lead investigator sat in his patrol car and pulled out a flask of whisky from his glove compartment. He took a long swig, then reached for the car radio to call police headquarters in Baltimore. "We found her and at least twenty, maybe more, bodies in the house. Just let the uncle know we can confirm the death of his niece, but he doesn't need to know the details. It will kill him.

29

House of Flames

Roscoe sits quietly at the kitchen table, coffee in hand. It's piping hot, but he doesn't care. He's numb. The news of Detective Albright's death at the hands of Nolan has left him feeling odd and a little displaced. He's relieved that Nolan is behind bars and will definitely be punished for his killing of Albright and Melanie, but what about his nephew, Jevonte? Since getting confirmation that Nolan killed Melanie, Roscoe has been searching for a place to put his anger and frustration. The police informed him that his nieces and nephew were among the bodies they discovered at Nolan's residence. Kim, Rickea, and James didn't deserve to die the way they did. Nolan must answer for all of them, but he holds a small glimmer of hope that his brother, Jedidiah, will turn up alive somewhere.

The doorbell rings, and Roscoe rises to answer it. RhaShawn is standing at the door. He is devastated, and Roscoe knew he needed someone to be with, so he called him over. The door barely finished opening when RhaShawn fell into his arms and started sobbing. The two men held each other tightly as they stood in the doorway. Melanie's brother looked haggard and drained. His eyes were bloodshot, and his hair was uncombed, stuffed under a skullcap. Roscoe had called him right after receiving the news that Melanie's body had been found. The news rocked him, but RhaShawn agreed to come over. He told Roscoe that he didn't trust being alone.

The two men walked into the sitting room and sat in silence for a few moments, then Roscoe began the difficult task of talking through everything he was feeling, giving RhaShawn an opening to do the same. They wept openly but not in a hopeless way. In their tears were the formations of hope and restoration. Sharing their pain openly, without masks or judgment, steeled the men in purpose. Roscoe pulled RhaShawn close and took his hand, then met RhaShawn's eyes with his own, sealing the moment.

"I've made up my mind. I wish I had moved sooner, but I can't worry about that now. I'm going to get Jevonte and bring him home. I'm not waiting on the cops. I'm not waiting anymore," said Roscoe flatly. "I'm going to their house today, and I just wanted you to know."

RhaShawn looks down, his eyes still wet with tears. "I want to see Jevonte, too. I want to go with you, Uncle, but I don't know how much help I'd be."

"Son, you don't have to do anything. If you want to be there to support Jevonte when I bring him out, that's ok. Look, I know what I am about to do may cost me, and our family has just suffered a horrendous loss. This whole year has been hell, so I understand. I intend to end this nightmare today, though, so come rain or shine, this family's story is going to change for the better."

"What are you planning to do, Uncle? I mean, is anyone else going with you? Did Uncle Jedidiah come back home yet?"

Roscoe exhales slowly. "I still haven't heard from my brother, and I can't know for sure whether he is another victim of Nolan or if he's just MIA. I will have help, though. You remember Marcus, my private investigator friend? He's coming too. In fact, he's supposed to meet me here in a few minutes so we can go over the plan."

"That's good, but what about the police? I know that Albright guy is dead, but they have to have assigned someone else to the case by now."

"Shit, they did, but they aren't really looking into Talaitha and her role in all this mayhem. They have Nolan in custody, so everything else is slow-rolling through the courts and the DA's office. They aren't in a hurry to look into her, so I'm not going to fuck with them anymore." Soon, Marcus arrives, and the three of them discuss Roscoe's plan to get Jevonte out of the house.

"Are you sure about this, Uncle?" "RhaShawn?" he asks, alarm in his voice.

"Neither of you will be breaking the law or put in any kind of danger. I'm going to be the one the police look at if anything goes sideways today. Just stick to the plan. I'm fine with whatever consequences there are," Roscoe replied.

"Well, let's get moving. I'm sure she has heard by now that Nolan is in police custody. She might try to get out of Dodge before they come questioning her," offered Marcus.

"I'm already loaded and ready. Let's go in separate cars. RhaShawn, you come with me, and we'll follow twenty minutes after you leave, Marcus."

Slowly and painfully, Talaitha sits up from the floor. She has no idea how long she's been out. Her head is still feeling woozy, and her vision is clouded. On the floor, there is dried blood from her side. Her wound has stopped bleeding, but she knows it won't last because she's going to have to get some stitches put in. She moves gingerly and stands on wobbly legs. Her cell phone has new messages and a missed call. The caller ID says Baltimore Police

Department, and her thoughts begin reeling in new anxiety and trepidation. After listening to Detective Albright's message, her worst fears begin to manifest. She hobbles to the bathroom and gathers towels to wrap around her side. She ties them off as tight as she can and then sits in the den, where she turns on the TV. The apprehension of a serial killer makes the news on all three local stations. When they provide the name of the suspected serial killer, Talaitha's face blanches. It's her, Nolan. She sits calmly, not alarmed by the crimes he committed but by the fact that her brother is gone and won't likely come back to her.

Talaitha picks up her phone and begins dialing.

"Hello, this is Dr. Robinson. How can I help you?"

"It's Talaitha. I need help, please."

"I assume you've seen the news?"

"Yes, and I don't know what to do now."

"What do you mean, Talaitha?"

"My brother is gone now. Who's going to protect me from her?" Talaitha cries.

"Talaitha, we have talked about this numerous times before. Noelle is not going to harm you. They have Nolan now, which means they have Noelle too. You don't have to worry about her ever again."

"Are you sure, doctor? Occasionally, I see her, or I hear her in my house. It's like she's hiding in the shadows, waiting to destroy me. For some reason, she just hates me. She never liked me. She's always wanted me dead. I think that's why she kept trading places with me when the men would come for us when we were little girls. She made sure that I was the one who had to service them. She never got picked," Talaitha said, her voice tiny and far away.

Sensing that Talaitha was about to have a psychotic break, Dr. Robinson began urging her to come into his office. "I really think you need to come in, Talaitha. Let me help you. This is a highly stressful time in your life, and you need to be in my care right now. Would you be able to come to my office now?

"Yes, I think so. It might take a while, though, because I'm badly injured."

"You're injured? How? Would you like me to arrange for someone to assist you?

"No," Talaitha nearly shouted. "I can come to your office. I just have to take my time. I've lost a lot of blood, and I can't see very well."

"Talaitha, you can't possibly drive in that condition. I will come personally to fetch you. Just drink some water and get under a blanket to stay warm. I am on my way."

"I said NO, Dr. Robinson. I will be there when I get there, so stop pushing me," Talaitha said, her old fire sparking within her.

"Very well. I will make preparations and meet you in my office. Please be careful..."

Talaitha hung up on the doctor and rose to change clothes in her bedroom. She passed by the basement door and then stopped. She had completely forgotten about Jevonte. He's probably dead by now, she thought, and proceeded down the hall to her room. Had her head been clearer, she would have heard the sound of water filling the basement and that of a vehicle pulling up to her house.

Marcus waited for a few minutes, then exited his vehicle. His gut told him to contact some friends on the force for backup, but at the same time, he didn't want to create an unnecessary stir by flooding the neighborhood with a swarm of police vehicles. He would play it the way Roscoe outlined it and see it through. As he walked to the front door, he couldn't help the eerie feeling seeping into his thoughts. Marcus didn't get nervous when he was doing a job like this. He'd done it so many times in his life as an investigator, so it was strange how this time, he felt off. He couldn't tell what the feeling was, and it wasn't fear, but something, some kind of alarm bell, was clanging away like crazy inside of him. He pushed it down the same way he did when he was in uniform and about to enter a kinetic environment. Snipers, roadside improvised explosive devices, and ambushes by forces lying in wait. All of those dangers created a sense of impending doom that Marcus had long since learned to suppress. He had to if he wanted to complete his mission, so he treated this moment the same way.

With a few deep breaths, he rang the doorbell. There was no response. He knew the bell was working, though, because he could clearly hear it inside the home. He tried ringing again, but there was still no response. Marcus waited, then he turned to walk away, thinking that maybe Talaitha or Jevonte was in the back and out of earshot of the doorbell. He pulled out his phone and was about to call Roscoe to let him know when the front door opened, and Talaitha stood just behind the opening, her face peering around the edge of the open door.

She strained and squinted hard to see who it was at her door, then squealed, "Nolan! What! How are you here? Hurry, get in here before someone sees you."

Marcus was floored and confused, but he played along and hurried inside. He turned to face Talaitha but didn't say anything. He was frozen in place by her appearance. Her midsection was wrapped in bloody towels, and one side of her face was badly swollen. Her eyes looked glossy, and explained why she couldn't see him very well. This plan might just work after all, he thought. Just got to stall her long enough for Roscoe and RhaShawn to arrive.

Marcus remains silent and then points at the sofa as if hinting that they need to sit down. Talaitha is hobbling and teetering on the brink of falling, but she sits, and leaning to her left, she tucks her arm into her side to put pressure there. "I saw the news, brother. I was sure I would never see you again. They said you had been captured, that you were a serial killer, but I'm not concerned about that. All I care about is that you're here with me, finally."

Marcus faked a cough as he responded, "Naw, I got away."

Talaitha began sobbing uncontrollably. "I don't know what I would have done had they gotten you. Jevonte left me, and I have no one now except you, brother. Jevonte really hurt me, but he won't do that again. I made sure of it, but we can't stay here. We have to leave right now because I know the police will be coming here soon."

Marcus's heart started racing. What did she do to Jevonte? He thought, worry starting to bubble to the surface of his mind. He didn't answer her; instead, he started scanning the room, hoping to find some sign of Jevonte, something that would let him know he was alive.

Talaitha started looking around nervously, then she crooked her head to one side, listening to something just out of Marcus's hearing. "Nolan? Nolan, are you there? Noelle is here! I can hear her. Can't you hear her? Do something!" she yelled.

Marcus looked around and then cleared his throat as he spoke. "No, Talaitha. I don't."

"I can hear her. She's right over there," Talaitha said, and she rose from the sofa and shambled off toward the kitchen. "Noelle, I see you, bitch. Come out and face me, you whore!" she yelled into the empty kitchen. Marcus followed her, not sure of what was happening but realizing that this opportunity was his chance to look around even more. "Nolan, my brother, can you see her?" Talaitha raved. She stopped suddenly and whirled around and looked directly at Marcus. Her eyes were empty and cold when she looked at him. Marcus slipped and spoke again without obscuring his voice.

"What is it, Talaitha?" Marcus asked as he casually glanced at the basement door.

"Who are you, and what have you done to my brother?" Talaitha demanded, her voice suddenly strong and quite clear.

Marcus walked to within arm's length of Talaitha. "Can we sit down for a moment? I just want to talk. I apologize for making you think I was—and he hesitated—your brother, Nolan. Please, Talaitha, can we just…"

Diminished though she was, Talaitha found a flash of speed and, without hesitation, plunged the kitchen knife she had lifted from the knife cart deep into Marcus's throat. A fountain of blood shot across her face as the blade cut across the jugular vein. For a moment, both were stuck, frozen in the shock of the attack, Marcus's eyes wide with disbelief and Talaitha's with vengeful joy. Marcus fell backwards, his body reacting in shock, and crashed to the floor—the kitchen knife still sticking out of his neck. Talaitha fell upon his dying body, her strength quickly fading from the effort. She pulled the knife from his throat and plunged it again into his chest and stomach. On her final thrust, she rolled off the private investigator and passed out next to him.

Talaitha recovered after a few minutes, but the loss of blood was wreaking havoc with her senses. She was weak and exhausted from the killing. She stared at Marcus' dead body and spat. "You thought you could fool me? Did you think I wouldn't know my brother's voice?" she whispered to the corpse. Talaitha stands, almost falling back down. There is blood everywhere, but she isn't concerned about cleaning up or hiding anything. She knows that she has no choice now but to run, to find somewhere to begin again. She decides to dump the body in the basement. This will give my lonely husband some company, she thinks to herself, and begins dragging Marcus towards the basement door. She doesn't make much progress and stops to rest a few feet away from the basement door. She's on one knee, panting and sweating profusely. "Maybe I'll just leave your ass right here," she says.

Roscoe and RhaShawn reach the back door just as Talaitha begins dragging the body again. At first, Roscoe peers through the door's window, and he sees his friend, bloody, dragged as a lifeless piece of meat across the floor, and with a roar, he begins banging on the door. Roscoe throws his shoulder into the door, but the frame only shudders. He starts kicking and kicking and kicking until the whole frame comes loose. With a final shoulder thrust, he throws his whole body into the door, and the entire thing comes free and crashes onto the kitchen floor.

Talaitha, startled by the explosive force of the door hitting the floor, falls backward and then screams in rage.

"Who the fuck do you think you are, breaking into my home like this? Get the hell out of my house!" she yells.

Roscoe steps onto the fallen door, breathing heavily, his eyes locked on the dead body of his friend. The image of his comrade and friend laying lifeless on the floor, fixes Roscoe in space and time. His brain refuses to register what his eyes are seeing. A deep rage begins boiling inside of him. "Bitch, I'm going to make you pay for this. Where is my nephew? Where is Jevonte?" he yelled back at her.

The booming voice of his uncle sent Jevonte reeling in the basement. He had passed out from the splint he used to force the bone sticking out of his leg back inside. At first, he thought he was hearing things. Was that really Uncle Roscoe? Was he really here, in his house, in his kitchen? Jevonte was so weak that he couldn't move, let alone call out to his uncle. He wanted to scream and yell and find some way to tell him where he was, but the water gushing out of the wall made more noise than he could muster.

Talaitha stood over the dead body of Marcus with the kitchen knife in her hand. She pointed it at Roscoe threateningly. "I'm not going to say it again. Get out of my house, or I will cut you like I did this intruder," Talaitha said weakly.

Roscoe, shocked by the sight of his friend and comrade in the throes of his final moments, withdrew his Smith & Wesson snub nose from his waist belt. "Bitch, I wish you would. What have you done? Move away from him now and tell me where my nephew is, you psycho piece of shit, before I make you dead."

"You can't do this. He tried to hurt my baby— Jevonte's baby. I had no choice!" Talaitha cackled.

RhaShawn stepped into the house just then and stood next to Roscoe. "Your baby?"

"Yes, you dumbass. I'm pregnant with Jevonte's child. You want to shoot me? Go right ahead and do it. Kill Jevonte's child!"

"Unc., let's go. We can call the police and let them straighten this out," RhaShawn pleaded.

"Bullshit. We're not leaving, and I don't believe this crazy bitch." Roscoe raises his weapon again and points it directly at Talaitha's face. "Tell me where Jevonte is now, you worthless bag of shit."

"Your precious nephew isn't here. Go and look for yourself. Like the coward he is, when he found out that I was pregnant, he left me. I don't know where he went. Isn't that his pattern, after all?"

"Let's go, Unc." RhaShawn turns to leave through the back door.

Roscoe stares hard at Talaitha, then he starts calling loudly for Jevonte. Over and over again, Roscoe calls his name, each time his voice rising in volume until he is almost screaming his name in one long resounding roar. He walks through the house, searching room by room, and then returns to the kitchen. Looking at RhaShawn, then back at Talaitha, Roscoe growls, "I am all out of patience. Tell me where Jevonte is right now. He's here somewhere; I know it. Drop the knife, or I'll put a bullet in that busted forehead of yours. I'm through playing with you."

Jevonte answers his uncle back, but his voice just isn't strong enough. Jevonte slaps at the water around him, and then he grabs the vise from his minibox and attempts to toss it toward the stairs, but it slips out of his hand and careens against a gas can that's sitting atop the workbench. The gas can doesn't budge after being struck, and Jevonte can hear the liquid sloshing around inside it. Quickened by the plan to get his uncle's attention, Jevonte angles his body to start floating toward the workbench where the gas can is sitting. They can't hear me, but I bet they'll smell this if I can find a way to set it on fire, he reasoned.

The basement was filling more slowly with water now, and Jevonte hoped that the rags piled up at the end of the workbench hadn't become wet. He reached the pile and grabbed the driest set he could find. He could barely reach the gas can with enough leverage to tilt it over, but after failing a few times, he got the can to fall over, and some of the gasoline started spilling out of the nozzle into the water-filled basement. He acted as quickly as his injured body would allow, soaked the rags, and then scrambled to find the lighter he used for lighting incense while working in the basement. In a matter of seconds, the rags ignite, and Jevonte desperately pushes away from the bench and the fire that's growing there. His body is soaked, but gasoline is also in the water.

Roscoe cocks his revolver and takes a step toward Talaitha.

"Uncle, don't do it. She's done. We have solid evidence against her for murdering Marcus. All we have to do is wait. Hey, do you smell that? It smells like something is burning," RhaShawn says.

"I smell it too. Talaitha, what is that? Nephew, go back through the rooms and check for smoke," Roscoe asked, pointing down the hall. Talaitha was silent, but her eyes flirted suspiciously around the kitchen as though she was trying to locate the source of the smell too. The smell of smoke is heavy and acrid. Roscoe's eyes begin to water, and then he sees it—wisps of smoke begin seeping from underneath the basement door. Roscoe points his gun at Talaitha and orders her to move toward the far side of the kitchen. Opening the door, the smoke from the basement spills out into the kitchen, and Roscoe catches a lungful. He starts coughing and waving at the smoke, trying to get a clearer picture of what's going on in the basement.

Something urges him to try one more time, and he calls out Jevonte's name. "Jevonte? Are you down there, nephew? Can you hear me?" Silence and the rumblings of a growing fire are his only answer. "Don't you move, witch," Roscoe says to Talaitha, and then he heads down into the smoky blackness of the deep. He holsters his revolver and takes a few cautious steps. Water has risen to the first five steps in the basement, and when Roscoe reaches the floor, it is almost to his knees. Knowing that he can't stay too long, he scans the room, trying to make out various objects in the space. He can see the fire and watches it carefully as it advances up the basement wall and begins to tickle the rafters above. Some parts of the water are covered in flames, and Roscoe knows that some kind of burning liquid is on its surface. He tries calling Jevonte again. "Jevonte, can you hear me, son?" Suddenly, a hand grabs him behind his knee, and Roscoe turns to find the face of his nephew, covered in black, oily soot.

"Hi, Unc. Can we go home now?" A small weak voice cried. Jevonte was floating on his back and had managed to push far enough away from the fire to keep from burning, but the smoke was spreading faster than he could move. He had heard his uncle calling for him and coming down the stairs for him, but he had nothing inside, no voice, no life left, and he had consigned himself to perish by either fire or water.

Roscoe, overcome with joy, reached down into the water and hauled Jevonte up into his arms. Jevonte screamed in pain, but no sound escaped his mouth—he was just too weak. "Let's get you out of here." Roscoe surveyed Jevonte's body quickly. The splint had fallen off, but the twine Jevonte used to hold the bone in place remained, although it was sagging and wouldn't hold the bone in place very long. The water had soaked all of Jevonte's other bandages off, and his wounds seeped badly. It was just too dark to tell what condition he was in, so Roscoe scooped Jevonte up into his arms and turned to head back upstairs. Roscoe couldn't believe he was holding another human being in his arms.

Jevonte's body was emaciated and bony. He had so little meat on his bones that Roscoe feared breaking something just by carrying him. His anger flared, and he was determined to blast Talaitha when he got back upstairs.

The flames reach the fuse box on the wall and begin melting the metal hinges holding it in place. The flames rise bold and furious, engulfing the ceiling and spreading to parts of the walkout door that were sealed shut. The air and open space in the kitchen begin pulling more and more smoke up from the basement. The smoke engulfs Roscoe's body, obscuring his vision. He just trusts the steps in front of him and moves carefully, one foot at a time. The smoke nearly overcomes him. Jevonte has passed out in his arms, his face serene and childlike under the grime and smudges. With all of the chaos swirling around him, amazingly, he looks at peace in his uncle's arms.

Like a wounded animal, Talaitha throws herself screaming at Roscoe as he emerges from the basement. The suddenness of her attack surprises Roscoe; blinded by the smoke and struggling to breathe, he absorbs her lunge while trying to hold Jevonte, causing all three of them to tumble back down into the smoke-filled basement. Thankfully, half the stairs are submerged, and the trio splashes into the water with little more than disoriented senses. Roscoe held Jevonte in his arms securely, regained his balance, and started back up the stairs. Talaitha rose from the water like a possessed thing out of a children's horror story. With a knife in hand, she darted for Roscoe's back, but he saw her coming and sidestepped enough for her to miss. His hands were full, and the only thing he could do was use his booted foot to stomp on Talaitha's knee. She crumpled in pain. Roscoe started advancing back up the stairs.

"Please," Talaitha groaned in agony. "Don't take my king away, please don't. Jevonte, why are you leaving me, my love?" Talaitha sagged against the banister. Roscoe stepped out of the water, took the next step, and turned to look at Talaitha. He glared at her in disbelief. "I see how you are looking at me, like I'm some kind of monster, but you just don't understand, you don't," Talaitha sobbed.

"What I understand is that you are going to pay for what you've done to my nephew, and you're going to answer for taking my friend's life. I can't prove that you had anything to do with the death of Jevonte's mother, but we have your sister, and she's going to pay for that. Both of you can rot in a cell together for the rest of your lives," Roscoe said before turning to resume his ascent up the stairs.

Behind Talaitha, the fuse box finally succumbed to the heat of the flames and fell off the wall. The entire wall was nearly engulfed in flames when the bracing bars holding the electrical wiring in place snapped, sending live wires into the water. The gasoline on the water's surface ignited instantly with a spark and flash. Electrical sparks showered the gas can, causing it to explode. The force of the blast slammed Talaitha from behind, sending her wrecked body flying out of the water and into the opposite wall. She bounced off the wall and landed in the middle of the spreading surface fire. She lay there, floating on the surface of the burning water, barely conscious, trying to avoid the burning fuel.

The explosion sent burning debris at Roscoe's back and legs, but he shielded Jevonte from most of it and quickly climbed the last few steps and into the kitchen. RhaShawn came running into the house through the back door, phone in hand.

"Uncle, what was that? What just exploded?" he asked, then he looked at what Roscoe was carrying in his arms and said, "Oh my God. Is that Jevonte? Is he alive?"

Roscoe nodded and said, "We have to get out of here. The whole house is going to burn to the ground, and we have to get Jevonte to a hospital, like right now!"

"I was outside calling the police, but I forgot to inform them that we also needed the fire department. Let's go, and I'll make a second call. What about..."

RhaShawn was cut off midsentence by a banshee-like howl escaping from the basement. "Jevonte! My King, Jevonte! Help me, please! Please, help me! It hurts so bad. I'm burning, lover. I can't..." A second explosion in the basement silenced her voice. The blast blew the basement door off its hinges and rocked the kitchen floor where the men were standing.

"The gas lines in the basement! Run, nephew, let's go!" Roscoe shouted. The two men dashed with all possible speed, Roscoe cradling Jevonte in his arms, and RhaShawn leading the way around the house and into the street. When they got to the front, Jevonte started regaining consciousness. RhaShawn opened the backseat of Roscoe's truck and made a space where Jevonte could lie down. In the light of day, they saw the full extent of Jevonte's injuries and were horrified. "Lay still, nephew. You're safe now. We're going to get you in the ambulance as soon as it arrives, so don't move."

"What happened? Uncle Roscoe, is that really you?" Jevonte responded slowly.

"Yes, son. RhaShawn is here, too."

"Where is she?" Jevonte asked, his voice weak and sorrowful.

"Don't worry about that witch; she can't hurt you anymore." Just then, another giant explosion blew out the home's windows and sent the roof and parts of its interior rocketing skyward in a brilliant cascade of orange, red, and yellow. Flaming debris fell to the ground all over the immediate area, and some of the trees caught fire in the yards of the neighboring homes. "That had to be the gas line or something in the basement," Roscoe commented.

"No, uncle. We didn't have gas lines. Talaitha kept a lot of ammonium nitrate in the basement. The basement had a garden full of various organic materials and fertilizers. Something may have mixed or ignited down there, who knows," Jevonte said.

"Nephew, just lie back. The ambulance will be here soon. You've been through a lot."

"When did she leave the house?" Jevonte asked weakly. "I know she's going to be furious when she finds out that her house is now a pile of ash," Jevonte half-grinned.

"Son, she didn't. She was still in the basement when everything blew up. She's done," Roscoe said. Jevonte just stared at him in disbelief. Was his wife really gone? he thought. The nightmare is over, finally.

Jevonte grew quiet and sullen, reflecting on the finality of his uncle's statement. "Uncle, I thought she was my forever, you know? I thought she was the last love I would ever need. She cost me everything and everyone who truly mattered to me. If I had never loved, or wanted to be loved so badly, Mom would still be here. This is all my fault, Uncle. It's all my fault. I'm so sorry." His voice began to trail off as the darkness of unconsciousness loomed.

"Son, we are still here and still standing with you. All is not lost, so just rest, you are safe now," replied Roscoe in a gentle, soothing voice.

"Uncle, what about Mel? Do you know that she…" and Jevonte passed out. In the distance, sirens grew louder as emergency vehicles drew closer. The entire home was now in flames. Neighbors had begun congregating outside their homes, trying to see whose house was on fire. E.M.T.s soon arrived, and Roscoe waved them over to his truck. Within an hour, Jevonte was stabilized and loaded into the ambulance and headed to Sable Ridge State Hospital, where a shock trauma team was standing by.

Roscoe informed the police that his friend and private investigator, Marcus Drummons, was dead, killed by the homeowner, Talaitha Mercedes. They would find two bodies inside. The police already had warrants to visit the home and conduct a search, and had scheduled to visit Talaitha later in the week. Roscoe told them he'd give them a statement later. He and RhaShawn needed to follow the ambulance to the hospital. Jevonte was not out of the woods and would need all the support he could get.

30

The Last Vow

Jevonte lies in his hospital bed, depleted and small—but alive. His mind has been in a fog since he was awakened from the medically induced coma the doctors put him in. He has no awareness of time, and most of his body is numb. Nurses have been coming in and out of his room, changing dressings and updating his chart. The days come and go, and he has no idea what day it is. Roscoe and RhaShawn have also come and gone through the days, and today, when he is most lucid, he finds Roscoe asleep in the visiting lounge chair near his bed.

"Hey, Uncle," he says sleepily.

Roscoe wakes in a fit. "You're awake! Hey there, nephew," he says, a look of relief and joy spreading across his face.

"Yeah, I had to, what with all of that snoring you were doing over there," Jevonte teases.

Roscoe smiles broadly, so relieved that Jevonte's sense of humor is coming back. "Hey, you haven't heard anything yet. Just wait until I get you home. I'll be waking you up with the roosters every morning like clockwork." The two men smile, and Roscoe can see it in Jevonte's eyes; the health and vitality are starting to return. "How are you feeling, nephew?"

"My head feels like it's full of molasses. I feel dull, like I'm still asleep, walking in a fog or something. My mouth is so dry, like my tongue is stuck to the roof of my mouth."

"Hold on, let me get the nurse in here. You've been out for two weeks."

"Two weeks! How?" Jevonte asks, astonished, because he doesn't remember that time.

"Well, you were in serious condition when we got you here. They were operating on you for almost twelve hours, and you actually died twice on the operating table, but God, nephew, but God," says Roscoe in reverent appreciation. Roscoe begins heading out of the hospital room when Jevonte begins struggling to sit up in his bed.

"Uncle, what's wrong with my legs? I can't sit up," Jevonte cries out. He can't reach down because of the body cast he's in. He keeps trying to extend his hands far enough to touch his thighs, but can't.

"Nephew, don't try to move. You've been through a lot, and although the doctors worked tirelessly to save your life, they couldn't save your leg. There was just too much damage from the compound fracture in your femur. They fixed the break and stabilized the leg with pins, but the lower left leg was badly infected, and most of the bone and muscle had become septic. It would have been fatal, and according to what they told us, you were just days away from dying from the infection when we arrived."

Jevonte looks at his uncle, and a single tear escapes his eye. "I'm grateful, Uncle. I'm alive, and I'm free. I have a chance to rebuild my life, and I will."

"Now that's the spirit, and I want you to hold on to that. The doctor will be in to give you all of the details and a plan for your rehabilitation. I'll be right back, and know this: I am so proud of how you fought to stay with us. You are the man your parents raised you to be; never forget that." Roscoe continues out of the door and heads to the nurses' station.

Alone with his thoughts, Jevonte plays distant memories over in his head. Melanie's round, joyful face is one of the first images running through his mind. She was always so happy for him and with him, always the person he needed when he needed someone. He regretted not listening to his mom and appreciating the joy that was always there.

Momma. What do I do now? I can't believe you're gone. Fate can be so cruel, but I know you're looking down on me and watching over me. I promise you, I will make you proud, and I won't give up on my dreams, dreams that your prayers and love made possible.

There is a knock at Jevonte's door, and he opens his eyes to see his father, Jedidiah, standing in the doorway. "Son, do you mind if I come in?"

"Dad?" Jevonte cries and lifts one hand, beckoning his father to come inside.

Jedidiah rushes over to Jevonte's bedside and wraps his arms around his body cast, being careful not to put too much weight on Jevonte's body. Father and son begin crying, Jedidiah kissing Jevonte's face and head. Jedidiah caresses his son's face and kisses him continuously. "My son, I'm so, so sorry," Jedidiah cries.

"No, Dad. There is nothing to be sorry about."

"There is, and I will never forgive myself for not being there for you when that woman was abusing you. I hate myself. I truly do," Jedidiah wept.

"Dad, there was nothing you could have done. I decided to stay, despite the advice you and mom…" Jevonte paused. "Do you know what happened to Mom now?"

"I do. The police finally got their heads out of their asses and found that your wife's sister—may she never rest in peace—caused her accident and murdered her."

"Yes, I was the one who decided to stay with Talaitha. That wasn't on you or Mom; that was me."

"I'm just so ashamed of myself. I couldn't handle Ruby's death. I didn't know how to function on my own, let alone be there for you or any of the family."

Roscoe paused just outside Jevonte's hospital room, listening and not wanting to intrude.

"Dad," Jevonte tried to interject.

"No, son, it's true, and I have to face that. I was a coward, and I failed you and the family. Your mom and I had a complicated love, but it was love through and through, and when she died—no, when she was murdered—it destroyed me on the inside. My anchor was gone, and I didn't have her faith. I didn't have the words for the prayers. I didn't have any songs inside of me, and I couldn't see my way anymore. I loved that woman so much, and it still hurts. I wanted to die myself, but your uncle found me. He stood in for me, and I will never forget what he's done for our family."

"Hey, everybody, what's with all the boohoos in here? No more tears today, ok? We're done with that because I'm already dehydrated enough as it is," Roscoe laughs out loud as he walks in with a pitcher of water trailed by two nurses and Jevonte's doctor. Jedidiah and Roscoe embrace deeply and step aside as the nurses begin adjusting Jevonte's monitors and bedding. Doctor Brandly Carmichael, clipboard in hand, moves to the side of Jevonte's bed once the nurses have made some adjustments and raised him to a sitting position.

"Mr. Greene, we're so happy to see you are awake. How do you feel?" asks Dr. Carmichael.

After Jevonte tells the doctor how his body feels, the doctor begins going over his chart, the necessary procedures, and the full extent of his injuries. The doctor explained that they needed to remove a few ribs because they were severely compromised and would probably never offer his chest cavity the support and protection needed. Those ribs were replaced with a new carbon fiber mesh that would last the rest of his life, he explained. The doctor also discussed the amputation with Jevonte, explaining that they had done everything humanly possible to save his leg, but it had been subjected to too much trauma and infection. A prosthetic was already ordered and sized for him, the doctor shared.

In more sad news, however, the doctor informed Jevonte that he would probably never sire a child. They had to remove one testicle, and the other was almost crushed. They left it in place, and with more surgeries and time, it might become functional. Blood flow was good, so the doctor assured him that an active sexual life was still possible. He would just need to take it slow and let the healing process run its full course.

Doctor Carmichael finished his examination and left some final instructions and guidance concerning the next steps for Jevonte's recovery. He and the nurses left, and Jedidiah and Roscoe resumed their positions around Jevonte.

"The medical staff let us know that, depending on how rehab goes initially, you could be released from the hospital in a few weeks. Just keep getting stronger and stay positive, and we'll have you home in no time," said Jedidiah.

"And we'll be here with you the whole way, nephew. You can bank on that, ok," said Roscoe.

Jevonte nodded in response. He remained quiet and reserved. In his mind, he was thinking more about the loss of one testicle rather than his leg, and started laughing hilariously. "My ball is gone?" Jevonte laughed, looking dead-eyed at his dad and uncle. The two men just stared at each other, then burst out laughing.

"He's back!" Roscoe laughed. "You got one good leg and one good ball, nephew." The three of them laughed loudly, their raucous laughter filling the room and spilling out into the hallway.

Over the next week, Jevonte has nearly doubled his body weight. He's eating without too much pain, and he can inhale deeply without agony. The rehabilitation process has been arduous and stressful. The prosthetic leg had to be refitted and resized multiple times, and Jevonte was having difficulty using it. With Jedidiah's help, he has been walking the length of the ward with assistance. The headaches have ceased, and his vision is back to normal. His doctor informed him that he was making such excellent progress that he believed that he could sign discharge papers sooner than expected. It was early on a Friday morning, and Jevonte was preparing for his morning rehab session when Dr. Robinson stopped by to see him.

Dr. Robinson walked into Jevonte's room and waited for the younger man to acknowledge his presence. Jevonte finished strapping his prosthetic leg on when he looked up to see Dr. Robinson. "Oh, hey, good morning."

"Good morning, Mr. Greene. I hope I'm not interrupting this morning. Do you mind if I come in and have a little talk with you?"

"No, not at all. Please come in," said Jevonte as he completed securing his leg in place.

"I hope you got my message about wanting to speak with you," Dr. Robinson asked.

"Yes. My Uncle Roscoe told me that you might be stopping by. What did you want to talk about?"

"As you may know, I have been treating your wife on and off for the past twenty years. Although she has passed away, I am unable to discuss her case or treatments; however, I want you to know that if you have any questions about her that I can answer to help you find closure, I am available to talk."

"I believe I know a lot about her, especially her childhood. I mean, I came across a journal of hers and read what she said about her parents and what they did to her."

"Yes, all of that was true. Talaitha was a victim of extreme brutality and horrific child abuse. I wouldn't have wished what she survived on anyone. The fact that she managed to come through that episode of her life is truly amazing, and it's a testament to her strength. Unfortunately, she was also affected by a new and rare mental health condition I have termed "effective symbiotic transference movement," or EST-M, that turned her relationship with her twin sister into a kind of psychosis that made her want to destroy her sister. This, in turn, also affected Noelle's psyche, leading to a mental breakdown. Her sister Noelle tried to counterbalance Talaitha's illness by changing her appearance to become acceptable to Talaitha, but the effort shattered her grip on reality, and she became the serial killing monster we know as Nolan."

"I never heard of EST-M, but that explains a lot. I mean, her journal did too, but why couldn't you help her more, and wasn't she a psychiatrist too? I would have thought she saw what was affecting her in some way."

"Talaitha wasn't an actual psychiatrist. She was just smart. She made it through university and passed all of her boards, but she wasn't committed to the science or profession. In reality, her practice served as a tool to achieve her goals. Part of her psychosis involved exerting control over people and manipulating them. She fueled that need by controlling her clients and programming treatments that made them dependent on her for help. She fed off of their need for her, and that drove her to experiment with different means of control."

"I couldn't see that. I guess I was just blinded at first. I just wanted to be with her because she seemed to be everything I wanted or needed. I mean, I was always depressed before she came into my life. She seemed like the perfect match for me, and honestly, she was in the beginning."

"But, you now know that all of that was just part of a ruse, right? I can't say why exactly she chose you, but I can say that you weren't the first man she pulled into this reality she constructed for herself."

"She was married before?" Jevonte asked, suddenly shocked.

"No, but there were multiple instances where she tried to pull men into her world of manipulation. I managed to intervene in those until she left the country for a while. I'm assuming that's when you met her?"

"I met her on a cruise, and according to the journal entry I read, she had been targeting me all along."

"That tracks, especially if what you're sharing is true about your depression. She probably keyed off of that and began checking you out, stalking you before the cruise, or maybe while she was on the cruise. Given your depressed state of mind, she may have perceived you as highly malleable and the perfect victim."

The rehab nurse arrives, and Dr. Robinson rises to shake Jevonte's hand. "If you need to talk further over the coming months, please give me a call. Here's my card, and my direct line is on the bottom."

"Thank you, Dr. Robinson. I'll keep that in mind. Now, I have some work to put in if I want to get out of this place," and smiles at the nurse.

Spring has come early to the city of White Marsh, Maryland, and Jevonte, Roscoe, and Jedidiah are in the backyard relaxing around the fire pit. Jevonte has taken his prosthetic off and is warming his stump in the afternoon sun. Jevonte's body has responded well to the rehabilitation and physical therapy, but his mental state is still untethered at times. The nightmares persist, and he hasn't disclosed to anyone how frequently they disrupt his nights. Dr. Robinson's card is still in his wallet, but he hasn't placed a call yet. He's hesitant to do so for reasons he can't pin down, but he knows that he's going to have to talk to someone soon.

"Nephew, you really look worn out. Are you getting enough rest? How are you sleeping?" asks Roscoe.

My uncle has always been able to read me like a book, Jevonte thinks to himself. "I could get more sleep, but it's just not coming to me as easily as it used to. I've been taking sleeping pills once or twice a week, but I hate doing that because they always leave me feeling drugged out and disoriented in the morning."

"Son, what about doctor Robinson? Can he prescribe something for you that is less addictive?" Jedidiah asked.

"No, Dad. I haven't reached out to him. I don't think I want to deal with any more psychologist-type people for a very long time, if you know what I mean?"

"Well, you have us, ok. After all you lived through, it's got to help to talk to someone instead of keeping all of that bottled up inside. We're here anytime you want to talk and unload," Roscoe said.

"Definitely. I appreciate that. Just knowing that I have that option is comforting, and I will reach out if things get too heavy," Jevonte lied. He knew he would need their support, but he would rather not burden them with what he was feeling. Melanie would tell him often that one of his problems was that he didn't give the people around him enough credit, that they could bear more than he thought. She was right, of course. He would figure it out on his own, but then he stopped in mid-thought.

I'm not going back to that life. I tried figuring things out on my own before, and it led to Talaitha. The mere thought of her and her name fills me with chills. No, I didn't come out on the other side of this mess because I was lucky; although I was fortunate to have a praying mother and family that cared enough to put their lives on the line for me. I don't have to do this on my own, and I won't.

"Guys, as I'm thinking about it, I will need your help. Maybe we can do this once or twice a week, and I can just talk about how I'm feeling and get it off my chest. I'll start looking for a therapist tomorrow. There has to be someone out there I can halfway trust," Jevonte chuckles.

"I'm down for that. I could use that too, son. It's still hard being in the house without your mom. Some nights," and Jedidiah lowers his head, "I still cry myself to sleep like a big old baby."

"Brother, I miss her too. There are days when I'm on my way to work, and it hits me that she's really gone. No more texts in the morning reminding me not to be mean to idiot drivers or to have patience with the dumbasses on the city council who couldn't lead their way out of a paper bag. I can't tell you how many times she would pray me off the ledge when I was ready to confront the skinheads on the city council who were trying to block city projects intended to help our young people. Your mom was a real force of nature. She is missed," said Roscoe.

The three men grew silent, each recalling a dynamic and powerful mother, wife, and woman of God. A man in a suit rang the front doorbell, breaking the silence. The bell echoed into the backyard, where the trio had been conversing. Roscoe got up, walked to the side of the house, and peered around the corner.

"May I help you?" he asked.

"Good morning. My name is Detective Manning with the Baltimore Police Department. Is there a Jevonte Greene here?

"Why?"

The detective walked off the front porch and approached Roscoe. "I'd like to speak with him and relay some information. It's not something I wanted to do over the phone or via the mail."

Roscoe looked at him with suspicion. "Badge?" After the detective showed him his credentials, Roscoe opened the side gate and escorted the detective to the fire pit area. "Nephew, this is Detective Manning, and he wants to share some information with you."

"Hello, and thank you for seeing me. This is a bit sensitive, and I'd like to speak to you in private, if possible, Mr. Greene."

"Whatever you have to say, say it here. My dad and uncle can be here for whatever you want to say. Take a seat," said Jevonte with some authority as he gestured at an empty seat.

The three men sat facing the lone seat occupied by the detective, who began speaking. "I don't know if you've seen the final report regarding your deceased wife, Talaitha, and if you haven't, I will see that you get a copy of it."

Jevonte shook his head and looked at his uncle and father. They both shook their heads as well. "No problem, I will get you a copy as soon as tomorrow. The short version of the investigation determined that your wife was not involved with any of the murders attributed to Nolan, I mean Noelle. This report includes his murder of your wife, Ruby," he said while looking at Jedidiah. "We have solid evidence that helped us convict Noelle of her murder, but she would not implicate her sister Talaitha in that act."

"We knew she wasn't in a simple car accident, but you guys didn't believe us," Roscoe grumbled.

"I know, and for that, I apologize on behalf of the department. We should have dug deeper."

"What I don't get is, how did she find us? How did she know where my wife went to church and when she was going to be there?" asked Jedidiah, frustrated.

"Apparently, Noelle had been stalking Melanie for some time. We believe she came to Noelle's radar when Noelle returned to Talaitha's life. Something came out of that interaction between Talitha and Noelle because, as far as we've been able to determine, Noelle started looking into Melanie right after one of her meetings with Talaitha. We've examined Talaitha's medical files and footage from her office. We saw that all three of them had a tense meeting at one point, and Melanie and Talaitha exchanged hostilities. It wasn't physically violent, but words were said."

"My wife and Melanie also had an encounter at the hospital the first time I got sick. I saw then that my wife didn't like Melanie, but I couldn't see why. I think she didn't like the idea of anyone else caring for me, or maybe Mel was just a threat to her for whatever reason."

"Your wife certainly did not trust you. Are you aware that she had recording devices in the house, and she could monitor everything you did from her office?" Detective Manning asked.

"I knew about the security cameras in the house, but I didn't know how or where she was seeing the feed. I always thought it was bizarre the way the cameras were positioned in the house. Although the cameras were mostly hidden, I discovered a few of them. She never explained them."

"From her office, she had views of all of the living spaces in the home, and she had months of recordings dating back to the beginning of 2018."

"2018, damn! We hadn't started having any issues then, and she was still recording and watching me?" said Jevonte, astounded.

"We subpoenaed the company that did the install, and we found that she used the same company to install cameras near your home in Middle River, Maryland."

"What the actual fuck!" Roscoe exclaimed. "So that's how she started tracking my nephew?"

"We're not sure, but we believe Talaitha was initially interested in another target in the area; however, at some point, Jevonte became her primary focus."

"Wow," said Jevonte. He shook his head in disbelief. "I had no idea, none. But why me? That's what I don't understand."

"Dr. Robinson has helped us piece together a profile for Talaitha, but in the end, none of that quack stuff makes sense to me. A very sick person locked onto you and fixated. It's as simple as that in my estimate. There is one more matter I need to relay to you. You are under no obligation to act on this, but I was instructed to pass this information to you to help us solve a few more murders committed by Noelle."

"Sure, what is it?" asked Jevonte.

"She wants to speak with you."

"Aw, hell no!" barked Roscoe. "That crazy woman can rot in her cell until she turns to dust."

"Wait, uncle," Jevonte interjects. "Detective, what does she want to talk to me about? I don't know anything about her other than she's Talaitha's sister."

"She won't say. She has stated through her attorney that she won't give us any more information about the missing persons we suspect she killed unless she can talk to you. We can't make you do this, so it has to be voluntary."

"Son, maybe you should. If it helps bring closure to the families of the missing, it might be worth doing," Jedidiah said.

"I disagree. Let me go and talk to her, detective. Jevonte doesn't need the reminder of what Talaitha did to him. Plus, I want another round with her ass, and this time I'll finish her," Roscoe growled.

"She'll only speak with Jevonte, and it has to be in person," replied the detective.

Several minutes passed before Jevonte responded. Looking at his uncle and then his father, he said, "Ok, I'll do it. Unc. I know you don't like the idea, but I believe this is my chance to speak to Talaitha as well, even though it won't be her I'm dealing with, if that makes sense?

"Well, you're not going alone. I hear you, but those two are still master manipulators, even though Talaitha is gone. You don't become a serial killer operating this long without being deceptive and cunning. I feel like even behind bars, Noelle is a threat, and we shouldn't take any chances when it comes to her," stated Roscoe.

"I promise you, Noelle will be in restraints. Her hands and legs will be bound, and we will have uniformed police present. Your nephew will be safe, and if it makes you feel better, the two of you can watch from our observation room." Roscoe and Jedidiah appear satisfied with this arrangement and look once more at Jevonte, who also nods in agreement.

The detective provides his business card and gives Jevonte instructions on when to come to the station. After he leaves, the trio returns to the fire pit and discusses dinner plans at the house. They agree that the best option is to keep Jedidiah away from the stove and the kitchen. The Street Fair diner seemed like the better choice for the evening.

Patuxent Institution wasn't on Jevonte's bingo card today, but after deciding to visit Noelle, he started to believe that it was just what he needed. He had no idea what to expect, and he knew very little about Noelle, despite all he had read in Talaitha's journal. He was glad his dad and uncle were accompanying him because he didn't think he'd want to do it alone. As he walked on his prosthetic, he thought about what he'd like to ask Noelle. He knew she had asked to speak to him; about what, he could not guess, but he had been putting together a few questions of his own that he wanted to ask her.

Jevonte knew his uncle was still skeptical about the visit, and no assurances from Detective Manning made him feel any better about seeing Noelle. Noelle would always be on Roscoe's shit list. Jevonte watched him and his father as they walked into the facility, looking for clues on how they were going to react when they saw the man—no, the woman—who took Ruby away from them all. Having lost his mother to this person made him feel like taking a hammer to Noelle's face, but he wasn't as angry as he once was. Maybe it was the therapy. Some of the hate he had been holding onto was fading. It was still there, but its grip over him had lessened. The one person he really could not forgive or forget was dead and beyond his retribution.

The trio checked in at the visitor's center and were met by Detective Manning, who escorted them to the observation space that had been prepared in advance. Dr. Robinson and a few other police and Patuxent Institution personnel waited inside the room. Detective Manning went over the ground rules and procedures Jevonte would need to follow once he was face-to-face with Noelle. Jevonte asked for a bottle of water while they waited to bring Noelle into the examining room. His throat had become exceedingly dry all of a sudden.

The door of the examining room swung open, and two burly guards walked in with Noelle handcuffed between them. They maneuvered Noelle into her seat and secured her wrists to the topside of the table. They finished by securing her legs and ankles to the leggings brace on the floor under the chair where Noelle was seated. Detective Manning motioned for Jevonte to follow him, and the two men left the observation room.

Roscoe looked at one of the staff members in the observation room and asked, "So, how fast can you all get in there if something goes haywire?"

"Sir, we have staff positioned right outside the door, and they can be in there in a matter of seconds. Those cuffs are steel, too. She's not getting out of those. Mr. Greene is perfectly safe."

"Ump, I wish Detective Albright were here to hear that. I doubt he'd be convinced," Roscoe replied dryly.

Detective Manning walked into the examining room, followed by Jevonte. The detective directed Jevonte to his seat and motioned for the guard to remove the gag from Noelle's mouth. They had gagged her because she was biting the staff and spitting at the guards. Her eyes looked a little glassy. Jevonte remembered what Dr. Robinson had said, that they might have her medicated because of her outbursts, so she might not appear coherent. Detective Manning gave Noelle some instructions and reminded her that she was on the clock, then he walked out of the room.

Noelle sat motionless across from Jevonte. Jevonte didn't shy away from meeting her eyes. He stared back at her and took her whole face into his view. He traced every line and curve of her, trying to see what connection remained to Talaitha. It wasn't until he locked eyes with her that he recognized Talaitha in her. The surgeon, or whoever had worked on her, could not do anything to mask the hazel-green eyes common to both sisters. As Noelle sat in silence, Jevonte also noticed how similar her collarbone and shoulders were to Talaitha's. Both held postures that emoted strength and power. Noelle, even shackled and dressed in prison colors, exuded an air of quiet confidence and menace.

"So, Noelle, you wanted to see me, and I'm here. What do you want?" Jevonte said coldly and flatly, never taking his eyes off of her.

Noelle did not immediately respond, and then a slight grin crossed her face. She glanced at the video camera in the ceiling against the wall and spoke into it. "Well, I did make a promise." He turned back to face Jevonte and asked, "So, how have you been, Jevonte?"

"Cut the bullshit, Noelle. What do you want? I have better things to do than waste my time with you."

"Don't you have some questions for me, dear brother?" Noelle said, cocking her head slightly to one side.

"Oh, I have some questions, but since you asked me to come and see you, I will let you go first. Remember, the clock is ticking, and I couldn't care less about what deal you may have worked out with the DA's office. You're done for what you did to my mother, Ruby, and Melanie. You're never going to see the light of freedom again."

"How thoughtful and true. I requested you, and I'm glad you accepted. What I have to share with you is going to change your world, just as it did mine. Are you ready?"

Jevonte folded his arms impatiently. "Any day, Noelle."

"Talaitha and I were twins."

"I know that."

"We had a brother, too. He was taken from the home when we were little, and we never got to know him at all. He escaped most of the abuse we suffered. He was the lucky one, you know what I mean?"

"I didn't know that, and Talaitha never mentioned or wrote about this brother in her journal before. What was his name?"

Noelle said nothing in answer. She lowered her face, and when she lifted her head, she said, "His name was Trevon, but after I did some digging, I found out that they changed his name to Jevonte."

Jevonte sat unmoving, then he burst out laughing. He slapped the table and laughed out loud. "Jevonte? Really? You are a nutcase, Noelle. You really need some help. I mean, I guess that could be a coincidence, that is, if you are telling the truth about having a brother. So what am I supposed to do about that? You have a brother who shares my first name; does that really matter?"

"Why would I lie? I have nothing to gain. I wanted to see you because now that our sister is gone, you are all I have left. I wanted, no, I needed to see you one more time before things go black for me."

"Noelle," Jevonte said as he sat up straight, "I am not your brother. I hate to break it to you, but I was born to Ruby and Jedidiah Greene. You are really delusional. Did you really think you could bring me here, claim that I'm your relative, and expect me to believe it just like that?"

"After I told Talaitha, she ran a DNA test on you, and you were a match to both of us. After she got the results, she stopped having sex with you. Did you notice how all of that passionate lovemaking came to a screeching halt all of a sudden?"

"You need to stop. You are digging yourself a giant hole, but I don't care. You can rot in that hole for the rest of your life. Neither of you crazy people has anything to do with me. You're just trying to fuck with my head one last time, but I'm done here," Jevonte said and then started to stand.

"Brother, wait," Noelle suddenly pleaded, his eyes wet with tears. "They have been lying to you all of this time. You were taken from Latriece and Rufus when you were little. They sold you to a Black couple here in Maryland. It was all done under the table, but I got the records from your real, biological mother, Latriece. I have the receipts and the letters they exchanged with Ruby and Jedidiah before you were sold to them. All of these papers are locked away in a safety deposit box, and I'll give you the key so you can see for yourself. I'm not lying to you, brother. I swear."

"I know you're lying, you piece of shit. I know you're just trying to manipulate me, but what your dumb ass doesn't realize is that I saw my birth, you idiot. My mom and dad had my delivery recorded. I saw my life begin as I came out of my mother's body. I saw the event with my own eyes, and even if I hadn't, I know where I came from and from whom. Nice fucking try."

"Get your DNA test then. My sample is with the police. All you have to do is get tested and make a comparison. I dare you to do it. You'll see that what I'm saying is true."

"I'm not doing any such thing. I don't need to. I know who I am, and I'm not your brother. But let's say for a moment that I believed you. Talaitha tortured me and nearly beat me to death. Why would she do that if she thought I was her brother?" Jevonte said while standing in front of the table.

"Our sister was not well. She hated me until I was transformed, but she hated me before my shift because I left her behind. I think that's what got her the most incensed. People leaving her behind triggered her madness more than anything else, and when you left, she hated you too, even though in your case, you were taken."

Jevonte just shook his head, amazed and bewildered. "Noelle, you are a real sociopath, or something like that. I can see how you got away with all the murders you're accused of. You know how to get inside people's heads better than Talaitha did, I might add, and she was a trained psychiatrist. Well, I'm not playing that game, and this meeting has been a complete waste of my time. I hope Dr. Robinson can help you once they get you checked into Sable Ridge." Jevonte looked at Noelle in the face one last time and then shook his head again before walking to the door.

"This is a shame, brother," Noelle said quietly, turning her head to follow him to the door.

"What's a shame, Noelle?"

"This. This hollow vow. It turns out that the promise I made to Ruby before I shoved her head under the water and choked the life from her body was empty. I promised her I'd send you on to see her, but I failed—for now," and Noelle began laughing hysterically.

Jevonte was shocked by Noelle's admission and stood paralyzed at the door. When he snapped out of it, he found himself pummeling Noelle over her head with his freed prosthetic. He swung the fake leg in wide sweeping arcs, hammering Noelle's head into the tabletop again and again. Her hands were fastened tightly, and she couldn't block or prevent the blows. Her nose was a bloody mess when the guards got into the room and pulled Jevonte off of her. One guard grabbed Jevonte, and his prosthetic went sailing across the room. The other guard stepped in to block any further strikes by Jevonte. They eventually hauled Jevonte out of the room and placed him in another interview room while they retrieved his artificial leg. Roscoe and Jedidiah soon joined him.

"Nephew, are you ok?" asked Roscoe. "We heard everything she said. I'm glad you beat her shit in because that was crazy."

"Son, I'm glad you didn't buy any of that nonsense for one minute," spoke Jedidiah. "It's madness, and she really believes it."

"She's sick. I think she just wanted to get to me and find a way to hurt me because it was what Talaitha would have wanted. Let's go home. I'm ready to put all of this crap behind me and start over fresh."

The three men leave the facility after the guards return Jevonte's prosthesis, and Detective Manning discusses possible charges that Jevonte might face for attacking Noelle. The ride back to Middle River is short and quiet. Jevonte isn't worried about the charges. He was justified, and no jury would convict him; he was sure of that. There was one thing that he wasn't entirely sure of, and he hadn't mentioned his thoughts to either Jedidiah or Roscoe. He hated that the idea was in his head, but he never really saw Ruby's or Jedidiah's face in the video of his birth. Thinking back on it, he strains to remember if he saw their faces when he was born. He can't be certain, but he can only remember them holding him when he was brought home as a baby. He didn't actually see the live birth, but he shook the thought out of his mind. It just couldn't be true; it couldn't.

As Roscoe's truck coasted over Highway 40 East to Middle River, Jevonte made a mental note to dig up the VHS tape of his birth. He just wanted to be sure because if what Noelle said was true, this terrible nightmare was not over. It was just beginning.

31

Epilogue

Months have passed, and Jevonte stood alone on the bow of the Harmony of the Seas. Finally, he booked a trip to the Mediterranean after his uncle bought him a Royal Caribbean cruise ticket. Upon receiving the tickets, he decided to take some time to reorganize his contracting business. His former clients were more than pleased to rehire him, and he had plenty of new projects lined up. He planned to travel abroad for a few weeks to see Europe, and at some point, he would visit Gabon, maybe Ghana, and other destinations, because the time had come. It was time to do something just for him.

The sun was just beginning to drop beneath the edge of the world when Jevonte leaned into the breeze. The sea stretched out in all directions—blue melting into gold, waves flickering like slow applause. Behind him, the music of the cabana party thumped softly. Voices laughed, glasses clinked, and someone was shouting over a card game. He had been invited and welcomed. But he'd told them, maybe. He didn't owe anyone an explanation. Not anymore.

EPILOGUE

He was barefoot, with a linen shirt open at the chest and wind traipsing through his beard. There were no bruises. No shackles. No shadows in the corners of his mind.

He smiled—not for anyone watching, not for approval. He was smiling because he felt like it. For the first time in a very long time, he didn't need to be needed. He no longer reached for love like a life raft. He didn't perform kindness so that he could be chosen. He didn't twist himself to fit into someone else's hunger. What he'd endured would never vanish. But it had shaped him into something stronger than survival: a man who belonged to himself.

He looked at his reflection in the darkened glass of the deck rail—still him, but new. Not perfect. But present. He was whole in ways he never thought possible.

The ocean didn't ask him to be more. It didn't judge the scars. It didn't want anything but his breath, his heartbeat, and the space he took up in this moment.

And for Jevonte Greene, that was enough.

After a few incidents at Patuxent Institution that delayed Noelle's treatment, transfer day finally arrives, and the orderlies arrive at her room to prepare her to go to Sable Ridge State Hospital. The security service handling the transfer could not explain to the warden or Maryland State investigators how it happened, but the vehicle used for transport was involved in an accident on its way to Sable Ridge. Both the driver and the orderly riding along were killed in the accident, and Noelle escaped. The vehicle was found on its side along an empty stretch of Highway 68, pointed west.

Weeks after the accident, a lone stranger stood quietly in front of 52 Riverrun Drive in the town of Accident, Maryland. All that remained of the once-occupied home on that lot was a blackened, empty crater. Her sister used to call that place home. Nothing remained. What did remain was Noelle's promise, and it burned hot in her chest and spirit.

"I will see you avenged, sister. Our brother will see the light and will be called upon to pay his due, as we did."

Acknowledgements

To my wonderful friends, whom I love dearly, I salute you all for letting me be me. You helped me live out my dream and showed me unconditional love and support. Faith and LaQuanna, your friendship has been unwavering and unconditional. Your presence and steadfast commitment to our friendship have been affirming and necessary. Dr. Wauseca Briscoe, when I needed a critical eye and an uncompromising reminder that Black excellence is not a byword, I knew I could turn to you. Thank you for being a listening and patient ear, always there to talk me down from the ledge. And to my business operations teammates—Jesse, Danny, Francis, Yvonne, and Franklyn—you may never realize the profound impact you have had on me in supporting this work. Thank you from the bottom of my heart.

Bryant, my brother, I am deeply grateful for your unwavering prayers and unending love. I appreciate how much you sacrificed to be there for Mom when I couldn't. You have been standing watch for so long, and I know you are worn out, but please know that I see you. I want to be just like you when I grow up!

I must give my publisher, Rise2Write, LLC, some flowers. Dee, you rock! I hadn't imagined that I could get this book done, but you came through and supported the work. You provided me with the motivation to persist, continue writing, and dedicate myself fully, and that's precisely what I did. You played a crucial role in realizing my dream! I appreciate you more than you know.

To my family, both far and near, on the East and West coasts, I say thank you.